Hers²

Hers^2

BRILLIANT NEW FICTION BY LESBIAN WRITERS

edited by Terry Wolverton with Robert Drake

Faber & Faber Boston • London

First published in the United States in 1997 by Faber and Faber, Inc., 53 Shore Road, Winchester, MA 01890.

Library of Congress Cataloging-in-Publication Data

Hers 2 : brilliant new fiction by lesbian writers / edited by Terry Wolverton with Robert Drake.
p. cm.
ISBN 0-571-19909-7 (paper)
1. Lesbians—United States—Fiction. 2. American fiction—Women authors. 3. Lesbians' writings, American. I. Wolverton, Terry. II. Drake, Robert.
PS648.L47H48 1997
813'.540809206643—dc21 96-37877
CIP

Jacket design by Susan Silton
Jacket photographs by Valerie Galloway
Printed in the United States of America

Contents

Introduction
TERRY WOLVERTON vii

Betty Grace Goes to County
HANNAH BLEIER 3

Perfectly Good
ELIZABETH CROWELL 8

Dance of the Cranes
DONNA ALLEGRA 17

Processing
MARY GAITSKILL 32

Green Toads of the High Desert
JUDY GRAHN 48

Ghosts and Bags
NANCY AGABIAN 62

Family
RONNA MAGY 71

Victor the Bear
PAT ALDERETE 81

Rain
CARLA TOMASO 88

Caravan
GERRY GOMEZ PEARLBERG 100

Safe Sex
WENDI FRISCH 112

Love
MARY BUCCI BUSH 117

Breakfast at Woolworth's, 1956
AYOFEMI FOLAYAN 127

Noise
ELLEN KROUT-HASEGAWA 140

Vegetative States
NONA CASPERS 145

Rachel
MARTHA K. DAVIS 156

Sex Less
TERRY WOLVERTON 183

Breasts
ELISE D'HAENE 190

Memory Like Ash Borne on Air
ROBIN PODOLSKY 196

Learning the Hula
ALICE BLOCH 215

Poker Face
ROBIN STROBER 234

Notes on the Contributors 245

About the Editors 253

Acknowledgments 255

Introduction

"An artist is now much more seen as a connector of things, a person who scans the enormous field of possible places for artistic attention, and says, 'What I am going to do is draw your attention to this sequence of things. . . .' You have made what seems to you a meaningful pattern in this field of possibilities. . . . This is why the curator, the editor, the compiler, and the anthropologist have become such big figures. They are all people whose job it is to digest things, and to connect them together."

Brian Eno, interviewed in *Wired,* April 1995

To edit a literary anthology is a tremendous opportunity, as well as an immense responsibility. It is the chance to survey the field of creative prose at a given moment in time, to revel in anticipated pleasures and to discover unknown (at least to myself) treasures. I am then given the power to create a public venue for writings about which I feel passionately, to vindicate those writers I believe are deserving of more recognition, to declare the validity of my taste.

Those very elements that make it an honor also make it a burden: the task involves reading hundreds of stories, making the effort to approach each and every one with care and respect and an open mind. While it's rewarding to bring some writers to wider attention, I cannot escape the awareness that I am at the same time the instrument for denying such attention to many more. And, of course, putting forward my taste is an irresistible invitation to have that sensibility challenged, even disparaged.

To be a *writer* and to edit a literary anthology only exacerbates the issues. It's inevitable that I will read work that's better than mine, and it's a challenge to try to learn from it, instead of feeling defeated by it. It's also inevitable to read some work that seems less developed than my own, and it's crucial to retain humility about this, knowing that another editor might not find it so. I'm forced to question the hundreds of hours spent away from my desk; am I doing a disservice to my own work? Do I risk becoming identified as an editor, someone whose role is to help other writers, while my identity as a writer becomes subordinate to that? And I still can't put a rejection letter into the mail without feeling the sting of all such letters I have received, the just and the unjust, the carefully worded or the terse and impersonal.

Still, I wish every writer could have the experience of editing an anthology or magazine. It's enormously instructive to one's writing—where do stories seem to go wrong? what subjects are written about too often? how does my work stack up against the other submissions? It also provides useful insight for the writer engaged in the laborious task of trying to market her work; having experienced firsthand the arbitrariness of the editing process, having been forced by space limitations and other agendas quite extraneous to quality to reject perfectly wonderful stories, I can never again take a rejection of my own work so personally.

To be a *lesbian* and to edit a literary anthology of works by lesbian writers adds again to the pleasure and the pain. The sense of purpose, to introduce to readers the wit and brilliance, the depth and heart of lesbian writers, is invigorating, as is the chance to further the ongoing investigation of the ever-expanding lesbian imagination. But there are pitfalls to working within a politicized community, wherein agendas have already been forged and wherein some have already decided what the lesbian imagination may and may not encompass.

Some reviewers of the first volume of *Hers* expressed frustration that the collection had no narrative thread, no common definition of "lesbian," no identifiably "lesbian" subject matter that bound together the diverse stories found within its pages. For me, that was the point. The Lesbian, as a distinct being with that consciously claimed identity (as opposed to an individual practicing lesbian behavior) is an invention of our century, and even in the brief time of her existence, she has undergone some radical redefinitions. As that century draws to a close, definitions are exploding all around us and I, for one, am not interested in closing down possibilities at this late hour. I want to see who that Lesbian can be, in all her contradictions and dimensions, to see if and how she exists independent of the multiple oppressions that define her parameters. But then, that's my taste.

So this lesbian writer who edits a literary anthology of work by lesbian writers thought it might be useful to demystify the process, to let the reader know how *Hers,* and its companion, *His,* have come to be. Beginning with the fact that this lesbian collaborates with a gay man, my invaluable co-editor, Robert Drake. I know there are a not inconsiderable number of lesbians who might take offense at the idea that their work is being evaluated by a man, but without Robert's encouragement, I would never have begun editing.

In 1989, Robert attended a reading of my students in the Perspectives Writing Program of the Gay and Lesbian Community Center in Los Angeles. Impressed by the display of their abilities, he approached me about collaborating on an anthology of literary fiction by gay and lesbian writers from the west coast. That anthology, *Indivisible,* had the goal of introducing the gay and lesbian writers and audiences to one another.

That goal persists in *Hers* and *His.* I read to enlarge my world, to learn about and empathize with experiences beyond the limits of my own life. Yes, there are times I want fiction to provide a mirror, to reflect my own culture, values, and place in the social order, but an exclusive diet of this seems restrictive and diminishing. So the co-gender aspect of the collaboration between Robert and myself is central to our vision, as is the inclusion of multicultural authors, and for the same reason.

In soliciting work for the second volumes of *Hers* and *His,* we made the following outreach. We sent flyers to all of the writers in our own databases, Robert posted the "Call for Submissions" on America Online, we placed an ad in *Poets & Writers* magazine, and Robert took copies of our flyer to the OutWrite conference in Boston. From these sources we received submissions of nearly 450 stories for the two books.

Then we read them. All of them. Each story was read carefully by both of us, and given a preliminary vote of "yes," "no," or "maybe." This took months, as each of us hold down multiple jobs in addition to editing, not to mention that both of us write. I know from my own experience that I read at night in bed, I read at the hair salon, I read on the Stair Master at the gym, I read while waiting in the dentist's office, I read on a fifteen-hour flight to Hong Kong. I was almost glad when I got the flu last spring; it meant I could read for hours uninterrupted.

With some stories there was immediate recognition—yes, this story has my pulse racing; yes, this story has made me laugh out loud; yes, this story brought tears to my eyes; yes, this story shows me the world in a way I've never seen it before. Others required more consideration; there was some quality, sometimes indefinable, that worked its way under my skin. I'd find myself still thinking about it days later, despite the fact that it hadn't seemed to make an overwhelming first impression. Then, inevitably, there were stories I just didn't care for, some because the story did not compel me, others because they were not written with a sense of craft.

In each case, subjectivity comes into play. *My* taste. What *I* find stimulating or fresh, what strikes *me* as funny, what moves *me*. What *I* consider to be well crafted. There's no getting around this.

Some of my internal criteria remains, no doubt, unarticulated to myself, although I do take seriously my responsibility to be conscious of my own biases and preferences, the elements that constitute my "taste." I know that I am a sucker for well-used language and a definitive style, evidence that the writer has carefully chosen her words. It's hard for me to warm to lackluster prose, no matter how unusual the plot. I also look for stories that show me new views of the world, or bring me back to familiar subjects with a fresh point of view. I also tend to have an appreciation for stories with an edge, with attitude, but I can be won by a "nice" story every now and again. And I have a great interest in experimentation—with form, with structure, with language—and wish I saw more of it that's done well.

Finally, the reading complete, Robert and I compared notes, and here's where it got interesting, because we don't have the same taste. Robert tends to have a more commercial sensibility (he freely admits this) and doesn't often warm to formal experimentation. Friends have joked that we're the "Scully and Mulder of gay and lesbian literature," and in this comparison with those inveterate seekers of truth from television's "The X-Files" is revealed our different approaches to our task.

There were a few stories that were undeniable yesses for both of us, as well as some stories that neither of us had chosen to include. That still left a large number of stories about which one of us felt positive or even passionate and the other felt negative or at least indifferent. Over our years of working together we have evolved an elaborate courtesy; each of us does our best to defer when the other feels passionately about a given story; we allow each other vetoes; sometimes we bargain. Each of us gives up some of the stories we feel deeply about, in order to make room for pieces to which the other is committed.

Inevitably we end up with more stories than our editor at Faber and Faber will let us include, and we have to let go of a few more of our favorites. But the process makes, I think, for a more textured and varied set of books than would exist without this process of collaboration.

A common critique by reviewers of literary anthologies is "Some of the stories worked better for me than others," but among these reviewers there is rarely agreement about which stories those are. This is as it should be. If an editor has done her job, an anthology will, like a Whitman's Sampler, contain enough variety to whet the appetite of a wide range of readers. Chocolate-covered cherries will appeal to one; caramels to another; still a third will savor the almond roca. Somebody's bound to be allergic to the coconut cream. It's my hope that within this second volume of *Hers* there'll be something to appeal to every taste.

But more than that, I hope this compilation will yield a picture—complex, contradictory, provocative, and continually unfolding—that expands the possibilities for who and how a lesbian can be and amplifies the lesbian imagination.

TERRY WOLVERTON, 1996

Hers[2]

Betty Grace Goes to County

HANNAH BLEIER

Here's what happens. When some girls come, they shoot. Naturally, no medical studies of this phenomenon have been done because whatever comes out of them isn't shlong juice, isn't a river of those infinitesimal creatures so lionized in the minds and hearts of breeding men everywhere, the doughty spermatozoa. Whatever it is, though, I wish the One Eye Jack had it on tap. I'd be belly up to the bar every afternoon at five, sucking it back. Especially when those girls haven't been eating red meat or taking antibiotics, because then the juice is light and sweet, then it tastes so good it makes me want to cry. Even if I'm an arm's length away from a shooter's cunt with my fingers or my hand or my whole fist up inside her, the delectable stuff spurts out of her and hits me on the tits, belly, cunt, and thighs.

One night one of those girls was over me like a dark, four-legged animal and she came straight into my face when my eyes were open. That didn't sting my eyes, but then she pissed a little and that stung a lot. After that she threw me on my stomach and fucked me from behind until she made me come so deep inside myself my guts felt molten and I thought I couldn't possibly take any more, and she said, "Say, 'Thank you, sir,'" and I knew if I didn't she'd stop so I opened my mouth and gasped, "Thank you sir, thank you daddy," and she said, "That's a good girl," and fucked me even harder so I couldn't have talked even if she'd told me to and she knew that so she didn't. When we were resting I said, "You know, you shouldn't piss in someone's face without letting them know you're going to do it beforehand." I thought the pissing had been some kind of dominance thing; I thought she had been improvising. Usually I enjoy extemporaneous moments, but the piss had really burned. "Look," she sneered, "do you think I can control what comes out when I shoot? I didn't even know it happened." I don't often kiss tricks, but when she said that I believed her so I kissed her, and she sucked my tongue into her mouth with her sharp little teeth, like a snake swallowing a whole mouse. We went to sleep.

The next morning my right eye, the one that caught most of the piss, was red and swollen. It itched like crazy. I washed it out with warm water and went back to sleep. When I woke up that afternoon my eye was completely swollen shut and there was yellowish pus oozing out of it. The trick was gone; she left me this eye and her phone number. I didn't call her. I called Bobo, not on the phone but the mental way we call each other that I used to think only happened in bad sci-fi movies, and he phoned me from the downtown library where he was no doubt reading some rare esoteric thing no one else gives a fuck about. I told him I needed to go to the hospital. By this time my eye was the size of a small egg and it throbbed.

Bobo drove over in his van and took me to County because, naturally, I had no insurance. It was Cinco de Mayo and there were about twenty-five heart attack victims in the emergency room with twenty or so gunshot wound victims, and they all had to go first. I started to get dizzy. Bobo sat on the plastic bench reading to me from a porn book I had in my jacket pocket called *Her Huge Meat* from the "Chicks with Dicks" series. He also told me to breathe and chant, and for a change I was too scared to argue with him and tell him I didn't believe in that shit. I do believe that it kept me from jumping out the window.

When a nurse finally called us over to a desk, she said, "What's the problem?" I whipped off the dark glasses I'd been wearing and curled my lip at her. "Omigod," she said, and led me to a room. She told me to sit down in a red vinyl examining chair. Bobo sat on a stool in the corner. Then two nurses and three doctors grabbed, wiped, poked, prodded, and measured my eye for about ten hours. Then they forced it open and made me read an eye chart for another five hours, and then they decided I needed to have a CAT scan to see if the infection was in my optic nerve headed for my brain. Bobo trotted alongside the wheelchair when they wheeled me to the CAT scan room, and all this time I was thinking how the fuck am I going to pay for this, because even at County they bill you for special tests. Then we got to the CAT scan room and the tech wouldn't let Bobo stay in the room. When Bobo tried to get into a philosophical discussion with the tech about the meaninglessness of the statement, "That's the policy," I told him not to worry about it and that I'd see him later if I could see at all, ha ha.

The tech made me lie perfectly still while he very slowly wheeled me in and out of a little tube and I felt nothing except for a weird jittery buzz all around me and the pain in my eye which was now pain in the entire right side of my face. The whole side of my face seemed to be filling slowly like a water balloon. I had no trouble holding completely still because when the butch tricks fuck me they make me hold completely still and if I move they stop.

After all that, all the doctors did was tell me to go home and put these orange, burning drops in my eye every half hour. A tiny bottle of the drops was $40 and we didn't have any money, so Bobo said, "Wait here," and I knew he was going to go give a blowjob. I hoped he found a doctor or someone else with money because otherwise he was going to have to give a few of them to get forty bucks and I didn't want him to tire himself out too much. Also the more blowjobs he gave the more likely he was to get the crap kicked out of him by one of the johns, and in fact I knew he hadn't blown guys for money in over a year for just that reason.

I felt like I was going to pass out. We'd been in the hospital over ten hours and the emergency waiting room where I was again was still filled with bleeding, moaning people, some of them little kids. Bobo must have found a doctor, god bless him, because he came back quick, walking toward me making a big thumbs up sign. He had no visible bruises. We bought the drops and got out of there.

I had to stay in my apartment for nearly a month while my eye healed. During the first week I had to pry it open to put drops in it. When I woke up in the morning I had to wash it with soap and hot water before I could open it because it was solidly crusted over, as though my eyeball lay underneath a pus meringue. Slowly it decreased from the size of an egg to the size of a golf ball. When it got to golf-ball size I could open it without using my fingers if I willed it to open. I couldn't read or watch TV, and I got dizzy every time I stood up. I jerked off and listened to the radio. The radio was old and only picked up one news station and the geriatric station. It took a lot of concentration to come with news about Bosnia or "Girl from Ipanema" in the background.

County called to tell me that gonorrhea grew out of my eye culture. Maybe that was another present from the trick, or from some guy, or maybe I'd had gonorrhea "down there," as the doctor so clinically put it, for a while and the bacteria finally made it up to my eye. It can happen. Many people have no symptoms of gonorrhea until something particularly gruesome happens, bulging eyes or pelvic inflammatory disease or sterility. I had to take oral antibiotics that nauseated me and killed my appetite. I couldn't smoke weed to get my appetite back because that dried out my eye and made it itch.

Bobo came over as much as he could to read to me, but he needed money and had taken a temporary job giving talks about HIV prevention at skid row shelters. Every day there was some tidbit on the news about THE HOMELESS, some tearjerking story about the nobility of their plight. Bobo said that was a way not to have to think of bums as real people, like straight guys putting their wives on pedestals one day and beating the crap out of them the next. A lot of people read as much as Bobo and many have seen as much, but not many can put the two together. When he wasn't there I felt like I was losing my mind.

I was in the middle of a pretty good nap one afternoon when I was awakened by the sound of one of my neighbors yelling his head off. I couldn't hear what he was saying, but the tone in his voice was the one men have before punching their fists through the wall or their women's guts. After a while he shut up and, since I hadn't heard any screaming, I went back to sleep on my lumpy couch. I had just started to dream about eating out a sixteen-year-old blonde girl who was nervous but unimaginably turned on by me when I heard this Neanderthal banging on another neighbor's door, screaming, "Come out of there, you fucking faggot! Fucking longhair! Fucking pussyboy! I'm going to kill you!" Normally I try to be patient with the heartbreakingly obvious cock-lust of guys like this, but I was not in the mood. Bobo would say I had a lapse in compassion. Whatever it was gave me a burst of energy. I got up off the couch, slipped on my work boots, and stalked out of my apartment wearing a huge, graying t-shirt with a silk-screen of a butch eating out a femme. It said, "POWER BREAKFAST." My eye oozed green pus down my face.

The guy was banging on a door four units down the hall from mine. He turned around when he heard my door slam and he paused, momentarily dumbfounded by my appearance. Even with one eye I could see that, like most of the men in my building, he looked like the lead guitarist for a 1970s southern rock band—scruffy beard, pot belly, matted hair, pasty complexion. The pussyboy he was yelling for must have been visiting from somewhere, because no man that pretty was in residence.

I took advantage of the guy's disorientation and charged down the hall toward him. I grabbed both his shoulders and yanked him toward me, and I pressed my right eye hard against his left one. Then I slapped him as hard as I could across the face, screaming, "You woke me up, you dumb redneck fuck!" I boxed his ears so he'd stay dizzy while I made it back into my apartment and grabbed the Smith & Wesson Bobo says I shouldn't have. I hurried to my door and looked through the peephole. The guy was standing back from the door getting ready to run toward it and break it down. As he charged the door I opened it, and he fell head first into the edge of my coffee table. I pointed the gun at his cock. "Go back to your fucking apartment," I said, "or I'm going to waste that puny thing, and then you won't have to worry when it stands up for longhair faggot pussyboys."

The guy turned pale. He got up. He raised his arms and moved very slowly off my floor and out the door, his head bleeding like a sieve. "Better see a doctor about that eye," I yelled after him and then slammed my door. I got so dizzy then I barely made it to the couch, where I collapsed. Fortunately, just then Bobo yelled my name through the door. "Come in," I said weakly, and he did. He looked alarmed. I was too tired to smile at him, but I tried. "Looks like I'll be moving again soon."

Perfectly Good

ELIZABETH CROWELL

My parents, who live in Ipswich, seldom come to my lover Melanie's and my apartment in Jamaica Plain. We meet them in the North End for dinner, or at the theater, or for some shopping on Newbury Street. "We won't bother you at home," my mother always says. So I was surprised when I ran downstairs to answer the doorbell one winter afternoon, and my parents stepped in, all dressed up. "Don't you ask who it is first?" my father said. "We could be pillagers!"

"Jennifer," my mother kissed me. "You should be careful."

"What are you doing here?"

"Who is it?" Melanie called up from up the stairs.

"Melanie's here?" my mother asked.

"As you might recall we've lived together for several years," I said.

This fact rested in the air, where it always did. My mother took an exaggerated sidestep, as if to walk by it as she passed me and started up the stairs.

"The most incredible thing has happened!" my mother cried, her blue heels tapping onto the stairway.

Once upstairs, my parents looked around as if they had been set loose in a museum gallery. My mother stopped by a quilt. My father looked at the books and magazines. I stood still as a guard, seeing how my mother and father did not touch. They wandered by bookcases, paused to look at pictures of the two of us, at the Homer print of women in billowing skirts playing croquet that my mother had gotten me for Christmas, and our college diplomas. They leaned forward and backward, and slipped by each other.

"We can't stay. We're on our way to a funeral," my father said.

"I'm so sorry," Melanie and I murmured together.

My parents sat on the couch. "We have bad news. Miss French died."

"Who's Miss French?" I asked. But then I remembered. On the nights my parents went to the Boston Symphony, I'd wait with my father downstairs as my mother finished dressing. He paced in his bright black shoes, stopping before his leather-bound books, picking one out, slipping his long fingers through the gilded edges. He would read a sentence of Tennyson or Austen aloud, and then put it back. He always wore a dark blue wool blazer, a light blue oxford, gray flannel pants, and a red tie. "Miss French is waiting," he would tell me. "Honey," he'd cry up to my mother. "We don't want to keep Miss French."

"Miss French has—had—the seat in front of my parents at the symphony," I told Melanie.

"Which is why we're here." My mother snapped open her purse. "The funeral is at five-thirty."

"I still think it's a misprint." My father put his gloved hand into his pocket and pulled out a ripped paper clipping. "French, Matilda. Beloved sister of Benedict and Eustacia. Librarian of Saint Agnes Academy for forty years. Services five-thirty Saint Bartholomew's Episcopal Church, Boston." He looked up at all of us. "Isn't five-thirty a strange time for a funeral?" he asked. "Oughtn't I to call the church?"

"You're welcome to the phone."

"Your phone is broken," they said together.

"We tried to call," my mother added. "We didn't mean to surprise you."

I went over to the phone. It was off the hook. "It's off the hook."

"That explains it," my father was entirely satisfied.

"We thought that something might have happened. You might have fallen or something. We've been trying to call you all day."

"But we live together," I said. "Melanie would pick me up."

"Or leave her," Melanie joked. "And run off with all her money."

They frowned. They were just rich enough to not joke about money.

"Coincidentally," my mother began, getting up and strutting

back and forth, "Miss French's funeral is tonight, and we have our tickets to the symphony. We've had season tickets for thirty years," she said this to Melanie, as if to indicate that this was why money wasn't to be joked about, since it could be the source of tremendous privilege. "So we have these tickets, and they're perfectly good."

My mother pulled the tickets from her purse, fanning them in the air and then placing them solidly on the coffee table. I had seen these season tickets for years, laid out on the Belgian lace of my mother's dresser as she prepared to go to the Symphony. She would spray perfume in the air and I would run through the rain of it. I would always try to reach for the tickets, but I was not allowed to touch them. "They'll bend and seem used and we won't be able to get in," my mother used to say, so convincingly that I believed it could happen. I even hesitated before taking them now.

"That's very sweet of you," Melanie said.

"They're perfectly good," my mother said again, sitting back down. "And we won't be able to use them, unfortunately."

For a moment the four of us sat looking at each other. "I was making cookies before you came in. Would you like some?" Melanie asked.

"Making cookies? For what?"

"For us," I said. "Homemade."

"For goodness sake." My mother rose and followed Melanie into the kitchen.

"What kind of retirement plan do you have?" my father asked immediately.

"Dad, I'm twenty-eight."

"It's not too early. And with social security going down the d-r-a-i-n. Does your landlord know?" he asked.

"Know what?"

"That you and Melanie are?"

"Are what?"

He squirmed. "I just hope that it's her," he murmured.

"Who?" I asked.

"Miss French. We think it's her, but we never knew her first name."

My mother came back out smiling and biting into a cookie.

"It's none of his damn business whether we're gay or not, Dad," I burst out.

"Jennifer," my mother said, "what is this about?"

"I was only saying," my father said, "that everyone has rental rights, no matter what."

I opened my mouth to protest, but they were late, already. They had to go find parking, at which point we suggested that they simply leave the car here. In fact, they were welcome to come back here afterwards, for the night. They could let themselves in with the extra key they kept for emergencies.

"Oh, we'll get home tonight, all right," my father said.

"That won't be necessary, but it's kind," my mother bubbled. We walked them down the stairs.

"Sorry to hear about Miss French," I said.

"She was just the most charming woman," my mother said. "We're so sorry she's gone." We watched them go halfway down the steps. Then my mother stepped back up.

"Please, no hand holding in public. There are people there we know." She said it the way she might say, *Check the oven before you leave the house.* I felt my hands open and close again. Melanie and I walked back up the stairs.

The tickets my mother had left for us were lying on the coffee table. I picked them up and inspected them, surprised how stiff and sturdy they felt. "Lately, they keep giving us things."

Recently my mother called to tell us they had chairs to give away, so we drove to Ipswich for dinner. Afterwards, by the dull ray of a flashlight in the garage, we inspected the mahogany chairs. My father helped us pack them in the car. Then, a month later, he called to say they had found some bookcases while cleaning the attic. So we went up for lunch and to get the bookcase. Only on the third trip, when my mother said they no longer had room for an old coffee table that rested on the landing to the third-floor hallway, did I realize they were giving things away to see us. They were pulling tables from the attic, china from the cabinets, old tools from the cellar. They were naming what they could lose, and they were using these words to call me home.

After we got dressed, Melanie and I pressed each other's faces with powders and blushes. As I ran the lipstick pencil over her lips, I remembered how my mother would stand in the mirror in the front hall and pucker her lips. "You look fine," my father would say. "Miss French is waiting."

"You know they had plenty of time to get to the symphony too," I said. "They could have gone after the funeral."

"Jennifer," Melanie batted her eyes to dry her mascara, "your parents only do one thing at a time."

I fluttered before her in my black dress. When her pale arm reached out to take me, I felt an impatient panic. "We're going to be late," I murmured. "I would say that Miss French is waiting. But I guess she isn't anymore."

I got up to inspect myself in the mirror. I remembered how my father would stand beside my mother in the front hall, ready to put on her heavy camel's hair coat. My mother kept looking at herself in the gold-framed mirror. She felt both her ears, to make sure her earrings were on, rubbed her hands along her neck, to double check for her necklace. She tapped each button on one of her many thick, wool suits. I still don't know what she thought she might have forgotten, but I felt, too, as if I had forgotten something, as if I had missed a way to make it not matter that when the music murmured toward crescendo or slowed, I might reach to hold the hand of the woman I loved.

How many times had I stood at the doorway of my home and watched my parents slip across the wintry, blue lawn, toward where my father had the car parked, already warming up? Halfway down the walk, they would suddenly hold hands, as if once away from the house and me, they could come together. I imagined running after them, meeting Miss French at last, but I never went farther than the porch, as if I had been left in charge of the walls they left behind.

"Oh, my God, it's Miss French," I murmured as we headed toward our seats. The chandeliers had the effect of candlelight and they shimmered off the deep red velvet curtains and wine-colored seats. An old woman dressed in purple was sitting in front of my parents' seat.

"How do you know it's her?" Melanie whispered.

"Miss French always wears purple, so I'm told."

"Oh, maybe you're wrong," Melanie said, as Miss French rose to straighten her skirt. She had on a purple blouse and stiff, wool suit, with an amethyst brooch that dimmed at the blink of the lights signalling others to hurry to their seats.

"I don't think so," I murmured. "Sssssh . . ." Melanie put her arm around me. "Not now," I said. "Half my father's law partners have season tickets. There's George Fenfield the tax attorney, over there." It seemed a major victory, proof of the danger, to see George's black wool coat and silvery hair across a nearly full concert hall.

"Oh, Jennifer," Melanie said, disappointed. "I hardly think your father will have to tender his resignation."

During the intermission, Miss French turned around. "Where are the Churches?" she asked.

"I'm Jennifer Church," I said.

"Jennifer," she smiled. "Why, I've heard so much about you over the years. How nice to finally meet you!" She pressed her hand in mine. Melanie's palm had stayed open all the way to intermission. She watched me shake Miss French's hand. "And who is this?"

"This is my lover, Melanie," I said it so unconsciously, I didn't know I'd said it, until Melanie pressed her hand in mine.

"Well, how nice to meet the both of you. Are your parents busy with other things?"

Melanie and I looked at each other and tried not to smile. "They're at a funeral."

"Oh dear, someone close?"

"Not so close, apparently," Melanie murmured.

"Well," Miss French sighed. "How very nice of them to give you tickets."

"They'd just go to waste," I said.

"I could never get my Millie to go to the Symphony." Her Millie? "She just didn't like music. Imagine that, I spent my whole life with someone who didn't love music. I don't know why it didn't matter, but it didn't."

Melanie and I looked at each other, stunned.

I leaned over and kissed Melanie right there. I felt like I was sailing through space. Out of the corner of my eye, I could see Miss French fade to a blur of purple, her brooch dead center and spinning. That jewel blurred with the soft peach of Melanie's skin. As I kissed Melanie, I wondered what I would have to give away after this. What would I part with next? What corner, or door, what memory, pressing like a window that won't open, but that you can still see out of, like the memory of symphony nights?

Yet Miss French only sighed sweetly. The bows bounced on the strings. Drums were tapped and tested. Soon we were all where we were before. The concert master tuned them up, and the conductor came onto the stage, smiling as if he had just heard something wonderful about all of us.

When we got back to the apartment, my parents were there. My mother was scrubbing in the kitchen. My father was scrutinizing our magazine collection. He frowned and tapped his pipe. "Well, how was the Symphony? Was the Beethoven good?"

"Oh yes." Melanie took my coat and winked at me.

"Are they back, Henry?" my mother cried from the kitchen, as if it was their house.

"We only just got back ourselves. I came in to use the bathroom, and your mother got started in the kitchen, and you know how it is."

"How was the funeral?" we asked in unison.

"Oh, it sounds like she really was quite a woman. You know," my father said. Melanie and I sat down together, arm in arm, next to him on the couch. I realized he may have never seen us this way. He frowned and got up. "She was somewhat of philanthropist—I always suspected she had money. Of course, it's not the kind of thing you ever say."

Melanie and I looked at each other and breathed out. "Dad, it wasn't her."

"Who wasn't her?"

"The woman who died wasn't her. Miss French was sitting right in front of us at the concert."

"What?" He seemed more upset that she was alive.

"Miss French. She introduced herself."

"From a field of purple," Melanie added.

"What are you talking about?" my mother called from the kitchen, but none of us answered her.

"Oh, Jesus," my father said. "You mean, it wasn't her, who—" Then he threw back his head and laughed. "I talked to her brother for over an hour . . . He said she was a great fan of music."

Melanie giggled. I smiled. "We gave them a two hundred dollar check for the Matilda French Memorial Fund at St. Agnes Academy." He slapped his hands together. "Well, I suppose we deserve to pay at least that much for making such jackasses out of ourselves."

"Dear, what on earth is it? Girls, you really need to watch this floor. My heels are sticking . . ." My mother emerged from the kitchen.

"The kids saw Miss French. She was at the concert, in her regular seat. Right where she always was—or is."

"What?" my mother repeated. "For goodness sake, what will people think? I talked to her sister. She's a butterfly collector . . . Oh, Henry!" We all laughed.

Melanie patted me on the back as I tried to catch my breath. "She was highly suspicious of us," Melanie contributed. "Sitting in your seats. She asked us some pressing questions."

"I hope you didn't tell her where we were," my mother gasped.

"We told her it was no one close," I said. We laughed all over again. "So Miss French had a lover?"

My parents gasped for a moment, and then settled together on the other couch. They had dressed for the funeral the same as they dressed for the Symphony, as if in their lives of pleasure, they were close to mourning something.

"So we understand. Milly or Lilly. They had a Boston marriage," my father said. "The old-fashioned kind. You couldn't tell," he said, "that's how you knew."

My parents looked at their hands. I wondered how Miss French's true life had never come up in their house. Home pressed against home, I imagined walls would certainly fall. These were our Boston marriages, theirs with its dark-clothed seams, ours with its airless indiscretions.

"Oh, Henry," my mother said with relief, "remember the canoe."

"That's right. We were wondering if you would like the canoe. We don't use it and it's perfectly good."

"Dad, we live in the city."

"But sometimes you go on those woman wilderness trips. The ones I don't approve of," he reminded us.

"When we go on those trips, they give us the canoes."

"It's a perfectly good canoe," he repeated.

"We don't need it," I said. "We really don't."

"Well, I don't know what we're going to do with it then," my mother said a little helplessly.

I reached out for Melanie's hand. "We have what we need," I said.

My mother gazed at our entwined hands. "I hope you didn't do that at the Symphony . . . we'd hate to lose those seats."

"Well, I'm glad that Miss French is still alive. She's so easy to see over." My father slapped his hands on his knees and got up. He went over and pulled her camel's hair coat off a director's chair.

"Lock the door behind us. There could be pillagers," my father said. I stepped with them outside. I felt lost without Melanie, who was more tenacious with my parents than I could be.

"The canoe is a nice offer, but we can't use it," I said firmly.

"You want some wine," my mother decided, buttoning the last button on her camel's hair wool coat. "We have so much wine from the University Club auction . . ."

"That's right." My father smiled at me. "Why don't you come up and we'll give you a few bottles?"

"You could come down here," I suggested.

"We wouldn't want to trouble you girls. You're so busy." She wrapped her scarf around her pale face.

My father said, "Pull the chain behind us."

"There isn't a chain on the door," I said, but I followed them down the stairs, to make them feel as if a chain were there, as if there were an extra lock, something to keep me in or danger out.

"We really do wish you'd come over for dinner sometime," I said.

My parents blinked, smiled oddly. "Maybe we will."

"We're together for good," I said. "This is how you'll always see me."

"Well, yes, of course," my father said. "Of course dear, it's just that . . . we'll come soon."

When I closed the door behind them, I could hear their shoes plodding sadly out to the car.

I remembered how I tried to stay awake until they got home from the Symphony, how I could hear the TV, and the babysitter munching on the pretzels my mother had left out for her, how every car whispering down the street might be theirs. Yet, after the promise of their return fell away, a dream began to bloom from the sweet perfume I'd run into as if it were spring rain. My body grew heavy with itself, and I woke the next morning, surprised by the light, by the good smell of breakfast downstairs and the lingering perfume, by all the things that had stayed, despite the dimming and faltering and the dreaming, perfectly good.

Dance of the Cranes

DONNA ALLEGRA

"It's my mother's favorite dance," had become Lenjen's standard response. She was used to the suspicion that accompanied, "What kind of name is that? What's it mean?" It irritated her that people frowned because her name wasn't one they could recognize; but without waiting for interrogation, she'd patiently reply, "It comes from a West African dance."

Lenjen spent a large part of her childhood traveling to West African dance classes where her mother's passion for Senegambian dance from the Old Mali Empire could be satisfied. As a baby, Lenjen would lay quietly in her bunting, absorbed by the hypnotic drum rhythms. The growing girl ran and played with other small children whose mothers had also brought them to class. Lenjen would watch with a smoldering interest when the adult women danced their way across the studio floor. She stared like a mesmerized cobra into the circle these women formed at the end of class when everyone had a chance to do a solo within the volcanic ring of dancers.

Eventually Lenjen joined the children's line of dancers and the fire for West African dance caught her in its grip, first as a playful tickling at her toes, then consuming her in its wake.

At thirteen, Lenjen stood tall, awkward, elegant in her long limbs fitted for the dance of the cranes—a bird more known for wading in the water than sailing on its wings through the sky. She never truly understood the full extent of her name until the Wednesday evening Senegalese dance class when Sulaiman explained that the movements for lenjen mimicked a crane's behavior in a marsh. This made sense to the girl, who'd already concluded that African people liked animals, particularly birds, to shape their dances.

Lenjen turned fourteen six months after she and her mother, Cayenne, moved from Newark to Harlem, primarily because it'd be easier to get to dance classes. Mother and child duly went everywhere in Harlem, Brooklyn, and Greenwich Village that Cayenne could find to take class.

Lenjen was by then a solid folkloric dancer, though not always obedient to hold to the traditional styles that African-Americans took up as the African way. More often than not, she would refuse to wear a lapa in dance class, aggravating Cayenne.

Cayenne had specially bought fabric made in Senegal from one of the merchants who sold jewelry wares, lapa outfits, and American-style dresses sewn in African fabrics. The woman had even shown Lenjen how to wrap the fabric around her waist for a lapa. "Like this . . . ," the woman demonstrated with the two edges of fabric she pulled first across her backside, then around the front of her waist to tie a knot, ". . . so the extra cloth won't get in your way when you dance with those long legs."

Noting the sweat pants and t-shirt Lenjen placed into a Capezio dance bag, Cayenne simply snorted over how once again, Lenjen completely disregarded yet another womanly way.

But Lenjen knew she didn't want to end up as some man's woman. Somehow she couldn't convince her mother that she wasn't like the sisters so eager to have babies. Even so, it pained her that she went against the grain of right and proper African womanhood—that is, in the ways that the grown-ups she was most familiar with would have a right and proper African womanhood be.

Trying to soothe her mother's irritation, Lenjen tried telling Cayenne, "Ma, I hate it when the drummers hoot and holler when I dance."

Cayenne rolled her eyes to the ceiling. "They're paying you a compliment, honey. You should be glad that the men like you." Lenjen sucked her teeth with ingratitude.

"I know I can shake a tail feather and I'm fast on my feet, but I'm dancing for the other dancers and the fellas just make it into something stupid." Lenjen stopped short of saying how eagerly she looked to the women for their approval. She longed for their encouraging attention as the dancing circle at the end of class settled down from being like a boiling caldron to a calm, hot soup.

"You won't feel that way much longer, missy. I'll bet my bottom dollar on that." Cayenne spoke with finality, certain that she knew the last word to this story.

"I'm not like that, Mommy." She hated the pleading tone that trailed in her voice, but Cayenne had already left the room.

Lenjen wanted to make her mother understand how she drank from the current of energy that came from the dancing women, that they were the ones who enriched her blood. She wasn't putting her passion in dance on the floor for some mating game. But Cayenne's mind was set and Lenjen didn't want to end up whining after her mother to explain.

When Cayenne returned with her own dance clothing in hand, mother and daughter let the matter rest so they wouldn't be late to class. They kept the peace on the common ground they held around the dance and music from the fourteenth-century Mali empire and other regions of the Senegambia in West Africa.

"You have your bus money?" Cayenne prompted.

Lenjen sent her mother a scolding look.

"Don't give me those eyes. We don't want to be late," Cayenne exaggerated her defensiveness.

"Hurry up, Ma. I'm waiting and you're the one who's not ready."

"All right old lady. Fourteen going on forty," Cayenne grumbled.

They always arrived among the first of those who would regularly gather together at the armory in Brooklyn or at the Sounds in Motion studio on Tuesdays on 125th Street. On Sundays, the community of dancers went to a recreation center in Newark and this evening, they'd join the dancers at the Cathedral of St. John the Divine.

As the bus lumbered down Amsterdam Avenue, Lenjen thought how she missed people when they didn't come to class; even women she didn't particularly like pained her with their absence. When a woman with the slightly sad and dreamy face had started showing up to Wednesday night classes, Lenjen recognized her as a new person. This woman too had a name taken from a dance of West Africa. She'd heard a woman call out to her in surprise, "Lamban!"

Lenjen had always favored lamban, the social celebration dance for different rites of passage in life—birth, puberty, marriage—but now that dance took on a whole new meaning for her. She found herself drawn to the woman—allured by the way Lamban would carry herself and be a part of the group but somehow kept to the sideline.

Lenjen first thought the feeling of kinship was on account of the genesis of their names—both from West African dances—and the similar sounds of "Lenjen" and "Lamban." But what she really loved was that Lamban wore African pants and wouldn't hold back from trying the men's steps.

As the bus neared their stop, Lenjen hoped Lamban would start coming to Tanya's class on Fridays and prayed that she not miss Sulaiman's class this evening. Maybe Lamban would be in the sabar class next Tuesday. She'd have to start coming to the Armory on Saturdays. That was the class of the week. All the African queens went there.

But maybe, Lenjen reasoned, the woman went to Newark on Sundays. Clearly an accomplished dancer, with movements articulate and strong, she always put her own vibe onto the steps. She *had* to be taking class somewhere regularly, Lenjen argued with herself. It took a long time to learn West African dance. Good Haitian and Brazilian dancers came across awkward and stupid-looking when they first started in the West African tradition. Even though some of the Haitian and Brazilian dance steps were similar, a whole different energy would spin the West African movements in motion. You had to learn the alphabet of each particular people's dance language before your body could say its words and form sentences.

Lenjen excited herself as she pondered where this eccentric woman had been taking class. I could ask her, she hesitantly proposed to herself. Grown-ups think teenagers are children anyway, so I could ask her as if I really were younger. I can make like I do to get people in class to show me steps so that I can catch their phrasing. Then I can ask where she takes class and I can ask her to show me some stuff about lamban!

I like that she's so strong and handsome, not pretty and silly about it. That stupid drummer, Ralph—always with something to say about a woman's body after she passed out of earshot—has a point: she *is* juicy delicious, and I think she's dreamy.

"Lenjen, wake up, little sister. Here's our stop!"

During the warming-up calisthenics that Sulaiman directed, Lamban, twice Lenjen's age, sensed someone watching her. She knew she had drawn Lenjen's eye.

She moved with caution when it came to revealing her interest for anyone in class, but she liked the teenaged girl who was all limbs and as quick to frown someone off as grin them in. Lenjen tickled Lamban with something familiar about herself. In class the previous week Lamban had asked her line partner, a Bajan woman called Merle, "Whose daughter is that bean pole?"

"Lenjen? She's Cayenne's girl. She has gotten big all of a sudden," and Merle frowned at this recognition that the girl was now a teen.

Lamban tried to cover up her curiosity by hastily saying, "That baby face on stilts is so open and alive when she dances. She has a sweet feeling to her." Merle had nodded and Lamban marveled how Lenjen could remain quietly self-contained among so many boisterous people. Maybe she's given up on being taken seriously around all these adults. Lamban mused that Lenjen was the rare bird who didn't wrangle for attention and demand that she be noticed. The girl had a quality to her that Lamban valued.

She felt pained to imagine that Lenjen probably kept herself quiet because otherwise the men in class would never leave her alone. Lenjen could at moments look like some imagined African royalty—delectable as she blossomed into a young woman's tantalizing beauty.

Lamban also found that she envied the fact that Lenjen had grown up with African dance and didn't have to start in the folklore as an adult. Not all people took to West African dance's demands, but those who did, held tight.

As Sulaiman guided the thirty dancers through a series of hip rolls, Lamban savored the interest she felt emanating from Lenjen. Probably doesn't know the half of her beauty, Lamban thought. Young women could look so unearthly at times.

She once again praised the powers that had brought her back to the African dance scene. She'd left, needing a break from the frustration of caring so strongly for women in a community that valued only male-female couples as the important pairings. It bewildered her that even in this day and age so many women still left themselves by the wayside. Why did those sisters pump up boys already overblown on a sense of themselves? These were the very men who didn't allow room for the women supporting them to have space on stage.

Lamban wondered if she could see this pattern of the heterosexual social dance because she entered the world as a lesbian. But she was also a dancer and West African folklore gave her heart its rhythm. She'd stayed away from these dance classes for several months and a few women let her know that they'd noticed and were glad to see her return. That first evening back, the woman who became her line partner for the night said, "Hello stranger—haven't seen you in a dog's age. You been busy, huh?"

Lamban heartened that she'd not been forgotten, surprised that she'd even been missed. As much as she chafed against the ultra-heterosexuality of the African dance community, she did love the people. They'd all been taking classes and sharing high energy for years now. She knew individual spirits, had watched their children grow and her own soul had mingled in the communion of rhythms for dance.

Still, the boys could be a real pain in the ass when they paraded their notions of manhood. "Hold back, girl, you're making me look bad. I'm supposed to be the strong one. You chill out."

Lamban felt she couldn't be as freely loving to the sisters as she wanted—she didn't want anyone calling her "queer," in that tone of contempt she knew so well, having heard it applied to others. She cringed at the disdain straight women could put forth.

She'd felt yet again bewildered by attitudes such as she overheard that evening in the dressing room. "That sister should know better, men can't help themselves."

But the African dancer in her could be fed only within this sphere. And not all the women were "black-maled" into keeping themselves back so that some men could keep an illusion of feeling superior, she countered her gloomy thought. Sisters weren't stupid. It was just that misguided and loud-about-it few who let themselves be quelled and who then energetically tried to herd other women astray.

"Jumping jacks," Sulaiman ordered. He simply smiled at the groans that issued from around the room.

Lamban knew as well as Sulaiman did that these women welcomed the good feeling that came with pushing their muscles. She felt so good to be back in this class, that she wondered why she'd ever left. No, she knew the reasons—they just weren't tormenting her like a headache fevered by the devil's hammer.

She'd been through the fire, sorted through her ashes and determined that she wouldn't hurt herself ever again by denying her lesbian self. She'd tried to hide this truth from anyone who got friendly with her. When she couldn't pretend anymore, instead of going to class, she stayed home and cried night after night for a week.

She'd switched to Haitian and Brazilian classes downtown. These fed another part of her soul, but her spirit longed for the dances of Senegal, Mali, and Guinée. She ached to do djola, mandgiani, wolofsodon, goumbe, lenjen, sabar, and her beloved lamban. Some part of her spirit throbbed at not getting its full extension, just as her muscles would want more stretch when she didn't work her body to the full range that she was capable.

Lamban grieved that being a lesbian could make her such an outlaw to a group of people who did the most spiritually sustaining thing she knew in life. She'd needed all those months away in order to love herself again. Being away let her grow a perspective, like new skin. That's how lobsters did it—when the old shell became too small for the mature body, they went to a protected place where they could shed the old covering safely. They'd have to be naked and vulnerable until a new one grew to fit.

"Are you getting warm?" Sulaiman asked the group, who responded with, "Yeah," "Give us a break."

It had taken time for Lamban to understand what had bent her so far out of shape. She'd ignored the many off-notes she felt as she smiled eagerly to people who gave her suspicious looks. She'd remained fervent in pursuit of the dance and felt she couldn't afford to challenge a woman who, when Lamban came into the bathroom, had self-righteously declared to another, "There's no funny women in Africa, you know."

Were they talking about her? Lamban's armpits grew moist. She wasn't sure and had been afraid to look up and regard the speaker, to somehow put her in check. Wasn't this the woman who'd once bragged, "I changed that AC-DC into a real man and he's my husband now." The man had left her not so long ago,

Lamban remembered as she'd hurriedly gotten dressed. Still, she hadn't opened her mouth to wrestle with the woman's distorted viewpoint.

Lamban couldn't admit that, as much as she loved her lesbian—a favorite part of herself which she would swear before anyone that the African powers had made of her—she did buy into straight ideas about how she ought to be. How many times had she heard, "Friends are okay and all that, but every woman needs a man to be complete." The brain-twisting occurred almost by osmosis, but not having any other visible lesbians and gay men to join with made it all too easy for her truth to be silenced.

For a long time, it had been all right with Lamban not to ask for anything, to be nurturing to the sisters when they talked about their men and babies. But after a while, she saw that she too had needs, just for simple recognition that she, a lesbian woman, was one on a scale of dissonant notes that Black Americans could always harmonize. She needed for someone to ask her about her girlfriend or give her a touch of sympathy if she mentioned having trouble in her relationship on the home front.

Fear kept her opinions unspoken. It didn't take long for that poverty of speech to make Lamban feel shut off from the people she mingled with. When her well ran dry, that's when she'd cried all those nights: hurting because she didn't like feeling left out and maligned.

During that time away she realized how strongly she loved West African folklore and in that culture were the people she most wanted to dance with. Maybe most wouldn't welcome her as a lesbian and she'd have to resign herself to getting a family embrace elsewhere. But by the same token, she didn't have to till the land for their heterosexuality either.

When a woman in a Brazilian dance class complimented Lamban on her samba step, "Work them hips, girl. That's the action that brings the brothers around," she found herself shaking her head and saying, "Hey, it's not about that for me." She felt her cheeks heat up, but didn't rush to assure the woman that men mattered for how she danced. Lamban decided right then and there that she needed her own encouragement more than she wanted to give it away to women who pledged themselves first to men and abandoned sisters to sink at sea. Let the ones who'd shrink from her do so, but she wouldn't stay away from her rightful place in this world and resolved to get back to West African dance. She was one of the multitude of rhythms that African people the world over could work through their bodies all at the same time.

Having a stronghold on hard-won knowledge, Lamban had earlier this evening packed her dance gear—leotards, leg warmers, tights cut off above her knees, and a piece of fabric to tie in a wrap she liked. She'd taken care to drape the fabric wrap almost like a baby's diaper, giving herself room to move freely and feel all her strength.

"Let's do some last stretches, you're almost done," Sulaiman coaxed.

"You're killing us before we even started, Sulai," a voice in the back of the room warned.

"This is it, I promise," and he put a hand on his hip in a classic black woman's body posture, queening it up, making everyone grin.

Lamban re-entered her old stomping grounds with a mind set to make herself comfortable. It was a freedom to no longer care so much if she didn't behave like the American-style traditional African woman. There'd be no rewards if she pretended to be anything she was not. She stopped wearing lapa or dress outfits; instead she wore the dabbas, the shokotos, the African pants that the men and some few women wore.

In her new ease, she marveled that she loved the people in class. She still recoiled from the just plain jive of some folks—and she could see they weren't the majority—but she could love the dance, the beauty of her classmates, the drummers, and the spirit that brought them all together.

"Okay, you're done," Sulaiman told the group, who grumbled at him good-naturedly for making them sweat with the warm-up exercises.

As women adjusted lapas and the drums gave off warm-up cries, Lamban felt triumphant in her awareness which knew all too well that Lenjen was drawn to her, and she knew the reason why. She vowed to the spirit of a young girl she carried inside herself that she would show forth proud as an example for this teenager if Lenjen needed one.

Lamban shook her head in wonder at the paradox that it was

only by taking a resting space away that she was afforded this freedom to grow firmly into herself. She could now say, this is who I am and I am a part of you people.

She particularly liked this Wednesday class in the Cathedral of the Church of St. John the Divine. Sulaiman had been teaching for the past few months. He was gay, she thought with defensive feelings to a disapproving audience. Lots of us are gay and you know it, so don't try to act like we don't exist or that we're too weird for you to even conceive of, she wanted to say to everyone.

Scanning the room to see who else was in class this evening, Lamban felt at home. She knew the routine of changing her clothes, warming up, learning the steps to the dances. The thought made her smile as she skipped downstairs to the lavatory. Before the night ended, she'd rise to the tide of rhythm the drums called forth as dancers unfurled in a wave of prayer.

When she returned from the bathroom, her African fabric wrapped like a diaper, Lamban heard Sulaiman saying, "Pat Rollins is our guest teacher tonight, so I'll let her speak on what she is teaching us. Pat."

Lamban looked approvingly to Pat. She'd taken a number of classes with that Brooklyn-born-spirit-of-Guinée girl. Pat embodied a Guinée folkloric dancer to her core—strong, faster in movement than the neighboring Senegalese style, and so much more exciting.

Pat's father was a master drummer in New York. Papa Rollins had been into the African folkloric arts as a drummer for years before the current generation, but Pat owned a reputation in her own right as a dancer, independent of her father's Nigerian cultural focus. The woman could move from liquid lightning to fiery steel, Lamban thought. If she weren't beautiful, she'd be ugly. The French had an expression for her—*belle laide.*

Lamban saw in Pat a hearty and outspoken woman whom some drummers would complain about behind her back. "She's the kind who puts fear in black men's hearts—always speaking her mind," a songbe drum player said to the others only half-jokingly. Lamban had surprised herself by turning to a woman standing nearby, "Well, Pat knows what she's talking about when she calls drummers on not playing the rhythms she wants."

The woman, her stance as sturdy as a market woman's, had nodded and whispered to a nervous-looking woman beside her,

"Sometimes these drummers they don't understand what the dance teacher is asking for. Some of these brothers act like women don't know anything about the drum. They think they can get away with playing any old beat they want—probably because they don't know how to do what the teacher asked." The woman was even getting into a huff.

Lamban wanted to further the whispered conversation, as the group waited for Pat to finish instructing the lead drummer. "Pat's father taught drum to a lot of these young brothers," she informed the women nearby, whose eyes regarded Pat approvingly.

Lamban liked how Pat wouldn't hesitate to pick up a djimbe and replace a drummer without apology to show up anyone who wasn't doing what she asked. Pat even made the men shut up when she explained something to her dancers. Lamban saw how she wasn't the only one appreciating Pat in this.

The woman she'd just spoken to, dressed in a lapa-and-matching-top outfit, said to her timid friend—clearly a newcomer to class—"There's another thing about Pat—she's really into her dancers and will not treat the drummers as if they were the high and holy be-all and end-all of the class. She wants the music exact and will make those men play harder until they get it right."

Lamban knew well that some men resented this, but they'd play harder and afterwards be glad they had to work their best energy to meet Pat's demands.

"Ms. Mister," Ralph, a djimbe player, called Pat behind her back as she left the drummers to ask Sulaiman a question. Lamban figured Ralph had heard the excited rumor that Pat was working on getting her own group together to perform traditional dance. Even he voiced no doubt that this group would be mighty.

Sulaiman, rounding up dancers, said to someone, "Pat is so knowledgeable about the folklore and such a blazing rock of a dancer that . . ."

Ralph's cramped eyebrows showed he disliked Pat. He could barely keep his opinions to himself. Still, he hoped to play with her group. Lamban wondered if he'd also heard the rumors that Pat was looking to have women compose her drum orchestra.

"Hi everyone," Pat addressed the gathered community of dancers and drummers. "Today we're going to work on saa."

Lamban wanted to hoot her joy as she thought, I am in heaven.

The very idea of saa sends my heart soaring. Thank God I came back to class.

"Saa is from the bush of Guinée," Pat explained. "It used to be a secret women's society dance. The women played the drums in the bush. Saa was like the strength dance for the women to keep themselves together. The sisters marched saa from Guinée to Mali and back again, protesting what we nowadays can talk about as too much 'macho' or 'the patriarchy.'" The room quieted with attentive interest.

"Saa was a dance to show that the women were just as strong, if not stronger than men. And like I said, the women played the rhythms," Pat said with a chastising look at those male drummers who made faces of disbelief.

Lamban nodded her head almost imperceptibly. She noticed how several feet away, Lenjen's expressive face showed keen interest in Pat's preface. She understood how a teenager like Lenjen might yearn to hear the greater truth behind what Pat was saying—that there is a wider realm for African women to range than the limits of what men who wanted to herd women fenced around them.

"Some of the brothers say that for women to play the drum is taboo, but you have to ignore these brothers. Have you ever heard of Makeda?" People nodded, some women smiling with a hopeful expression. "She's one of the best drummers—man or woman. A lot of brothers don't like her 'cause she's so good, and that is just their jealousy."

"And that little ego thing," someone called out. Several women, Cayenne among them, raised a chorus of "Um hm" that broke into tolerant laughter. Lamban nodded enthusiastically now. She ached to connect with the smile widening on Lenjen's young face. Pat changed directions slightly. "The saa steps are strenuous, ladies. It's a military dance—I'm talking serious war. Don't cheat on the step. You have to smile when you march it." She then flashed a challenging brightness of teeth, as if opening her mouth set free a small flock of white birds to suddenly fly around the room of respectful listeners. Lenjen could tell Pat was readying to show the steps now, as Pat adjusted her lapa around her hips for a looser fit.

"Like I said, saa was a women's secret society dance originally, but like a lot of things, the brothers peeped it and now it is everybody's dance." She added, as if this were a discovery to her, "Women's secret societies testify to the fact that it is important for us to get together as women to share what we are strong with. I'm ready—I hope you are."

As the dancers lined up in rows of three to go across the floor, Lamban let two women move ahead of her and quickly stepped in place so that she stood in Lenjen's line. She smiled at the girl—open and freely. "Come on puppy, this is the women's dance of strength." Before Lamban could continue or Lenjen could answer with anything more than her own smile of delight, Pat was demonstrating the steps to saa and both dancers set to work.

At first Lenjen was annoyed that she wasn't picking up the movements with her usual ease. Distress changed to horror as the rows of dancers sailed across the floor stitching the step securely to the music, but she just wasn't grasping the needle of movements that Pat had shown. Lenjen had to work hard just to do it all wrong. Somehow, when she did get a slight grip on the footwork, she had a difficult time holding on to its thread.

Her mind kept repeating the enthusiastic words, "Come on puppy, saa is the women's dance of strength." Lenjen felt near panic; she had to get this. The sisters had marched saa from Guinée to Mali and then back again to make a point to males whose egos had taken them unaturally out of line.

Halfway through the class, Lamban took Lenjen's hand and drew her to the side of the room to help Lenjen learn the transition which made the saa step so troublesome.

"It's a rhythm thing," Lamban said. "Count it: one and uh, two." Lenjen felt grateful for this instruction even as she felt shamed that this reserved woman translated little break-downs of the movement to help Lenjen understand the steps into her body.

Lenjen badly wanted to look good, was flustered by her mistakes and hated each and every one. She kept a thin grip on her belief that she was learning something important. She paid heed to what Lamban pointed out and let herself be a child who had something to inherit from a woman she favored.

She rallied herself like a coach on the eve of a playoff game. Every class humbles me, she thought. Every class brings out my weakness, shows me my power, tells me my name. It's the same for anyone else here. I'm not going through anything different than the rest of the folks trying to learn this stuff. But damn, I hate that I've got to sweat for it today.

The class didn't do saa for much longer after Lenjen had her thoughts acknowledging the need to struggle. Pat motioned the drummers to go into a new rhythm for the next dance they'd do in the class. The drum call tickled Lenjen just short of recognition. Her body could practically taste what dance was about to come next, but her mouth couldn't quite call it by name.

Pat motioned like a choir director to the group of attentive women, eager for her every word. "Let's slow it down some now. We'll do a lamban next. What I teach is from Guinée. This lamban is for a rite of passage from girlhood into womanhood."

Pat narrowed her eyes into the group of dancers, and when her glance caught Lamban, she signaled the woman to come to the front line.

Lamban felt her blood course both humble and proud. She put more than her body into the steps that Pat laid out, aware that people watched her so they could learn. She danced full-out and deeply into each part of the movement. People needed clear demonstrations, she thought, especially in African dance where every movement could not be counted and broken down. She consciously offered herself as the strong pattern for anyone who looked to pick up the impression of her footfalls.

The music of the drums drove line after line of dancers. After what seemed a flicker of time, the hurricane of dance let up from a storm to a shower of raining arms and legs. Lamban looked forward to the ending circle where they'd probably do the social dance, mandgiani, but instead, Pat signaled the drummers to play yet another different rhythm. After a false start with the music and a moment of confusion, Pat sang out a rhythm that the lead drummer tried to catch, while Ralph made a face of non-comprehension. Finally Pat just called out, "I want you to play lenjen." The lead djimbe player smiled in quick recognition and apology.

Pat skipped around the semi-circle she had directed the dancers to form around the drummers. She then she paired people off. Lamban caught the moment of irony when Pat recognized how she'd just put together the two dance-named women. Pat's face startled in that look of uncertainty, then sureness, when someone realizes that she has sensed a family resemblance in two people who are sisters. Pat's face flared with bright teeth that she'd made Lamban and Lenjen partners.

She then went center-circle to say, "Here's what I want: come out together with your partner in an opening step. Each of you will do an individual solo. Then you leave together doing the same step. Take a minute to work it out, okay?"

Lamban, her flesh heated, body confident and spirit strengthened from dancing, felt privileged to partner with this teenager. She said "Yes" to all of Lenjen's suggestions for the steps they would do. Lamban went gladly into a listening stance, knowing that she could channel greater good from that position. She also knew she would take in more and connect with greater ease as she deferred to someone who had greater knowledge.

The woman and teenager worked out and rehearsed their duet and solo steps. When Pat called the dance circle to order and it came their turn to ride out on the lenjen rhythm, Lamban felt herself barely more than a shadow. Lenjen danced as if she had no bones in her body to hamper its fluidity and indeed sported wings instead of arms. Her steps took her high into the air, as close to flight as was humanly possible.

Lamban sensed everyone else in class look with wonder at Lenjen's solo, which soared the group to a climax. On Lenjen's last go-around at jumping into the circle of paired dancers to do a solo, she pulled Lamban in with her and danced elaborate patterns around her partner. In finale, she angled her body into a sequence of steps everyone could join in on, then broke off with steps like a kaleidoscope discovering it could also be a rainbow.

As always at the end of dance class, faces glistened with the sweaty joy fashioned from something cleansed and set free. Lenjen and Lamban smiled shyly at one another. Lamban pulled Lenjen to her and held the teenaged woman in a long strong hug. She felt people smiling their way. And why not smile upon them?—the community had just witnessed a mighty rite of passage this class. Two queer birds had stretched their wings, each finding a new level of flight in the dance of the cranes.

Processing

MARY GAITSKILL

For several days afterward, the memory of my encounter with Frederick lingered like a bruise that is not painful until, walking through the kitchen in the dark one night to get a drink of water, you hang it on a piece of furniture. I would be talking animatedly with someone when I would suddenly realize that I was really talking to and for Frederick, as if he were standing off to the side, listening to me. This was a nuisance, but a mildly advantageous one; my efforts to communicate with the phantom Frederick gave my conversation a twisted frisson some people mistook for charm.

The week after I met Frederick, I went to a party celebrating the publication of a book of lesbian erotica. I was talking to two women, one of whom was facetiously describing her "gay boyfriend" as better than a lover or a "regular friend." She said he was handsome too, so much so that she constantly had to "defend his honor."

"You mean he's actually got honor?" asked someone.

"One should always maintain a few shreds of honor," I remarked. "In order to give people something to violate."

"I don't know if that qualifies as honor."

"It's faux honor, and it's every bit as good for the purpose I just described."

"Can I get you a drink?" There was a woman standing off to the side, listening to me. I was startled to see that she was the woman who had taken a Polaroid of Frederick and me. Even in a state of apparent sobriety she emitted an odd, enchanting dazzle. "Yes,"

I said. We took our drinks out onto the steps. A lone woman was sitting there already, smoking and dropping cigarette ash into an inverted seashell. When she saw us, she said hello and moved to the lowest step, giving us the top of her head and her back. Because she was there, we whispered, and our whispers made an aural tent only big enough for the two of us.

"I wondered if I'd see you again," she said. "I wondered what happened with you and that guy."

"Nothing," I said. "It was a one-night thing. We didn't even have sex."

"I also wondered if you like girls."

"I definitely like girls." I paused. "Why did you want to get me a drink just now?"

"What do you think? Because I like your faux honor."

"Because it has cheap brio and masochism?"

"Exactly!" I felt her come toward me in an eager burst, then pull away, as if in a fit of bashfulness. "But we shouldn't be so direct," she said. "We should maintain our mystery for at least two minutes."

I felt myself go toward her in a reflexive longing undercut by the exhaustion that often accompanies old reflexes. "I'm Susan," I said.

Her name was Erin. She was thirty-two years old. She was trying, with another woman, to establish a small press and, to this end, was living on a grant that was about to run out. She was reading a self-help book called *Care of the Soul* and also *Dead Souls* by Gogol. She had been taking Zoloft for six months. She seemed to like that I'd written a book of poetry, even if it had been ten years ago. She said that she sometimes described herself as a "butch bottom" but that lately she questioned the accuracy of that. I told her that I was sick of categories like butch bottom and femme top or vice versa. I said I was looking for something more genuine, although I didn't know yet what it was. She said she thought she probably was too.

"That picture you took of me was sad," I said. "I look sad in it."

I expected her to deny it, but she didn't say anything. She reached between my legs and with one finger drew tiny, concentrated circles through my slacks. It seemed a very natural thing. It seemed as if she thought anyone could've come along and done that, and it might as well be her. This wasn't true, but for the moment, I liked the idea; it was a simple, easy idea. It made my genitals seem disconnected from me, yet at the same time the most central part of me. I parted my lips. I stared straight ahead. The silence was like a small bubble rising through water. She kissed the side of my lips, and I turned so that we kissed full on. She opened her mouth and I felt her in a rush of tension and need. I was surprised to feel such need in this woman; it was a dense, insensible neediness that rose through her in a gross howl, momentarily shouting out whatever else her body had to say. I opened in the pit of my stomach and let her discharge into me. The tension slacked off and I could feel her sparkle again, now softer and more diffuse.

We separated and I glanced at the woman on the steps, who was, I thought, looking a little despondent. "Let's go in," I said.

Inside we were subdued and a bit shy. We walked around together, she sometimes leading me with the tips of her fingers on my wrist or arm. I only knew one person at the party and she had a lot of friends there. But being in such a bare way made me feel mute, large and fleshy next to her lean, nervous form. I think it made us both feel the fragility of our bond, and although we spoke to other people, we said very little to each other, as though to talk might break it. We assumed she would walk me home; when we left she offered me her arm, and I fleetingly compared her easy gallantry with Frederick's miserable imitation of politeness.

As we walked she talked about people at the party, particularly their romantic problems. I listened to her, puzzled over the competence of her voice, the delicacy of her leading fingers, the brute need of her kiss. Her competence and delicacy were attractive, but it was the need that pulled me towards her. Not because I imagined satisfying it—I didn't think that was possible—but because I wanted to rub against it, to put my hand on it, to comfort it. Actually, I wasn't sure what I wanted with it.

We sat on my front steps and made out. "I'd like to invite you in," I said, "but it would be too much like that guy—I meet you at a party, bring you home." I shrugged.

She nodded solemnly, looked away, looked back and smiled. "So? I thought you said nothing happened anyway."

"Well, it was weird. I sucked his dick, well, sporadically, and then he wouldn't fuck me."

"That's sort of harsh."

"Yeah. He acted like he was being nice and I believed him, but then when I saw him again, he acted like a weird prick."

She embraced me sideways. "That sort of turns me on," she said. She nuzzled my neck, and the feminine delicacy of her lips and eyelashes was like a startling burst of gold vein in a broken piece of rock. I slid my hands under her shirt. She had small, muscular breasts and freakishly long nipples and there was faint, sweet down all along her low back.

I invited her in. She entered the living room with a tense, mercurial swagger that pierced my heart. We sat on the couch. "So," she said. "Do I get to be the bad boy? Are you gonna suck my cock?"

"Wait," I said. "I don't . . . um . . ."

She knelt between my legs with her hand on my thighs. Her fingers were blunt and spatulate, with little gnawed nails. "If I say something wrong, it's because I'm not sure what to do. I'm not used to this. I want to please you but you also make me want to . . . I don't even know."

"I'm not sure what I want either," I said. "I think there might be something wrong with me."

She held my face in her hands. "Let me make it better," she said. She looked at me, and her expression seemed to fracture. Abruptly, she struck me across the face, backhanded me and then struck me with her palm again. She checked my reaction. "Open your mouth," she said. "Stick out your tongue." I did. She started to unzip her pants, then faltered. "Um," she said, "Susan? Is this cool?"

"Yeah."

When we were finished, I walked her out the door onto the porch. Using her ballpoint we wrote our numbers on scraps of paper torn from a flyer that had been placed on my doormat to remind me to fight AIDS. She held my face and kissed my cheek and left.

When I woke the next day I didn't think of her but I felt her, and I wasn't sure what she felt like to me. I was acutely aware of the artificiality of our experience. It felt like a dollhouse with tiny plastic furniture and false windows looking out on mechanically painted meadows and cloud-dotted skies. It felt both safe and cruelly stifling, and both feelings appealed to me. More simply, I felt as if some habitual pain had shifted position slightly, allowing me to breathe more easily. As the day went on I thought of her, but gingerly. The thought was like a smell that is both endearing and faintly embarrassing. I remembered how she had knelt and said, "I'm not sure what to do," and I remembered her reckless blow to my face. She seemed split in two, and the memory split me in two. But when she called me, I was happy; I realized that I had not expected to hear from her.

"I would've called earlier," she said. "But last night was intense for me and I had to process. Like I said, I usually bottom."

Her voice was bright and optimistic, but there was something else in it too. It was as if she'd made an agreement with somebody to supply all the optimism required on a general basis all by herself for the rest of her life, and that the strain of it had become almost anguishing. But when she opened the door of her house to greet me, it was with brash, striding movement, and she was elegant and beautiful in a sleek suit.

We went to a Thai restaurant for dinner. It was a cheap place that maintained its dignity with orderly arrangement and dim lighting. Little statuettes and vases invoked foreignness unctuously yet honorably. The other diners seemed grateful to be in such an unassuming place, where all they had to do was talk to each other and eat. Erin pulled out my chair for me.

A waitress, vibrant with purpose, poured us water in a harried rattle of ice. We ordered sweet drinks and dainty, greasy dishes. Erin's smile burst off her face in a wild curlicue. I imagined her unsmiling, wearing lipstick, with her hair upswept, in a hat with a little veil; she would've been formidable and very beautiful. Her jaw was strong but also suggestive of intense female sensitivity and erotic suppleness. Then under that was a rigidity that made me think of something trapped. I reached across the table and took her hand. We were both sweating slightly.

"I haven't been involved with a woman for a long time," I said. "Mostly I'm with men. Although I haven't been involved with men lately either."

"I don't care," she said. "Basically I'm a dyke but I like sex with men sometimes, so I can understand."

I asked her if she always needed to role-play in sex. I said I was trying not to relate to people in such a structured way. "I mean, I can do that kind of sex, um, obviously, and I can like it. It gets me off and everything. But it's a mechanical response. It's not deep."

"Well," she said, "I hope you didn't feel like what we did was mechanical because it wasn't for me. I hardly ever top anybody so it was really new." She drank her sweet iced coffee with ingenuous relish.

"It wasn't really mechanical, because I could feel you under the fantasy. But I've done those fantasies all my life, and I want to try to be more genuine and direct, so whatever we do, it'll really be us. Emotionally, I mean."

"I can respect that," she said. Her voice was like that of a little girl trying to be good for her mother. It gave me a strange, sad pleasure. It made me want to pretend to be her mother, just like another little girl.

Erin was from Kansas. She used to be an Evangelical Christian. She wasn't raised a Christian, but she had converted on her own initiative when she was fourteen. Her parents had separated when she was ten because of her dad's unearthed pedophilia, and her mother had to work brutal night shifts that made her more disappointed with life than she already was. Erin spent most of her time with ardent Christian boys with whom she went to religious meetings. She was occasionally moved to give bouquets of handpicked flowers to various bewildered girls, but it wasn't until prom night that it hit her that her repeated daydreams about the elaborate scorn of a certain beautiful brat were actually erotic in nature. She made a successful pass at a drunk, pretty little mouse in the restroom and never wore a dress again—although she valiantly tried to be a queer Evangelical well after she realized it would never work.

I pictured her standing alone in plain neat clothes in a landscape of dry sunlight and parched yellow earth. Vague shapes were present in the distance, but I couldn't see what they were. She was extending her arm to offer a bunch of flowers to someone who wasn't there. The expression on her face was humble, stoic, and tenaciously expectant, as if she was waiting for something she had never seen yet chose to believe would someday appear. It was the expression she had on her face while she was talking to me. She was telling me that when she told her mother she was gay, her mother said, "I could just shit," and went into the next room to watch TV.

She had other expressions, too. When we talked abut the ongoing rape trial of a pop star, I made predictable sarcastic comments about people who said that the girl had probably brought it on herself. Erin first agreed with me, then reversed herself to say that maybe the girl had asked for it. Her expression when she said that was rambunctious, with a sensual shade of silly meanness—but mostly it was the expression of a kid with her hands in Play-doh, squishing around and making fun shapes.

After dinner we went drinking. As we walked down the street, we held hands. There was real feeling between us, but it was unstable, as if we had been rewarded with a treat of flavored ice, which we wanted to put off eating for as long as possible so that we could savor it, but it was already melting anyway.

We went to a bar where people in various states of good-natured resignation sat in the dark under crushing disco music. I ordered drinks with lots of amaretto in them. The sweetness gave my mild drunkenness a pleasant, miasmic quality.

Erin said she liked what I had said about trying to be more genuine. She said her therapist had recently suggested to her that it might be good for Erin to spend at least a few weeks getting to know women before she had sex with them, and that, although she hated the idea on principle, she was considering it.

I reminded her that we'd already had sex.

"But we could start fresh," she said. "And get to know each other before we do it again."

I thought of going with her to restaurants and movies. We would sit and discuss current events, and under all our talk would be the memory of my open mouth and exposed tongue. I moved close to her on the banquette and put my head on her slim, spare shoulder. She held me. Her hair had a tender chemical smell. I pictured her washing it, bent naked over a bathtub, moving her arms with the touching confidence of rote grooming practices.

She walked me to my door and we kissed. Her kiss felt honorable and empty. I asked her in. "We don't have to have sex," I said. She came in and we lay on the living room floor with our arms around one another. We touched each other gently and respectfully, but with each such caress I felt as if we became more separated. That made me touch her more insistently and more intimately. I felt her neediness rise through her abdomen in a long pulse; we brushed our lips together in a stifled dry kiss and then opened our mouths to feed.

"I want to do what you said," she whispered. "I want to just be us."

I took her face in my hands. I wanted to say "my darling girl" but I hardly knew her. I pulled up my shirt and pulled my bra down. I pulled up her shirt. I knelt over her and rubbed against her chest and belly, just touching. She closed her eyes and I could feel her waiting in her deep body, wanting me to show her what "ourselves" might be. And I would've done that except that I didn't know. I could remember her at the restaurant, talking about her mother and religion, expressing her opinions. Again, I imagined her standing alone, offering her flowers to no one. She was very dear and I wanted her, but I could only see her in pornographic snapshots, stripped of her opinions and her past. I unzipped her pants and pulled them down. I turned her over and positioned her the way I wanted her. Her breath subtly deepened; she was taut and vibrant and absolutely present. I lightly rubbed my knuckles against her genitals. I felt an impersonal half-cruelty that was more titillating than real cruelty.

But she wanted to be cruel too, or rather to pretend that she was. She would take her artificial debasement to a certain point, and then she would change direction. She would kiss me and I would feel her tender self in a burst of nakedness that stopped my breath—and then she would veer away, immersing herself in some internal personality that didn't know or care about me. She was a nasty teenage boy, she was a silly kid, she was a full, deep woman all the way down to her private organs. She slapped me and she pulled my hair—but she demanded that I beat her between her shoulder blades. And when I did she whispered "Thank you," her face transfigured with sorrow so abject that I was for one violent second absolutely repelled, and then drawn back with equal violence.

Afterward, we lay against my throw pillows, cuddling and drinking chocolate milk. "Well," I said. "I guess that was us." She giggled and rubbed her nose on my stomach. My feral kitten crept round the bedroom door and peered at us, her wide eyes wistful, curious, and scared.

Later in the week we took a nighttime walk. We walked uphill to Noe Valley, talking through strained waves of breath. She talked about a book she wanted to publish, even though the author was a nut who called every day to pester Erin with questions about how best to advance her career. Her stride was long and confident, but the inclination of her head was mechanical and deferential. She asked me if I would ever again dress the way I had dressed when she'd first seen me. I said probably, but not to take uphill walks. She told me that a previous girlfriend who had been molested by her father when she was little had liked Erin to pretend to be her father while they were having sex; she asked me if I thought that was creepy. I said it definitely didn't seem like they were relating directly as their real selves. She laughed and said it sure felt real to her. She pushed me against a car and tried to make me turn around. I snapped at her to cut it out; there was hurt feeling in her retraction, and I put my arm around her.

We walked downhill and came upon the slovenly burghership of Twenty-Fourth Street. People dressed in floppy clothing and carrying lumpy handbags walked up and down in complicated states of distraction. Two men were standing on the corner, each with a telescope, offering people the chance to admire the planets for fifty cents. One telescope was labeled "The Moon" and the other "Venus." A group of children stood around them looking as if they were willing to be delighted but weren't sure that the moon and Venus were quite delightful enough.

"Do you want to look?" asked Erin.

I said yes because I could tell she wanted to. I did enjoy waiting in line with the kids; their hope for enchantment, glimmering just faintly through their premature disaffection, was poignant in its secret tenacity. Their mothers sat drinking cappuccino on the outdoor bench of an expensive coffee shop, looking pleased to see their children engaged in such a good, simple activity. The moon was the cold orb it had been represented to be.

We held hands as we walked back up the hill. The city was sparkling, calm and beautiful in panorama. Erin told me that she'd fantasized about adopting kids one day, but she knew she needed to "work on" herself before that could happen. She asked if I'd ever wanted to have a family.

"No," I said, "not for its own sake." I paused, watching my shoes crease with each steep step. "If, when I was in my twenties, I'd fallen in love with someone and he'd loved me, I would've wanted to have children with him. And I probably would've loved it. But that didn't happen, and I'm not going to be running around trying to get pregnant just to do it."

"It doesn't make you sad?"

"No. Although sometimes, when I hear friends talk about their babies, or other friends talk about how they desperately want to have babies, I wonder if I'm really sad and am just pretending I'm not." My breath chugged earnestly. "I think I'm sadder that I don't write poetry anymore. Although I've been thinking lately that I might start again. Not now though. Maybe when I'm old."

"Cool." She paused. "I just felt like pushing you up against a car again. But I won't."

Erin shared a large flat with a former girlfriend named Jana and Jana's girlfriend Paulette. The house had a tiny yard full of flowers, with the saucy attitude of a picnic. Erin's two large cats sat on the pavement blinking, or bounded and promenaded about the area. I loved coming to Erin's house. Every time I rounded the corner and saw it, I felt I was approaching a place where tenderness and good humor prevailed.

One night I came unannounced, surprising Erin in her lavender thermal pajamas. We sat together on her bed and enjoyed the garish comfort of her electric fireplace. To entertain me, she brought a large cardboard box out of the closet and showed me what was in it. There were somber albums of family pictures (tiny, troubled Erin in a ruffled swimsuit, handsome dad looking absently at something outside the frame, towering, pissed-off mom), a plaque that had been awarded her in a high school photography contest, a track team trophy, a bracelet her brother had made for her in junior high, love letters, an artificial penis made of rubber, an apparatus with which to strap it on, an odd assortment of small plastic animals and some Polaroids of Erin naked except for a dog collar and leash around her neck. She explained that the pictures had been taken by a heterosexual couple whom she had met when she'd answered their advertisement for a "slave girl."

"They totally loved me," she said. "It was great, but I got tired of it before they did. They dragged it out too long. They kept making it a big deal that he was eventually going to fuck me with his cock—the way they went on about it, I just lost interest."

I looked at the Polaroids. I was slightly discomfited by her thinness; her ribs showed and her eyes looked starved and abnormally luminous.

"I forgot they even took those pictures until they sent them to me a month later." She put them in a pile and placed them back in the box. She indicated the rubber penis. "I was going to use that on you," she said. "But it reminds me too much of Jana. You deserve your own cock."

Maybe because she had told me a story, I told her one about myself. It was something that had happened when, as a teenager, I had tried having sex for money. I told her the story to excite her, and I could see right away that it did. At first it excited me too; I had never told anyone about it before.

"He didn't want me to take my pantyhose off, he just wanted me to bend over and pull them down to about mid-thigh, which sort of embarrassed me. But I did it, and then I bent over and waited, and he didn't do anything."

"Yeah?" We were lying together, Erin up on her elbow, her eyes dilating slightly as she went into the rigid psychic suspension required by the schema of fantasy. She was, I thought, the only person I could tell this story to.

"Well, it was weird because on one hand I was embarrassed on account of the pantyhose thing, but on the other hand, I was very matter-of-fact, I guess teenagers just naturally are. I said, 'Um, are you, like, doing something or what?' And he didn't say anything, so I said, 'Well, what are you doing?' And he said, 'Shut up. I'm doing what I gotta do.'"

"Which was?"

I realized that I was not excited anymore. I was not embarrassed either. I didn't know what I felt.

"What did he do?"

I put my face against her chest.

She ruffled my hair. "C'mon."

I tilted my head up and whispered in her ear.

Erin yelped with glee. "He jerked off on you?" She fell down on her back and roared with laughter. We rolled around laughing, me tickling her, her little chin pointing at the ceiling. Then she grabbed me and held my head against her chest and I felt, under her quick breath, her radiant tenderness; it was as if some secret part of her had come out to touch me gently and had then drawn back into its hiding place.

The next day I was shopping in a clothing store and daydreaming about Erin, when a pop song on the sound system took my imagination in a facile grab. It was a flimsy love song, sung in a high, caressing register. There was real feeling in it, but the singer had tortured it into deformed and precious shapes that debased his own emotionality with a methodical viciousness that was quite breathtaking and gave the song a strange, obscene jolt. It reminded me of Frederick and the artificial civility just veiling his furious contempt. It also reminded me of Erin, offering her flowers to no one. These images seemed opposite each other, but at the same time locked together in an electrical stasis, each holding the other in place.

It was a very popular song. I had seen the singer interviewed on TV. He was a foppish young man who seemed thoroughly disgusted to find himself so liked.

We no longer talked about trying to have sex as "ourselves." Sometimes this was all right with me; we could find a little slot to be in and frantically wiggle around in it until we were both satisfied. Other times I felt disgruntled and ashamed of myself. On those occasions I was aware that I was offering her only a superficial tidbit of myself, a tidbit tricked out to look substantial. It was dishonest but our tacit agreement to be dishonest together at least allowed a tiny moment of exchange that I wasn't sure was possible otherwise. And perhaps it was not fair to call her behavior dishonest, since she was so used to it that to her it felt true.

We saw each other two or three times a week, usually for dinner or a movie. Sometimes we went out with her friends. They were loud, lewd, exhibitionistic, and kind. They were a comedienne, an office worker, a photographer, and a waitress who wrote acerbic short stories. They were mostly ten tears younger than me, and in their presence I felt enveloped in bracing female warmth that I did not experience with most people my own age, certainly not with my august colleagues. I loved standing around with them in the dark of some bar, talking sex trash. They made fun of me for having sex with men, although most of them occasionally did too.

"When I have guy fantasies, I want it to be a frat boy thing," said Gina, the robust waitress. "I want them to call me bitch and make me suck their cocks and all that."

"I like something more refined myself," I said. "Cruel, but refined."

"I'm the reverse about guys," said Lana. She was a curvaceous girl with loud clothes, severe hair, and signifying glasses. "Women can degrade me, sometimes, if I really like them. But if I'm with men I want them to get on their knees and worship it. And they have to mean it."

Their talk was like a friendly shoving match between giggling kids, a game about aggression that made aggression harmless. Although I wasn't sure it was completely harmless. It was fun to say that I liked something refined and cruel, but under the fun was an impatient yank of boredom and under that was indignation and pain.

One night Gina wore a rubber cock strapped onto her body under her pants. She clownishly pressed it against the rumps of men, who laughed and jovially explained that she was doing it wrong. She pressed it against my thigh and I cooed and groped the rubber thing, arching my back and butt in a satire of narcissism and subservience.

"I'll give Erin ten dollars if she'll get on her knees and suck Gin's cock," said Donna.

Erin smiled, and began to move forward. "She doesn't need ten dollars," I said.

"Just for you, baby," said Gina.

"She doesn't need it," I said, and put my arm around Erin's waist. Erin's smile stuck and she halted uncertainly.

"Aww, Susan loves Erin," said Donna.

We all went to dance, our movements sloppily describing friendship sex, display, and animal warmth, all in a loop of drunkenness that equalized every sensation. I loved these young women.

But the next day, our posturing seemed stupid. I sat in my office between hours, thinking of the moment when Donna had offered Erin ten dollars, and I felt embarrassed. I imagined my office mate, a hale critic in her fifties, witnessing the exchange in the bar. I imagined her smiling gamely, eager to approve of these young women who were, after all, gender bending. I imagined her smile faltering as she registered that Erin's eager response had nothing to do with sex, or even with fun. I imagined her frowning and turning away. I closed my eyes and felt this imagined rejection. I wanted to protect Erin from it, to make my office mate see her in all her different aspects, her brave flowers, her swagger, her private tenderness. That way I made my oblivious office mate hear the discomfort I didn't want to feel.

When I got in bed that night I thought of Erin erotically, but my thoughts quickly became inarticulate. I pictured her staring at me like a frightened animal. I imagined a deep, perpetual moan that racked her body but did not come out of her mouth. I pictured the organs in her abdomen dry as old roots, parched for lack of some fundamental nurture that she had never received and was trying futilely to find.

The next night we had dinner together. She pulled my chair out for me as she always did. Her gestures and expressions were piquant and feisty, but for me they were occluded by the way I had imagined her the previous night. What I saw in front of me and what I had imagined both seemed real, yet one seemed to have nothing to do with the other. I was appalled to realize that I didn't want to see her again.

Still, I invited her into my apartment. We sat on my living room rug and I brought us dishes of tapioca pudding that I had made. There was subtle discomfort between us; I wondered if she had sensed the change in me, or if there had also been a change in her. She tried to kiss me and I said I wasn't sure I wanted to have sex. She said okay. We ate our desserts and talked. I said I didn't think I wanted to stay in San Francisco. I said I thought my apartment was beautiful but that it seemed to me like a way station.

"There are so many doors and hallways in this place," I said. "It makes it seem like a crossroads."

"Is that how you think of me?" asked Erin.

Her question startled me. I said no, and took her hand and kissed her, but I wasn't sure if I was telling the truth. She kissed me back as though she knew this. Kissing, we toppled onto the floor. The moan I had sensed in her was nearly palpable, but I knew she didn't feel it. My kiss became an escalating slur of useless feeling. I kissed her to locate her, but it was no good; she was all in fragments. I took her wrist. "Don't slap me," I said. "I don't want that." She disengaged her wrist and pulled up my skirt. I knew I should not let this happen. She pulled my pantyhose and underwear down. Inwardly, I rushed forward, trying to engage her, to find one tiny place we could wiggle around in together. She flew by me in an electrical storm. She had discovered that I didn't want her, but she was ignoring her discovery. Without knowing why, I ignored it too. I rifled my memories of her, all her different faces; none of them stayed with me. She handled me roughly. Tomorrow, I thought, I would tell her I didn't want to be intimate anymore. I closed my eyes. She was doing something strange. I opened my eyes.

She slapped my crotch with a handful of tapioca.

Jerkily, I sat up and stared. "Erin," I said, "what are you doing?"

"Sorry," she said. "It just felt right." She giggled nervously and contracted herself. Her open hand sat in her lap, wet with beads of tapioca.

Absurd tears came to my eyes. I felt almost as if someone had thrown a pie in my face, but that wasn't why the tears had come. "What a gross, inconsiderate thing to do." But that wasn't right either.

"Oh, Susan, come on."

She reached for me and I pulled away. My stingy little tears went dry. Erin shrugged and self-consciously ate some tapioca off her hand. Then she rubbed her nose with the back of it.

"I'll get some paper towels," she said. "I'll clean the carpet."

"I'll be right back," I said. "I'm going to take a shower."

When I came back into the living room, Erin was seated on the couch, her limbs held tight into her body. Even in the dark, I could see she wore the starved face I'd seen in the Polaroids that the swinging heterosexuals had taken of her.

"Do you want me to go?" she said.

"I don't know." I knelt and put my hand on her foot. "I think so."

"I'll go if you want. But I don't want you to think I'm a jerk. I didn't do that to be a jerk."

"I know," I said. "I know, Erin."

"You know, you seem so vulnerable," she said. "You say you want to be real. But you don't. Not really."

I took my hand off her foot and turned my head away. The silence held varied beats and long, slow pulses.

When she left she held my face in her hand and kissed me. "I probably won't call you for a while," she said. "But you can call me, if you need to process."

After she was gone, I lay on the floor until I noticed that my old cat was eating leftover tapioca from a dish. I got up to put the dishes away, and then got in bed. I had a puzzling sensation of triumph at finding myself alone, a sensation that took me happily into sleep.

But I woke in two hours, sweating and throwing off the blankets. I wondered if Erin had thrown the pie in my face because she had been secretly angry. Or perhaps what had felt like anger was just the random overspill of a ceaseless internal spasm. I imagined the terrible moan inside her, like an endless, coughing dry sob. I imagined it so acutely that I was transfigured by it. The pain of it was so ugly it was almost revolting, and yet there was something desperately vital about it. I tried to think what "it" was. My kitten woke and touched me with her small muzzle. She allowed me to stroke her; even in her slumberous state, her small body was quick and fierce with life. She felt her life all the way down to the bottom. Everybody wants it, I thought. Erin has it, but she can't bear it. Again, I saw her low internal organs, parched but tough and fiercely alive, holding on.

Green Toads of the High Desert

JUDY GRAHN

My mom giggles like a little kid who has gotten away with something naughty when I ask her whether she has stopped writing to everyone or just me. I haven't gotten a note from her for three weeks, and I don't tell her I am worried, I just ask the question and then listen to the giggling. She is taking open delight in not writing, that much I can tell, even over the telephone.

"Who is this?" she asks after we exchange a few more how-are-you's. Usually I respond with "Judith," which with her particular hearing problem is almost guaranteed to make her guess "Edith?" She says the name very slowly, like "E-space-space-dith?" in two ascending high whole notes. She has been talking slow-syllabled like that all year, effortfully, as though the jaw is on strike and taking over the company.

Edith was our neighbor and close family friend who has been dead for seven years, a crossing which doesn't seem to have impressed my Mom. Time has become compressed for her. Or maybe she's right. Maybe it is Edith on the phone sometimes, calling to remind her of her immortality. This time it is me.

"I'm calling from California." Let's give her a big clue.

"O-hh." I hear wheels clicking across the miles between our two minds. She's going through a short list of names that includes her older sister, who moved to Bakersfield twelve years ago. And then the explosion of pleasure: "Ju-dith!"

She is ninety-two this year, and busy giving up one thing or another, a matter of "going light" I should say, the way birds do when they lose weight in certain seasons. Except she is also becoming luminous and high-humored. "How's Kris?" she asks, immediately adding, "She's your other part." This is not how she was ten years ago, when I first took Kris out to meet my parents, the year before my father died. By the time Mom and I have said our half dozen "goodbye-I-love-yous" and hung up the phone I am remembering that trip.

We'd only been together a couple of months when I wrote Mom and Dad that I had a new friend who was a mechanic and we were coming to visit. My folks live in the high desert of New Mexico and we took off in Kris's avocado green VW bus. We weren't yet living together, and full of hesitations about trying it, and nothing lets you know whether you can live intimately or not as completely as being nose to nose for ten days in the confines of a vehicle.

I thought this trip would give us plenty of time to talk, as there were so many subjects we had been avoiding, but the first day's drive told me different. With no air conditioner to mediate the August heat blast we had all the windows down, a favorite way for her to drive anyhow, and in all seasons. In the roar of moving air and shrieking trucks she put Bonnie Raitt on the tape deck and cranked up the sound till we were splitting the sky open with enthusiastic harmonics to Bonnie's sweet dark country western. Endangered by the dry oven blast, we guzzled water and citrus drinks across the chest-searing sauna that is an unairconditioned car in the Mojave desert in summer and then turned south along the brilliant blue knife of Colorado River across the Arizona border.

Gila Bend is a tiny town in a blistering bit of road in southern Arizona. It was named for a colorful and rare huge lizard which had become exotified and demonized. In my childhood, roadside sheds with screaming red and yellow signs had featured them for voyeuristic scrutiny, along with rattlesnakes and other hapless desert creatures who happened to use venom in their own defense. Tourists were enticed to stop and spend money to gape at the little dying prisoners in their cages, feeling grateful not to be stepping on them. I had always hated these displays, and still had an attitude toward the town though now such misuses of creatures were illegal.

So it seemed to me our journey turned ominous when the bus lurched and Kris guided us with a deflating tire to the exit for Gila

Bend late in what remained of the blistering August afternoon. The station attendant was amiable, and the amount of sweat pouring off us all day had made us dull-headed, so we decided to stay overnight and the gas station guy recommended a motel.

My first shock once we were in the room was noticing some kind of steam coming off the toilet water, so that for a second I wondered if I hadn't overheated my bladder and my own pee was steaming the commode like a radiator in the desert. The second shock was turning on the cold water tap and nearly scalding my hands. "What the hell is this?"

"All the water in town is the same temperature—ninety-two degrees," the motel manager reported to our inquiry. "Just don't ever turn on the hot water at the same time as the cold and you won't really scald yourself," he assured us.

We watched as buckets of ice vanished into the steamy vapors of the "cold" water before we could get a cold sip to the lips. Setting down our cups, we looked at each other. The unspoken question of whether we were going to make love at this stop hung in the air for a moment, as each of us searched inside, finding the reality of our tiredness. This was the disappointing part of the trip—I had imagined that we would be steaming lusciously skin to skin in motel beds or even the bus, which featured its own bed. Instead, this trip was steaming us.

"Let's try the swimming pool," Kris suggested hopefully, so we grabbed suits and towels and followed the signs along the broiling cement driveway.

The motel had two pools, one big steamy one and a glimmering shallow wading pool. "This could be sort of like a hot tub," I suggested doubtfully. The shallow pool did look inviting with its blue and cream tiles, despite the warm mist lifting off its surface.

"Why don't we relax in warm water in the evening when it's cooler?"

Okay, I agreed.

In the late evening, though it wasn't what anyone would call "cooler," we put on suits and nestled together into the small pool. This was more than worth it for the rare chance to be close in semi-public, and the added exhilaration of being outdoors under the naked sky in an intimate situation. This didn't appear to be a popular tourist stopping place. No one was around so we treated the small pool like our personal bed, the water's calm seeping like deep psychic pleasure into sore muscles, our throats opening to long cold streams from the cans of pop we drank to cool our insides. She put her arms around me and we laid our heads against the slick tiles that rimmed the luminous silky water.

Our bodies were stretched out langorously floating in that idyllic state, the next best thing to sex, resting half-excitedly against each other when from the corner of my eye I saw a moving shadow and sensed a being rising from the lower depths of water. "Naw," I thought to my instantly pounding heart. "Now I'm hallucinating, the heat of the drive sure must have gotten to me." I nuzzled my chin against her shoulder and shifted so my head was leaning on her upper chest. Her breast fell along my cheek. I dropped into a doze, awakened by a sensation of a bumping from underneath, and instantly my childhood experience as a desert kid came skittering toward me with the Grade B movie experience of coming eye to eye with a tarantula in the public swimming pool or the sense my body gave of flying around the room the day the long segmented—very, very long segmented—centipede climbed out of the drain in the bathtub while I was in it.

As an adult I had used these fears to try to understand other peoples' fears of me as a lesbian. I had figured, if I can learn to get over my fear of a centipede, others can learn to get over their fears of me. Not bad reasoning, as far as it went. And I'd discovered that centipedes were good mothers, wrapping those long bodies protectively around their broods. Somehow that made me like them better. But those were real insects, not some phantom seen from the corner of a sleepy eye.

Then I believed I felt her hand approaching my midsection, and thought how daring the woman was, out here in the open to hold me and now to reach to fondle me. I opened my eyes to smile at her. Then I clutched Kris and let out a shriek, limbs flailing and neck stretched far away from a scratchy insistent and very concrete monster that had just crawled onto my stomach.

"What is it what is it what is it!" I cried out, thrashing my way out of the pool like a panicky poodle.

"I don't know," Kris said, "you tell me—I didn't see anything, my eyes were closed. I was napping." She had climbed out with me, somewhat disgustedly, I thought. I thought how undignified I must look with my eyes popping out of my head, shrieking. Oh no, she's going to think I'm a hysteric who can't be trusted in difficult situations. Calming down now that I saw the mysterious stranger was not following me, I peered back into the water. "Where did it go?"

"Where did what go?" Kris still looked skeptical. Not only was it not following me, now it didn't seem to be anywhere and I worried she would think I was the kind of woman who would wake her up every other night expecting her to explore mysterious house noises with a flashlight.

"There it is!" I pointed to a slight shadowy pale form hovering in the silky pool light and began to laugh, then got back into the water. "It's a little toad. Must have been trying to climb out. Must be trapped in this little pool." I slid my hand under the eagerly swimming body, barely visible as an outline in its watery camouflage.

"Oh, how beautiful it is," Kris exclaimed over what has to have been the palest shade of green anyone ever wore, even the gold eyes were light as mineral shavings. I turned the little creature loose on the paving and we watched as she hopped away. "Why does it look like such a ghost?" I wondered.

"The hot water turns them pale. They live in the pipes all over town," the motel manager said later in answer to our question. "You wouldn't think they could survive in this hot water, but they do."

When we filled up with gas in the morning the gas station guy explained more about the water. "Used to be eighty-seven but everybody in town believed the hotshot engineering advisors and drilled a new deeper well at more than anyone could afford and now it's five degrees hotter. See here. The water stains everyone's teeth and erodes them away," the gas station guy said. He showed his own poor teeth, dark stubs in a trapped mouth. "S'ruined the town. I'd move away too, but this is my business and I can't leave it," he mourned.

"Oooh," I said sympathetically.

I thought about him on the mountainous drive over the New Mexico border to the town of Lordsburg, where we spent our second night. How a person can get fatally wrapped up in what they have already done, as though life is a fishnet we weave around our own feet. This reminded me of my last relationship, how I could never please her no matter what I did. And the more I tried, the more tangled I got. Until I was doing things I hated myself for, her displeasure the hook taking me deeper and deeper. The memory made me uneasy as I stared out the window at the saguaro forest around us.

That night once again Kris and I did not make love, though the motel room was pleasant and even air conditioned. Road tiredness, I thought, though our seriousness seemed to be made of something more profound. I debated wearing the new white Levis I had bought to impress her with, and then slid them back into the suitcase in favor of plainer travel pants. The white pants could wait, and I would know the right moment. After dinner we went for a walk, and to our delight we discovered a park. Even though it was nearly pitch dark we crossed the thin grass to a playground.

"Look at the swings," Kris said, "I love to swing." She sat down on a wooden seat and grasped the chains, which creaked. "Come on," she urged, "don't you like this? This is fun." At first I felt foolish, then I got into the swaying motion with her and forgot my self-consciousness. The creaking chains created a song I found myself examining for hidden meaning.

In the dark, she began to talk earnestly about her past relationship, how she had felt inflexibly identified. Her face was shadowed between the chains of the swing, which glinted every so often, and her voice was all the more easy to listen to because I couldn't see her expressions. I could hear the lyric qualities in it, and the basic optimism.

"I don't want to be that hurt again," she was saying. "I'm not willing to be anything except exactly who I am in a relationship."

"I'm not sure I even want a relationship," I said. Then, to fill in her overly long silence, "I mean, I'm just not ready quite yet to fall over any cliffs." I didn't say, and you don't seem substantial to me; I want someone to rely on, someone with big strong shoulders to lean against. Her shoulders are narrow, her face and neck delicate. My last relationship had worn me out too, I realized.

The moon broke through clouds in a dazzling display of directed light that enveloped us, so I felt we were in a bubble together, and separately, each watching the other. The chains continued to creak as we rocked back and forth, and though we had resolved nothing whatever, a tenderness came between us. We walked out of the park hand in hand, and I was so oblivious to the earth I nearly stepped on a small shape in the road, and I hopped awkwardly over it at the last moment before the crush.

Laughing and puzzled, we turned back to find a small toad,

dark olive green and fearlessly possessive of the road. "It's rained here, too," I said. "Look, there's another one, the town must be full of toads." I remembered my childhood in Las Cruces, how welcome and exciting the brief season of toads was, coming in the late summer rains. "They lie deep under the clay," I explained, "for years if necessary, waiting for a season of wet. Then they just explode all over town. I brought a few tadpoles home once and we put them in a tank—an old Coca-Cola case behind an abandoned store. We watched them get fins, and then legs—it was so exciting."

We walked on and suddenly car lights lit us up, with our hands linked. I cringed as a carload of teenaged boys slowed and began to holler insults. We separated and walked quickly, faces turned alertly to the threatening car. It passed, became more noisy, and swayed to turn. The boys in back were pounding on the sides of the car. I searched the road for a stone or board, anything, frantic that we had left ourselves wide open, weren't even carrying knives. And then the car straightened and rode on. We breathed again. The insults themselves didn't bother me. They were names for who we are together, and ordinarily I love hearing them. And you could turn even the word "milk" into an ugly name if you holler it angrily enough. But, I wondered, what if they had gotten out to beat us, could we really take care of ourselves, each other, in this world? And fell asleep with this question.

We crested the mesa overlooking Las Cruces from the west around ten in the morning. We would visit my parents only a few hours, partly because in their eighties they grew irritable from too much company, and partly because Kris had to get back to work on Tuesday morning, and it was already Sunday. Whatever happened among us on this first visit would have the rarefied effect of severe compression, making each moment an event and each event momentous.

My mom was outside her apartment door. She walked haltingly toward us as though on stilts that reached deep under the earth. When we were close to her she flung herself into Kris's arms. "*Judith!*" she cried.

Kris hugged her back, then gently turned her and guided her in my direction. "I think this is where you want to go."

"It's me, Mom," I said.

"Oh!" she said. "Oh, your hair!"

Puzzled, I patted the top of my head. "Hair?" I asked.

Just at that moment Marian came out of her own apartment, downstairs from my parents'. Marian is my mom's age. She wobbled toward me, hand outstretched.

"Congratulations, dear," she said, in tones she reserved for graduating students and blushing brides.

This puzzle was followed by another. Once we were each situated in seats upstairs in my parents' living room, my white-bearded father in his wooden arm chair and Kris and I on the rose couch, my mother stood up in the middle of the floor and surprised us all by bursting into tears.

"What is it?" I asked with concern. My father said nothing, just stroking his beard reflectively. He couldn't see anymore, so only his ears could tell him the course of history. My mother doesn't hear, necessitating repetition and sometimes yelling. Their twin conditions had led them to heights of cooperation unimaginable in their younger days, so that watching them cook a dinner together was like watching an intricate dance of the senses turned into two characters on stage. However, we had arrived so late in the day they had already accomplished the cooking, as I could tell by the delicious smells wafting from the kitchen. Meantime, I was worried that Mom was going to burst out with some dire medical prognosis or other crisis.

On my third query she sobbed, "Oh, it's so awful to be old. Don't ever get old."

I was not satisfied with this as it is her standard answer when she really cannot say what is bothering her, and since her crying persisted, so did my question. Finally she blurted out, "It's your hair, what have you done to it?"

My hair again. I looked at Kris and shrugged in puzzlement. We had both cropped our hair in preparation for the hot trip. She crops her hair all the time and much shorter than mine, a butch look I find endlessly exciting and challenging. "Don't think this means I am always the butch," she had said emphatically, early in our getting to know each other. "I don't want to be cast in stone or have my tender side overlooked."

Still baffled, I followed my no longer crying mother into the kitchen where she completed preparations for dinner. I knew "what have you done to your hair?" was shorthand for something else, a shorthand she had often used when I was living under her roof. Meantime we were immersed in the mechanics of finishing gravy and mashing potatoes and getting Kris to arrange the TV trays that passed for the dining room table and its trappings. My mother filled the plates to her own specifications, and then handed me a full one.

"There you are," she said. "I'll take Elmer his plate and you take Kris his plate."

For once I was the deaf one. "What was that again?"

"I'll take your father his plate and you take Kris his plate."

"Mom," I said, "Kris is not a his."

"Eh?"

"Kris is a she."

"What is it?"

"Kris is not a he—Kris is a woman—a she."

"What are you saying? I don't hear so well." As though I didn't grow up knowing this every day.

"Kris is a SHE." I could hear attentive silence from the living room.

By now I was genuinely shouting: "Kris is a SHE!" And the fifth or sixth time around my mom suddenly got it, throwing her hands to her face and rocking backwards, all the bad aura stuff leaving in a flash of lightning understanding that illuminated her face with a lively glow.

"Oh, I'm so glad to hear that!" she said, her joy and relief transferring yet a new puzzle to me. "I'm so glad to hear that." Totally changed, she wiped her face with the bottom of her apron, and then peeked guilelessly as a child around the corner to peer the twelve feet into the living room where Kris sat with a beatifically controlled face and body language that said, "Later I will explode and bend over laughing, but not now."

"I thought she looked awfully cute to be a man," my mom finished, handing me the plate of food with finality of purpose and settled accomplishment.

From the living room I could hear my father begin to laugh, a cascade that began at the throat and worked its way down to big guffaws and finally toe-rocking spasms that he enjoyed thoroughly for several minutes until the emphysema took it up and turned it painful and he stopped, wiping water from the corners of his bright, round brown eyes and holding his chest with the flat of his hand saying, "Oh Lord. Oh Lord."

Kris stayed cool as a cucumber through dinner, balancing her plate on her knee. When Mom and I were in the kitchen finishing washing the dishes I could hear Kris and my dad talking, and from various words that drifted in I could tell they were talking shop and talking about crafts, and then wandered off from that vantage point into their views of the world.

When I walked back into the living room to my surprise they were both standing up, hugging, Kris the taller of the two.

Two hours later, in the green bus traveling north, Kris and I continually howled with laughter over my mother, over my shouting "Kris is a SHE!" and we'd put the greater picture together, that I had written in my note only that "Kris was a mechanic and would be coming with me."

"The way you spell your name!" I added.

"My occupation and my haircut," she continued. "And how she thought I was you."

"And all that crying about the hair, she always used to rag on me about my hair, that was the one place where she knew that she had to socialize me and make me do it right, and be a real woman, or she would have failed her mother mission for certain."

We decided she had been upset because if Kris was a man, how could I do anything so shameful as to drive across the country with him before we were married?

"That must have been what she herself made certain not to do, it's as though she had memorized that particular morality all the way to her bones, whereas the lesbian thing—"

"You said she talked it through with a neighbor—"

"Yes, when I was eighteen, by the time I was living with my first lover and she had met her, you know she loved Von. She took me around the corner into the kitchen after five minutes of the first visit and whispered to me: 'How can I not like her? She's just like you.'"

"Through all her socialization, your mom sees what is really there."

"Yes—except for the hair thing, and the business about riding in a car overnight without being married." As though morality settles out as a few emotionally memorized injunctions, different for each generation. They should come with labels: "Caution: in certain circumstances, this may not apply." I thought about my father wasting no time during our visit, getting out of his chair to hug my new woman after talking to her for only half an hour.

"What did my dad say to you?"

Her face moved to the tender end of the scale, "Well—he—he said, 'I love you.'"

"My goodness," I said. "He's hardly ever said that to *me*."

"First he said, 'Kris—tell me—what do you look like? I'm too blind to see you.'"

"And you said—? You said, 'Oh, I look like your average handsome dyke,'" I joked.

She looked very serious. "I said, 'I look okay. I like the way I look.' Then he stood up and gave me a big hug and said, 'I love you.'"

I saw that she was very moved by this. As so was I.

Our drive north had brought us to a right hand turn, the entrance to a portion of New Mexico called El Coronado Del Muerte, The Plain of Death. A group of black vultures stood to the left of the cattle guard that marked the beginning of the dirt road. We stopped to admire them, aware that for us they did not so much signify death as transformation.

The summer rains had saturated the plain, bringing out the vivid redness of the bittersweet clay stretching out on either side, and thousands of yellow, pink, and blue wildflowers. All day our eyes feasted on the silhouettes of distant mountain ranges and the vivacity of desert sage in the middle of flowering enticement, cleared of dust by the showers, stroked by the recent thunders, burgeoning with sap under the thick skin of resistance. We ate my mother's turkey and margarine sandwiches without pulling the bus over, wanting to reach Santa Fe for dinner and rent a beautiful motel room, maybe stay an extra day and have some time to rediscover each other.

About six o'clock a broad puddle reached across the road toward us and Kris steered down the wrong edge of it, thinking it was shallow skim on hardpan. The road melted out from under her and turned into pond, sluicing the bus off to the left and deep into the thick entrapping juice, stopping the engine. We looked at each other and got out.

The red mud stretched indefinitely into the future as I looked at the depth of hub cap sinkage, seeing the white sparkle of my brand new Levis in the same field of view. I had worn them this day finally to celebrate our trip, and one thing for sure, I was not going to be the one getting into the mud to dig us out. Kris was the mechanic, let her figure it out. I stood waiting, withholding myself from the problem.

She revved. The bus lurched feebly, sank deeper; she revved again, the bus swept forward, sliding further off to the left, stalled in yet deeper mud. I glowered. She was the butch, she had gotten us into this, now she could damn well get us out.

"What's your plan now?" I snapped as she gave up the driver's seat and came to join me. The sun had lowered dramatically.

"Why don't you dig us out while I steer," she said.

"Me? Me?"

"You have the shoulders for it," she observed. She handed me the little trench shovel. I bugged my eyes at her. I slapped the shovel handle with my other hand. Looked at the gathering overhead blue darkness, felt its deep quiet.

I sighed. Went through a number of inner adjustments. I gave my white Levis one last admiring glance, and then surrendered. I felt the surrender all the way to the base of my spine. I wondered just what it was I was surrendering *to.* I hoped I would like it.

I knelt, looked under the car, feeling the water squeeze from the mud onto my knee and down my calves. She touched my back, ran her fingers up the back of my thigh and when I turned my head her lips were there to meet mine and her tongue was hot and alive.

"Let's make love first," she said.

"Here on the road?" I asked, already climbing into the bus.

"If anyone does come along they'll be too preoccupied trying to drive through this stuff to notice," she reasoned, helping me off with my red stained jeans.

"I got these pants to impress you," I laughed.

"I'm very impressed," she said, running the flat of her tongue up the inside of my naked thigh before reaching to tug off her own shirt. Her breasts tumbled out like two new friends and I spent some time getting to know them. The first star had appeared to mark the opening of night. By the time we were sex traveling to constellations the sky was beading up millions of stars, each a glistening drop of intensity. Blessed under the blanket of their certain light pulsing in that certain dark I lay in her arms thinking about how easily we exploded together, about the stunningly beautiful visions that spontaneously appeared between us, the inexpressible sweetness of her tongue on my clitoris, her underarm smell of mesquite wood, my age-deepening musk, our easy fit in the narrow confines of the vehicle, how my parents had responded to her, how she moaned my name when I slid my fingers into her.

Soon I would be under the bus sweating and swearing, my Levis completely saturated in the red juice of earth, its iron smell wrapping around me, mud in my hair and mouth, mud on the sweet apple she fed me around ten o'clock to keep me going. She would cheer me on, her face smeared with clay from hugging me, her hands sturdy on the steering wheel. I would dig with big strong motions and lie down under the back tires fitting the one palm-sized flat stone and the one-foot-long rotten board we had found to give the back wheels any kind of traction in the slip-slick road. My sandals would be sucked off into the cloying soup and I would dive for traction with my toes, seeking bedrock. She would drive as she had never driven before, pelvis and knees working, skillfully rocking and shimmying us forward six or ten inches at a time while thick drops spun out and splattered the windows. In exhilaration of the effort I would shove my weight against the rear frame timed with her shouts of now! until my muscles went numb and capillary vessels burst in my hands and legs. I would lose the stone and board in deep mud, search the bus to find a glove and one tire chain to substitute, then lose them as well. We would dig and drive a foot at a time through a half mile of road, until two o'clock in the morning when we reached solid ground. And in these simple actions we would know one simple thing. We would know we could get married. We would know she could drive us through and I could dig us through, we would know just how big a distance we could go together in our lives, in this avocado green bus or out of it.

For the moment I lay love-spent in her arms, cheek pressed against her sweet mouth as, their voices rising out of small pools, the whole Coronado began to thrum to the rhythms of green toads, gold-eyed and piping their lovesongs to the heavens, celebrating the end of their waiting, celebrating their climb out of solitary slumber into the time of expressing and connecting. And in that holy time I felt completely enveloped in love, love arriving from every side, pouring over us where we lay together, two women in a timeless covering of the approval of red mud and live reptiles, of insensate but loving parents, and vibrant, vibrant, vibrant stars looking at us, in their reflection of the earth's precession, exactly as though seeing us, from all around the sky.

Ghosts and Bags

NANCY AGABIAN

There are a lot of dead Armenians. There are more Armenians dead than living. I suppose you could say that at any given moment in time there are more dead members than living members in any ethnic group but it's different for Armenians because Armenians are aware that they have dead people attached to them. The dead Armenians died from genocide and massacres and earthquakes and religious wars. The living Armenians carry these dead Armenians around in guilt and shame and anger-crafted bags. The bags emit an odor that, when detected by living Armenians, creates a voice in their inner ear that rants like this: "People are out to get you, people want to take your values and ideas away and you better hold on to them tight because I died for you and you are responsible for my death pain. You just better survive, I don't care how you do it, I don't care if you have no love in your life, if you are miserable and hate everybody, even your parents and children and brothers and sisters. If you don't survive with your values intact then you will be a disgrace to us." This voice makes the Armenians so defensive that they wear blue and white glass evil eyes to ward off badness, as opposed to carrying good luck charms to attract hope or goodness. As you can see, Armenians are negative, hurt, and broken people. I know I am generalizing. I know I have anger towards Armenians. But don't blame me. The bags of the dead are making me do it. I have to be angry so that I can survive. I am Armenian. See how aware I am of my dead Armenians.

There are also Armenian ghosts. The ghosts are the positive energy shades of the dead that naturally rise out of the bags to care about us. The ghosts like to whisper in our living Armenian ears. If they don't whisper, they just watch us and nod with recognition. They look sad, but they hope for us. They see us carrying the bags, and they understand because they used to lug them around when they were living. They are the ones who gave the bags to us. They want to see our bags go away, but they can't lift them off. They cry when they see us perform desperate acts; they see us trying to hide the bags underneath coarse blankets of pride.

One of the Armenian ghosts is my grandmother. She died recently, a couple of days before the day she believed to be her birthday, February 12. She wasn't really certain of what her age was either; the family told people she was seventy-eight when she passed away but she could have just as easily been eighty, or seventy-nine. Her birth information got destroyed when her family got destroyed. It was also documented on the inside cover of the family bible in the house in the village where my grandmother lived until the Turks came to town and seized all the valuables and burned all the homes and bibles. When I think of that bible being burned I get angry. That bible held all kinds of family knowledge, all the secrets to my blood vessels and my hair color and my weird lips and crazy voice and other inherited traits and talents, at least the imprint of those things. That bible is in my bag.

My grandmother died suddenly, from the major artery to her heart backing up. She wasn't feeling well after dinner one night and she went into the den to rest and she took off her pantyhose. My aunts who lived with her knew something was fatally wrong when she did that because my grandmother had a decorum that prohibited her from doing such a thing as removing her pantyhose in the den. My aunts called the ambulance and took her in to the hospital and called my father but by the time he got to the emergency room she was gone. My mother called me when my father was on his way to the hospital. She said, "Nancy, your grandmother is sick, it doesn't look good, she's in the hospital." Then she told me how my grandmother had been going to doctors the past month or so and the doctors had told my aunts she wasn't going to live much longer, maybe six months, a year. No one told me. They didn't tell my grandmother either. I couldn't believe it. What were they thinking? How could they have treated my grandmother like that? They should have told her so that she could have known. They should have told us so we could have said goodbye to each other.

I immediately got on a plane from Los Angeles to Boston. When my father picked me up at the airport he looked fine; he was smiling and he hugged me, and he looked pretty much the same as any other time he had picked me up at the airport, with his gray jacket, his gray wool cap. We were driving through the city traffic which was also gray and he told me what she looked like when he got to the hospital. "Her mouth was still open, her eyes were closed, she looked pale and terrible," he said, and then he started crying, which I have never seen him do before or since. I said, "It's okay, Daddy," and he said, "I know, honey," and he held my hand and he's never done anything like that before or since either. I wanted to ask him, "Daddy, why didn't you tell me she was sick? Why didn't anyone tell me she was gonna die soon?" but the power of his moment of crying made me benevolent. We were both grieving her.

My grandmother was special. She was old and funny and I communicated with her through her broken English and through the soft and tasty Armenian food she made. She came from a foreign other world where people killed each other brutally. My grandmother was a little girl when the Turks came to her village and she marched around a desert with them for months, losing her mother and sisters and father and brothers along the way. She had a whole story on how it happened, the atrocities and her survival, and she told it over and over and over again, getting her dead out. Mostly her children heard it, but after a while the story was just a story, and it ended with her arrival in America.

No one cared about the story of her early life in America. Getting here was the big amazing struggle, and my aunts and father knew what had happened once she got here. My grandmother used to try to tell me the rest of the story: how her brothers who saved her from an Armenian orphanage basically sold her to a man twice her age for marriage and children when she was only sixteen. She really wanted to go to school and learn, she wanted to drive a car.

Whenever she told the American half of her story to me, my aunts would yell that she was full of shit and would remind her of the time my grandfather tried to teach her how to drive. She backed into a tree and jumped out screaming that she would never get into such a crazy machine again, and she cursed him for making her get behind the wheel. "I would never have married him if we had been in Armenia, my family wouldn't have allowed it, he wasn't good enough for me," my grandmother would say and my aunts would all laugh. "Ma, you were lucky, LUCKY, to get him." My grandfather ran away from my grandmother a couple of times, for a few days. My mother said she drove him crazy; "She would drive anyone crazy."

My mother always told me growing up that if she had known what my grandmother was really like she would never have married my father; his mother made their marriage miserable. "But you were with him for two years before you got married, wasn't that enough time to find out what she was like?"

"No, she didn't act like that for two years, she behaved herself. Your aunts kept her in line so I would marry him."

"But if you didn't marry him I would never have been born."

"Yes, you would have, you would just have had a different father."

"What? Who would be my father?"

"I dated other boys before your father, you know. There was one who was very smart. He wanted to marry me but I wasn't ready yet, I felt I was too young to get married, so we broke up. He is a professor at Harvard now. You would be going to Harvard now if I hadn't married your father. He was more like my family; he was more refined than your father. Your father's family is from the villages, whereas mine is from the city. My family is more genteel and educated, whereas your father and aunts and grandmother are vulgar and loud."

"That's terrible. I wouldn't be me if you didn't marry Daddy." I'd be some half version of me, I'd have a different consciousness, I'd probably be some snotty, upper-class, nose-jobbed Armenian girl. But maybe I'd be smarter. Maybe I'd be a boy. This is sick.

The last few years of my grandmother's life were stupid. She didn't like living with my aunts. She resented them for not allowing her to move back to the old farmhouse she owned in rural Massachusetts. My grandmother was obsessed with that house and she wanted her freedom. She kept a bag packed under her bed. She'd take me up to her room and show it to me and tried to convince me to drive her to Oxford. My grandmother raised her family in Oxford; I think she looked back at that time as being a happy one, although I'm sure she was complaining then too. I don't think she loved her children enough when they were growing up. In their old age my aunts took out their childhood pain on their mother by screaming uncontrollably at her about anything: how to set the silverware on the table, the location of the birdseed, inviting company over for dinner. They drove each other nuts the last few years. I hate telling this part of the story. I hate the fact that I have three old unmarried aunts. I hate saying that my grandmother told the neighbors my aunts were beating her up. I hate saying that the State of Massachusetts tried to intervene and failed. I hate saying that my aunts admitted they pushed my grandmother around. How do you explain that? We would go for visits and there would always be some kind of blow up. People were always screaming at each other. I hate screaming. I hate them. I hate them for never looking into their fucking bags and now I have to do it.

My grandmother used to accuse my aunts of poisoning her. "You can't wait till I'm dead," she'd say. She also accused them of having midnight rendezvous with the postman and the lawnmower man. "Ha ha ha, Ma," they would say and shake their heads. My grandmother was not well liked by her family. Except by me. She chose me. She chose me to love in the most unconditional way possible. When I walked into a room, she smiled like the sun. She would tell me, "You are my favorite grandchild." I felt guilty when she said that but I never told anyone. I think she chose me as favorite because I was the youngest and had long Armenian braids growing out of the sides of my head, just like her before the genocide disrupted her. I think the most Armenian things in the world are braids, pomegranates, and Mount Ararat. And ghosts. Anyway, I miss my grandmother and her love that I could depend on. She is watching me, I am pretty sure. She is hanging out, crocheting some huge, never-ending afghan. She is seeing my fingers move and is happy I am working. Maybe she thinks I should be with my family, or maybe she is glad I am away from them, I don't know, but I am surviving here. I've got her ghost in me and around me. I've got her heavy dead anger here in my bag too. The ghosts can't rest till we get rid of their big bags. I don't know what I am doing.

Another one of the Armenian ghosts is Mr. Stambolian. He was my teacher at Wellesley College in Wellesley, Massachusetts. He was in his fifties, I think. He seemed to be around my parents' age, and he was gay. He taught a class called Lesbian and Gay Fiction. It was great to know someone of my parent's generation who was Armenian and gay. I haven't met another such Armenian since. There are probably a lot of gay Armenian dead people. I suspect they don't come out until they are up there in the Mount Ararat in the sky. Anyway, it was great to have a gay role model who was Armenian, and an Armenian role model who was gay.

The class was great because it was campus-condoned study of gay life. There was no other gay class on campus. It was the first of its kind. In the course catalogue it was listed as New Lit. and the students were fond of calling it New Clits. Mr. Stambolian explained that it was the administration's idea to give the class a different official name, so parents wouldn't get freaked out and cut off tuition when they saw it listed in their daughters' transcripts.

Mr. Stambolian was very honest. We didn't just study literature, we learned all about gay history in America. Mr. Stambolian told us lots of stories from his life that related to what we were reading: Stonewall, Fire Island, the seventies, etc. He was open about his sexuality. He was an invaluable contributor to my education and development as an artist and a gay person and a bisexual Armenian princess freak.

I took his class because I wanted to be known as gay without owning up to it myself, without directly coming out in words to friends and acquaintances. All my close friends knew about the love crush I had had the year before on another art major girl and the women's college gossip mill had gotten the news around to lesbians who knew my name and face and major and said hello to me on the paths to the quad. But I hadn't asserted my sexuality yet, I hadn't found it, I hadn't flirted. I kept it all within my body and I was hoping some miracle (i.e., a cute dyke) would grab it out of me, for me. I took the class because I thought enrolling automatically meant I was a lesbian, and I would be made more visible to the lesbian eyes on campus, cuz I wanted a lesbian to sweep me off my feet, to teach me all the lesbian ropes. It never happened. I was so lame. No, I wasn't; I was just wanting something, and there is nothing lame about wanting.

The fact that Mr. Stambolian was Armenian was an added incentive to sign up for the class. My parents had instilled in me a belief that Armenians stick together, they help each other out in the diaspora. So I thought Mr. Stambolian would automatically like me since I was of his ethnic group and I had gayness to boot. One day before everyone had gotten to class, Mr. Stambolian made a point of coming up to me and asking me where are your parents from? "Oxford, Massachusetts, and Cranston, Rhode Island," I said.

"Where are your grandparents from?"

"Armenia," I said, matter-of-factly.

"Where in Armenia?" he persisted.

"I don't know," I said.

"You should find out, it's important," and he walked away and started class. I felt so stupid and apathetic that I called my grandmother after class and asked her and she said Sepastia and I kept forgetting when other people asked me too, and I had to ask her again a couple more times before she died and then she died and I don't forget it now, although there is a blank moment right after someone asks me and I want to pronounce it correctly. It is a beautiful word, Sepastia, and I don't know if she is whispering it to me, or is it my pride?

Mr. Stambolian died of pneumonia I think, but you know, it was due to complications from AIDS. He took the semester off before he died and there was a rumor going around that he had AIDS and then he died. He had talked about AIDS in class all the time, and I always wondered about him: was he safe? was he okay? I just assumed he was, he wouldn't have been able to talk about it so objectively the way he did if he had the virus. And I felt stupid when he died. Why didn't he tell us? No one tells me anything until it's too late. But I guess I know why he didn't tell us. It was the first gay class at Wellesley. They need an AIDS class there now.

My mother told me about his death. My parents are on Armenia-alert. They see an Armenian name somewhere, in the paper, on TV, in the phone book and they perk up. My parents saw his name in the obituary. "Nancy," my mother said, "did you know this man George Stambolian?"

"Yeah, he was at Wellesley, why?"

"He died of AIDS." Oh no. Empty pit stomach death feeling. "That's too bad," my mother said. It said in the obituary that he was a French literature professor, he had written a book on Jean Genet. It also said that he taught the gay class and he edited *Men on Men 1* and *2*, anthologies of contemporary gay male fiction. My parents knew I never took French, I was thankful for the New Lit. cover up; I couldn't tell them that he was a most important teacher to me or that I was bisexual. I couldn't tell my family who I was, who I am, and I still don't. Sometimes I choose to say the words, "I am bisexual," but that is as far as I can get. That's not everything about me to tell and many times they don't even seem to want to know who I am. You are our daughter, they tell me. You are our lovely Armenian daughter and we love you, we would never do anything to harm you. You are Our Daughter.

I went back east for what was to be my grandmother's last Christmas with me. At the dinner table at Grammy's house Mr. Stambolian's name came up again. My aunts were talking about him, saying it was a shame that he had died. He was a very handsome man. I thought to myself they probably wish they could have married someone who looked like him. It was a shame that he was gay; a wasted Armenian husband. My mother told them a lot of alumnae had written letters to the Wellesley magazine of their memories of him, giving him honor. My parents and aunts love to talk about Armenian successes because it makes them feel better. Our ancestors were victims; they were massacred for their faith, but success is in our genes. I felt compelled to put my words in, to be more than just a part of the Armenian appreciation group. "He was a great teacher," I said, and then I swallowed my bottom lip. Oops. "What?" my father said. He looked at me suspiciously. My parents aren't just on Armenia alert, they are on gay alert too. Although they are on Armenia alert constantly and it is a positive thing, gay alert is more of an apocalyptic type of thing. My sister came out to them about ten years previously, and the world came to an end. So my parents were scared their other kids could be gay as well, and if we showed any signs, they were on to us, ready to fire off the anti-gay warnings. They didn't want the world to end two more times. My father asked me, "Did you have a class with him, Nancy? I didn't know you took French." No one else caught my comment, the conversation had moved on. My family is loud and everyone talks at the same time. "No," I said pathetically and looked away to jump into another conversation. My grandmother sat quietly in her corner seat at the table, to the left of my father's head-of-the-table chair. She was trying to palm off her turkey to someone else. It was always too much for her. The last couple of holidays she was very quiet and lost at the table. I kept forgetting she was there. Everyone else made a huge noise but she didn't know what was going on in the conversation or didn't care. I kept forgetting she was there and felt terrible when I noticed she was falling away from me. At those times I would try to ask her questions. "Grammy, how're you doing?" Everyone would shut up so we could hear her. "Oh, honey, awful. I'm awful." And my aunts would yell at her and at me. "Just ignore her, Nancy, she's doing just fine," and the conversation would swirl around the table again, louder and louder and my grandmother was becoming a ghost. Mr. Stambolian was whispering to her. He just watched me that day.

Family

RONNA MAGY

1

I like them, they are family. They live in decaying houses on nice streets in Los Angeles. Yucca plants and shaggy banana leaves grow next to their dirty water swimming pools. Bathrooms sinks are cracking and dusty, corners of silver-flowered paper peel back from their walls, uncovering layers of phoenix birds rising. When I visit them on Mother's Day, my family talks of dead relatives as if they were alive. "Aunt Harriet," Uncle Jerry remembers. "Go to her house, anytime. She makes a meal fit for a king." And we are taken back through Harriet's apple pies and peanut butter cookies, lamb chops and baked potatoes, until our mouths water.

Still, no one knows what to do about cousin Sylvie. She is just recently out of the hospital. Neither my aunts, uncles, or cousins gathered for Mother's Day. I am connected to skinny Sylvie, the problem cousin, through my mother's line, through Aunt Harriet. Exactly how, I'm not sure, as with other things in our family, but we call each other cousins. Her mother and mine being dead, we are the ones left. Sylvie and I have birthdays in the same month, February. We always send each other cards around birthday time, unless one of us is too busy or forgets, in which case we call. We are both women approaching fifty, premenopausal. She is married, I am not.

"Sylvie doesn't eat anymore," Aunt Fran begins. She's addressing the audience on the floral couch and a couple of leftover relatives seated on card chairs enjoying pimento-flavored cheese-and-cracker appetizers. As she says this, Fran shakes her head and purses her lips in a frown. Fran wears a long purple flowered apron over a pair of pink slacks and matching top, the square apron bib covers her sagging breasts. "She was sixty pounds in the hospital in March, couldn't even get out of bed to go to the bathroom. It hurt her to walk. She had to use the bedpan!"

"Remember when the nurses tried to fit her in a children's gown?" Jerry looks at Fran and then at the rest of us. He is paunchy, wears polyester pants with pleats that bulge around the waist and tucks his shirts in to maintain the svelte look. "Mickey Mouse and Donald Duck across her flat chest. The nurses ended up putting her in a small adult gown and pinning it closed so the neck wouldn't fall off her shoulders!"

Uncle Jerry says Sylvie looks like she came out of Buchenwald, a survivor, and I imagine her sleeping on a wood frame bed, no mattress, no pillow, in a room patrolled by armed Nazis. Barely moving, she is all skin and chicken bones, no muscle. They feed her gruel.

Apparently the psychiatrists at Kaiser tried to talk her into eating, tempted her with milk shakes, sodas, cookies, cake, ice cream, sweets. She refused everything. I hear Jerry's frustration. "You know, she's gotten to be a real mental case, a nut, *meshuggeneh*."

According to Jerry, the psychiatrists examined Sylvie's hollow eyes, probed her dreams. She talked to them of shadowy forms running across endless spaces, escaping persecution. They asked about her father, abuse, life as an only child. Eventually she pulled the IV out and left. No one chased after her. After all, she was an adult. In the chart the doctor wrote, "Patient released self, refused appropriate treatment." There was an additional note in the margin, "Do not re-admit without permission."

Fran talked to Sylvie three times last week to invite her to Mother's Day. The first time, Sylvie answered her old black dial phone and said she didn't want anyone to see her, she'd lost too much weight, she'd already started to disappear. The second time Fran ran into her at Ralph's in the health and ethnic foods aisle. Fran is sure of the aisle because she passed it looking for regular canned tomatoes and came back to compare Del Monte and Health Valley. Sylvie was there both times gazing at cans of chicken broth and lentil soup. They chatted for a while. Fran urged her again to come to Mother's Day. Sylvie declined, said she would hide in the bathroom.

"Well," Fran says, "what could I say back to that?" She throws up her hands. "At least she was looking at food! It was like she was a kid, lost in the pictures on the label. I wondered if she would get home okay."

The third time Fran called, Sylvie said she had nothing to wear that fit, everything hung. This was probably true. And there really was no point in her buying new clothes if she didn't want to live.

That's just it; I think Sylvie believes there is no life after cancer. Last week on the phone she told me that for her, having cancer was the same as dying. We were taught that in the fifties, but some of us outgrew it like a wading pool too small to swim in. When Sylvie came to my house, scrawny change-of-life baby of maybe eight or nine, she played with imaginary friends. She preferred books to bicycles, didn't know how to yell and scream, had been kept separate from other kids too long. The world told her cancer killed people, like Aunt Dottie, the chain smoker, cousin Bobby's mother. When Dottie's lungs couldn't get air anymore, she died. Like Uncle Sam who owned the dime store, another smoking addict dead from clogged lungs. No airways for the oxygen to get through. And on top of that, Sylvie's husband Joel has cancer. I try to tell her it isn't contagious, but there is no arguing with Sylvie.

2

I am in the bathroom washing my hands after Aunt Fran's meal of brisket and stuffed potatoes, iceberg lettuce and cherry tomatoes with cream dressing, and cooked zucchini. We have been eating these same foods on holidays for years with little variation. Sometimes it is green beans with almonds, sometimes candied carrots. The first taste of the meat on the tongue is a ritual, shredding the fiber between the teeth, juices trickling down the throat. Suddenly Aunt Dottie's spirit is next to me as I remember this, standing over my left shoulder in a green linen dress covered by an organdy apron. We have just finished the crisp lettuce. She is offering me brisket on plates special for Passover. Onion slices flavor the juices. I inhale the aroma, take a piece of meat from the plate, cut it, gnash it. Some of the shreds get stuck between my teeth and flavor the rest of the meal with a brown meaty juice. When I come back from this reverie, I realize our family has grown smaller. Aunt Flo died this year; Dottie, before I left home.

The towels in the bathroom are black and white, their paisley does not go with the metallic wallpaper flowers nor the brown bar of soap on the sink. I wonder what is happening to my relatives. Things used to match in these houses and be ordered, no dust.

Outside the bathroom hang rows of family pictures. As I look at them, I hear strains of Benny Goodman's clarinet, music of the forties. The bodies begin to move, voices talk. When the dead's names, *alashalom*, are called out during our conversation, even in passing, their spirits float in and hover round us. It is the custom. In the respinning of story, names, streets lived on, stores frequented, weddings, synagogue walls are opened again like unused back porches smelling of must and mildew. Called on, these spirits float through the narrow hallway, into the rooms, out through the open door of the patio, rise higher toward heaven. There is no knowing which of us will go next, who will need to be named by the ones who live after.

I go back to the flowered sofa where the living sit. They are Fran and Charlotte, who wears a red neck scarf tied in a bow over a white cardigan, Jerry and Lou, Charlotte's husband, and my cousin, Bobby, in his late forties. He and I were children once. There are pictures of when we were four and eight and played in lilac-filled yards back home in Detroit. There is a black and white of me and him standing together; he is four. I am three heads taller, in a gathered skirt with matching blouse, straight hair down to my shoulders. We look at the camera, smile. Bobby really doesn't want to remember four; he was cross-eyed before his surgery.

Bobby wears the bottle glass lenses the optometrist tried to make look thinner, but they are really double magnification and dizzy him when he glances sideways, make him squint when he smiles. Bobby says he thinks family can bring Sylvie back to life. He believes we can revive Sylvie's lungs, liver, heart, vital organs, cells, make her want to live. "Family is life blood," he says. "We just need to talk to her, make her remember the old times." His voice trails off here. His mother, Dottie, had one lobe removed from her lungs and was still overcome by emphysema eating up the leftover spaces. Bobby still believes in family. He says this looking at no one in particular and no one looks directly at him as he speaks, either. Like with that old bicycle pump he always carries in his car,

I imagine him pumping family into Sylvie's arm through an IV tube. Her body slowly inflates, face fills out.

Sylvie has not wanted to live for a long time. She told me this when I visited her after she was at Kaiser. We sat in her living room sipping Diet Cokes, on those square fifties chairs with the black wood frames and motelish foam rubber cushions. She said she just never liked being a wife and mother, felt trapped by Joel and the boys. She attributed it to their yelling and drag racing, to taking the car without permission and returning at four in the morning, to raging testosterone. She told me she couldn't stand their energy. I told her to be more tolerant, but she didn't listen.

"But Aaron is a wonderful store manager, and Jason is going to be a great architect, they're terrific boys," Aunt Fran remarks, wiping her hands on the purple apron. "Who could ask for better?"

Sylvie said she did not want to live after her best friend, Judy, died of cancer two years ago. After Judy died, I remember, her husband and son appeared again at a Mother's Day, talked of Macintosh and IBM compatible, Sony and Panasonic, electronic male things. Someone brought up Judy. Tears welled up in her husband's eyes, his eye sockets reddened, voice choked. We all looked away. Lou told a joke about hens and chickens crossing the road.

Aunt Fran doesn't want to gossip about Sylvie. "I told myself not to talk about her tonight," she says. "She's not here, can't defend herself."

"We're not gossiping," I say, "we're trying to help the way we always do." We examine Sylvie like a frog pinned down and cut open in a biology class, her problem, our specimen. As we do the dissection, we recount the facts of her life since childhood. Then, we construct a découpage doll, gluing on dried pieces of Sylvie's wedding cake, family photos of her mother, father, and us cousins, holiday dinners of *gefilte fish* and *matzo balls*, and family outings, until there is some likeness of the way we all remember her. It is a composite, one we all feel some connection to, each of our truths layered over by another's glue until this molded doll of material things and memory is complete.

3

No one wants to discuss Joel. He is her husband, not family blood. There is that distinction. Nice guy, but always a little odd, my mother would have said. Plays classical violin and listens to opera, a little too cultured, out of the range of family poverty and practicality. He is the one with cancer.

Recently Joel stopped playing romantic operas like *La Bohème* and *Madame Butterfly*, and began turning up the volume on *Rigoletto*. Blasted it with all the doors and windows open until the next-door neighbor, Bob Leimert, called the police. Afterwards, Joel ran outside screaming at Leimert's closed door, "Leimert, you asshole," he said. "You try having cancer. You try being irradiated and turned into a hot microbe."

Sylvie doesn't know what to do. Cancer is not visible in her body, but she's afraid it will enter her, undetected. She said this in one of our phone conversations. Since there is already cancer in the family, Sylvie thinks it is passed on through the DNA, down along the twisting chains inside until muscles and bones and organs revert to womb curls. Until morphine is the only end to suffering and later, only death. We all write in "family history of cancer" on our medical questionnaires, lung cancer, colon cancer, throat cancer. We hope the doctors know what to look for, how to treat us.

4

Before Aunt Fran serves the coffee, the doorbell rings. Nine P.M. on Sunday? No one comes to the door at this hour, only kids from other parts of the city collecting money for trips to camp or Magic Mountain "to stay out of trouble," but that's at dinner time.

"I don't know who it is, but I'll check," Jerry yells back over his shoulder as he heads for the door. To his left is a picture of Joel and Sylvie taken three summers ago at the ocean. Sylvie's dark eyes peer out from a matching top and pants the color of faded coral. She looks like an aging flamingo, all neck and skinny arms. Joel is grasping a volleyball, which he aims at the photographer.

Jerry looks through the peep hole and sees only dark until he remembers and flicks on the porch light and yells, "Who's there?"

"It's me, Sylvie," the voice comes back.

"Sylvie," he shrieks as he opens the door. We hear his gasp back in the living room.

"Oh, my God," he says and there she is standing on the other side of the white burglar screen in the shadow.

"Can I come in, Uncle Jerry?" she asks.

"Of course you can," he says, welcoming her like an expected visitor even though the meal is already completed. Jerry loops her small right hand through his bent elbow and pats the top as if she were five. "Look who's here," he says to us. It feels like we are doing show and tell.

I am standing in the kitchen doorway drying my hands on a blue waffle square dishtowel. Embedded in it are snags from the washing machine and old grease spots. I grip the towel tightly as if it were the baby blanket I used to carry around for protection. The spaces between the towel squares absorb the water leaking from my fingers. My mouth opens, "Sylvie," comes out.

Sylvie stands in the living room and says, "Sorry I'm late, everyone," as if nothing were wrong. Perhaps she just got caught in traffic. She is wearing mourning black leggings under a loose black shirt. Across the front is a large skull with crossbones. It has a Halloweeny skeleton look, dark eyes peering out from a white face. A face like that used to guard the treasure chest bank on my dresser. I used to tell people, "Woe be unto you if you touch it. Ho. Ho. Ho." There is a long moment when we are all silent, looking at Sylvie. She is the real skeleton walking around with a leering skull on her chest.

Fran, hostess in the long apron, welcomes Sylvie as if it were six in the evening and we were just about to sit down to dinner. "Well, Sylvie, I'm glad you could be with us. Would you like some coffee or tea?"

"Nothing thanks, Aunt Fran."

Bobby stands up abruptly from behind the coffee table and says, "Welcome, Sylvie." He stumbles over Lou's legs in an attempt to get out and hug her and splays himself on the carpet. He says, "Oh, sorry," and we all groan.

"You have to be more careful, Bobby," Charlotte reprimands. "Remember when your cousin Morty hit his head on the coffee table? He hasn't remembered much since."

Bobby gets up from the floor, his hands shaking as he dusts off his plaid polyester jacket. "Sylvie," he tells her, "We've missed you." He wants to infuse her with family love, give her an injection of his survival of cross-eyed persecution and mother-loss. Instead, he puts his arm around her shoulder like a distant brother. "Are you back to join the family?" he asks. I imagine Bobby, a camp counselor, taking out his clipboard and checking her off as part of the family count.

"I just wanted to see all of you one more time," Sylvie says. As if we are supposed to know what one more time means.

Charlotte picks up the framed picture from near the door. "We were just talking about what a wonderful day this must have been for you and Joel." She fibs about our discussion as if lying were the connective tissue pulling Sylvie's existence onto the side of the living and away from the closeness of death.

Sylvie's eyes are black as papaya seeds and big as sunflowers as she stares back at us. "I thought you should be the first to know," she begins. "I've willed my sons to charity and my husband to drugs." She laughs and pulls out a folded paper that snags on the peeling gold clasp of her clutch purse. It looks like the word WILL is printed across the paper in bold black letters. She obviously has taken time to work on this. Sylvie backs up a little so she is partially in the hallway near the old pictures and partly in the living room with us. She perches herself up on a footrest and clears her throat. Her refrigerator and all the food in it, all the vegetables and fruit, mayo, mustard, wine and cheese, her favorite Cokes, meat and fish have been donated to the West Valley Center for Anorexic Women, in case the women ever want to eat again. The ten pound bag of sugar, jars of orange blossom honey, Equal, malt, fructose, and other sweeteners in her cupboards go to the Overeaters Anonymous meetings on Wilshire Boulevard in Westwood. To the psychiatrists at Kaiser she has given a lifetime subscription to *Mechanics Illustrated* and the Deluxe 200 set of Sears Craftsman Wrenches so they will have the right tools to use when they tinker with patient's brains.

She has given up all her real property. Since she is planning to predecease all of us she says, her relationship, the house, the bank account, the furniture, and the children roll over to her husband, Joel. She says it is a relief for her not to have to take care of these mundane issues.

Charlotte says, "You can't do this to yourself, Sylvie. You can't kill yourself off because you're upset about Joel. What a stupid thing to do! Women always outlive their husbands. Don't you remember your mother lived a long time after your father? That's the way it works. When Joel dies, the boys continue the blood line. You have to be around for them. You have to accept it and go on!" She throws down her dish towel.

Everyone moans, "Charlotte!" like a chorus of seals barking on the rocks during high tide. "That's enough," Lou tells her. To which Charlotte responds, "Oh," and clasps a hand over her mouth, but the words have already been let out and there is nothing more to shut off. I imagine Charlotte's words separating into letters, trickling out the kitchen faucet I have left running, until water seeps over the sink onto the floor and floods up on the toes of Sylvie's shoes and wets her socks.

"How could you, Charlotte?" Fran says, putting her hands on her hips.

"That's what my mother would have said, too, Aunt Charlotte, but I've been thinking," Sylvie says. "It's really time for me to leave. You remember my friend, Judy, the one who always came for Mother's Day?" Of course I remember Judy, she died of cancer. "She called me this morning," Sylvie continues, "and asked me to come join her. After all, it is Mother's Day. What better day to depart? I'll be going on a vacation. My things are in the car. Want to see?"

We all look at Sylvie and then at each other. What does she have in her car? According to the will, she's given away all her clothes, food, and relationships. We follow her down the cracked walkway to the driveway where she's pulled her sky-blue Corolla with the bashed headlight up behind Jerry's old Mazda. I hear the rusty hinges groan as the trunk opens. There is a huge teddy bear, a pair of bedroom slippers, a robe, a sleeping bag, a toothbrush, and no toothpaste. She shows us each of these things, one by one. Judy is going to meet her in the desert near Twenty Nine Palms. The things are all in case she doesn't find Judy the first day.

There is her box of 45's from the fifties in case she wants to hear some music, record sleeves filled with the Motown sound, but no record player. There is her mother's family album opened to a picture of Sylvie's seventh birthday party. All of us are there, standing around her lit cake, waiting for the gangly girl to blow out the candles. The rest of the page is black and empty, except for yellow glue marks where other pictures were and have been removed. There is a long scarf to wear around her neck for warmth in case she gets cold, but no jacket. There is a butcher knife large enough to cut food, but there is nothing to eat. As she pulls out each of these things, it dawns on me that with the scarf she could hang herself and with the knife, slash her wrists. I whisper this to Aunt Fran.

I try to lead Sylvie away from the trunk. "Show us your new stereo," I say, but she slams the trunk down quickly so that no one can reach in and remove the seemingly benign weapons. We have seen depressives and alcoholics in our family, ragers and smokers, but there has never been a suicide.

Aunt Fran says, "That's nice, Sylvie," and pulls me into the house to call Kaiser Psychiatric. "My niece is a former patient. She's about to commit suicide," she tells them. When the nurse asks, "How?" Fran explains the crazy behavior and the weapons. The nurse checks the patient computer list. "We'll have to get authorization," she tells my aunt. Fran puts down the receiver. Her face is white. We return to the group in the driveway.

I look at Sylvie. She is fighting so that death will take her, take away the loneliness of the one who lives afterwards. If death won't take her, she will help it. We, family, are trying in our bumbling way to maintain her connection to the past. We throw her a lifeline in a tug of war over which we have no control of the other side. On the one end is Sylvie's desire to make herself disappear. On the other end is us, family, kids she grew up with, people who know her history, the things traditional women of our generation are supposed to be and do. We pull one way, she pulls the other. Sylvie roots herself in the concrete. Cracks spider out from under her feet, between her toes. More of the rope is pulled by the lightweight woman to her side of the line. Eventually each of us is pulled forward by the force of her inner will. One by one the rope slips through our fingers and we let go. Aunt Fran and Uncle Jerry are the last. They are too old to hold on any longer. As the pull of family weakens, Sylvie drops the rope in the driveway and gets in the car. Bobby stands near the car door with his tire pump in his hand. Sylvie starts the ignition.

Victor the Bear

PAT ALDERETE

I didn't know I was going to meet my father's latest girlfriend that evening. We had planned to meet for dinner at his favorite Mexican restaurant, La Parilla, in Boyle Heights. He was waiting inside for me and I smiled at him as I pushed the heavy door open.

"Hey, mija!" he yelled, jumping up to hug me.

A woman sitting next to where my father had been was looking at me.

My father waved her over and said in Spanish, "Ven aqui, Leticia."

She was an attractive woman wearing a red dress that had a slit up the front. As she walked over to us I noticed with faint interest that she was at least ten years younger than me. She extended her hand and said, "Que gusto conocerte, your father has told me so much about you."

"The dress is pretty, huh, mija? But check out her falda." And he pulled her dress up at the slit to show off the frilly pink slip she was wearing.

Embarrassed, I nodded at him and said, "C'mon, Dad, let's sit down."

We walked over to the table and I looked around. It was an old establishment with tattered papel picado fluttering down from the ceiling. The overstuffed vinyl-covered booths had seats that practically pushed your face into your plate.

About twenty feet from us knelt a worn-looking woman, slapping tortillas together and cooking them on a smoking grill. When she saw us she pulled herself up and brought us a basket filled with tortillas. My father pressed some money into her palm and admonished her to keep them coming, fresh and hot. She nodded humbly and returned to her station. All the waitresses seemed to know him as they came by to greet us.

My father pulled out a packet of photographs and I could see they were nude shots of Leticia. The picture on top had her bare breasted and he flashed it at both me and the waitress. Leticia did not flinch and I realized she had been around him long enough to be used to his ways.

Seeing my chance to change the subject before he really got going, I said, "Hey, Dad, remember Victor the Bear? I brought that . . ."

"Ay, mija!" he interrupted. "How'd you know what I was thinking? Just the other day I was watching a talk show on TV and one of the guests had a bear with him."

"You mean like that Mutual of Omaha guy?" I asked.

"Yeah, but this pendejo didn't know what he was doing and the bear got away from him. It jumped on a lady in the audience and shook the hell out of her." Wrapping his arms around me, my father swayed me back and forth in the booth, growling in my ear.

His arm still draped on my shoulder, he asked, "Do you want a beer?"

"Oh, no thanks Dad, I haven't had a drink in almost a year now."

"But mija, they have your favorite here. Señorita," he flagged the waitress.

After placing our order, I tried again. "Dad, remember Victor? I was going through some of my things the other day and I found this picture you took of us."

Leticia's eyes widened as she picked up the black-and-white photograph. Its edges were curling and it had the glazed finish of early Polaroids. "Ay mira que gigante el oso y tu tan chiquita. Que edad tenias?"

"I think I was about nine," I answered.

Shaking her head, Leticia said, "Ay, he told me you were a daredevil."

My father smiled at me. "Te recuerdas how you use to ride on the roof of the jeep, mija?"

"Sure do, Dad," I answered. "I remember how you used to ride up and down the sand dunes out in the desert and I would be sitting in the tire on the roof."

Leticia looked at my dad. "Que barbaro!"

Looking at the picture again, she said, "But why were you in the cage with that bear?"

It happened on a Sunday morning when we had driven to church in our new 1964 red Corvair Monza. My father had taken special care to teach me to always say Corvair *Monza,* not just Corvair. The Monza was supposedly a step up from a plain old Corvair but aside from a lip pouting out from the back of the roof they looked and sounded identical. It had its engine in the rear which meant that any trip longer than ten minutes left my brother and me with ringing ears.

Driving into the church's parking lot, we saw a raggedy banner that said "Victor the Bear." A section was being fenced off and I was curious to see what was going on. Reluctantly I followed my family into St. Alphonsus, the nicest church, according to my mother, in all of East Los Angeles. It was cool inside and rapidly filling for the mass that was about to begin. Stained glass filtered the light reaching us and it threw shadows on the dark paneling of the confessionals, enhancing their serious nature. Up on the ceiling above the altar was a painting of a huge dove caught in mid-flight, its wings outstretched and its beak holding an olive branch. Staring at it, I'd often wished I could jump up on it and fly away.

It was one of those rare Sundays when my father had forsaken the sport of the season to attend mass with my mother, brother, and me, for although the ritual could only be led by men, the duty of attendance fell on the women and children. Maybe the men knew Victor was in the neighborhood because it seemed there were lots of dads there that day.

I was happy my father was there and I made a point of coughing loudly during the service so that my friends and neighbors could see him with us. I smiled proudly and sat as still as I could, relieved also that my brother could not so easily hit me nor my mother pinch me with him there.

The priest commenced the ceremony but the parishioners could sense a commotion outside the sanctuary and we were anxious to escape its solemn confines. The priest mistook this anxiety for enthusiasm and threw himself wholeheartedly into the service. At the end of mass we screamed, "And peace be with you, Father," so loudly that tears came to his eyes as he reluctantly closed the rite.

As we exited the church and saw a crowd gathering in the parking lot I was again grateful for my father's presence. I knew he was curious, just like me, and he'd want to see what was going on. To my delight, we pushed our way through the crowd.

A squat, weasel-faced, middle-aged man was standing in front of the cage. We knew he was the bear's owner since he was the only white man there. He was bald except for a tuft of sand-colored hair that ran around his head like a horseshoe. I wondered if his feet ached because he kept shifting from one foot to the other. His hands were thick and callused with dirty little slivers for fingernails and he kept wiping his palms on his shabby khaki-colored pants. He had on a polo shirt that was so old it seemed the lizard on it should be belly up.

Behind him was Victor the Bear, rocking on his paws and looking very alone. He kept shaking his head from side to side but I couldn't figure out what he was saying no to. Victor had fur that was as black as my father's hair but Victor's was matted and looked like it wouldn't smell good if you got too close to him. He was wearing a frayed brown collar that had a length of heavy chain attached to it with the other end tethered to a flimsy looking stake. He had amazing rubber-like lips. They seemed completely detached from his face when they moved, like Mr. Ed's, the talking horse on TV.

Once a respectable crowd had gathered, the owner stepped up on a box. "Ladies and gentlemen! Here before you is Victor the Bear!" When the crowd remained quiet he continued, "The famous wrestling bear!"

The owner tiptoed and waved a ten-dollar bill in his left hand and pointed with his right. "Are any of you men *home-bray* enough to try your luck with Victor or are you scared? This ten-dollar bill goes to the man who's strong enough and brave enough to win a round of wrestling with Victor!"

I don't know if it was his challenge to their manhood or his terrible pronunciation of "hombre" that angered the men more but a rumble came forth from the crowd and a man in his twenties wearing a lime green striped shirt and blue work pants shoved his way through.

The owner looked him over. "You seem healthy and strong, young man, what's your name?"

"Hector," the man sneered.

"OK, Hector, do you dare take on Victor?"

"Just let me in the cage, mister. I'm gonna punish that stupid bear."

The owner smiled. "OK, Hector. Five dollars and he's yours to punish all you want."

"Whatta ya mean, five dollars?" Hector sputtered. "What about the ten dollars you promised?"

"It's yours," the owner assured him. "There's no doubt you'll win a round. But if we didn't charge five dollars any little weakling who's had a bad day would be beating up on my poor little Victor. But why bother you with my sad story? You're strong and you'll double your money!"

Somebody yelled from the crowd, "Orale, Hector, give 'em the money! Go on, man, show that payaso you ain't scared of no bear."

Another voice yelled, "I've got five dollars here that says you'll pound Victor to the floor. I'll back you up, compadre!"

The crowd surged and pulsed with men yelling and waving money.

Smirking disdainfully, Hector handed a five-dollar bill to the owner and entered the cage. He walked directly towards Victor, fully expecting to immediately pin the bear down.

The first thing Victor did was rip off Hector's lime green shirt as casually and easily as a mother changing a baby's diaper though not quite so gently. Then the bear wrapped his shaggy arms around him and swayed to a deadly dance, slow and grotesque. Though Victor had only stubs left where his once mighty claws had been, they were still able to slash wide red streaks across Hector's back like a kind of signature.

Hector's eyes were huge with fright and disbelief as Victor slammed him into the fence, nearly knocking it over. Everyone was amazed at Victor's quickness; that bear could move.

After flipping and spinning Hector around to the delight of the crowd the owner mercifully pulled him out as Victor waved his paws in triumph.

Somebody yelled, "Orale, Hector, you sure did show that bear a thing or two."

Hector didn't look towards the voice but just staggered away.

The owner smiled at the crowd. "Victor's ready, men! Who's next?"

The crowd did not stir and the owner astutely sensed the change in mood.

"All right then," he announced, "how about some of you kids feeding him? Just twenty-five cents and you can feed Victor yourselves!"

My father smiled at my brother. "How 'bout it, mijo? You want to play with the bear?"

"NO!" my brother yelled, moving away from him.

Seeing my chance, I started jumping up and down, yelling, "I do, Daddy! I do! I wanna play with the bear!"

My mother immediately elbowed my father. "Estas loco, honey! She shouldn't wrestle bears, it's not ladylike!"

My father laughed at her. "Aw honey, she's just going to feed him. It'll be fun for her."

"But I wanna wrestle Victor," I cried, "not just feed him like a sissy!" But the owner muttered something about insurance and handed me a soda bottle filled with heavily sugared water.

When the owner closed the gate behind me, I could hear murmuring and gasping from the crowd and several people were crossing themselves. Looking up at Victor, who was tall even sitting on his haunches, I suddenly felt small and very alone.

Smiling, I began walking slowly towards him, holding his drink up and out like a crucifix. The mumbling of the crowd was soon drowned out by the pounding of my heart as I realized that Victor was unmoved by my silent offering of friendship. He was huge and shaggy and his nose was wet in a nasty-looking way. He was sniffing the air all around and I wondered if he was offended by his own stink. My feet became heavier the closer I got to him, but my fear of being afraid kept pulling my body along. Slowly I offered the bottle to him and in a flash he snatched it with a swipe of his huge arm, covering the bottle entirely with his paw. He quickly guzzled it and then looked expectantly at me.

It reminded me of the Frankenstein movie I had just watched on TV the night before. Something about the way he looked at me made me think of Maria, the little girl Frankenstein threw into the lake when they ran out of flowers. Spittle dripped from the side of Victor's snout and he was twitching nervously. His chain rasping against the gravel made a sound that turned my stomach sour.

I wasn't having fun anymore. His breathing was heavy and hot and I became overwhelmed. No longer caring, I turned to escape the cage.

"Wait, mija!" my father yelled. "Let me get a couple more pictures of you with Victor. Smile, mija, turn towards me now!"

It seemed a lifetime was passing me by while he clicked away. Rubbing my hands together for warmth, I could smell Victor's rancid breath and my stomach started hurting. I wanted to look at Victor but I knew better than to expect any help from him and so I lowered my eyes until my dad finally called me out of the cage.

My father thought it was great fun, the sort of thing every little kid should do. He told me how lucky I was, how I had it so much better than he ever did.

Leticia's voice startled me. "You looked like your father even then. This is really a wonderful picture."

"Mija," my father was tapping me on the shoulder. "You're not paying attention to me. I been trying to tell you that Leticia bought that dress 'cause she wanted to make a good impression on you."

"I was looking forward to meeting you," Leticia said softly. "Your father is so proud of you."

I smiled appreciatively at her, happy that my father finally had a girlfriend that cared what I thought.

The waitress appeared with our dinner and drinks.

Waving his glass of beer under my nose he said, "Are you sure you don't want any? I know how much you like a good cold beer."

"I'm really sure, Dad," I said, pushing his glass away from me.

"Are you feeling okay, mija?' he asked. "You don't seem to be in a very good mood."

Taking a deep breath, I looked at him and smiled. "But Dad, remember when you took this picture of me and Victor?"

He looked at me with a serious expression on his face. "Oh mija, I didn't take that picture."

"Whatta ya mean?" I stammered. "Of course you did."

"Oh no, mija," he answered. "I never would have let you in the cage with that bear."

Rain

CARLA TOMASO

In the middle of the night, that's when it all happens. It's a big time for dreaming of course. But it's also when people tell things they shouldn't tell, or kill each other, or do the sexual stuff they'd never do during the day.

If you're dreaming, it's when you dream about shouting obscenities at your mother, the first person who broke your heart. Or about the toddler running across the street to pet a dog and getting hit by a car. You wake up screaming or crying, snot all over your face, your throat raw from calling out—"Stop, stop, stop."

In the middle of the night, people whisper and the world is dark. It's all so secret.

And, Freud be damned, I think it's a good thing.

I went to a psychiatrist once. I was desperate, the only reason you'd pay $150 to tell a stranger nighttime information in the middle of the day.

You're praying they can make you like you were before, before you lost your head. You're hoping this period can turn out to be an interesting learning experience, not a permanent condition of your life.

Of course, they can't. There's no magic left on anybody's clinical couch. There hasn't been for years. Besides, they're just as crazy as you are, those psychiatrists. And that's the twisted key. Once you figure that out, it's all you need to know. Once you realize you're the human condition incarnate, no better, no worse, you're healed!

When I went to the psychiatrist I thought I was the crazy one. I wasn't looking at life like everybody else.

The main thing I wasn't looking at right was rain.

I was terrified of it. I was powerless.

"Do you think it will kill you?" the doctor asked, as if death at least is a reasonable thing to fear.

"No," I said.

"So?" she said.

"I think it's going to flood my basement or leak through the roof. I think I'm going to have to go to sleep soaking wet."

"So you're afraid of discomfort?" she said, capping a yawn.

Was she bored with me already? I'd only been in her office ten minutes.

"Have you ever had a patient with a phobia like mine?" I said.

"Fear of flying is quite common," she said. "Myself, I don't drive a car."

"Someone drives you?"

"Yes," she said. "I stopped driving when all I could see ahead of me were fiery, tangled wrecks about to happen."

"But rain . . . I watch clouds gathering overhead. I dial the National Weather Service five times a day. I'm obsessed. I'm consumed with terror. You can't escape the rain."

"Move to the desert," she said. And, just like that, I was cured.

I didn't tell anybody anything else for years. Because, in truth, I missed that phobia like a limb. I missed the chest-throbbing rush every time a dark cloud passed overhead, every time the news reports predicted precipitation, every time my expensive all-weather barometer pointed to rain.

I learned my lesson. I was a lot more at home with my nighttime dreams and fears than I was during the day. The unconscious was my private roller coaster and from now on I was determined to enjoy the ride.

So I didn't move to the desert.

Instead of that, I married my dad.

I know it sounds incredible but what can I say? At the time it seemed inevitable, preordained, like we'd both been touched on the shoulder by fate. We moved in together on my thirty-fifth birthday, when he was seventy-one. After the van unloaded all our boxes and furniture in front of the house we'd decided to rent, he took me in his arms and carried me over the threshold (he could do that because he still lifted weights at a gym). Then he barbecued steaks and opened an antique bottle of port.

"To your birthday, darling," he said by way of a toast. "You've made me the happiest man on earth."

"Me too, Daddy," I said, and for now, it was true.

My father's real name was John, but I called him Daddy even though I can't remember much about living with him as a dad. He moved out the spring of my seventh year when he fell in love with someone else, that is someone other than my mother. I never blamed him for it in the least. My mom is the worst combination of every bad trait in the book.

But back to my dad.

Three months after his second wife Sally died of organ failure, Daddy and I fell in love. He was still traveling all the time then and he asked me to join him for two weeks in the south of France.

"Sure, Daddy," I said, like an aging whore, like someone who could be bought and sold for the price of a trip abroad. Not that I was, of course. I did have a life of my own, although it was easy enough to leave.

And the trip hadn't really cost him a thing. His company, an international textiles firm, had already paid for the two of them, Daddy and Sally, to go. Daddy was supposed to pick up a couple of original Gauguins his company could copy for its Tahitian line and then display in the corporate lobby. Sally got to go as a bonus. Daddy was good at his work.

He looked like David Niven and he was somewhat of a thief. The owner of the paintings would never press charges but eventually he'd sell Daddy the masterpieces for little more than the price of a meal. Daddy's was obviously a nighttime job.

How did it work?

Who cares? He was my daddy and I loved him no matter what.

The house we moved into was beautiful. Driving up at night after work, I felt like I was coming home to a castle, not a house. There was even a two story turret in front where the stairway ran up to the second floor.

For a long time this is how it went.

"Daddy, I'm home," I'd call out. "Daddy, I'm home."

I'd take off my shoes and run into the kitchen for a cookie and some milk. John would wipe his hands on his apron and then take me in his arms like in a film.

"How was your day?" he'd say.

I'd make something up to entertain him about my boss, Ms. Sackville-West, or my co-worker, Mr. Henry Jones. He particularly enjoyed stories where I described my walking in on them doing something despicable like cleaning each other's ears with Q-tips or popping pimples with their nails.

"How disgusting," he'd say. "Why do you put up with it?"

I think he missed a sense of colleagues, his work for the textile company being as solitary as it was.

"She pays me well," I'd say. "Blood money maybe. Because of what I've seen."

"Well, you relax for half an hour and then I'll slice the roast."

In spite of all the crappy p.r. lately about father/daughter love, it sounds damn good, doesn't it? None of my girlfriends ever had cookies ready or paid my way through France. And I don't think anybody'd ever thought to let me rest before a roast. So had I just now invented a new way of life? Was I going to get away with living out a dream?

Absolutely.

What wine we drank! What food we ate! From France Daddy had brought back several cases of local Merlot to go with the meat, local Sauvignon to go with the fish and fowl. All morning long he watched the cooking channel on cable. All afternoon he'd shop and chop to make the meal he'd seen that day on TV. Our senses sang. Our heartbeats hummed. We were living so much in the present that we didn't have any leftovers to clutter the view.

I took them all to work.

Over delicious lunches provided by me, Ms. S.-W. and Mr. Jones began to ask about my living arrangements.

"You live alone, dearie?" asked S.-W., stuffing an artichoke heart into her mouth. "When do you find the time?"

"To cook, you mean?" I said.

"And how can you afford it?" said Henry.

Ms. Sackville-West pinched him under the table. She paid him more than me of course, but what did I care?

I cut my chilled lobster tail in half.

I couldn't decide if they really wanted an answer or if they were just passing the time, feigning interest because of the free food.

"No dependents," I said, evasively.

"Lucky you," my boss said. It was clear she was thinking of her boy Henry the way she giggled and then touched the back of his neck. I felt a frisson of jealousy and then I let it pass.

What did I care? I had my dad.

And soon we were three.

Dad, me, and the baby.

There was plenty of room, no problem with that. Plenty to eat. The same interests, similar taste in clothes and art and evening TV. It should have been perfect but something was wrong. Nothing you could put your finger on really. It was the details. The smells. The sounds. The way the two of them looked alike in a certain light. In the dark.

I began to feel left out.

Now when I came home from work and called out, "Dad, I'm home," it was never just Dad who greeted me, it was the two of them. And what they said was hardly a greeting; it was more like a double grunt. Could they be bothered to raise their heads from the board game they were playing, the puzzle they were putting together, the train engine they were building from scratch?

When I was growing up, I'd never had a dad who played with me like that.

For the first time in ten years, I wanted to speak to Mom.

Divorcing your mom is more common than you might think. In fact, I read about a group for people like me, D.O.N.E., Daughters Overcoming Neglect and Exploitation, made up of women who need to feel they aren't the only ones. Women who get together regularly to talk their mother stuff through.

Obviously I didn't join. My mom's buried deep down inside me and that's where she's going to stay.

She's always ill and yet, unlike poor Sally, she never dies. I don't think. No notice of that had come to me and my new address, the one with my dad, was listed in the book.

"Passive aggressive," the shrink had said. "Very common." We were supposed to be talking about the rain but mother had gotten tangled up in the discussion the way mothers always do.

"Not exactly. She's helpless but she's mean," I told her. "Needy but withholding. Demanding but cold."

"Hmm," she'd said. "That's even worse."

"Can I dump her?" I said.

"Well," she hedged, "she is your mom. The loss of her might be more difficult than dealing with her crap."

"That's OK," I said. And then my time was up.

"Mom?" I said. Over the phone, we'd agreed to meet at one of those soup and salad places but I'd forgotten to ask her what she was looking like now.

"Yes," she said. She was sitting in a wheelchair near the door.

"Are you my mom?" I said.

"Could be," she said.

"You once married to a man named John?"

"Ran off with somebody when you were seven. Never forgave the son of a bitch."

"Mom!" I said. "It's you." I leaned over and tried to hug her.

"Don't," she said, brushing me away. "I haven't forgiven you either."

"You're looking well," I said, "except for the chair."

"You're not."

"Oh come on. Don't be mean, Mom. I need you."

"Now?" she said. "When you feel like it? Did you ever think about what I might need? For ten years I've had to pay people to push me around. My own daughter should have been doing it for free."

Then she neatly spun her chair around on its back wheels so that I couldn't see her face.

"You do that good, Mom," I said. "Like a pro."

"Don't flatter me," she said.

"Are you leaving? Don't you at least want lunch? I'll pay. See, I've got two-for-one coupons."

"Typical."

A businessman opened the exit door for her and she rolled out towards the street.

"Don't call me again," she said.

"But Mom," I shouted after her. "I finally understand how you feel. Daddy is a son of a bitch. Now he's gone and left me too."

But I wasn't ready yet to be an orphan. I went back to Dad.

He hadn't actually left me for one thing, although he and the baby slept in the same room now. Dad's excuse was that you never knew when a baby might stop breathing.

"Put a monitor near its crib," I said.

"It's just for a little while, honey," Dad said. "Until it grows up."

And we still did family things together like rent videos or go out to breakfast on Sunday mornings. But it wasn't the same as it had been when it was just Dad and me. There were all these damn interruptions in the flow. At breakfast the baby's toast falling on the floor and Daddy bending over to pick it up. And Daddy rewinding the video over and over to the part the baby liked best. The thing that got to me was that Daddy enjoyed doing it, honest to god!

When I began to have serious fantasies about murdering them both I got scared. Was there anything as bad as me in the Greeks? Had any woman in Sophocles ever killed father and baby in a fit of pique? I ran through the tragedies for a comforting classical precedent but I couldn't remember a thing.

Crazy as I felt, this time, I didn't go near a shrink. I didn't want to get healed. I wanted to get even.

Every day it kept getting worse.

"Daddy," I said. "We have to talk."

"Sure," he said. He looked up from bottle feeding the kid.

"It's it or me," I said.

"It won't be much longer," he said.

"That's what you said last time and that was ages ago. Look, by now its feet are dangling on the ground."

"You're right," he said and he flipped it over for a burp.

A few months later, I tried it again. This time Daddy was giving it a bath.

"Daddy," I said. I averted my eyes discreetly as he washed its privates with care.

"Yes, dear."

"The neighbors are talking. They say your relationship with the baby just isn't right."

"Fiddlesticks," he said. "I'm its father. They aren't used to modern parenting where the dad does his equal share."

"It's more than equal," I murmured.

"What?" He couldn't hear me over the hot water running into the tub.

"It's more than equal," I yelled.

"They're threatened," he said. "Change always threatens people. At first."

He was giving me a message, that much was clear. I needed a change. He wanted me out of the house. He didn't love me anymore.

One night I looked in on them in the den, the orange/blue light of the television screen reflecting off their twin smiling faces. I never saw them again. The next morning, I left before they got up for breakfast. I left before dawn.

I didn't pack a thing except the last bottle of Merlot and the money I'd saved working for Sackville-West. I wanted to take something that would hurt them and show them what they'd done to me but I couldn't think of what. My picture? That would only make me easier to forget.

I wandered the streets. I became a character in French film noir, full of secrets and self-pity and angst. I wore dark turtlenecks and forgot to wash my hair. Almost immediately I turned to drugs.

Then I went clean. It was the shortest addiction on record, one month to the day. The trouble about drugs was that they dulled my senses and numbed my pain and the pain was OK with me. Plus the people I had to hang out with to score were sordid and boring as hell.

In rehab I met this woman named Nicole. She wasn't anything like my dad.

When we became lovers I made her promise there would never be anyone else. She thought I was nuts.

"Like another lover besides you?" she said.

"Like a baby," I said.

She thought I was a comedian. Lots of people in rehab are.

"That I can promise," she said. "Unless you've got something I didn't notice inside your pants."

I took her for a ride past the castle I'd lived in with my dad. There was a For Sale sign on the front lawn.

"I used to live there," I said.

"Yeah, sure," she said. "And I used to be Hillary Clinton."

"I did. I have quite a past."

"I'll bet," she said and then she kissed me so hard I tasted blood.

"Ouch," I said.

"It's been a long time," she said. "I'm sorry I'm such a klutz."

"You're going to be good for me," I said, "believe it or not."

After we got out, Nicole and I moved in together. They warn you not to do that. They mention Liz and Larry and shake their heads but we persisted. What harm could there be?

"Can we afford the castle?" she asked.

"No," I said. "Not in the least."

"What can we afford?"

"Something sweet," I said. "Something more like a home."

And that's just what we got, an adorable guest house, a tiny love nest for two.

Nicole carried me over the threshold of our little cottage but she dropped me near the stairs. She hadn't worked out in a while. "Welcome home, darling," she said.

"What do you mean by that?" I said. I sat down on a box and stared up at her. I noticed for the first time that she had the beginnings of a double chin.

"You still miss your dad," she said. It wasn't a question. Already she knew me through and through.

I looked at her some more. I noticed that she had several black hairs sprouting near her mouth.

"What a thing to say at a time like this."

"Let's unpack and then grab a Whopper or a Big Mac or a Chicken McLean."

"You're kidding," I said. And then I tried to laugh.

We lived like that for a long, long time. Almost as long as with my Dad. We ate fast food and pizza and things we microwaved after work. We drank beer from the bottle and Coke from the can. I gained a lot of weight. So did Nicole. When we walked down the street people turned to look or they stepped off the sidewalk to get out of the way. We were Liz and Larry after all, but without the dough.

One time this supermarket checker asked me when my baby was due.

"Never," I said. "No baby." I patted my stomach. "It's all fat in here. No brain, no eyes, no teeth."

"I'm sorry," she said.

"Don't be. I'm happy as I could be."

But I wasn't. I wanted more.

I shouldn't have been surprised that the kid came into my life again. All the hard stuff rolls around at least twice. To give you another chance maybe, like reincarnation or a recurring dream. I looked through the fisheye peephole one Saturday afternoon and saw it standing there, all grown up with a little suitcase hanging from its hand.

"Nobody's home," I said.

"Dad died."

"So?" I was talking through the door because Nicole would be home any minute and I didn't want the kid getting too comfortable inside. We had some nice furniture, a good hard couch, and a big chair with an ottoman that drew you down into it so far you almost couldn't get up.

"Let me in. Can't you see I'm grieving?"

"How'd you get so tall and skinny?" I said. I opened the door. "You can come in, but only for ten minutes. Is it money you want or what?"

"No. In fact, Dad gave me some for you if I ever found out where you live. We were loaded, remember?"

I brought us a couple of Cokes and we sat down next to each other on the couch.

"So what are you going to do now?" I said.

"I don't know. I was hoping you'd tell me."

"What a big baby you are," I said. Maybe because so much time had passed, maybe because of the resemblance to Dad, this feeling was welling up I didn't even know I had. I made the mistake of affectionately ruffling the kid's hair before I noticed the front door open up again.

"Hey," said Nicole, home early from bowling a few lanes, "think fast." She tossed the ball in our direction. Luckily the kid had fast reflexes and caught the damn thing before it knocked us out.

"Buzz off," I said. All of a sudden I couldn't help but see her through somebody else's eyes. She sure wasn't David Niven, that much was clear. She wasn't my dad. She was a big-hearted jealous ex-junkie who'd found me ruffling somebody else's hair.

"Yeah," the kid said and threw the ball back. "She's leaving with me."

"Who are you? Her new secret lover?"

"Let's go," I said, and we picked up our Cokes and left.

It was so ironic, living with the same baby who'd ruined my life with Dad, that it came full circle and began to make sense. Plus, it wasn't like we'd fallen in love. We were just sharing our lives for a while, until both of us figured out what to do next.

I stayed cool. I knew that someday the kid would grow up and want to make a life of its own. Get married, have kids, own a house. I didn't want to get too attached or hold it back in any way.

But I couldn't help myself, I kept having dreams for the future. It's a classic cliche but I kept wanting the kid to have everything I never could. Graduate school in art history, a competitive tennis game, fluent French, world travels, a tendency toward philanthropy of the liberal sort. The kind of stuff Daddy would have wanted if he'd lived long enough to see it all through.

One rainy evening after scallops *a la coeur* and a sweet little truffle *pâté,* I couldn't hold it back anymore. I had to say it out loud like a big bubble of intestinal gas.

"So, you thought about what you want to do with your life?"

The kid looked at me with those big, deep eyes.

"Never mind," I said. "It's none of my business. I've got to go out and check the rain gutters anyway. There's a flood watch on the other side of town."

I'd recently begun to worry about rain again, like the old days, as if I was in danger of some kind.

The kid looked at the ground and said, "Maybe we should get married."

"What the hell," I said. "OK."

We shook on it and I couldn't help but notice how soft the kid's skin was. Like a baby's, more or less.

Then I went out into the rain, using a ladder to climb onto the roof. The kid offered to help, but I needed to check on things for myself. Once I got up there, I used my hands to scoop the leaves and twigs from the gutters even though somehow I knew it wouldn't do any good. Finally I looked up at the clouds to estimate how much time I had before rain began to seep into the basement and leak through the walls.

Caravan

GERRY GOMEZ PEARLBERG

I am furious at my girlfriend today. Going over and over in my head, not the things she said, but the things she didn't, abscesses that cut me to the quick. When I am mad at my girlfriend, I do what everybody does, I try to erase her from my mind. From the streets I walk. From the sky above. From the bars we always go to, which I am passing now. Dark bars where we buy each other drinks and recline on Egyptian pillows, kissing, her hand sliding up my shirt, even as she apologizes for her lack of restraint in a heterosexual public place—"forgetting" herself, as she likes to say.

I am trying to forget her too, but it isn't easy when you have a famous girlfriend, because then she's everywhere, the whole world is perpetually memorizing her, she is remembered by newsstands, TV sets, the very atmosphere. Case in point: I'm walking past a bookstore, the window stocked with good ideas I didn't come up with: books by cagey girls in acrid dialects, 'zines for adherents of this or that psycho-sexual persuasion, slickly packaged audiocassettes of long-dead poets reading their poetry. And there, a magazine with my girlfriend's picture on the cover—and then another, and another, and another. High up on the very top shelf, glaring down at me. Glossy and inevitable.

My girlfriend is famous and that makes her look more real from the outside in than from the inside out. When I see a photo of her on the cover of a magazine—which is often—I am amazed at how definite she looks. How on the page there is a beginning, a middle, and an end to her. And yet, in real life I cannot escape her because there is no end to her—she is everywhere, larger than life, and this is the defining element of her life's elixir, Fame.

She shines on the covers of those slick magazines, and it's more than the effect of paper treated with chemical compounds. Her desire to shine becomes incarnate on the page. She glows and is beautiful, like a 1950's rawhide lamp, the kind with stenciled cowgirls and laced-up edges. When her full body is shown, her legs dangle boldly off the sides of chaise longues, swimming pools, and queen-sized beds, like smooth souvenirs floating far from the shallows of time. It is, in part, her hourglass figure for which she is so well loved. The way she holds time by the scruff of its neck, shaking it to bits in the jaws of her extraordinary self-confidence in the potency of physical being.

I am amazed at how definite she looks on the page because in my heart she is an umbra, her suggestiveness her allure. Like a magic trick, the secret's all in the wrist: she does not insist, she implies. *Embodies.* On the page she seems realer than she has ever seemed in my arms, my shower, my bed. Perhaps that's what happens when light hits glossy paper. Perhaps it's all that light refracting back from her image, so precisely framed. It gives her a dimension distinctly lacking in our interactions; a sense of permanence, finality.

In the beginning, Darka undid me. On our first date, we met at a seedy bar on the fragrant edge of the city. We had barely touched our lips to the salted rims of our cocktail glasses when she leaned toward me and whispered, "I want to enjoy your body and all its ramifications."

Her tongue was a stallion of muscle galloping across my river. Her breath in my ear a book I could not open. Who could have known that would be our metaphor? And why are books so often the metaphor?— Good Book, Open Book. I once heard the story of a lover spurned, who not only read her boyfriend's journal, but actually wrote in it—not concealing her invasion of privacy so much as formalizing it. She crossed out whole sections of his diary, rewrote the stories she did not want to hear, adjusted his syntax, and annotated his margins with her own interpretations of the truth of the matter. The Real Story, Whole Story, Story Thus Far.

Darka was wearing old-fashioned earrings, clip-ons encrusted with faux jewels of powder-puff pink and incision red, the kind that transform the outer ear into a stardust ballroom, a glimmering arcade of music and dance. A whirlpool of skin guards the secret corridor in which love's hot breath blows and whispers are entrusted, and the earlobe becomes a velveteen love seat, a magnificent parlor of ardor and perfume. My grandmother had such earrings. She called them costume jewelry. In that phrase was the suggestion of a ruse or charade. And grand seduction. Darka was wearing shiny earrings, those old-fashioned clip-ons encrusted with faux jewels of viscous pink and decision red. She wore them that first evening. I never saw them again.

That night at the bar, our bodies were infused with time. The sexiest song in the world was playing: Ella Fitzgerald's swooning rendition of "Caravan." Neither of us wanted the first kiss to end; we knew it would be all downhill from there. So it was only after a long, long time that she broke away—as she put it—"to visit the powder room." I waited for her on my barstool, feeling off kilter without the pressure of her body spilled against me like a ladder. I'd grown accustomed to the texture of her flesh, addicted within moments.

Time passed. She did not return for what seemed forever. She did not return at all. I decided to go after her. I paid for our drinks, grabbed my jacket, and dashed down the long spiral staircase—perpetuity incarnate—that she had disappeared into. There was a long, slate-colored corridor at the foot of the stairs. It twisted and turned, a viaduct. I followed it. Through the narrow streets of ancient Chinese cities, along the paralyzing catwalks of industrial capitalism's end-stage fortresses, across the claustrophobic caverns where naked bat-pups by the thousands clung to the ceiling like lumpy pink wallpaper, chirping for their milky mothers' return. For what seemed forever I walked, crawled, climbed, pursued.

There, at the end, in a little arena, was Darka, splayed out on a chartreuse velvet couch with goat-horn feet, drunkenly gorgeous, a flagrant Cleopatra.

And there, on my knees, I caressed her, by the gate to the Ladies' Room, that great Forbidden City. Made love to her again and again with parts of the body I didn't know I had. Like a movie star, she returned only the favor of her presence in my arms. But her moans collected in my eardrums, riveting themselves to my spinal column like a liquid string of black barnacles. Her flesh smooth against my fingers, a pink pearl bubble bath—slippery, feminine, deliciously short-lived. She was a genie in the lamplight, a genie inverted—rub her the wrong way, and she'd surely disappear.

We went to the corner and hailed a cab. Inside that dark cradle, she leaned down to retrieve a fallen jewel and bit my thigh, brutally hard. Then laughed when a gasp escaped me. The bite left a bruise the shape of a semi-colon, suggesting more to follow. "Why have a segue when you can have a non sequitur?" that bruise seemed to say. I studied it every day for a week and was sad when it faded, end of an era.

On every corner we sped past, stood the statues of the New Plague. The plague that zapped people while they hurried to work, ran out for groceries, took out the trash. But mostly on their way to work. They'd stop in their tracks, just up and die, like pillars of salt, *X* marks the spot. And like an evil spell in a fairy tail, touching or attempting to move their statued bodies would unleash so potent a hailstorm of bad luck and furies upon the interlopers, that before long the corpses were simply left where they stood—in peace, as it were. Odd term, "up and died," isn't it? And how the passage of time renders old expressions new.

In this City of Statues our bodies sought each other out. She took me back to her place, though I hardly knew her, except from magazines and the Big Screen, mid-morning infomercials, and late-night appearances as everybody else's Special Guest. I knew what she looked like on the glossy page, on newsprint matte, on billboards, in Garamond #3, in 16-millimeter, and Panavision. The body looks different from each of these vantage points, but I wanted her in every conceivable dimension, first through fifth. And every position. Every proposition I made her, she accepted with glee.

In real life, up close, she was pure, unadulterated Technicolor. One hundred percent Red reds, one hundred percent Blue blues. Her colors popped out of themselves, *saturated.* Something about her whispered, *1957.* She was an anagram of seduction. And I, a glass of water into which she lowered her smooth red stems.

What becomes a legend most? she asked.

A sexy, dangerous woman.

What becomes a legend most? she asked.

The one who makes love to your body, but not to you.

What becomes a legend most? she asked.
You do. You do. You do.

Fame, while commonly perceived as an acquisition, gift, or achievement, is actually an accumulation of losses. First you lose your privacy. Your face and body become public property. Next, you lose your friends. You lose the privilege of honest speech; anything you say can be used against you. You lose perspective on yourself, then humility, and ultimately, heart. In time you become a vessel, an open secret for pouring other secrets into.

Secrets are a dime a dozen, but here's a word that's gone out of style:

INTEGRITY

That first night together, while she lay sleeping, I thought about how some words you just want to reach out and touch, to make a part of your life. *Integrity* is a range of great mountains: difficult to attain. I remember encountering the Himalayas for the first time. It was like meeting a famous person—the way those mountains went on and on, the way they shone in the day and glowed in the dark, the way their faces were etched in blue shadow, and how differently they appeared from every vantage point. But there was one important difference: meeting them in person wasn't a bit anti-climactic; it was the experience of a lifetime. There are thrilling experiences—like encountering a star of stage and screen—that you can embellish upon and mythologize. And there is mythic experience—like being in the presence of a great mountain—that does not fit within the confines of language, and is best left to swelter and swell in the personal canals of memory and nostalgia.

Sometimes I feel I am being watched by them. The city is claustrophobic with the dead and their memories. It's true what they say about the dead taking their secrets with them, but no one ever mentions how many of our secrets they take as well. City of a Thousand Watchers. A thousand listeners and thinkers and rememberers. I do not believe, as many do, that the statued dead are angels in our midst, put there to help or judge us. But I do believe they are watching, with aching comprehension.

Sometimes I long to be witnessed, sad and unadorned. So I visit Cyclone's statue. Lay flowers at her feet. Or just stand nearby, watching and being watched. The expression on her face seems different every time. Sometimes sinister, sometimes serene. Sometimes familiar, or a dialect of fear. Cyclone was my lover. The plague overcame her near the movie theater. I like to watch the crowds coming out of the movie, parting to either side of her. Making way for her. My Cyclone, like so many others, halted in time.

Each succeeding love is a paradoxical culmination of the laws of chemistry and physics: greater in mass and volume, less stable than the one before. I love Darka more than all the others combined, and so differently from how I've loved the others. But each time is so different as to be virtually unrecognizable from the time before. After biting my thigh she said, *Your heart needs no lifeboat, it's dying to drown.*

For the second time, I am on my way to see her, wearing my Walkman, riding the rails. Speeding uptown to a girl named Uncertainty. When I am certain of her, the invisible timer in my heart will click, and I will be compelled to move on. That is my pathology; love having become not a form of hope but a gorgeous futility, like gunning the engine on the Möbius Strip. But tonight I am the picture of earnest pursuit, on my way to her on a magic carpet of unadulterated desire. I am standing between the subway cars, dancing, listening to music and the howling wheels upon the ancient tracks, leaning into the fast black wind of the tunnel, wondering how it can possibly be that in Spanish, this word—*el túnel*—takes the masculine form.

Sometimes the train sidles up alongside another—a local, perhaps, or one that will split off at the next station in another direction—and like a glimpse into a parallel universe I see my fellow riders sitting and reading, napping, or staring blankly into the empty spaces that are fast becoming the fragments of their own accumulating lives. Not one of them is on their way to see her. Not one will kiss those lips tonight in the candlelight, not one will touch her there, and there. I am listening to music and howling into the darkness that I wouldn't trade these gifts, the gift of my life for any of theirs, for immortality, or heroism, or for anything I could name. I am grateful for this night, for the lurching subway cars that catapult me toward her, along the underground of this harsh, handsome city of cigarillos and peppermint sticks, manhole covers imported from India, alligator rumors in the slime—and women who wear the caps of matadors, reducing leather dykes, lathering butches, bulls, and bulldaggers like myself to their most essential tinctures: skin and horn and baited breath. I am grateful for such women, like the one I am careening toward. And for this, my night, advancing through the dark chasm between the well-lit cars' glistening slide show of normalcy's demise.

"Know what makes a whip crack?" Darka asked, and of course I didn't. "The momentum of the tip as it breaks the sound barrier. That's the kind of speed I want to come at you with."

"Breakneck?" I asked.

"Oh, my poor baby. Breakneck is just the half of it," she purred, her intentions glistening through her black lace underwear, a socket of bioluminescence.

Where I live, there is a distant bridge that only appears at night, a piece of rock candy. I do not know its name, but long to lay lips upon it. I imagine my mouth will stick there, as if to dry ice, and that in time I will be absorbed into its catenaries and suspenders, made whole and nocturnal and useful at last.

She sleeps like a statue, still as a stone. I lie beside her and listen to her breathe. It is an obsession, wondering when it will cease. I listen to my own breath and bloodstream, the sounds of the world entering my eardrums. There is a part of me that is always awaiting the end: the end of the sounds within, the bloodstream's thrum, the ample humps of breath. And the end of the sounds outside, the world pouring in.

I watch Darka sleep and imagine her dreaming of her hero, Max Factor. To make it shimmer on the silver screen, Max Factor sprinkled gold dust in Marlene Dietrich's hair. For the sake of modesty, Max Factor created fur pants for the chimpanzees in *Tarzan* to wear. To make him more memorable, Max Factor created the famous ring around the eye of Petey, the dog in Spanky's Gang. Hollywood created the dreams on which our lives are based, and recycles them now, endlessly. For this reason, she is fond of telling me, fame and glamour—not adventure and honor—are what we long to reach out and embrace. I wonder what she reaches for in dreams, where all things are equal: a cyclone, a lion, a kiss, cologne. I wonder what the famous dream of, residing as they do in a world where stars are made and ground to dust and made again, through ruthless pressure, like diamonds.

I watch her sleep. How far she has gone from me. Drifting, a statue floating on a river. An impossibility, this dead-weight buoyancy in the ecosystem of sleep, where Darka's body is a cool marble canoe, parting the smoke-grey reeds, pushing the limits of surface tension.

Every gift she gave me was a dream sequence, strange and absorbing. Like the Animal Drawing course she signed me up for at The Museum of Natural History. I remember the first class, wandering the Hall of Mammals late at night, long after the museum had closed, the sound of our footsteps echoing in the shadow of an enormous sperm whale suspended from the ceiling. How that strangely lit hall evoked for me the sensation of the first time one kisses a lover after having begun, almost imperceptibly, to fall in love with her: thrilling and desolate.

The overhead lights were off, but achingly bright fluorescence emanated from each of the mammal dioramas, like a series of slides projected at equidistant intervals along the wall. Within those boxed perimeters of light, water buffalos, orangutans, a herd of giraffes, and other once warm-blooded creatures were poised for all eternity in habitats crudely reproduced in plaster and paint. In places the walls—on which were rendered desert backgrounds, or jungles, or plains—were cracked and chipping, a ruination of faith. I remember thinking that the world's most enervating loneliness must surely reside in the dust-filmed frames of those exquisite creatures, and how much *this* sensation precisely mirrored those produced at a love affair's end.

The teacher had us pause to sketch a pride of lions in the Hall of African Mammals. A fallen aura of pulverized plaster illuminated the male lion's overblown mane. It made me think of a Nepali legend I'd once heard about a king who'd ordered the creation of great stone lions to guard his domain. They stood in pairs, potent and enormous, at the gate of every temple and palace. In ritual ceremonies, the king's priests were instructed to imbue these lions with "life." But the king, cowering from what he himself had wrought, grew fearful of these empowered stones, and ordered that they be placed in chains to ensure that they would never turn against him. Hence, the ancient lions of Nepal are bound forever in chains of stone.

I'll never forget what the Animal Drawing teacher said on the very first night of class. He was discussing spined animals, as compared to invertebrates like insects, clams, and snails. He pointed out that virtually all vertebrates—a vast category of living things—have a spine from which legs, and in some cases arms or fins or wings, extend outward, so that whether the creature is a biped or a quadruped, the fundamental "design" is remarkably constant. "Biologically speaking," he observed, "we have infinitely more in common with a bear, a bat, a shrew, and a whale, than the surface details—mere variations on a theme—might suggest."

If this is true—and I believe it is—how can she and I be so infinitely far apart?

Whereas once her cunt perched on my outstretched finger like a little wet sparrow, all heartbeat and hidden heat, now my heart has slipped from inside me and into her open, unsuspecting hand. She does me so perfectly that when she is finished I pull her up to lay upon me, my heart outside of me, stretched along my skin like a wetsuit, shimmering. She is on top of me with her eyes closed, her hand still penetrating me, and I am watching her. Her eyes are always closed when she makes love to me, or rather, to my body.

"Look at me," I say, wishing I didn't have to ask. And when she does, her stare is so intense and scrutinizing, her eyes so dark and empty, it makes me shudder. Dislodges something inside me I didn't even know was there.

"I'm going to cry," I say, as the tears begin rising.

She holds me with a tenderness that is entirely new. And I begin a silent cry, stifled like a moan passed into a pillow, and then I am sobbing, tears skating down my cheeks, infusing the pillow of stifled moans. Her hand is still inside me, still nursing the wetness there, and realizing this makes me cry harder, I who have never cried during lovemaking.

"Why are you crying?" she whispers. Her soft cheek, that smell I love, the flavor of her are pressed against my ear so that I can taste and smell her with my earlobe. *Why are you crying,* she wants to know.

I am crying because you don't love me, I think, *from the frustration of making love to you and knowing you don't love me.*

Instead I say, "Because I miss Cyclone."
Instead I say, "Because I'm exhausted."
Instead I say, "Because you move me."
Instead I say, "I really don't know."

I wonder what she expects to hear. Does she suspect and dread the truthful answer? Or crave it?

She pulls out of me and we fall asleep, locked in each other's arms. In a dream she tells me, "Being in love is like being in an airplane. A marvelous takeoff, full of expectancy and new sensations. Once in the air, the view alternates between exquisite and desolate. One anticipates glorious arrivals, face pressed against the window. Then the flight becomes bumpy, hazardous, frightening. The crew will refer to this as 'turbulence.' There is a long period of uncertainty, when prayers you didn't think you remembered find themselves crammed in your throat, along with your heart. At last the plane descends. The wheels touch the runway, and there is relief bordering on ecstacy. The passengers applaud. The plane bursts into flames."

In the morning, well before sunrise, I wake up beside her apathetic body, a warm loaf of sweet deviled bread. She is sleeping with her face turned away from me, as she always does and always will, a movie star with her eye makeup still on. I'd never kissed a girl with eye makeup until her. So much I never knew. Her back to me, her makeup and cologne, parted lips and attitude. Beyond asleep: oblivion personified. It's what makes a star: the capacity to suggest so much more than you actually are.

I reach around in front of her, touching her nipples almost imperceptibly, as if trying out a Ouija board. When she moans, I know I've reached the spirit world. It is precisely this implausible contact I seek with her, as if to speak to the phantom of her deepest passions, the ghost of who she was before disappointment rendered her so remote. What is it about this emptiness that draws me? The desert's apparent desolation, and the subtle riches therein? The sheer enormity of its scope and mystery? Waking up to her is an adventure, every night a narrative. Unpredictable as a candelabra plunged underwater, a shipwreck submerged in flames.

She moans herself awake, nipples stiffening in my fingers, and for a moment I feel like a victor, except I'm not sure what I've won. Or that I *have* won. Or that there is even such a thing as winning. What does one long for in the desert? Water. Shelter. A fire at night. A variation in the landscape. The most fundamental of elements. Even a mirage seems too much to hope for. Even the intimacy of off-Broadway.

With her I found that Orgasm could mean Epiphany. The very first time we got into bed together she spoke about the holiness of lovemaking between women, the irony of our stigmatization. She made it quite clear that it was nothing personal, that she was simply articulating a general principle: that what our bodies did together encompassed—and was encompassed by—the sacred. *Wine, flesh, fish, women, and sexual congress: these are the five-fold boons that remove all sin.* So say the practitioners of Tantrism, and rightly so.

When Darka fucked me, she fucked my heart, drawing her hand in and out of that membrane shallow, my hollow squid, my squirt gun, my gumshoe chiton. And my heart rose through my porous flesh, enshrouding me like gelatin. Her knuckles chafing at my heart, chafing against it, was an epiphany, and that epiphany made me weep: *That nothing—save sex—would ever be right between us. That I might never find love again. That I, and all my friends and lovers, would die someday. That loneliness would be the chandelier, half-lit, illuminating the path toward a nostalgic yellow future without Darka in my arms.*

Sandoval the poet wrote, "Nostalgia is porous."

Sometimes I wonder what would happen if Darka disappeared one day as Cyclone did. How could I rescue her disappearance from her famousness? The famous never disappear; in the eyes of the world, they intensify. Death is merely an enhancement. How would I reconcile the intensified, famous Darka from the disappeared Darka who drifts to sleep in my bed each night, who is warm if not real, tangible if not actual?

I kiss her while she sleeps, but she is still as stone. I caress her, but she doesn't stir, a lioness battened down. I leave my lips upon her like a sugar maple leaf drifted down upon a bridge of sugary ice. I am trying to get somewhere, trying to get somewhere with her, but where? I want to retrieve her from her drifting, to awaken her or something within her. To offer and receive a kind of recognition that only lovers give. Is it simply a matter of reassuring myself of her warm presence, her blunt existence? Or attempting entry into an even more desolate landscape, like a searchlight skidding across enemy territory? What do I expect to find there? A crimson polygraph, set to stun? A turbulent creature enchained by stone? A queen-sized bed where Pleasure and Time sleep with their backs to one another? Or a porous passage back to that first kiss in the bar—our one great moment of certainty: the sure sensation of her leg touching mine, a bruise soon to be embedded like a jewel in my thigh.

Safe Sex

WENDI FRISCH

"She's a real pistol," E.J. says to me, nodding at a woman on the far side of the dance floor wearing a tight red minidress. Her long black hair is tousled to give her an appearance of nonchalance that's almost convincing. Right away I notice that her dress clashes with the red of the hearts stuck to the walls in honor of Valentine's Day, like she planned it. She looks like the type who insists on standing out in a crowd.

It was E.J.'s idea to hit the clubs on this official night of romance. "The hunting's always good on Valentine's Day," she said, flipping me an invitation to a party "for love slaves only" being held at a woman's bar. The invitation had a picture of a pouty lipped woman dangling a pair of handcuffs from one wrist. I could almost hear her whispering, "Be mine." I keep telling E.J. I'm not interested in hunting, but we've been friends for so long she knows she doesn't have to listen to me anymore.

I imagine the woman of the red minidress and E.J. naked in a bedroom with crushed velvet walls. They're stretched out on the red satin sheets of a heart-shaped bed, and E.J. is between the woman's legs, working. Some embers glow in a fireplace beyond the foot of the bed. Rain drums against a pair of French doors that open onto a small balcony. The woman arches her back, and a crucifix hanging from a gold chain around her neck falls across her left nipple. Steam rises out of her head as she comes, like smoke from a loaded gun, cocked, then fired.

The club's all dressed up for Valentine's Day and looks the way

I imagine a lesbian bordello would. A blonde go-go dancer and a brunette gyrate in a cage by the dance floor. A sign underneath identifies them as "Prisoners of Love."

"She's so hot, you could fry an egg on her ass," E.J. says staring at the woman in the minidress. She licks her lips as if she can taste it. She's looking sharp tonight in black baggies with red suspenders and a bolero jacket. She and red mini would look good together.

I picture E.J. in a red-and-white checkered apron, standing over the steaming woman with a spatula. A couple of eggs sizzle sunny-side up on the woman's backside. A little chorizo crackles and spits next to the eggs. Tortillas warm on the woman's shoulder blades. To the right, a wicker table in a breakfast nook is set for two. From a clock radio sitting on a window sill, a voice announces the time as 8:00 A.M.

"What is it about red?" I wonder to myself. I try to get a closer look at E.J.'s infatuation, but a cloud of disco fog obscures my view.

Just then Marguerite strolls by with a glass in her hand and her nose in the air, looking better than an ex-lover has any right to. She's wearing the cowboy boots I gave her, and her long hair is darker and even more lustrous than I remember. I pretend I don't see her. She's acting like she doesn't see me either, but I know it's an act because right away she's on the dance floor with a short woman wearing a tuxedo. Marguerite hates to sweat and only goes near a dance floor if she's trying to seduce somebody or make somebody jealous. From the looks of her dance partner, seduction's out, unless Marguerite's standards have really slipped.

I wonder if the burning in the pit of my stomach is jealousy. I remember how she could drive me crazy with even the most casual remark. "I went shopping with a *friend*," she'd say, breezing into the apartment on a Saturday afternoon. I'd start a slow burn, wondering what kind of nameless *friend* she was referring to. No matter how many arguments it caused, Marguerite always had to maintain an air of mystery.

The runt dips Marguerite, and Marguerite bites her earlobe. I decide the burning in my stomach is probably anger that two years after she moved out we're still playing games with one another. For about the millionth time I decide that I'm better off without her.

I glance toward the bar, which is littered with red and pink streamers. A blonde in a black bodysuit eating candy hearts there catches my eye and smiles.

E.J.'s still focused on the woman across the dance floor. "What I wouldn't give—" She lets the thought dangle. "Yeah, she really lights my fire." She runs her finger under the collar of her shirt to demonstrate her comment. The woman pulls out a compact and dabs at her lipstick with a tissue. Under the blood-red paste, her lips are a little too thin for her face.

I imagine them in an alley, E.J. tied to a telephone pole, nude except for the unlaced combat boots she wears. The woman is dressed entirely in leather, and kneels before E.J. with a lighted torch. A smile plays around my friend's lips as if she doesn't believe the woman will go through with it, or as if, maybe, she looks forward to it. A breeze stalks down the alley and blows the woman's hair across her eyes. The flame of the torch surges toward E.J. who smiles a little more broadly, showing teeth. As the woman touches the torch to some old newsprint crumpled around my friend's feet and ignites a flame, E.J. cries out. In pleasure? In pain?

I used to appear in my own sexual fantasies, but since Marguerite and I broke up, it feels too risky to fantasize in anything but the third person. The blonde at the bar is still watching me, so I take a second look. Her face could belong to an angel, but it's the glint of mischief in her eyes that captures my imagination. Her look says "fun." My stomach clenches involuntarily. I'm not sure if it's from desire or fear. She's got to be at least ten years younger than me and, as E.J. says, "The young ones always break your heart." With a little effort, I set my face into a mask of indifference.

E.J.'s fixation is dancing a quick cha-cha. The lights spattering the dance floor reflect pink and white spots on her bare arms. She has circles under her eyes that are only partially covered by a base makeup that doesn't quite match her olive skin. E.J. and I go back a lot of years and I'd hate to see her get hooked up with another bloodsucker, but I don't comment on any of the woman's obvious flaws. That saves E.J. from snarling at me, "And you wonder why you've been single for two years?"

The blonde heads toward the rest room. I know if I followed her we could strike up a conversation and perhaps more. But I'm not looking for "more" these days. I glance at my watch and wonder how soon I can leave without getting a lecture from E.J.

E.J. pulls a comb out of her pocket and slicks it through her short black hair. She makes big eyes at the woman who makes big eyes right back and blows a kiss in my friend's general direction. "Oh, you got me, you devil! Right through the heart!" She crosses her hands over the spot in her chest where presumably her heart resides and smiles widely at the woman. A cardboard Cupid grins demonically from the ceiling above her heard, looking more like Satan's bastard son than a guardian of romance.

I picture E.J. standing nude before a stone wall, a cigarette dangling from the corner of her mouth. The woman, also nude, faces E.J. with a pistol. Beyond the wall, the sky is as gray as slate without even the promise of sunrise. Smoke from E.J.'s cigarette partially shrouds her face, and she closes her eyes. Somewhere a factory whistle shrieks. The blonde in the bodysuit steps from behind the wall. A moment later, Marguerite steps from behind the same wall and moves to take her place next to the blonde. At a prearranged signal, both women nod at the woman holding the gun. As the woman leisurely takes aim at E.J., E.J. opens her eyes and smiles.

Marguerite walks by and leans in to murmur, "Happy Valentine's Day." She gives me an inscrutable look before she stalks off toward the bar. I remember how when we lived together, she would surprise me with a chocolate éclair or cream puff whenever she came home from shopping. Sitting on my lap, she'd feed me the pastry bite by bite, her long hair tickling my neck. After I swallowed the last bite, she would kiss any traces of sugar from around my mouth. For about the millionth time I decide I never really knew her.

"Hey, wasn't that Marguerite?" E.J. asks. Then, gazing back at the object of her desire, she mutters, "Just one night. I'd sell my soul for just one night." Her voice is loud enough for me to hear, but not the woman. The woman beckons with a wag of one of her crimson tipped fingers, then stands facing us with her hands on her hips. My friend dusts off the right lapel of her jacket and pulls in her stomach.

"See you in Hell," she says to me over her shoulder as she begins striding across the room.

I watch as E. J. reaches the woman and the woman touches her arm. They do look good together. A few minutes later, they dance and I see the woman pressing her vampire lips into my friend's neck. Then the two of them head toward the door, their arms twined around one another as tightly as nooses. As they step over the threshold that leads to the street, I think I see a flicker of flames encircling their ankles. I shiver with envy. They may be crossing through the gates of Hades, but I know that it's warm there and there's always something good to eat.

Out of the corner of my eye I watch Marguerite leaving through a side exit, alone. Before the door swings shut, she swivels once and looks directly at me. Two years of resolve crumple to my feet, discarded as easily as a candy wrapper. Almost involuntarily, I'm across the dance floor and out the door after her. Once the door locks behind me there's no turning back and I figure I'll know what to say when I catch her.

On the sidewalk, I find myself facing the woman I followed who's not Marguerite at all, just somebody who looks a little like her. It's only standing this close that I notice she isn't wearing cowboy boots and that her eyes are gray, not brown. She looks at me quizzically and turns away, tossing her hair over her shoulders and zipping her leather jacket.

A love song that I recognize is playing in the bar, but I can't quite make out the words. The woman mounts a motorcycle parked at the curb and guns it down the boulevard. I stare after her until she disappears and there's nothing left to look at but the street lamps holding up the sky. Then I keep staring until the fire tickling the edge of my vision begins to recede again.

Love

MARY BUCCI BUSH

September 1907

Birdie was always off working with that boy Shake, or sneaking into the *bosc'* with him, the two of them laughing and tugging at each other, acting like they *liked* to work, like they liked to be out in the scorching sun in the middle of the day lugging a croker sack of cotton through the dusty rows. There went Birdie now, hurrying down the road to the Titus fields, singing like she was the happiest girl in the world. She didn't even look over at the Pascala land to see if Isola was out picking.

It had started in the spring, then got worse over the summer. Shake this, Shake that, like he was sugar candy and the holy angels all rolled into one. And like her best friend Isola was somebody she'd never even heard of before. Birdie didn't play with anybody anymore, except her cousin Lecie, who had a boyfriend too.

"I don't care," Isola told herself. "She's nobody anyway." She turned back to her own work, feeling the tightness in her throat and the knot in her stomach squeezing at her from both ends till she couldn't help but cry out: "Uhh."

It seemed everywhere she looked now girls were eyeing boys, giggling, acting foolish. Isola would stare at Tobe Hall or even at her brother and ask herself, "What? What is it?"

Once when she saw Shake up close she stared so hard he finally asked her if she was okay. "You havin' some kinda spell?" he said. She turned away, embarrassed, while Birdie laughed at her.

She closed her eyes and tried to hold onto the picture of Shake in her head: a skinny, dark boy with scabs on his hands and dusty, knotty hair. Just another boy, that's all. Maybe, she told herself, she should get herself one, too. Then she'd know for sure what the fuss was about. And then maybe Birdie would pay her some attention again.

The only boy she could think of was Favo, whose father was a blacksmith without a barn, and whose mother always wore a dark shawl tied around her head. Favo was ugly and dumb, so maybe he'd be a good one to go after. But what would she do with him once she got him? She'd never even spoken a word to him before.

Isola dragged her croker sack to the end of the row, down near the lane. Favo's farm was way over on the other side of the plantation, near the swampy end of the lake. She looked at the dirt road that cut through the cotton fields, and she looked out at the speckled green and white fields scattered with all the workers she would have to walk past in the middle of the day to get to Favo's farm.

When her family stopped at noon to eat she told her mother she was sick.

"Sick?" her mother said, putting her hand to Isola's forehead.

"I want to go to the house to lie down."

"You lie down here in the row where I can keep an eye on you."

"I have to get out of the sun," Isola said, and she put her hand to her stomach and sagged forward, thinking she really did feel sick just talking about it.

Her mother looked at her. She felt Isola's forehead again. "Drink some water," she told Isola.

Isola shielded her eyes with her hands. "I can't drink," she said. "I'll throw up."

Her mother took her by the shoulder and searched her face. She held Isola's chin and looked and looked. Finally she told her, "You go to the house for a little while. Then you come back."

Isola clutched her stomach and dragged herself through the field like a dying girl. Once she passed the house and was out of sight of her family, she ran through the field and out onto the road on the other side.

People worked slowly, black people in some fields, Italians in others, both together in others. They all wore hats to keep the sun from burning their heads, except for a few Italian women who wore kerchiefs tied around their heads. One family had rigged a tattered sheet on poles to block the sun and was sitting under it, fanning their faces with their hats. Wagons went by hauling cotton. A few white fluffs of cotton lay in the yellow dirt where they'd fallen from a wagon or been blown by the wind.

Favo's family was one of just a couple from Calabria. Isola could hardly understand them when they talked. But she understood enough to know that Favo's father was always complaining. She'd see him at the commissary with his family, his wife silent and unhappy under her kerchief and the children dull and quiet, the old man complaining about foolish things that no one else would ever think to find fault with: the coarseness of the flour, or how many frayed threads were coming from a rope he wanted to buy. Everyone else complained about the high prices or the hard work or the lies they'd been told or the malaria that killed so many of them, but Favo's father said his mule's bit had a nick in it.

And there they were now, scattered in their field, picking cotton. The sight of them stopped Isola. The mother moved quickly down the row, a big round figure under her dark kerchief. Favo's father worked the opposite end of the field. He was a short, stocky man with bushy hair that made him look like a walking haystack. Between the parents the children worked: the three girls Isola's age and younger, and Favo, who was a little older than her sister Angelina.

Isola moved cautiously into their field. Her stomach sank as she watched Favo. His hair was bushy like his father's, and he had long ears that stuck out from his head and a nose like a piece of gnocchi. He moved so slowly that at first she thought he was sleeping on his feet. At least with her brother or Tobe Hall she could go sneaking into the gin mill or hunting turtles in the swamp or listening to old Mr. Blue tell stories of the "hents" that lived in the woods. But what could she possibly do with a boy like Favo? Most people pulled as many cotton balls from the plant as they could before tossing the clump into their sack. But Favo picked one ball at a time and put each into his sack like it was an egg he was afraid of breaking. If she or Angelina or Osualdo worked like that their father would slap them and yell for them to get moving. "Work, or you don't eat," he'd yell, and he would mean it.

Suddenly Isola felt afraid. What if somebody saw her staring at Favo? What if he came over and talked to her? What if he tried to hold her hand? She shuddered at the thought.

Favo raised his head and Isola felt her face flush. He watched her a moment, then went back to picking one ball at a time, as if it were perfectly normal for a strange girl to be standing on his land watching him work.

When he didn't look up again, she moved closer.

"*Ciao,* Favo," she called to him.

He stared at her. Then he raised his hand, as if to wave. He had a blank, dull expression on his face, and for the first time Isola wondered if maybe he was like *La Vecchia:* not right in the head.

"You can pick faster if you get a handful and then throw it in the sack," she told him.

He looked at his hand, then back at her.

She wanted to shrivel up inside her clothes and disappear. It was a terrible idea to come looking for Favo. If she ran home right that minute he would never even know what she'd been up to and she wouldn't have to think about him again.

Favo's father was nearing the end of his row. Soon he would turn and head back toward them. Any minute his sisters or mother would look up and notice her.

"My mother says to come to our house tomorrow," Isola blurted. "She wants to give you an egg."

He looked at her as if she were some kind of horrible animal he had never seen before.

"Egg, from a chicken," she said, thinking maybe he could not understand her Marche dialect.

He started to shake his head.

"You have to come," she told him. "Mamma will be mad if you don't."

Favo turned to look at his father down at the end of the row, as if to say, "Talk to him, not me."

"She wants to give it to *you,*" Isola called to him. "Come alone. Come after picking. Okay?"

He scowled at her.

"Can't you talk?" Isola blurted. But then Favo's father reached the end of the row and stood up straight and yanked his croker sack behind him, and Isola turned and ran.

The next day she went out early so she could find an egg and hide it. She worried about how she would meet him without her mother and father finding out. What if he came straight to the door and asked for her mother? What if he brought his mother and father with him? And what would she say to him if he came?

As she picked a section of their land with her brother Osualdo, she tried to remember how Birdie and Shake acted together, what they said and did. Then she thought of other girls who had boys, but she couldn't think of any Italian girls her age who had them. Even Angelina, who was two years older and always noticed boys, never talked to one. She tried to remember if any of the other Italian girls who giggled about boys really talked to them. Their parents would probably beat them if they did.

So what, she told herself. So what if she was the only Italian who had a boyfriend? At least Birdie would be her friend again. At least they'd be able to see each other and laugh and play like they used to.

She picked the cotton absentmindedly. Maybe things wouldn't be so bad with Favo, she thought. He would be her boyfriend for a while. Then she'd marry him and Birdie would marry Shake and the four of them would live together in a big house across the lake in the village. Right after they moved into the house Favo and Shake would catch the fever and die and Isola and Birdie would have to live alone together.

When she thought of that, a wonderful feeling ran through her and she had an exciting new thought: Why would she and Birdie have to marry boys in the first place? Why couldn't they just marry each other? They could have some babies and play with them and then they'd all go out fishing on the lake in the priest's rowboat.

Before she knew it she was no longer picking cotton with her brother where their parents had left them. She was walking into Lud Titus' field where Lud and Birdie and her cousin Lecie were working, the three of them singing one of their strange work songs.

Isola stopped. She hadn't gone to see Birdie once all summer, she realized. And then she got confused. She couldn't remember who had stopped seeing who first.

Birdie looked up at her and scowled. "I seein' a ghost?" she said.

Isola blushed.

"You ain't done pickin' this early?" Lud Titus called to Isola.

"I'm taking a rest," Isola answered, and the woman muttered "rest" and shook her head.

Birdie narrowed her eyes at Isola and frowned. "What you doin' here?" she said. "I thought you gone back to Italy."

"Well, you never came to see me either," Isola answered. They stared at each other angrily. Isola didn't know what to do, so she started plucking cotton from the plants. She had wanted to tell Birdie her idea about getting married. But everything felt strange now. Birdie started picking too, stiffly, from the same few plants, neither one of them moving down the row. They rustled through the bare leaves, looking for cotton that was no longer there.

Finally Isola threw her handful of cotton into Birdie's sack. "Where's Shake?" she asked.

"Shake? What you talkin' 'bout, Shake?" Birdie said. "What you think, he work for me?"

"I don't know," Isola shrugged. "Every time I see you he's there." Her face was burning.

"So what?" Birdie snapped. "That why you so uppity lately?"

"I am not uppity, Birdie Hall," Isola shouted.

Birdie's aunt and cousin looked up from their work.

"Well, well, well," Birdie said.

"Anyway, Favo's coming to see me tonight after work," Isola boasted.

Birdie looked at Isola, then burst out laughing. "Favo? What that, some kinda dog?"

Isola glared at Birdie. But the harder she tried to keep her angry expression, the clearer the picture of Favo, with long ears and a snout, came into her mind. She felt her mouth start to loosen into a grin, in spite of herself.

"Issy got herself a boyfriend," Birdie called out to the others. "But she say he a dog."

"Honey, they all dogs," Lud Titus called back.

"*That* why you never come see me?" Birdie said. "You been too busy courtin'?" She leaned close to Isola and winked, then squeezed Isola's arm. Isola laughed in relief at the familiar heat and smoothness of Birdie's skin.

"Who this Favo?" Birdie asked. "How you find him?"

"My Papa knows his Papa," Isola lied.

It didn't feel right to be lying to Birdie. And it didn't feel right to be all of a sudden talking with her, either, close and friendly like they used to be. But she wanted to talk. She didn't want to be mad.

"How long you two been eyein' each other?" Birdie asked her.

"Not long," she told her. "I don't know what to do."

Birdie gave her a funny look. "What to *do*?" she said.

"I never had a boy before," Isola whispered to her. "What do you do with them?"

Birdie shrieked. "Aunt Lud," she called. "Lecie. Listen up. She wanna know what you do with a boy."

The other two laughed.

Isola felt humiliated, but excited at the same time. None of her aunts would ever talk to her that way about boys and girls.

"Anyways, you too young to be worryin' 'bout boys," Lud Titus told her. "You got a couple good years left before you start that trouble."

Isola wanted to point out that she and Birdie were the same age, but she was afraid Birdie would get mad at her.

After a minute Isola turned to Birdie. Birdie stood smiling, her face all shiny and bright, and Isola felt the ache of missing her all summer. And then she had a picture of Birdie and Shake early in the summer asking her to go fishing, and Isola's insides flaring up like the dried stalks burning with coal tar after harvest, her shouting no, no, and running away. She'd been furious that she couldn't have Birdie to herself. And she'd been aching from not being able to talk with her.

"He doesn't even talk," Isola murmured.

"He must be really took by you," Birdie told her.

Isola nodded. "I think he is."

She felt her insides twisting. "Liar, liar," they said.

"You got to get him alone somewhere, is all," Birdie told her. "Out at the lake. They git all loose up there."

Isola tried to picture herself and Favo doing the things Birdie and Shake did: walking down the dirt road together. Laughing and slapping each other and pushing each other away. Touching hands, then holding on for a minute. Isola made a face and shook her head. The picture she kept getting was of Favo's long dog ears and dumb, sad dog eyes, and long dog nose.

Birdie squeezed Isola's arm. "Things be all right when you alone. Away from this." She nodded out at the field. "Bright sun an' a million eyes watchin' you."

When she was back picking with Osualdo, she realized Birdie hadn't asked her one single question about her family or who she'd been playing with lately. All she'd cared about was that Isola was seeing a boy. And she hadn't even told Isola anything important: how you knew when to hold hands with a boy, how you kissed one, and what it felt like.

She looked up and saw Osualdo poking at the cotton plants with a dried stalk and she yelled at him to stop playing and get to work. He glanced up, then went back to poking at the plants. She rushed over and slapped Osualdo on the side of the head. "I'm sick of you," she yelled. "I always get stuck working with you, but you're a lazy bum. Get to work or we'll never be finished."

Osualdo wailed as he held his head. "I'm telling Mamma and Papa."

"Don't you dare go anywhere," she screamed at him. "Get to work. Pick. You want to make us end up in jail?"

He whimpered and turned his back on her.

"You better move faster than that," she yelled, "or I'll hit you even harder." He cried and started picking.

Isola gathered her sack and rushed down the row a distance, hating all of them, every boy that ever existed. She yanked at the cotton balls, scratching her hands and making them bleed. Finally she clutched a handful of the cotton to her mouth and sank to the ground, crying.

After her family had finished their evening meal, and their mother had scolded and slapped both of them for fighting while they worked, Isola sneaked outside.

She went behind the chicken shed and pushed away the dried grass and dug in the soft dirt for the egg she'd buried. She brushed the yellow dirt from the shell, then went to the road at the edge of their land, cradling the egg in her palm.

She looked up and down the road, but there was no Favo. It

was late, but she could still see a few people out in their fields working. Soon the sun would turn red, and then it would be dark. She looked back at her house, worried that her mother would see her at the road and yell for her to come in. All the time she waited she thought of Birdie's warm hand on her arm, and the way Birdie's face turned shiny and full of light when she laughed. And then she got mad again at Birdie for being friendly just because of Favo. The egg turned hot in her hand, and she realized she'd been squeezing it. She opened her hand, relieved to find the egg whole.

She headed down the road, in the direction of Favo's house. Step Hall passed her, pulling a wagon load of cotton, and looking weary as he leaned forward in his seat. He seemed barely able to raise his hand to call, "Hey, Missy." The sky was turning red.

And then she saw a strange, slumped figure standing down where the road crossed the old road to the lake. As she got closer she could see it was Favo, his shoulders hunched, his hands in his pockets.

She stopped a short ways in front of him and they looked at each other awkwardly. Finally, she stretched her hand out to him, showing him the egg. "I thought you weren't coming," she told him.

He looked at her hand. "What's your mother want to give me an egg for?" he said.

His voice startled her. It sounded husky, like he he'd had the influenza and lost his voice and it was just coming back. She took a step closer and he took the egg. He looked at it as if he didn't know what it was.

She noticed how square and dirty his hand was. But he doesn't even do any work, she thought. Her own gouged hands hung at her sides. She thought with despair of all the time she would have to spend with him before she and Birdie would be able to live together.

"Do you want to go to the lake?" she blurted.

He looked up at her with a startled expression. "Now?" he asked.

It was then that she noticed that the red sun had sunk and the sky was almost dark.

"I mean tomorrow," she stammered, ashamed. "After work, before it gets dark."

She waited for him to ask, "What for?" while she frantically searched for an answer to give him. But he didn't ask. Instead he said, "You're the one who runs around with the black ones, aren't you? I've seen you."

She was so surprised she couldn't answer. What did he mean, he'd seen her? What was there to see?

"Can you come earlier than you did tonight?" he said. "I've been waiting a long time."

"Waiting?" she said. "I told you to meet me at my house."

But then she stopped herself. He gave her that blank look that she'd thought meant he was stupid. But maybe he wasn't so dumb after all. She thought of all the things she had heard about boys: they were dangerous. They did things to you. You were never supposed to be alone with them. And then she remembered what Mr. Horton had done that time to Lecie Titus in the *bosc'*.

"I don't know," she told Favo. "I don't know if I can get away."

"Meet me tomorrow," he told her in his strange hoarse voice. "The trees at the end of the lake."

She didn't know what he was saying.

"Okay?" he said, squinting his eyes at her. They glinted like a plow blade striking rock.

She looked at the egg that he still held balanced in his dirty, square hand.

"I guess so," she told him.

He nodded at her.

She turned and headed down the darkened road to her house. Behind her she heard Favo padding away on the road to his house, Favo the dog trotting back home. She pictured the big house in the village across the lake, and all of them living there together. *Birdie, Birdie,* she moaned. She had not gone far when she heard the splat of something small landing in the dirt behind her.

Breakfast at Woolworth's, 1956

AYOFEMI FOLAYAN

Mt. Calvary Baptist Church was located at the far end of "The Bottom." It was built almost as an afterthought at the intersection of the two roads that bisect the colored section of town, like Christ nailed on the cross. It was not an imposing structure, appearing from the outside more like a small white house. Only the cross nailed to the eaves gave any indication that this house was reserved for The Lord.

Inside, wooden pews gleamed from many hours of polishing. The nails holding the pews to the floor were the only blemishes in an otherwise lustrous waxed surface. At the front of the room, a simple platform held a podium from which Dexter exhorted the congregation.

Dexter felt the spirit coursing through his body that morning, heard the voice of God whispering in his heart. He paced back and forth along the pulpit in the tiny church, his ministerial robe flapping wildly as he reversed direction. "I feel the presence of God in here tonight," Dexter roared, his voice rumbling deeply like an old diesel engine. "He is standing with us in our struggle. This is a just and righteous cause, and we must be willing to put ourselves on the line with God." As he wound his way through the thicket of sentences, his voice got higher, until he was nearly shrill by the time he cried, "I am here as a messenger for the one true General, the Lord God Almighty, who is calling you to enlist in His army of righteousness and become soldiers, soldiers, soldiers for justice!"

Verneta Porter called out a fervent, "Amen!" as she feverishly fanned herself in the late August humid heat. "Preach the word!"

As Dexter paced back and forth, rivulets of perspiration streamed down his face, collecting in a glistening pool around his chin that drained onto the collar of his shirt, which was barely visible under the thick, dark robe. He paused in the center of the pulpit to pound on the podium and glare at the congregation, a sea of faces blurred behind the motion of cardboard fans from the local funeral parlor covered with a beatific portrait of Christ.

Dexter looked out at the front row, focused on the glistening face of Betty Nobles and pointed a finger in her direction. "Stand up on the side of truth! Stand up on the side of justice! Stand up and face the wicked legions of Satan, who try to crush you and tell you that you are somehow not a child of God, not another brother or sister in the family of mankind, simply because you are not white. Stand up, so you can put on your armor, go into the fray, and defend your humanity against the enemy whose evilness would forget that we are all just a little lower than the angels in the sight of God. Stand up and stretch to your true stature, you who are built in the image and likeness of a magnificent and powerful God. Let me know that you are ready to fight this battle for justice. If you believe in yourself as a child of God, let me hear you say, 'Hallelujah!'"

Junior Nobles jumped to his feet and hollered, "Hallelujah!" He clapped his hands and shook his head as if to clear it of any unworthy thoughts. Two rows back, Henry Lee was also moved by the voice of his longtime friend. He waved his hand and called out a heartfelt, "Hallelujah!"

Dexter continued his call for recruits in this army of willing soldiers: "If you believe that we can be victorious as Christian Soldiers, let me hear you say, 'Thank you, Jesus!'" He paused to internalize the energy from the thunderous roar of voices, as the congregation swelled with response to his invitations.

Betty Nobles joined her husband Junior on his feet as she called out, "Thank you, Jesus.'" She seemed electrified as her body spasmed with the force of the energy that charged the room.

Dexter resumed his feverish pacing, shaking his head sadly, as if disappointed in the weak commitment of the congregation. "I don't know if I can believe you," he said softly, continuing to shake his head. "I feel like you don't really mean it!" He strode to the podium, grabbed both sides as if he might leap out into the congregation if he did not restrain himself. "I know you can give me more of a sign that you believe. Let me hear you!" Dexter ran to the edge of the pulpit and cupped his hand to his ear as the voices in the room screamed back at him, "Hallelujah!" By this time, nearly everyone was on their feet, clapping their hands or waving their fans. Robert Mason Carver and his wife Louise held their baby high in the air as they joined in the exultant chorus.

Dexter's face turned serious. "Don't get me wrong," he began. "This is not a carnival for those who want a good time. This is not a church picnic, with everyone getting together for fellowship. This is a battle for *freedom*!" Wesley Jones, Dexter's younger brother, began to play chords on the piano synchronized to the cadence of Dexter's preaching. "Let me ask you again. Tell me the truth that is in your hearts today when you answer me." Dexter fixed his gaze on George Williams before he asked, "Are you ready to stand up for your rights?" The congregation swayed on its feet like a tidal wave, a unanimous assent bellowing from their throats. "Are you ready to stand up for justice?" Once again the voices swelled around one syllable: "*Yes*!" Dexter stared hard at the crowd, sweat stinging his eyes so that he blinked rapidly. "Are you ready to march for freedom today?" Wesley played faster and faster under this exchange, virtually pounding the battered keys until the people screamed their reply, when he landed on a high chord and kept repeating it. It seemed as though an electric charge held everyone in the room suspended in this moment. Betty Nobles and Verneta Porter both fanned feverishly as the room temperature matched the inside of a blast furnace. Others clapped their hands.

Dexter broke the spell with a voice so small that everyone strained to hear. "Don't go out there today because I told you to. Don't go out there today with anger in your hearts. Remember, 'Vengeance is mine, saith the Lord.' We are going out there today to march for our rights, to show this town that there is a place for us at the table, for every one of us eats the bread and drinks the wine of the Last Supper. There has to be room for us at the inn, for every one of us is born a child of God. We are welcome in the Promised Land, for we are one of the twelve tribes of Israel. Don't carry anything but love in your hearts today. Take the hand of a brother or sister next to you and let's march downtown. Hold on to each other, children. March with the faith of the Israelites as they stepped between the waters of the parted Red Sea."

The pianist started playing march music, barely audible under the voice of Dexter, who prayed, "Oh, Heavenly Father, we ask you this morning to look down upon your faithful servants. Give them the courage to do Your Will." As he prayed, a hush fell over the room. Heads bowed and eyes closed as his words circled over the congregation like carrier pigeons bringing a message home. Ushers silently moved to open the doors of the church. "Oh, Mighty God, reach down and touch the hearts of those who would deny us and rebuke us, simply because of the color of our skin. We know that we are all equal in Your Sight. March with us, Oh God, and lead us to victory in this struggle for justice here on earth. Amen."

As they gathered up their belongings and began to leave the church, the music grew stronger, driving their feet into motion. The congregation began to sing as they moved onto the sidewalk in front of the church. Their voices sailed out on the slight morning breeze as they sang with fervor: *We are marching, marching in the army; we have to fight, we know we have to fight; we are holding up the blood-stained banner; we have to hold it up until we die!*

Out on the sidewalk, Betty Nobles led the procession toward Hedge Street. Her voice was clear and strong, as she stepped to the rhythm of the music. Behind her, Verneta Porter and Louise Carver shepherded several children into the column that was forming. When she reached the end of the verse, Betty Nobles started to hum the melody of the hymn softly as those behind her followed suit.

Once they got to town, Henry Lee Burnett paused with about fifteen of his comrades outside the Woolworth's on Hedge Street. They had been in that Woolworth's many times, to buy items that they needed, but never to sit down at the lunch counter to eat. Robert Mason Carver looked over at his good friend, Henry Lee, with an expression of concern etched on his face. "What's the matter, Henry Lee, don't you have the stomach for this?" he asked.

"Of course I do. Just give me a minute. I'm almost ready." Henry Lee knelt down as if to relace the workboots he was wearing under his overalls. While he was on his knees, he sent up a quick silent prayer. "Lord, please look down on your servants. Protect us in this mission of righteousness. We ask this in Jesus' name. Amen." He tugged on the shoe lace again.

Harry Bartlett was the manager of the Woolworth's in Homewood. He had worked hard to rise to this position after seventeen years with the store. His personal pride was deeply entwined with the success of the store. His sales figures had been the highest in the region for the past five years. His incidence of shoplifting was the lowest. As he prepared to open up on this Wednesday morning, he looked out the window and saw Mr. James Robert Buchanan, affectionately called Jim-Bob by his friends, who had been coming to the Woolworth's to have breakfast every morning since his wife Thelma had died two years earlier.

As was his custom, Harry dusted the window blinds with a feather duster before he opened them. He had already swept each aisle and dusted all the shelves. He personally believed that not doing so would contribute dramatically to a decline in sales at his store. The minute hand on the clock was exactly vertical when Harry Bartlett signaled to the other employees that the store was about to open. With a great flourish, he pulled the floor bolts and turned his key to unlock the door.

Jim-Bob Buchanan went directly to his customary seat at the end of the counter right next to the wall, pausing only to place his hat on the bamboo rack in the corner. Adjusting his glasses so he could see through the reading part of his bifocals, he picked up the menu and carefully studied his options.

"Jim-Bob, put that menu down and stop your foolishness!" Lurlene scolded him. She was the head waitress at the lunch counter, an honor which entitled her to fifty cents extra per shift. She had worked at the lunch counter so long, nobody could remember who was there before her. "You know perfectly well you can't read, so put that menu up!"

"I can so read." Jim-Bob's voice was petulant.

"Then why're you holding the dang thing upside down?" Although Lurlene had exposed his ignorance, Jim-Bob did not feel offended. It was a conversation in which they had both engaged before. Lurlene came up with a cup of black coffee and a pitcher of cream.

"I bet you didn't even leave me room to pour in my cream," Buchanan whined. "You always fill it way too full."

"Do not. If you drank coffee instead of a melted coffee milk shake you'd have plenty of room," she snorted. "So, will it be the bacon and egg special or the ham and egg scramble today?"

"It's Wednesday, ain't it? What do I always have on Wednesday?" His face glowed with satisfaction.

"That's easy. Ham and egg scramble," she replied.

"Well, stop wasting my time asking questions and get my order in," he grumbled.

On aisle twelve, Harry Bartlett was unpacking theme books in the stationery section. Mildred Paxton and her daughter Phillippa were trying to decide whether to get one with lined pages or one with graph paper. It was an important decision, as school was already in session, so there was no time for a delay. Phillippa still looked as pale as fading magnolia blossoms even though she had been over the chicken pox for nearly a week.

"I couldn't help but overhear your conversation," Harry said gently, "but I just sold one of these theme books to Margaret Sue Huntington the other day and she bought the one with the graph paper in it. Said that way she could use it for science class, too."

Mildred Paxton looked visibly relieved. "I swear, Mr. Bartlett, you are just the most helpful man. I was just telling Mr. Paxton over dinner the other night, when we were having chicken à la king and I used that wonderful recipe I found right here in the household section as a free gift in the American Home canister set? Anyway, I said that I would give up everything about Homewood except this here Woolworth's. Yours is the best store in the entire Rankin County."

Harry was virtually beside himself. While other men longed to hear something like "You are the strongest man alive," Mrs. Paxton had uttered his emotional equivalent. However, she would never know how he felt about her declaration because at that moment he heard Lurlene cry out, "Just what exactly do you boys think you are doing?"

It was not what she said, exactly, that hit Harry's ears like a dog whistle. It was something in her voice that sounded the alarm. Sprinting in the direction of the lunch counter, all Harry could think of was that whatever was going on sure as heck sounded like it could jeopardize his store's first-place standing. As he rounded the corner of aisle one, he nearly skidded into Junior Nobles.

There had always been rumors about Junior. He was tall and

very black-skinned, although both his parents were the color of cream. He had the body of a linebacker and talked as if his brains had been kicked in by a mean mule. "Excuse me, Mr. Bartlett," Junior said. "I think you should tell Lurlene to serve us some food."

Lurlene rolled her eyes. "I'd rather make love to a bull in heat than let some nigras eat off the same plates and cups as me. This here lunch counter has always been for decent white folks."

Harry moved around to the end of the lunch counter by Jim-Bob. He stood on the foot rail to make himself taller. "I know all you boys. Why, Henry Lee, you used to work for me, sweeping out the store and dusting all the shelves. I haven't found anyone else to help me since you went off to high school. Robert Mason, I can't believe you'd be a part of some foolishness like this! I have always helped your family when they needed things from my store, from school boxes to sewing supplies. How could you turn on me like this? And you, George Williams. I have known every single one of you as you grew up in this town. I'm asking each of you to be responsible and go around to the take-out window like you always have."

Lurlene stood with her hands on her hips sulking. Jim-Bob's toast popped up unnoticed in the toaster. His plate of scrambled eggs and ham sat on the ledge from the kitchen. Jerry, the cook, peered out over the ledge to see why everything had gotten so quiet. There was not a sound in the entire store as everybody waited. Harry stood his ground on the counter rail, his head cocked as if he could hear some secret sound nobody else could hear. "Alice Faye," he called out to the cashier. "Call Sheriff Briggs, please. Tell him we got some trespassers down here."

Alice Faye was trembling as she went into Harry's office and dialed the numbers for the Sheriff's office. A large horsefly landed on her white sweater, held together with a mother-of-pearl clasp. Normally such a sacrilege would have been immediately noticed by Alice Faye, whose cash register was virtually decorated with flypaper, but her concentration on this assignment was all-consuming. Finally someone in the Sheriff's office answered the telephone. "Come quick!" she shouted into the phone. "The nigras is sitting at the lunch counter. They want us to give them something to eat."

Lurlene emerged from the kitchen with an enormous cast iron skillet in her upraised hand. "Which one of you nigras wants to get your goose cooked first?" she demanded.

Henry Lee said quietly, "We don't want any trouble. We just want to be treated like human beings, same as you."

"Well, you can be treated like a human being out there in the parking lot, boy, just like you always have!" said Harry, his face turning red.

Robert Mason folded his hands on the counter and began to recite the Twenty-third Psalm. Soon all of them were reciting it together. It was like some primordial chant that had united their ancestors. When they came to ". . . and I shall dwell in the house of the Lord forever," immediately, without losing rhythm, they began again: "The Lord is my shepherd . . ."

Harry Bartlett's neck began to throb as the blue vein running from his chin into his shirt collar swelled and ebbed. "You have no business in here. Now just leave!" he screamed over the voices of the men. He stepped down from his perch and began walking from one stool to the next, repeating, "Just leave!" His frustration was so evident that he had to put his hands in his pocket so as not to strike one of the seated men. Each man had his feet firmly planted flat on the floor and his hands folded on the counter in a posture of control and unshakability.

James Lester Briggs had been Sheriff of Rankin County for almost ten years. The last Sheriff had lost his job and his life at the same time, and J.L. had been very careful to remember that. He didn't know exactly what was going on at Woolworth's, but he wasn't taking any chances. When Alice Faye called him and said the nigras was sitting in all the seats at the lunch counter, J.L. knew he needed help to control the situation. He called Milton Price and asked him to come over to the Woolworth's, along with his four grown sons. J.L. knew that Milt's Chevy pickup had a gun rack mounted behind the seat, and the Prices would not come unprepared.

J.L. then called Buster Williams, his deputy, who was home with his wife Mollie and their newest child, just eight days old. After expressing his congratulations to her, he said, "I hate to do this, Mollie, but the nigras have gone totally crazy, and I need every bit of help I can get. I promise I'll send Buster back to you and your little prince just as soon as I can, but I have to take him away for a little while right now. Put him on the phone, you hear?" he commanded as Mollie commenced to crying.

J.L. walked across Hedge Street and surveyed the front of the Woolworth's, while he waited for Buster and the Prices to show up. Outside the store, he could see about twenty or thirty nigra women and children kneeling and holding onto each other, forming a human barricade. In front of them an assorted crowd of whites were yelling and throwing raw eggs and ripe fruit at them. Briggs stepped up to the crowd and announced in his most "professional" voice: "I am going to ask everyone within the sound of my voice to disperse right this minute! Just do as I'm telling you, and there won't be any trouble."

He stood there with his arms folded across his chest in an effort to exude authority. Nobody moved. The heckling and pelting ceased, but nobody moved. After a few minutes, J.L. went up to Ray Bramford and asked, "Just what is wrong with you? Couldn't you hear me tell you to move out?"

Ray chewed on his toothpick for a long spell, then replied, "I guess I've been alive a long time, J.L., when I hear you asking me to move aside before these nigras got to move." At about this time Milton Price pulled up in his blue pickup truck and jumped down holding a double-barreled shot gun. As he did so, his four sons followed suit, climbing out of the bed of the truck.

"Hey, J.L.," Milton call out, as he fired his shot gun in the air. "Are you having any problems here?" Each of his four sons fired a single shot gun blast into the air. "Cause we came to help out, if you are."

As he spoke, Milton walked toward the people gathered in front of the Woolworth's. They had scampered away like rabbits at the first shot, but now they were beginning to peer around corners at the impending confrontation. The "nigra" women and children on their knees silently prayed for deliverance from the mouth of this ugly beast.

Inside the store, Harry ran to the glass door and pulled it wide open. "This way, Sheriff, this way!" When he opened the door, one of the women on her knees fell backward into his legs, knocking him backward into Junior Nobles, who remained solidly unaffected by the blow. He simply stepped aside, allowing Harry's head to slam into the store's tile floor, knocking him unconscious.

"Now, see what you've done?" cried Lurlene. She ran into the kitchen, emerging a few seconds later with a hunk of ice wrapped in a towel that she held against Harry's head. Junior Nobles stood unmoved, as she ministered to Harry, who looked as if he was peacefully asleep until the odd angle of the lower portion of his body was considered.

Briggs' other deputy, Johnnie Ray Plunkett, pulled up in the huge black paddy wagon, careful to set the parking brake. "Don't want this one to roll away, too!" he remarked, referring to the previous county vehicle which had rolled down Hedge Street, stopped only by the brick walls of the Rankin County Bank that demolished the front end. Johnnie Ray surveyed the situation and walked around to the back of the vehicle, where he unlocked and opened the doors in anticipation of human cargo. "Well, boss," he said to J.L., "ready when you are. I even took the time to sweep out all the dirt and spiderwebs before I brought it over, seeing as it's women and children."

"Menfolk is inside," offered Petey Price, Milton's oldest son.

"Sitting at the lunch counter," added his brother Paulie, in a tone of wonderment.

"Can you believe it?" asked Preston, shaking his head.

"No way! Nothing like this ever happened in this town," younger brother Purvis commented. Their father flexed the fingers of his right hand, as if eager to shoot the thick shotgun he held, but instead just muttered, "Why don't you magpies stop chattering?" When he spoke, his lips never moved, not even to slightly dislodge the toothpick that was always there.

J.L. stepped closer to the cluster of women and children kneeling in front of the store. "If you do not move this instant, I shall be forced to arrest you."

Betty Nobles, Junior's wife, began to sing in a strong, rich voice, "We shall not, we shall not be moved." The others joined in, a choir formed of urgent necessity. As she sang, Betty's face was tranquil, but there was a defiance in her eyes that directly challenged J.L. Her son Willis was on one side of her and her daughter Phyllis was on the other. The twins were fifteen but looked even older, having inherited their height and bulk from their father. Willis had played both basketball and football, so could run and jump easily. Phyllis was shy, often the tallest in her classes, boy or girl, other than her brother. Both joined their mother in singing "We Shall Not Be Moved."

J.L. lost his patience. "You are all under arrest!" he shouted. "Stand and put your hands against the wall." None of the women or children moved. Betty started to sing even louder, with the others adding their voices to her challenge. "I mean it. This is no joke. You have been ordered to move, and now you are under arrest!" Although a cool morning breeze still whispered along Hedge Street, perspiration streamed from his face, creating a pool of wetness around his open collar.

Johnnie Ray and Buster lifted Verneta Porter, who was at the end of the line, and began to half carry, half drag her limp body toward the paddy wagon. J.L. looked over at Milton and implored, "Can you give us a hand, fellas?" The Prices put their guns into the blue pickup truck and then began to haul others into the paddy wagon. All of the women and children offered no resistance but also supplied no cooperation. Their voices echoed from inside the hollow expanse of the paddy wagon. When only Betty Nobles and her twins remained on the ground, it sounded as if fifty voices were creating the music that filled Hedge Street. All eight men stood by the paddy wagon, immobilized by the force of the voices surrounding them. Even J.L. stood listening, his head tilted to one side. It was Milton Price who broke the spell and grabbed Phyllis Nobles, calling out to Purvis, "Git over here and give me a hand, son." Purvis shook his head as if trying to clear it, then moved to assist his father.

Harry Bartlett moaned like a wounded dog as consciousness returned and pain from his head wound surged. He sat up gingerly, assisted by Lurlene, his face nearly as red as a tomato. "Where is J.L.?" he asked, as his eyelids continued to flutter.

"Sheriff is still outside, busy arresting the women and children," replied Lurlene. The men at the counter, except for Jim-Bob, and Junior Nobles, who stood next to Jim-Bob's seat, all turned to look out the window just in time to see Betty Nobles being carried to the paddy wagon and to hear her unstoppable voice still singing. Without a moment's hesitation, the men began to sing "We Shall Not Be Moved," their rich tenor and baritone voices strangely incongruous in the Woolworth's.

J.L. entered the store and proclaimed, "You are hereby ordered to vacate these premises under Section *two point one zero nine point four-A* of the civil code, which forbids usage of these facilities by nigras." The men were unaffected by his pronouncement, singing as if they were in the choir loft on a Sunday morning. J.L. signaled to Johnnie Ray, Buster, and the Price family to begin arresting the men.

Since Junior Nobles was nearest and already standing, Paul and Purvis went over to grab him first, but as soon as they touched him, he went limp. His huge body as dead weight was more than they could handle, and all three fell in a mound of twisted arms and legs.

Milton looked at the tangle of bodies with disgust. "I swear, Purvis, some of my hounds are smarter than you!" He grabbed Junior Nobles's wrists and pulled them behind his back. "Give me some 'cuffs, Sheriff." Briggs tossed him a pair which Milton used to secure the gigantic man's hands. Milton planted his foot on top of Junior's feet and pulled him to a standing position. Then he put one arm under each armpit and proceeded to drag Junior through the door toward the paddy wagon.

Thus instructed, Purvis and Paul got up from the floor, ready to duplicate their father's feat. Petey and Preston were not exactly thrilled about getting that close to a nigra, but figured they would have to do so to avoid their father's wrath.

"Harry," J.L. called out, "Gonna need some twine or something to tie their hands. Ain't got that many handcuffs in alla Rankin County." Harry went off to aisle seven, where several thicknesses of cord could be found. He grabbed two balls and returned to the lunch counter where the fifteen remaining protesters sat, calmly reciting the Lord's Prayer in unison.

Challenged by the new obstacle of moving men so securely seated, Paul and Purvis watched to see how Petey and Preston would tackle the situation. Fortunately, J.L. Briggs had handled this problem before. Signalling to Buster Williams to give him a hand, he started with Robert Mason Carver, sitting on the corner stool. Smoothly, as if handling a life-sized doll, he spun the stool around and slid Robert Mason off the stool into a standing position. Then he held Robert Mason's hands behind his back while Buster tied the hands together and then dragged his captive person to the paddy wagon. In rapid succession, all the counter stools were similarly emptied, until they came to Henry Lee Burnett.

Just before Johnnie Ray and Milton came to his stool, Henry Lee folded his arms across his chest. "I am a man!" he declared. "I will not be tied and dragged away like so much cattle. All I want is to sit at this lunch counter and eat like a man." He glared at J.L.

and Buster who were now standing behind Milton and Johnnie Ray. The Price boys just gawked through the big plate glass window. "You don't have to tie me or drag me, I will go along with you under your arrest order, I will walk to the police truck, I will not give you any trouble. I just want you to remember that you arrested Henry Lee Burnett, the son of Patrick Burnett, a man." He slid off the bar stool and held his hands behind him. J.L. cut a length of rope and pulled it tight around Henry Lee's wrist before shepherding him to the paddy wagon.

As he went through the door, Milton asked the Sheriff, "Will you be needing me and the boys over at the jail, J.L.?"

"No, Milton, we're taking these troublemakers down to the state facility outside of Jackson. That way we can get help with all the arrest procedures. Y'all get on back to your place." He paused, as if trying to remember something very important. "Oh, Harry, I'll need to get a sworn complaint from you, pretty quick, so we can charge this whole lot."

As he walked out of the Woolworth's, Briggs snarled at the curious townsfolk peering from doorways along Hedge Street. "Party's over, folks, let's go!" He went over to Johnnie Ray, who was closing and locking the paddy wagon door. "You get on the road, Johnnie Ray. I'm just going to call Warden Luther Dawkins and let him know we're on our way, then I'll be right behind you in the car." He headed across the street to his office, waving to Buster Williams as he pulled his car away from the curb.

Williams rolled down his window and called out, "See you later, J.L.! Got to get back to Mollie before she gets upset." He started to roll the window up, then added, "What will these nigras think of next?"

Noise

ELLEN KROUT-HASEGAWA

Rhea stands in front of me. She is neither tall nor short but average height for a ninth grader.

—— What would you say if I told you I wasn't interested in boys, Mom?

—— I would say good for you, dear. Who's the lucky gal?

Her eyes roll heavenward. She's heard this all before.

—— No, I'm serious, she says, frowning at the ground. Her hands become small animals that burrow into her oversized jeans.

—— And so am I. I say it as calmly as I can.

She turns, chest sunken, shoulders hunched, fists bulging in pockets. She looks lost like a boy whose playmates have all moved away.

In truth, she says nothing.

She's busy adjusting the volume on her Walkman, now her constant companion, which I'm convinced is some new form of IV drip, responsible for keeping the young alive except that it plugs into the ears and not the veins.

It's what I imagine she wants to say, standing there, staring at me, smirking, daring me to say what I already sense is true: like mother, like daughter.

I gesture to her and point at my watch. I mouth, Get your things. Time to go.

—— O-kay, I'm not deaf, she says, over-enunciating every syllable.

She darts into the house and slams the screen door that I've stopped asking her to close gently.

I've heard it runs in families. Even so, should I blame myself? I know Bob will. He already does.

When I went to pick up Rhea for the weekend, all Bob could say to me was, See if *you* can get her to wear a dress. He said it in that accusing tone of his, narrowing those glacial blue eyes that he and Rhea share, glaring at me as if I were the one buying her boys' clothes ten sizes too big, the only things she'll wear. I tried to think of something clever to say. Still, I thought, if he thinks that just because I've given birth to her I can tell her what to wear, he has only once more confused me with his own mother. The story of our marriage. I smiled half-heartedly as if to say I'll try my best. Which now turns out to be a lie.

The weekend is nearly over without much conversation between us, let alone a discussion of what kind of fashion statement her father thinks Rhea should be making.

I myself have barely begun to discern Rhea's moods by the music she plays. She listens to bands with household names like Bleach or Sugar. I think there's even one called Medicine. But today, as for most of Saturday, she's been listening to her favorite band, which is tantamount to snapping around her neck one of those *Do Not Disturb* signs that used to hang from the door of her room. Which from what Bob tells me, she doesn't even bother with now. Once her door is shut, it stays shut, reports Bob, unless an offering of food is made. He says he's starting to feel like a zookeeper. I'm not sure how I feel.

When I first heard the band's name, I made the mistake of saying, Nirvana: does that mean they're transcendent?

Anything but, she replied and punched the volume on the car stereo.

I must admit I've given up trying to understand the noise she calls music. I've even stopped worrying whether MTV will rot her brain. I just hope she has some left for college and pray she doesn't grow deaf before I do. I do not think these are unreasonable expectations for a mother to have.

Recently someone did accuse me of being unreasonable, of caring more about books than people. After surveying a garage of half-unpacked boxes, their tops popped open, exploding with books, a woman told me that I had a fetish for printed matter.

She was right, of course, though I wasn't willing to admit it at the time. She herself turned out to be semi-literate, someone for whom reading was a chore.

But how could I have known? You can't give everyone you fall in love with a literacy test.

From within the house I hear a voice that doesn't sound like Rhea's, half-singing, half-shouting, WHAT IS WRONG WITH ME, WHAT IS WHAT I NEED, which I've come to learn means she's searching for something she's mislaid. Judging from the time of day it's probably her skateboard.

—— Look in the hall closet, I yell.

A door slams and the voice snarls, FOREVER IN DEBT TO YOUR PRICELESS ADVICE.

—— You're WELLL-COME, I sing back, not sure whether I like this new tongue of hers, this speaking in lyrics. Nirvana, no doubt. It reminds me too much of when she was two and *wee-o, wee-o* meant fire truck, making me realize how little ever changes between mother and child. I can just see myself twenty years from now still acting as translator for Rhea and her father.

Like me, Rhea is a voracious reader. Though it's been weeks since I've seen her with a book and even longer since she asked me which of Jane's books begins *It is a truth universally acknowledged, that a single man in possession of a good fortune must be in want of a wife.* It's a game we played, quizzing each other on the first and last lines of novels by Jane Austen, whom we would always refer to as Jane as if she were one of the help behind the bakery counter who had recently taken up writing.

It's not the hostility I mind so much, but the questions she asks, questions I can't possibly answer. Just yesterday, she asked what I thought would happen if Kurt Cobain died.

—— Kurt who? I blurted. Cobalt?

Only as the words left my mouth did I realize who she meant but it was too late. Her face turned away in disgust, as if I had betrayed some small confidence of hers.

It's as if she were trying me on, seeing how I fit, casting me aside as if I were a shoe that pinches her toes. Now I can't tell what's worse—to be a zookeeper or a pair of shoes she's outgrown.

I doubt Rhea and I will broach the subject of dress today. I still smart from what she said this morning as we drove to the farmers market in search of berries, the first of the season.

—— Something has to be at least a hundred years old for you to think it's important enough to remember.

Startled, I looked at her. She had been quiet until then.

—— At least fifty, I countered.

—— Same thing.

Our conversations echoed the ones I used to have with my mother, a parrying of tongues, words which came out in fits and starts. It made me wonder whether Rhea saw me in the same light as I did my own mother.

Granted, Rhea is right, I've lost track of pop culture and pop culture has lost track of me. It's certainly something I never thought would happen to me, and Rhea won't understand until it happens to her. It's not something I can tell her.

Just as I cannot tell her about the dream I had last night.

In the dream, I am outside my house. As I open the front door, Rhea appears in the doorway, arms folded, brow furrowed. She points to me and says she won't allow me inside unless I answer her question, and the question is always the same—Who is Kurt Cobain? In the dream world as in waking life, I know the answer but my mouth won't let me form the words, leaving me to stand mute before my own daughter. When it is clear I cannot answer, she tears me to shreds just as the Sphinx destroys all those who cannot answer her riddle.

I woke up to my own lowing, like a cow. It's as if my screams had become wedged in my larynx.

By now you can imagine I want to strangle this Kurt Cobain.

I hear the screen door slam once more and watch Rhea struggle with a backpack that looks large enough for her to live in. I know better than to help. I'm only allowed to unlock the car door. In this way, Rhea is a typical fourteen-year-old. She has a ritual for most everything. I notice how her jeans sag at the crotch and gather in folds at the ankles like wrinkled flesh. She totters forward from the weight on her back, and for a moment, looks something other than human, like a turtle, perhaps. I can't help but wonder if her dress isn't some means of camouflage, a way to disguise the transformation occurring in her body. The budding breasts, the thickening pubic hair, the widening hips. These clothes are her cocoon.

I wonder if Bob understands such things. Now, as before, Bob has difficulty hearing what any woman has to say, including a new wife who doesn't know what to make of me or my swaggering daughter; the one who stands before me, backpack at her feet, skateboard in hand, ready for the drive back to her father's house.

Eyes shut, she stands as straight as a stalk as she takes in the sun's last rays. I wish I could take her in my arms and hold her. But I can't now, she's too big for that. Still the desire persists and my arms ache to feel her weight against them.

I call out to her but she does not hear me through the noise in her head. Before I know it, my hand sneaks out to touch her face. As my fingers graze her cheek, her head jerks back as if I had slapped her.

I turn away, cut adrift as if I were an astronaut whose tether has snapped midstep in his spacewalk. But a whisper pulls me back to earth. It's Rhea, singing softly, over and over, the same words: *all are all in all is all we all are all in all* . . . I realize I've heard them before.

They're Cobain's.

Vegetative States

NONA CASPERS

I stand at my Auntie Jenny's hospital bed and watch her breathe. That's all she has to do—makes living look easy. Whenever Auntie Jenny forgets to breathe, a gray machine wheezes and feeds some mix of oxygen into her lungs. The air pushes her chest up and then her lungs slowly deflate. The machine breaths look the same to me as when Auntie Jenny breathes on her own. She looks like she's sleeping. According to my mother, sleep is something Jenny could never get enough of.

My mother and my Auntie Sal are sitting on green plastic chairs in the corner of the room playing five-card schmere. My mother has wound her rosary loosely around her wrist, so when she plays a card the black wooden beads tick against the table. Auntie Sal keeps her rosary wrapped in Kleenex in her coat pocket. In between the fifth and sixth games she wet a Kleenex and scrubbed the corners of the windowsill and the crevices of the radiator. Though it's only October and the room is overheated, both women huddle in their coats as if they are freezing.

Five days ago, in the middle of the afternoon, while driving from New Munich to Freeport on County Road 52, Jenny lost control of the wheel and smashed her 1976 Chevy convertible into an electrical pole. She flew twenty feet through the air and then her head hit a patch of concrete left over from when 52 was a highway. Since the accident, my mother and Sal, Jenny's older sisters by ten and twelve years, have been staying with Jenny during the day and sleeping at the Holiday Inn a block from Abbott North-western Hospital. I told my mother they could stay in the apartment with me and Selsa, but they are afraid of driving back and forth through the city at night. Last year my mother decided to visit, and drove up and down University Avenue for three hours looking for our street. Finally she stopped and called us from an Amoco station. Her voice on the phone sounded terrified.

Sometimes I picture her and Sal in their single economy room with royal blue carpet and matching drapes, sleeping in front of the TV in their coats, scrubbing sills and eating packets of beef jerky and Planters peanuts from the vending machines. They are country women—neither has slept in a motel before.

This morning, while Auntie Sal and I sorted through Jenny's mail, my mother bought two posters on sale at the gift center. She borrowed a roll of Scotch tape and a step ladder from the intake nurse and hung a poster of a dazzling orange sunrise on the ceiling over Jenny's bed. She taped the other poster—a rainbow—on the side of the respirator facing Jenny's pillow. Under the rainbow, white calligraphic words read, *Lord, help me hang in there.*

I pick at the tape on the corners of the poster. I am thinking that the rainbow may annoy the nurses when they check Jenny's blood pressure gauge and oxygen levels, though they haven't complained. The bright colors and delusional cheeriness irritate me.

"Mom, are you sure the rainbow is necessary?" I ask. "We're not in Oz, you know."

Sal sets down a queen of spades. I notice how worn the card is, as if she's been kneading the edges. "I told her it was a waste of money."

My mother picks up the queen. "Do you hear that, Jenny?" she says. "Our college girl says you're not in Oz." She sets down a run of three.

The next morning Selsa is banging around our bedroom, opening and closing drawers. It's Monday and I should be studying anatomy, but I lie in bed, my face buried in the futon. I hear Selsa say "Shit" under her breath. We've lived together seven years, since my first 4.0 semester as an undergrad, and this banging and cursing are new for her, like this lying in bed is new for me. She sits on the side of the bed and rests her hand on the back of my neck. "You are the slug of my heart," she says. "But have you been wearing my underwear?"

I don't answer. She sighs and gets up.

The clothes on the floor of our room are piling up, weeks of Haines underwear, cotton socks, slacks, button-down shirts. All mine. Along the wall near the bed and in the corners, piles of books gather dust: *Physical Chemistry, Gray's Anatomy, The Physiology of Ten Major Diseases, Your Skeletal System.*

On August first I started my second year of medical school at the University of Minnesota. Last year I recorded all the lectures and listened to them twice. I spent weekends in the library, ran five miles every morning, cooked supper three times a week, slept four hours a night. During the winter holiday and summer, I slogged baskets of French fries to high school students every day from noon to 2 A.M. at Embers on Hennepin Avenue. By the time school started six weeks ago I was so tired I took out a bread-and-butter loan and quit my job. I quit running, cooking, picking up clothes.

Through the futon I hear Selsa's nylon jacket swish down the hall. The front door opens. "Debra, you've got twenty minutes to get ready for classes." She pauses. I hear the door close.

I am thinking about my death; I am wondering if death hurts, what it feels like. I imagine the moment of death itself, and then, of course, after. I know this is pointless, unreasonable. I roll over in the sunlight, put the pillow over my face and hold my breath. My heart thumps dimly against my upper ribs. The carbon dioxide waiting for exhale presses against my cranium, my diaphragm, the roof of my mouth. My hands tingle. My ears buzz. But I hear no loud protests, no wild clamoring from my inner soul. It's all very quiet.

Death feels familiar somehow, as though I've already been there. Death is a mindless, reassuring drone. A dark luminous hum. A buzz.

I have seen dead bodies. I have sliced open abdomens, identified the bluish crest of the ilium, dissected the rectum. I have divided the reptilian R-complex of the brain from the mammalian limbic system from the primatial neocortex. The day before my mother called from the hospital to tell me Jenny had crashed, I stood in my blue gown in the dissection room and held lungs in my hands.

In my top dresser drawer next to our bed is a bottle of sleeping pills I got last year when I had insomnia. Now I sit up in the sunlight, take out the bottle, and read the label. I drag the phone from the hallway to the bed and call the medical library. The librarian is very sweet; she is sipping coffee and chewing on something. I tell her I am studying to be a doctor and ask her about the physiology of barbiturate intake. She tells me good luck. She finds a book on pharmacodynamics and explains in a factual voice that barbiturates selectively depress an area in the medulla oblongata which regulates respiration and heart rate. The excitable cells in your brain relax.

"The body falls into a sleeping state," she says. "Not a normal sleep, but a sleep uninterrupted by dreams."

"What happens with overdose?" I ask.

She hesitates. "The lungs give out; the esophagus closes in."

I close my eyes and imagine the afterlife as a clean room—my eyelids are a white wall. I imagine walking across this room and crawling into a wide bed between freshly washed sheets. I pull the top sheet up to my chin, lay my head back on the white pillow. I rest my hands at my sides. The shades in the room are drawn but the windows are open. A slight breeze touches my shoulders and face. I close my eyes and think of nothing. I breathe in and out.

That afternoon at the hospital my mother is hovering over Jenny's bed. Jenny opens her eyes and stares at the ceiling where my mother hung the sunrise. She closes them. She has been doing this for two days. Sal looks out the window at the gray paved top of the Sears building. Just before I arrived she had hand-washed Jenny's underwear and nightgowns in the sink because she doesn't trust the laundry to return them. The items now hang over the radiator.

"Jenny, who am I?" my mother asks. She waves her hand and the rosary back and forth in front of Jenny's face.

I sit on the end of the bed. "Amazing what we expect from the comatose," I say.

"The doctor says she's not in a coma anymore," my mother says. "She's in a vegetative state." She pronounces the words clearly.

"What's the difference?"

She raises her eyebrows at me as if to say, You're the medical student. "Coma is like sleeping," she says. "Now she's not sleeping, but she's not awake. Don't you have classes today?"

I shrug.

My mother explains that, according to the doctor, the swelling in Jenny's brain has gone down enough for her to resume consciousness. The fact that she hasn't may imply that her brain has gotten used to the non-active state; the normal chemical reactions aren't kicking in. But the doctor says it's more likely she's vegetative. Her reptilian trunk and mammalian midbrain coordinate enough to tell her heart to beat and her lungs to respire. But the frontal and parietal lobes—her memory, her thinking and knowing parts—are permanently damaged.

"We can't know how the brain will grow," my mother says. "It's possible that with prayer and time the damaged parts will repair themselves and branches of her brain will bloom back to life."

"I'm not sure you can talk about Jenny's brain as if it were a bush tomato plant," I say.

In the visitors' lounge my mother puts two quarters in the vending machine. A young man in a hospital gown sits on the only couch, drooling and staring at a TV commercial. Once when I was in the sixth grade, I woke in the night and walked into the kitchen for a glass of milk. My aunts and uncles were sitting around our kitchen table eating nuts and playing schmere. Jenny stood next to the refrigerator talking to my mother while she fixed butter sandwiches. I yanked on the end of the red belt Jenny had tied too tightly around her waist. "Who was the second president of the United States?" I quizzed. Jenny's face got red. She looked from me to my mother to the table and back. "I don't know," she said. "Herbert Hoover?" She threw her head back and laughed at herself; then we all laughed.

"Do you think Jenny would want to wake up without her thinking intact?" I ask. "I mean, her brain was never exactly blooming."

My mother glances at me. She smacks the machine and the bag of peanuts falls loose. "No, she was never smart, that wasn't her gift," she says. "But who's to say God values smart more than anything else?"

I put my quarters in the slot and a Hershey bar slides out. "Well, maybe she just wants to get the whole damn thing over."

My mother opens her bag of peanuts. She spills a few into her palm. She stares at them. "I have more faith in Jenny than that," she says.

That evening, other relatives arrive. They step shyly into Jenny's room, hang back in the doorway—two towheaded teenage second cousins and an older man my mother reminds me is my great uncle. They stand in the middle of the room with their arms at their sides and look at the floor. My mother and Sal give them a tour of the respirator, the glucose IV, the I&O chart.

We sit around Jenny's bed on the green plastic chairs. The two boys are sipping Cokes. The television is blasting.

"She was not wearing her seat belt," Sal leans forward and whispers. The visitors shake their heads.

"A man from Greyeagle once was pinned inside the car by the seat belt and became paralyzed from the neck down," my great uncle says. "It happens. You can't always tell."

My mother and Sal look at each other. "I suppose so," they say.

After the relatives leave, Sal tells me this man's oldest son, a brother of the towheads, once had shut himself in the garage with the car running.

"Did he die?"

"Oh no. Alquin found him and the next afternoon the boy was back on the tractor." She plucks Jenny's undergarments from the radiator and gives them a shake.

My mother and Sal believe that if Jenny had been wearing her seat belt she would not have flown and hit concrete but would have stopped with the passenger side of the Chevy hugging the pole in the ditch. Now as they sit in their chairs and deal out cards, they tally up the damage—broken ribs, legs, even a snapped vertebra—and weigh all this against the vegetative state. They pull their coats closer, pray, shake their heads, and click their tongues. They are women who gutted chickens and pigs before they learned to read; who at eleven and thirteen picked two acres of beans, put up fifty-six quarts of cabbage and tomatoes, baked eleven loaves of bread in a day. They raised Jenny. For them life is a series of small responsibilities dealt out by and owed to God. Shirking their duties, even through death, would never seriously occur to them.

On the way home I run a red light and a Jeep almost hits me. I pull onto the shoulder and lay my head on the steering wheel. I listen to the sighs of the radiator. I think about my skeletal system and the tired gray matter inside my skull. I think about how fragile a brain is.

Selsa is cooking biryani and spicy sweet potato pie. She is trying to draw me back into my life. Last week she brought home a bottle of fresh squeezed orange juice and a piece of almond cheesecake every night. The five boxes of cake are stacked in the fridge; half of the juice has turned acidic. She asks me if I'm hungry and I shake my head.

"Excuse me, doctor, I can't hear you," she says. "Could you try using language?"

I ignore her and open the vegetable bin. I take out a head of broccoli and go into the bedroom.

Selsa has made the bed. She has also folded some of my shirts and pants and set them on the edge of the bed for me to put away. I set the broccoli on my pillow. I pull the covers up over the stalk so the green head sticks out. I feel Selsa's hand on my shoulder.

"This is what our children will look like," Selsa says.

Holding a wooden spatula in my mouth to keep from crying, I cut up eggplant and red onions. Selsa fries the vegetables in olive oil. We eat at the kitchen table and I stare out the window. The sky is gray. When I was little my mother told me God's kingdom was behind the sky. I imagined the back of our sky was heaven's floor. Jesus walked in a white robe with his disciples. Moses and Joseph of the coat of many colors hung out at wells and rode camels. I never doubted that they were there, and that it was enough that I would someday join them. Then I learned that the sky is composed of gasses, the clouds are nothing but water vapor, and the blue is only a refraction of sunlight.

Perhaps our energy seeps out of us when we die. Perhaps the protons and neutrons from our cells leak back into the atmosphere and feed something.

But I am not thinking about the afterlife or Jenny when I look at the sky from the kitchen table tonight. I am thinking about the body itself. I know what it contains, but what makes us alive? This is what I want to ask someone.

After dinner, Selsa watches TV and I lie in bed next to the broccoli. I picture my second cousin crouched in the backseat of my great uncle's Pontiac. Wisps of his white blond hair stick to the vinyl seats, the exhaust drifts in the dusty back window, and his tissues and organs turn a deep, restful blue.

The next afternoon I pack one of the blankets from my bed into the Toyota. I think of Selsa and throw in one of the good bottles of orange juice.

Interstate 94 turns into suburbs, then into yellow ditches, low hills, Holsteins, fallow corn fields. The New Munich exit ramp has been repaved.

I park the car across from the electrical pole on the shoulder of County Road 52. I spread the blanket on the side of the ditch. I drink my orange juice and stare at the few cars that pass. The air is still and cool.

I lie on my back. I am wearing a short-sleeved shirt and the little hairs on my arms tingle. Ants crawl up my neck. Horseflies and mosquitoes that have somehow lived through the cool beginning of fall buzz.

I grew up on this land. It's flat and brown now that the leaves have lost their chlorophyll. But in the spring the green is brilliant. And even now I imagine the birch and maple forests behind the fields show hints of bursting into red.

The short yellow grasses around the electrical pole are flecked with blue paint and rust from Jenny's Chevy. I stand with my back to the pole, facing Freeport. I count twenty paces.

There is a brown stain the size of a grapefruit on the old concrete. Squatting next to the stain, I trace the blurred outline. A strand of short dark hair sticks up from a crack in the concrete. I put the hair in my pocket.

Selsa's voice booms on the answering machine. She's at work. "Debra, where are you? I called your mother at the hospital and she says you haven't been there, and your professors from school called this afternoon and said you better get your butt to some classes next week. If you're home, I want you to pick up the phone." I hear not only the anger in her voice, the frustration, but also the fatigue. "I'm sick of this, you asshole." She slams down the phone.

From the floor I pick up the rest of the shirts and pants and underwear, fold the clean ones and put them in drawers. I put my school books in a paper bag. I set the bag behind the shoes in the hall closet and take out the duster. I wipe off all the surfaces in the room. I sweep the floor.

In bed, the sheets feel cool under my chin. The ceiling is bare. I open the bottle of pills and pour them onto my chest. I count fifteen. I swallow one and then two. I picture my medulla oblongata and all the cells in my brain kicking back and relaxing. I think about swallowing more pills, the esophagus closing in. Then I see my mother at the hospital climbing the ladder she'd borrowed from housekeeping. She's wrestling with an armful of posters, tape tangled in her hair, the roll of tape between her teeth. Despite myself I laugh.

The doctor lifts Jenny's hand high into the air and lets go, the arm falling heavily to her chest. He asks her to blink; she stares straight up at the ceiling. He sticks a long pin into her toe, and her foot twitches. Only a reflex, the doctor tells us.

Tomorrow the doctor, my mother, and some of the other relatives are going to have a big powwow in the third-floor conference room of the hospital. I am not immediate family—husband, daughter, sister—so I am not invited or expected to participate, which is a relief. They must decide how long to keep Jenny on the respirator. The doctor sees no sense in pretending that science, in this case, can do more than maintain a body in a hospital bed. Auntie Sal, always mindful of waste, has already given her opinion: The body is made for work; shut the thing off. If they turn off the respirator, chances are slim that Jenny's brain will kick in and she'll breathe on her own. But it is possible.

There are rings around my mother's eyes, deep gray rings. She looks tired. Sal drove home two days ago to her farm and her chickens and my uncle Ralph. My mother wants to leave too—she has spent more money than she had all year, she misses my father, she is in the middle of a quilt. This waiting has become tedious. She sighs and picks at a fruit cocktail on the tray the nurse mistakenly dropped off for Jenny.

"Where were you yesterday?" she asks. "Selsa says you haven't been going to your classes. She says you're sleeping all the time."

"I went to the crash site."

My mother squints and looks at me, baffled. She shakes her head as if I told her I'd painted myself green and run naked down University Avenue.

She wipes her mouth on her napkin and stuffs it inside the plastic cup. She holds up a styrofoam bowl. "Soup?"

"Nobody likes hospital food, Mom."

"You did. In third grade when you were in the hospital you told me that you loved the soup and the desserts."

I don't remember ever being in the hospital. I remember that at the end of seventh grade, just before finals, I stayed home from school for a month. I lay in my bed reading one book over and over, a book about this woman who travels from her childhood home in Michigan to the Himalayas and single-handedly nurses a village of poor people who are dying of typhoid. I would read to the end of the book and feel this horrible pressure in my stomach. I felt terrified of having to get up and dress and start the day. I would turn back to page one and start the book again.

"What was wrong with me?" I ask.

My mother looks down and sips more of the soup. "The doctors said they didn't know."

"Are you sure it was me? Maybe it was Julie or Susan."

"No, it was you," she says quietly. "Looking back, I think you may have been depressed."

I expect my mother to look away when she says this—or rather I don't expect her to say this at all—but she has and she doesn't. She looks right at me and doesn't blink. In fact she looks a little relieved.

"Debra, do you think you're the only one in the world who's ever felt sick and tired of things?"

"Why didn't you do something?" I ask.

"I did. I brought you to the hospital."

"You should have brought me to a counselor."

"I know that now," she says. "Everyone knows about depression now. You think I'm a dummy?"

She opens her purse and starts to rummage. "Here. Have a piece of gum."

The flavor of Big Red Cinnamon shoots through my mouth.

"I just wish she'd do something," she says, and I know she's referring to Jenny. "It's just so sickening to see her lie there like that. Yesterday I was sitting next to her bed and I just threw up my arms." My mother throws up her arms and lets them drop to her sides. "Goddammit, Jenny," she yells. "Stop being so damned self-centered. Shit or get off the pot." She looks toward the door to see if someone is listening.

My mother sighs and leans over the hospital bed until her face hovers above Jenny's face. She takes her hand. "Jenny," she says. "You've got to make up your mind. The living or the dead."

My mother and the relatives are in the conference room deciding. Her rainbow hangs on the respirator, her sunrise on the ceiling.

The muscles in Jenny's face are going slack, as if her face is slowly spreading across the pillow. She looks rubbery and pale compared to when she first came in. Her eyes are wide open now, even at night. But they are glazed, unfocused, like fish eyes. For every five breaths the machine puts in her she takes one or two.

Everyone has brought fall flowers from their yards and gardens. Mums, purple sedums, zinnias. There are also the orange and yellow marigolds Selsa and I brought yesterday, the strawflowers from Sal's front yard which she sent with one of the brothers, the blooming petunia plant my mother bought at the gift center. The room smells like plants and earth and cooked air.

I imagine a miracle. Even knowing that her brain is squeezed and bruised, I picture Auntie Jenny sitting bolt upright and speaking. Not the laughing self-deprecating speech of the real Jenny, but long elegant sentences. I imagine her as an oracle, someone straddling life and death, possessing the knowledge that would end all the mystique and uncertainty and delusions about the meaning of our lives and why we go on living them. The bruises on her temples have faded, but a luminous gray color deepens around her eyes.

I have so many questions. What is it like not having to think about anything, living in a half state? What does it feel like when you know you are going to crash, to see that pole in front of you and feel your head finally hitting the concrete? What in the world will I do with my life if I can't make it through medical school?

I kneel down at the side of Jenny's bed and rest my arms on the mattress. My breath tastes stale and metallic. I hear a noise and look up. It's only air moving through her upper intestines.

I envy her, not because she will die, necessarily, but because she is removed from all this bright, insistent, blooming survival. I am doomed to go on like this, plodding through the ridiculous, mysterious gray areas.

I can feel myself careering through the air.

"Jenny," I whisper. Her eyelids flutter, or it could be only my breath against them.

Rachel

MARTHA K. DAVIS

Have you ever used intravenous drugs?

Are you a man who has had sex with another man since 1975?

What if I'm a woman who's had sex with another woman who's had sex with a bisexual man? The blood bank doesn't seem to have considered this possibility; there is no question here that addresses the sexual history of one's previous partners, or their previous partners, or theirs. There is nothing that reflects the complex and mutable sexuality of most people I know. I can't decide if it's ignorance that limits the scope of these questions or a failure of imagination. Maybe they're the same thing. For myself, I'm not really worried. Rachel slept with him more than four years ago, and she was tested at least twice before she met me.

But I think of it. For the first time, I see this questionnaire as something more than the annoying form I am asked to fill out every single time I donate blood despite the fact that my answers are always the same. It's designed to keep people from infecting each other, designed to save lives. I always thought that merely by offering my blood I was saving lives. Now that Rachel is gone I have to recognize that no interaction is as simple as one person giving and the other receiving, a vein opened and poured into someone else's body. I wanted it to be that simple. I still don't think I was wrong to want that.

The list of questions seems endless. I check off my answers in a neat column of boxes marked "no." In my hurry to get through, I almost miss the last question: Are you feeling well today? It stops me. Rachel would know immediately, without thinking about it. I check "yes" quickly and stand up. As I approach, the woman sitting behind the desk across the room reluctantly tears herself away from the soap opera she's watching on the ceiling-mounted TV. She peers up at me through thick glasses when I hand her my clipboard. She's probably in her seventies, volunteering her afternoons for something to do. She's wearing bright red lipstick that leaks out into the creases near her mouth. I try not to stare.

"Can I have your card?" she asks. She looks at it skeptically. "Are you from Seattle?" I tell her I just lived there a long time. She purses her lips and turns the card over. As she's filling in the date, she comments, "You haven't come in for a while. You were donating every three months, even after you moved. It's been almost a year now." She holds the card out to me, pointing with her pen at the last of the neatly listed dates like a dentist indicating on an x-ray the area of decay. She blinks at me, the motion slow and condemning behind the curved fishbowl of her glasses. She's waiting for me to answer. I don't have to justify myself. I wouldn't have come back at all, but one of my students is having surgery in a few days and asked me to donate. I couldn't refuse her. I stare back at the woman. She shrugs, clips my card to the form, and drops them in a box on her desk. "Take a seat," she tells me, already turning back to the drama on her TV.

I sit down in the first of a row of empty chairs, pull my Walkman out of my bag, and put on the headphones. For weeks I've been listening to a tape Rachel gave me last summer of her favorite Queen songs. She gave it to me because from the beginning she wanted me to love what she loved, or at least to know what that was. I was never much of a rock music fan; I took it home and played a few songs and then filed it in my tape racks between Puccini and Ravel. I didn't listen to it carefully, as I would listen to any other music.

It turns out the lyrics are sweet, funny, boastful, surprisingly ardent. The melodies swoop and swagger, the lead singer often veering off into a falsetto or a breaking lower register, as though he's unable to resist playing with the limits of his voice range. There are moments of aesthetic genius that I've come to crave: I stop the tape and rewind it to listen to a single phrase again. A few weeks after Rachel moved back to Ithaca, I read in the paper that Freddie Mercury, the lead singer, had died of AIDS. I knew Rachel must have heard. I even started to write her a letter telling her I was sorry about his death, but then I felt like a fool and tore it up. I found the tape and tried again. Now the only music I listen to are these songs Rachel accumulated for over ten years, since she was in junior high, and then gave to me. I play the tape over and over, the way Rachel played the tapes I gave her in the fall. My music was all new to her—classical, women vocalists I had discovered in the last year or two. She told me she could only stand listening to music she had never heard before, that carried no echoes of an earlier time, no memories. That made no sense to me. What I love about music is how vividly and precisely it can evoke the memory of a person or a moment. I didn't understand that Rachel and I were talking about the same thing, but for her the memories had been marred by her loss. Returning to the present, she couldn't help but fail to bring back with her what hadn't survived. I wonder if Rachel ever listens to my tapes anymore, or if the music contains its own memories now and, tainted, has lost its capacity for comfort.

I met Rachel ten months ago, in May. I had been hired by a small, private high school in a suburb outside of Boston to teach a music history class, give piano lessons, and lead the concert choir. The man who had been teaching music that year had come down with a sudden illness that kept him in the hospital for several weeks, so the school brought me in early to finish the spring semester. I didn't mind moving suddenly, with so little notice. In Seattle I had gotten myself involved with a married woman, and I was looking for an easy way out.

The only person I knew in Boston had moved away a couple of months before. Sheila was a close friend from college who had received her MBA from Harvard in the winter and gone to Los Angeles, a city she had always been infatuated with. She and Rachel had been seeing each other for almost a year. Even after it was over, Sheila described their relationship as sweet and undemanding, which at the time I though sounded very nice; mine all seemed to become muddy with expectations right away. She also told me Rachel was a painter and had been out of college only two years. From the way she said "only" I knew she thought that Rachel was young; we were twenty-nine. I told her I wasn't interested in meeting someone who was still idealistic and sincere. Sheila gave me Rachel's number anyway, pointing out that I needed friends. But I didn't want friends; I wanted to keep my life as simple and anonymous as possible.

I never got around to calling Rachel. I settled into a routine of teaching and rehearsing the choir at school during the day and at night hanging out in the living room with my two roommates—a straight couple—drinking beer and reading the paper. A few weeks later there was a message from Rachel on the phone machine. When I called her back, she told me she missed Sheila and wondered if we could meet. She thought that talking to someone who knew Sheila well and loved her too might make her seem less far away. I was surprised that she missed Sheila so much, and surprised as well to find that they kept in touch. My relationships had always ended in spectacular raging arguments which usually concluded with my slamming down the phone or slamming shut the front door behind me. I had never been able to become friends with my ex-lovers. Once the sexual involvement was over, there was nothing left, except perhaps bitterness and the determination to choose more carefully next time. I agreed to meet Rachel more for Sheila's sake than hers.

I was late arriving at her house. Despite her detailed instructions, I had gotten lost driving the one-way streets of Somerville. It was the first humid day of summer; the back of my t-shirt was damp with sweat when I got out of the car. Rachel lived alone on the top floor of a narrow clapboard building. I climbed the stairs past the empty porches of the first two floors until I reached hers. It was filled with plants hanging from the rafters and sitting on the railings and the grey wood floor, luxuriantly spilling down over the sides of the porch. Some of them were flowering—pink and red geraniums, blue African violets, white and orange azaleas. Carefully stepping in between them, I thought that Rachel must be extremely patient to be able to give them such consistent, devoted attention.

From what Sheila had told me, I imagined Rachel as small and delicate, probably with long, curly hair that she occasionally tied back carelessly, lots of bangles on her arms, and dangling earrings. When she opened the door I was surprised by how ordinary-looking she was. Her springy dark hair was cut close to her head. She had thick eyebrows and shadows around her deepset eyes. Her face was wide and round, like her body. She wore baggy shorts and a bright yellow tank top. I was aware most of all of the solid thickness of her body and at the same time of the way her brown eyes seemed glad—brighter, softer—when she smiled at me. "Kim?" she asked. Before I could answer, she pulled me into a hug as though she had known me a long time, as though I was the woman she missed. Then I stepped back and we became strangers again.

She showed me her apartment, four small rooms with large windows and lots of afternoon light. The couch and armchair and bed were draped with colorful hand-woven fabrics, but she had left the windows bare, without curtains. In the living room, books filled the tall bookcase and overflowed into piles on either side. The kitchen walls were mauve and covered with racks holding pots and cooking utensils. I could smell a faint odor of turpentine throughout the apartment. In the last room, more of an alcove off her bedroom, there was an easel set up in one corner, as well as several charcoal sketches, which I took to be unfinished, taped up on the walls.

Back in the living room, I tentatively studied the six paintings she had hung crowded together above the couch. They were filled with large, indistinct shapes moving off the canvas, light fading into dark, outlines breaking off into a wash of exuberant colors. I kept looking for figures or faces, objects I could recognize, that might be trying to emerge. Reluctantly, I admitted to myself that I didn't like them very much.

"I don't know how to look at these," I told her apologetically. Rachel was standing a little in front of me, looking at the paintings too. Her hair curled in short wisps on the back of her neck. I had a sudden desire to move up close, slip my arms around her from behind, and rest my lips where her neck was bare. She turned toward me. I went on quickly, "Do you show your work?" I had seen other paintings stored against the wall in her studio. Canvases languished in the corners of this room too, stacked upright like record albums. Her sheer output impressed me.

"God no, I haven't even tried," she said, moving past me into the kitchen. "I'm not anywhere near good enough yet. Do you like grape juice?" She held up a bottle, and I nodded and came in and sat down on a stool at the butcher block table, suddenly thirsty. "No," she said again, opening cupboards, "I sell theater tickets at Faneuil Hall for a living, if you can call it that. My parents help me out with the rest, so I'm not quite the starving artist." That explained all the new, tasteful furniture.

I was relieved, in a way, that as a painter she wasn't really good. More precisely, I was relieved that she knew she wasn't. She was ambitious. She was also willing to learn. I didn't think I could teach her anything about painting, of course, but I felt suddenly that there was room for me—for someone—amidst the crowding canvases and books and plants. It struck me that this was the first time since I had moved to Boston that I wanted to have anything to do with anybody else.

Rachel poured the juice into two tall glasses, adding seltzer and ice. As she turned and carried the glasses to the table, the rounded muscles in her upper arm tightened, standing out beneath her smooth, olive skin. She caught me staring and turned bright red. "Here," she said, and I took the glass she offered, but she wouldn't meet my eyes. Later I discovered her feelings were always close to the surface of her skin: embarrassment and anger turned her face red, and fear and sadness drained the blood from her face.

"Sheila told me you left a relationship to move here," she said, sitting across the table from me. "Do you miss her?"

"No," I said truthfully. "She was straight. Well . . . she was married. I couldn't understand why she wanted to stay with him after we started seeing each other. It's a long story. What about you? You told me over the phone that you miss Sheila's laugh, that you don't laugh so hard with anyone else."

She smiled, and her eyes got gentle again. I knew she was smiling at some memory of Sheila, something she would probably never tell me about, whatever happened between us. She said, "Actually, my sister and I laugh like that too, but I don't see her very often. I only go home three or four times a year." That sounded like a lot to me. Rachel continued, "You know when some tiny and absurd thing—maybe it's something you said that doesn't make sense, or you realize it has another meaning—when the hilarity of it suddenly strikes you? And you both burst into laughter at the same time, and can't stop laughing as long as the other person is laughing?"

Rachel was excited, leaning forward as she talked, and I think she fully expected me to nod vigorously, my face lit up with recognition. In fact, I wanted to be able to respond to her elation, to meet her halfway, but I was distracted: I had just realized that her feelings for Sheila went deeper than Sheila had led me to believe, than Sheila even knew, perhaps. I was busy telling myself I didn't want someone who continued to want someone else. I'd been through that already, several times.

I made myself nod. She went on, telling me about Sheila's generosity, her impulsiveness, her occasional moodiness, while I half-listened, sipping grape juice and wondering how soon I could leave without being rude. But Rachel was also talking about my friend, whom I had known longer than she had. After a while Rachel's anecdotes summoned my own memories. Our first year in college we hitchhiked along the west coast from Seattle to San Francisco and missed a week of classes. We were always taking study breaks to hole up in Sheila's room, where she kept a hot plate and a lifetime supply of Ramen noodles and popcorn. The spring of our junior year, after exams, we tripped all night long and by dawn found a way to climb to the top of the church tower to watch the sun rise and bring with it the lighted world. It was perched on that tower that we finally acknowledged our mutual attraction. We decided not to act on it, but I don't remember exactly why anymore. Listening to Rachel, I realized how much I missed that friendship. I felt a lot older, remembering what we had done then that wouldn't occur to me now.

At the same time, Rachel was speaking of Sheila as a lover, as someone with whom she had had a wholly separate and different relationship than I had, at a later time in Sheila's life. Rachel admired Sheila tremendously. She held no resentment against Sheila for moving away. I found that extraordinary. At times she described my friend as someone I had never known, someone I had grown apart from since college. As that woman emerged, separate from the close friend I remembered, Sheila became two people; the second one I would have loved as Rachel did, and now I was jealous of her.

The late afternoon sun had sunk below the neighboring houses, leaving the kitchen dim. "Do you want to have dinner with me?" I asked as Rachel rinsed our glasses in the sink. I wasn't even thinking of it as a date. Now that I was talking, I found I was starved for conversation.

"I can't. I'm meeting a friend." She wiped her hands on a dishtowel and walked me to the door. I stood on the porch surrounded by roosting plants.

"Thank you," she said from the doorway.

"For what?"

"For being Sheila's friend, I guess. I knew I'd like you."

"Why?"

"Sheila said you were . . . never mind, I'll tell you when I see you again."

But she didn't. She called me the next morning and invited me to a barbecue some friends of hers were having by the Charles River. After that we took a long walk beside the water, throwing a frisbee back and forth, then just talking, until it got dark and we had to turn back.

I recognize the young nurse who picks up my questionnaire and motions me into the next room. She's been working here at least a year. The two times I came in after moving to Boston, before I met Rachel and stopped donating, the blood bank was much busier, but I remember this woman. She was the only one who didn't seem to be exhausted. She asks me to sit at the first of a row of partitioned tables and seats herself across from me. I don't think she remembers me.

"I have to ask you these questions again," she says abruptly, unapologetic. I know she is following standard procedure. Even so, as she looks over my form, I feel as if she suspects me of lying. She wants to disqualify me, bar me from ever donating again. Maybe, she is thinking, I will remember something I didn't think of earlier. I know my blood is safe. Yet I feel accused, implicated. I am nervous answering, afraid of contradicting myself.

"All right," she says, unwrapping a plastic thermometer like a paper-thin popsicle stick with notches. "Under your tongue." The nurse holds my wrist, takes my pulse. She writes down a number, pulls the thermometer from my mouth, glances at it, throws it away and writes down another number. It's all very efficient, very impersonal. I could be anyone; it doesn't matter to this woman whether I'm comfortable, whether or not I've been happy today. She only wants to know if I'm well enough to donate, and if she can use the product I provide: my blood.

This never bothered me before; why does it now? I used to like giving blood mostly because of the anonymity. I wanted to be useful, to help someone in need, but without any continuing responsibility. I was afraid if I knew the person, I would always feel I hadn't done enough. I was committed to going in as often as the blood bank would let me. But it was a lot easier than some other kinds of service, and more gratifying. Today it only feels perfunctory, a tiny, perhaps insignificant gesture. But back then I liked possessing something important enough to save another person's life. Even more, I liked being able to give a part of myself to someone else and not miss it.

My nurse pulls on a pair of white latex gloves. She swabs the tip of my ring finger with disinfectant, then pricks it. As she squeezes my finger, a dot of dark blood appears and grows into a large drop. She tips a tube as thin as a hair brush bristle into the blood, drawing it up. I am fascinated by my blood's willingness to leap through another vein, to travel with unknown destination. She lets a drop fall into a vial of transparent blue liquid, watching the blood's progress as it disperses a little, wafting down through the blue. This tests the iron level. The drop rolls gently on the bottom of the vial. I wonder, Does all screened blood get used? Are the dozen or so pints I have already given circulating somewhere in the world through the arteries of twelve recovered strangers? Or does some blood wait, vital, life-giving, in those sealed plastic bags, until it goes bad and has to be thrown away?

I have always felt that I can love almost anyone, given her permission. And sex is the easiest and quickest way I know to obtain that permission. In friendship the work of loving is slow and arduous, and I am always brought up short by a solid barrier past which I cannot go. Perhaps I could in childhood, when I had a best friend—actually, three of them, consecutively. There was no question then of our mutual devotion: the person we always wanted to play with and tell secrets to was each other. I lost my last best friend in high school. By then everyone seemed to believe that best friends stepped aside unquestioningly for dates with boys or the need to stay home waiting for their call. I didn't recognize until years later that I wanted to love my friends the way they wished their boyfriends would love them. In college, when Sheila and I ran into the wall within our friendship, we started to flirt with the idea of sleeping together. The next friend I made became my first woman lover. I still believe in best friends, but not in finding them. Instead I look for women who are willing to be loved, and I make love to them. Then the boundaries confining friendship are broken down; there's room to move around in. I can love without restriction. At least, that's how it looks from the outside.

I thought Rachel and I would become lovers right away. It took us more than a month. "Why are you in such a hurry?" she asked me once, in her studio, stirring the brushes she had been using in a coffee can half full of turpentine. "Enjoy this. We've got time." I had wiped away a smudge of cerulean blue on her lip, then lightly kissed her where the smudge had been.

"It's what I want," I blurted out, confused. "Aren't you attracted to me?"

"Of course, you know I am. You don't have to rush it." She took the can and brushes into the bathroom.

On her easel, the painting she had been working on was suffused with beautiful shades of yellow and blue, but like all the others there was something unshaped about it, something lacking. Blurry. Her paintings frustrated me, and usually I didn't look at them. I could hear water running in the bathroom, Rachel humming to herself. She's afraid, I thought, eyeing the confusing mass of color on the canvas. She doesn't know what she wants. I had forgotten about Sheila, and about the woman I had left in Seattle and my vow that next time I would wait for someone who didn't have to be convinced.

We began eating dinner together two or three times a week. I was trying to make some money working for a temp agency until I began teaching again in the fall. I would drive from Boston directly to Rachel's house, or on weekends we would return from the beach or an afternoon concert or street fair. Often we took our plates outside to the porch and cleared a place among the trailing plants at the edge. We sat side by side, watching the sky lose its color and her neighbors below on the street walk their dogs in the cooling air.

One night, after piling our empty plates in the sink, Rachel asked if she could rest against me while I read to her. Two weeks before, I had bought Rachel an out-of-print children's book she had told me her mother used to read her and her sister before bed. Rachel remembered that Anna and she would jump up and down on Anna's bed, begging for the story, then curl up under the covers together to listen. Often Rachel fell asleep and found herself in her own bed across the room in the morning, presumably carried there by her mother. I had spent a whole day searching in used bookstores for a copy of this book. Whenever I visited, I had been reading a chapter or two aloud.

She remembered the story vividly: years ago, the king's son mysteriously disappeared, and a talking golden door at the court promised to reveal the prince's location only if it were told a story that pleased it. An old man has wandered the land, gathering many stories. In a remote village, he asks a boy named Tal to help him choose the best one as they make their way to the palace. Most of the chapters of the book are taken up with the stories themselves. When they arrive, because children are forbidden to enter the court, the old man hides Tal inside a crystal block he has brought as a gift for the king. He tells his story, but the door remains silent. The king orders the crystal block smashed and the old man killed. When the block is shattered, dazzling light from the golden door falls on Tal. "This is your son," the door intones.

We were near the end of the book, and I still didn't know what was going to happen. In fact, I had forgotten about the missing prince; I was caught up in the old man's fanciful and compelling stories. That night, Rachel was excited, anticipating my pleasure in the revelation of the boy's identity. On the couch, she contentedly cradled herself against me, leaning her head back on my chest. I rested an arm lightly around her, my hand on her stomach.

After I had read a few pages, Rachel began to stroke my hand. I stopped reading and looked down at her face: her eyes were closed and she was smiling. "Go on, this is the best part," she said. She stilled her hand, leaving it on mine. When I finished the last chapter, I closed the book, balanced it on the back of the couch, and put my arm around her. Neither of us moved.

"I can feel your heartbeat," I said, aware of its rhythmically drumming pulse underneath my hands. "Are you nervous?" I could feel my own heart beating too, much faster than hers. She turned her head and kissed me.

In her bedroom, we were awkward taking off our clothes. We undressed separately, watching each other. As I kicked my underwear to the floor, I was aware of stepping out of our established, familiar friendship at the same time. We stood naked in front of each other, not yet touching. I was drinking in the differences between our bodies. "Hey, you," Rachel said softly, and covered my breasts with her warm hands experimentally. My nipples tingled and hardened. I slid my arms around her waist, smiling. "This is a little strange," she went on, "touching you like this."

"I think we can get over that," I suggested, backing her up to the bed. I leaned against her until she lost her balance and we fell onto it together.

At first I thought Rachel was being tentative, perhaps out of inexperience. She lingered at my throat, my breasts, while I willed her on, impatient. "You've got ribs. And hipbones," she said, her hand on the ridge of my pelvis. She was lying on top of me, moving her face softly against mine. "Am I too heavy? I don't want to crush you."

"No, I like your weight." I did. I liked the creases at her thighs when she brought up her legs on either side of mine, and I liked her broad, smooth back. I liked lying helplessly beneath her, shuddering as she licked the soft pockets of skin above my collarbone. I began to realize that she was not uncertain or shy; slowly she was exploring my body, following every impulse she had. I was used to moving faster, especially the first time when what I wanted was most pronounced. I was used to balancing how much I gave with how much I received. Rachel wasn't keeping score. As she touched and tasted and came back to tell me what she had found, I realized that Rachel loved my ordinary body, enough to want to stay there as long as possible. I had never had a relationship begin like that before.

Later we lay holding each other. I traced her jaw with my finger, then the curve of her ear. Watching her face, inches from mine, blissful and sleepy, I was struck by how beautiful she actually was. I had never seen it in the sunny daylight of our friendship. She smiled, kissed my forehead tenderly, and closed her eyes. Almost immediately I felt her body twitch and her arms loosen from around me. I was wide awake, riveted by her face. Something about her moved me enormously. I didn't know what, exactly. All I knew was that now that I was here with her, I wanted to stay to the end.

The nurse wraps a Band-Aid around my finger, then pulls off her latex gloves and throws them away. She pushes two bar-coded stickers on peel-off backing under the paper clip at the top of my form. Under one bar code are printed the words *Do Not Use,* under the other, *Use.*

"See that booth? You need to put one of these stickers on this

X," she says, crossing out a rectangle in the corner of my form with her pen. She hands the form over, looking up at me for the first time since we sat down.

The booth is only a folding table with sides rigged up for privacy. As I stand before it, I have the uneasy sense of being at the last checkpoint before crossing over into another country. Do you have anything to declare? I look in the trash can below the table. The pile of discarded bar-code sheets are all marked *Do Not Use* below the remaining stickers. It seems incredible to me that this final precaution has to be taken, that someone might feel obligated to go through the entire procedure of donating, knowing that his or her blood might be—or is—infected. But I am the one giving, not receiving, this well-screened blood, the knowledge of its safety lost in the transmission.

The bar codes lie on the table, uncompromising. I peel off the sticker marked *Use* and paste it on my form.

It was the first Sunday in September. Rachel and I had been lovers for two months. We woke up late, sweating in the humidity. After eating a large breakfast at our favorite diner, we drove out to Walden Pond. We stayed away from the crowded beach, the water dense with screaming children. Instead we walked around the edge to swim across the far end of the pond and back. Then Rachel wanted to play Marco Polo, which I said you couldn't play with only two people. She insisted that you could, that Anna and she had done it all the time in the neighbors' pool when they went away in the summer. So I closed my eyes and called across the water, following the sound of her answering voice. I found her surprisingly fast, and we sank underwater clasped tightly together before separating and coming up for air. Even after she denied it, I suspected she had put herself in my way.

Back on our narrow strip of beach, we sprawled on our towels and fell asleep. When we woke up, the sun was going down behind the trees. The pond was deserted. We took off our bathing suits and swam one last time in the cool water, washing off the sand and sweat, then drove home in the gathering dark.

Back in June, Rachel had bought a couple of comfortable bean bag chairs for the porch. We often ate dinner sitting in them, or we would lie together after dark, quietly talking. That September evening we were outside eating cold chicken and corn on the cob when the phone rang behind us in the living room. Rachel got up to answer it. I put my plate down and lay back. The night air was warm. The hanging plants were in silhouette against the clear, black sky. I picked out a few stars. Rachel had been teaching me the constellations, but I couldn't identify them yet on my own. I tried not to listen to her conversation.

"Tell me," I heard her say. Her voice was suddenly hard and strained. I thought maybe something had happened to a friend of hers—someone had locked herself out of her house—and Rachel would have to go out and help with the problem. I looked in through the door. She stood with her back to me. Usually by now she would have signaled who it was and whether she was going to be on the phone for a while. Then she said, "Oh God," and I watched her body fold over, collapsing as she sat heavily on the floor. She had the phone crushed to her ear with both hands. She was crying quietly. I couldn't imagine what could be wrong. I thought it was best not to listen, to give her privacy. Gathering our plates and glasses, I went into the kitchen. I was still thinking about our leisurely afternoon at Walden Pond, how easy it was to be with her. I scraped the dishes and washed them, wiped off the table and counters, and was sitting on her bed trying to read when she hung up. She came and stood in the doorway. She looked bruised, as though someone had actually hit her and the swelling had begun. She wouldn't look at me.

"Anna died," she said. The two words sounded hollow, dried up. My mind flipped through names, trying to place this one. It took me several seconds to remember that Anna was her sister. This was not a momentary crisis, then; it was not going to go away. I thought, My life was going so well, why did this have to happen now? Immediately I felt ashamed of myself.

Rachel remained frozen in the doorway, not looking at me. I had never seen her look defeated before. I couldn't bear it. I pushed myself off the bed and went to her. As soon as I touched her she started to cry, hard dry sobs that grated through her body. I held her against me, silent. What could I say to her? She was still crying when she pulled roughly away, telling me she needed to breathe, to move, she had to do something, anything, she didn't know what, she would do anything, she would give up anything to have her sister back right now.

The night Rachel flew back from Ithaca, I picked her up at the airport and drove her out to Revere Beach. It was a chilly night, and the beach in the dark was damp and flat, but there was a sliver of moon that turned the surf a beautiful, shimmering white. I spread out a blanket and poured peppermint tea from a thermos. Rachel had been gone six days and I wanted to have a romantic reunion. In the car she had said almost nothing, agreeing to be taken to the beach as if she didn't care where she ended up. Sitting beside her on the blanket, I wanted to kiss her but I hung back, uncertain and a little afraid of her strained face, her stiff body.

The tea was too hot to drink at first. Rachel held the plastic cup in both hands, grateful for the warmth. She stared out at the phosphorous waves. She looked vulnerable and astonishingly young. I wanted to put my arms around her, but I could tell she didn't want to be touched, not even by a friend, and I knew that for me it would be impossible to keep my hands still, my mouth from her skin.

I didn't know what to expect of Rachel. At twenty-nine, I had never had someone close to me die, and I had never been a witness to someone else's grief. I was curious about hers particularly because I had grown up an only child. The closest I could come to fathoming Rachel's pain was by imagining how it would feel if Sheila died. I knew it wasn't the same thing, but I didn't know what was different. During the six days that she had been gone, I had decided that we would watch her sadness together, that it was something we could share the way we shared our favorite books and our dreams as we came out of sleep in the mornings, that it was something outside of both of us.

I put my cup down on the sand. "I'm glad you're back. I missed you so much," I said. I had. For those six days I hadn't known what to do with myself. Everywhere I had liked going with Rachel I didn't want to visit by myself. I even found myself wishing I had flown to Ithaca, just to be with her, even though she hadn't asked me to.

"That's what I kept thinking on the plane home," Rachel said, still staring out over the water. "I miss you so much." It took me a moment to realize she didn't mean me but her sister.

"I kept asking everyone questions," she went on, starting to rush her words, as though now that they had surfaced, an underground spring, she was afraid they might dry up before she had said them all. "I wanted to know everything they remembered about how Anna died. I mean, I took some things of hers, like clothes, her journals. But I wanted her. I want her back more than anything in my whole life." She swallowed. "I keep imagining it over and over, how she must have felt, falling, and hoping it was quick, that she didn't know—Can I tell you?" she asked suddenly, turning toward me for the first time since we had sat down. The movement pierced me with gratitude.

"Of course," I said. "I want you to."

She had told me some of it the night Anna died, but she went through everything again. It was a freak accident. Anna had been spending the morning mowing the lawn and trimming the trees around the house while her husband Matthew did household repairs down in the basement. This was how they liked to spend their weekends: working with their hands, making things sturdy and presentable. Rachel's visits alone with Anna had often taken place outside, where they would talk as they planted bulbs or raked fallen leaves in piles on the lawn. That day Anna was in a sycamore outside the second-floor bedroom window, sawing off the branches that had started to scrape against the house. Maybe the branch she was on was too fragile for her weight; maybe she leaned out too far and lost her balance. She fell onto the branches that were already littering the grass, and the jagged end of one punctured her chest, sliding between her ribs. Matthew heard the thump of her body landing while he was climbing the steps from the basement. When he found her, blood was soaking into the lawn; she was already unconscious. Matthew called an ambulance and then her parents across town.

In the hospital they were given regular reports, first by the surgeon who told them Anna was being given transfusions of blood, then by an intern who could only tell them that the operation was underway and that Anna was still in critical condition. Hours later, the surgeon reappeared. He told them Anna had lost too much blood; they hadn't been able to save her.

Rachel told me these facts flatly, as if she had learned them by rote and they had nothing to do with her. Then she told me everything she remembered of the last six chaotic days, hopscotching backward and forward in time as something she had left out occurred to her. Her mother had kept busy making phone calls and cleaning the house while her father sat in the armchair in their bedroom quietly refilling his drink. Relatives, neighbors, and friends came to sit shiva, and for three days the house was full of people and talk and food and occasional edgy laughter. Her father remained ensconced in the bedroom. Once when no one else was with him, Rachel sat with her father in complete silence until it grew dark, which she found oddly comforting. Later in the week she took long walks with Matthew, who was unable to cry over the death of his wife, and she helped him sort through Anna's belongings, most of which he wanted to get rid of as soon as possible. Anna's empty clothes, her tennis racquet, her drafting table—she had been a landscape designer—deprived of daily use, accused him of his failure to keep her safe. Shocked, unable to let go of anything that had been her sister's, Rachel packed up what he didn't want into boxes and stored what she couldn't take with her in her parents' basement. At night Rachel wasn't able to sleep, and when she woke up in the morning, groggy, disoriented, her dreams had been full of natural disasters and flattened animals lying in the street.

Even through her numbness, Rachel's pain was palpable. I listened quietly, gathering and ordering the pieces to help keep these memories intact for her, whole. I knew they, too, were part of all she had left of Anna. She kept backtracking to the death itself, lingering over the gruesome details: filling in what she had been told, imagining the rest. Was Anna conscious when she first lay bleeding on the lawn, did she know she was dying? Was she afraid? No one could tell her. She felt no one wanted her to ask. Every morning she woke up with dread coiled in her chest, squeezing tight: she was sure something terrible was about to happen, until she remembered that it already had.

The tea in both our cups had cooled, untouched. The wind had picked up. I was shivering, but Rachel didn't seem to notice. She said, "I forgot about the funeral. That was the first day, the day I got there. The rabbi had never met my sister, just my parents. A few people got up during the service and talked about Anna, her wisdom, her patience. Her sense of humor. I couldn't do it. I kept thinking about her dead. My family had gone early to see Anna laid out in the casket, before anyone else arrived. Just before we went in, my mother said to me, 'You don't have to look.' I couldn't believe she said that. Of course I wanted to look. I wanted to see Anna again, find some way to say goodbye. I keep thinking if I had been able to say goodbye it would be easier. I had to see her. My mother didn't seem to understand that."

"She wanted to protect you," I said, understanding her mother's position better than I understood Rachel's.

I expected her to answer. I looked at her hugging her knees. She had closed her eyes, tight, but tears leaked from under her lids.

"Are you remembering how Anna looked in the casket?" I asked softly.

She nodded, and swallowed. I had guessed right. "I still can't believe she's dead," Rachel said in a small voice, and then began to cry. I reached out and held her, soaking in the warmth of her body as my neck and the collar of my shirt grew sodden with her snot and tears.

In the time that Rachel has been gone, I have spoken to several people about their siblings. They all say they can't imagine a life without their brothers and sisters. Not that they necessarily live nearby or keep in close contact or like them very much, but they take for granted, even count on, their siblings' continuing presence in the world.

One man, a French teacher at the school with whom I eat lunch once a week, told me that his older brother died in a car accident when they were both in high school. A year later my friend was hospitalized after jumping off the roof of his house. Now, almost twenty-five years later, he still considers killing himself; the only thing that has stopped him from trying again is knowing how devastating it would be for his younger brother.

I don't have any siblings, and I've never regretted this. My parents treated me as an adult at a very early age, taking me on weekends to their friends' boisterous gatherings where I was the only child present, one or two nights a week leaving me at home, trusting me to practice the piano and do my homework on my own. I used to watch large families closely, disgusted at the children screaming for attention and teasing each other, banding together against the younger or slower ones. Growing up, I had the impression that most children hated their sisters and brothers from the way they treated each other. Rachel said she and Anna fought all the time when they were children; because Anna was older, she was always allowed to do things Rachel wasn't. Yet, as adults, Rachel and Anna had talked on the phone almost every week.

One Friday in October Rachel found me crouched on the sidewalk outside her building, correcting the alignment of my bicycle.

I had begun riding it in the cooler weather, in the afternoons before she got home from work.

"Have you always known how to do that? I didn't until Anna showed me," she said, kissing the top of my head and crouching down next to me. I fit the front wheel back on the frame, adjusted the brake pads. I was surprised at how easily she spoke of Anna, without pain or the relentless obsession of the last weeks. "You'd think my father would've taught me the grimy stuff. He's always liked tinkering with the furnace or the car or whatever before calling someone in to fix it. I guess by the time I got a ten-speed, I was spending more time with Anna than I was with my parents."

She picked up my faded cloth tool bag and followed me as I carried the bicycle up the three flights of stairs. On her porch, most of the plants had shriveled to dry, brown stalks. Even the autumn rains hadn't managed to keep them alive now that Rachel had lost the energy to water them. Inside, she sat down at the kitchen table. I filled the tea kettle and put it on the stove to boil. I was trying to gauge whether she felt game enough to go for a walk or see a movie. This had been a particularly bad week, and I was tired of lying around her apartment, reading or watching TV, her body next to mine weighed down, immobile.

"By the time I was in eighth grade, neither of us was home much. You know, she was the first person I got high with," Rachel told me. By now I didn't have to try to follow her train of thought; it was always focused on Anna. "Who knows where my parents thought we were. At school cheering for our basketball team or something. I used to hang out with her and her friends a lot. We'd drive around stoned, way over the speed limit. She taught me how to drive a stick shift, too."

I was still trying to understand. "Wasn't she ever mean to you?"

"Oh, sure. I mean, when I was about ten or eleven, she'd make me give her my allowance, and if I wouldn't she'd pinch me really hard until I cried. Stuff like that."

"And you didn't tell your parents."

"God no, I was too old for that. She would have despised me." Rachel was silent. I turned off the flame and made our tea.

"Damn her," she said quietly behind me. "Goddamn her."

I put the two mugs back on the counter and turned around. She was hunched over, her eyes tightly shut. She drew in a deep, shaky breath.

"Come here," I said, moving toward her.

I had never seen anyone cry as hard as Rachel cried. Her harsh, uncontrollable sobbing sounded as though her body were being ripped out from the inside. At the end of each long, heaving breath, she struggled audibly to pull air back into her exhausted lungs. I often felt I was literally holding her together. For several weeks the muscles of her abdomen were sore, painful even when she breathed deeply. She didn't cry for a minute or two and, comforted, wipe her tears away, thank me, then go on to something else; she cried until she was limp, sticky, and feeling no sense of relief, only emptiness.

It was easiest to be woken from sleep by Rachel's sobs, to roll over on top of her and hold her as tightly as I could. In the daytime I always felt a touch of fear, a jab of resentment—not again—before I folded Rachel into my arms. And yet I couldn't find her crying alone and not go to her, trying—wanting—to bear with her this unimaginable grief. Rachel said once it was like falling down a deep well, and my caring presence like someone from the lip of the well above reaching down to catch hold of her hand, keeping her from sinking below the dark, stagnant water at the bottom. I tried to lean farther into the well for a better grip, but I wasn't strong enough to pull Rachel out. Sometimes I became afraid I would get too tired and have to let her go. More and more, I felt her pulling me into the well with her, and I didn't want to drown.

During the fall I had made an effort to be more accessible to my students and more involved in faculty meetings. One day I had a very good rehearsal with the choir and afterward went down the street for a beer with the administrative assistant in the principal's office, a woman who, I had discovered, also loved opera. Altogether it had been a satisfying afternoon, and I wanted to share it with Rachel. I surprised her by showing up at Faneuil Hall when she got off work. It was one of her better days, and as we walked to Haymarket to buy fish, then back toward the T, holding hands in the crisp early evening air, I remembered the summer. I hoped that now we could find our way back to that time, reclaim it for ourselves. The rich scent of wood smoke from a nearby chimney drifted by. We inhaled deeply and swung our hands. Rachel was happy, so I was happy.

At her apartment she marinated the salmon steaks while I

made a salad. For the first time in almost two months she was genuinely interested as I talked about my work and my students. Throughout the meal we stroked each other's hands over the table, kissed an ear, a neck, before taking away the plates. I hadn't felt such aching desire for her since before we first slept together. For dessert she stood beside my chair and fed me peach slices and blueberries, slipping them into my mouth from hers. "Come on," she said. She picked up the bowl of fruit with one hand and took my hand with the other, leading me into the bedroom. "I know another way to eat these."

She showed me, and we quickly forgot about the fruit. Then we got silly, trying to balance the blueberries on different parts of each other's bodies. "Look, I've invented a new form of jewelry," Rachel said, admiring the slices of peach circling my breast. They made me laugh. Rachel ate the peaches, their juice dribbling down my side. She licked up the juice and returned to my nipple. She bit gently as though it were a fat blueberry, then tasted it with her tongue. I moaned. When she moved away, settling beside me, I put the bowl on the floor and reached for the light switch.

"Leave the light on," Rachel said raggedly. I looked back at her and saw in her face that it wasn't sex anymore but the grief again. She looked as though she were being beaten, cringing before the next blow, and I still couldn't bear to see her look that way. I reached out and turned the switch. In the darkness I rolled back and on top of her.

"I'm here," I said, burrowing my face into her curly hair. Feeling her shiver, I tried to kick the quilt up over us with my foot.

"No, don't move," she said, hooking my leg with hers, stopping me. We lay still. The day had been going so well. I felt sure that I could change how she was feeling, beat back her grief with my tenderness. Her skin was warm and damp and smelled faintly of peaches. I lay above her listening to the rhythm of her breath, her soft body lightly lifting mine up and carrying it gently down, and I felt suddenly what I realize now she often felt with me: the delicacy of her bones, the beating of her heart beneath mine, the aliveness of her. She would tell me sometimes, as we held each other, how fragile I now seemed to her, how astonishing she found the complex, vulnerable workings of our bodies. That night I knew what she had meant. I was holding a woman I truly loved, and it was occurring to me for the first time how easily she could die. At that moment, no one had ever been so precious to me. I wanted to cry, holding her.

Then, as my throat tightened, something inside me shifted, froze. My heart started pounding and I felt suddenly numb, as though my skin and organs, all the parts of my body, had separated from each other and hardened. She became alien, a stranger, no longer the Rachel I loved. I didn't know what I was doing there. I desperately wanted to go back to the feeling before her grief, back to our pleasure together, and I only knew one way. I turned my face toward her. Listening to the shallow rasp of her breath, I slid my tongue into her ear, delicately tracing its curves and hollows.

"Kim . . . ?" At the sound of my name, I began to move on top of her, slowly, rubbing my body against hers. I licked the side of her neck lightly. "Kim," she repeated, alarmed, and started to pull away from under me.

"Shh," I whispered, meaning that I would take care of everything, that I wanted her to receive what I had to give her. I turned her face back to me and kissed her. When my fingers slipped between her legs, her breath caught, and I felt exonerated. I kissed her open mouth for a long time, teasing her with my tongue and my fingers until she began to push against my hand. "Shh," I whispered again, and moved my mouth down her body.

Sex, when we had it, was even better after Anna died. For Rachel especially, it seemed to bring her to some other place, separate from the everyday world, where the usual roles didn't apply anymore, where nothing was out of bounds. I was glad of this wildness in her, a kind of hunger for the edges of feeling and a forgetting of self, as if she didn't care where it took her. In bed all her dampened energy gathered and poured out. Making love could become so exquisite that she would cry or laugh or hum with pleasure. But underneath our passionate exchanges there was always Anna, always. A few times I couldn't be sure that Rachel's orgasms weren't shouts of despair, Rachel calling after her sister, trying to push out of her body to the place where Anna was. I could only hold on to her to keep her there in the room with me.

This time Rachel was taking a long time to come. She seemed to linger at the edge, shuddering, and I tried everything I knew to help her. When I could no longer taste her, I lifted my head. "Rachel, it's not going to happen."

She let out a low groan. "Don't stop, Kim. You were the one who started this."

"Take a break," I said, and pulled myself up to her mouth again. While we kissed I straddled her thigh, moving gently then harder, grasping Rachel and rocking her with me while I came. I fell asleep not long after, spooned against the round curve of Rachel's back.

In the morning I wanted to cuddle. Rachel was awake but wouldn't roll over to face me. I put my arm around her waist, resting my hand on her breast. She was very still, barely breathing. "Are you crying?" I asked.

"Yes, but not for the reason you think," she said.

"It's not about Anna?"

"It's always about Anna. It was about her last night. I just wanted to be held."

I was silent. Fear that I hadn't done the right thing mingled with resentment that she hadn't appreciated what I had done. I had been trying to comfort her for months and nothing I did seemed to help. At least, not enough. "I wanted you to feel good," I said finally.

She pushed the covers away and sat up. "You can't make me, Kim."

"That's not what I meant," I said irritably. "It's horrible to see you in so much pain all the time. You never seem to get better. Why won't you let yourself be comforted?"

"Do you think I have a choice? Do you think I enjoy this?" She was as angry as I was.

"Of course not. I don't know. Do you want to know what I think? I think you're hanging on to Anna and losing the rest of your life. Maybe it's time to let go of her now and move on."

We were both silent. I rolled onto my back, closed my eyes. "Kim," Rachel said patiently, "sometimes I think I'm going to die from Anna's death, it hurts so much. There is no rest of my life that isn't affected by this. Everything has changed. I can't explain it. And I can't make it go away. I have to finish it."

"How do you know it will end?" My anger was slowly leaking away, now that we were talking. My throat hurt.

"I don't. I have to trust it will."

Suddenly tears were rolling down my face, dripping into my ears and onto the bed. Rachel must have noticed; I felt her lean over and tenderly wipe them away. When I opened my eyes she was putting her wet fingers in her mouth to lick off the salt. She held my gaze, brushing my hair back with her hand, waiting for me to speak.

I looked away. "I can't compete with Anna, Rachel. You love her so strongly, so emphatically." I tried to swallow. "I want to be loved like that."

Now she knew. Rachel looked at me for a moment, her gentle brown eyes unmistakably filled with quiet love. Then she lay down beside me and pulled me to her. I couldn't relax, even pressed against her warm, ample body.

"I'm sorry," she said. "You don't know how grateful I am that you're here."

Somehow it was no comfort.

I stand at the entrance of a room containing six vinyl chaise longues with adjustable table-arms. In the nearest chair, a woman lies with her eyes closed, a plastic cord dark with blood running from her outstretched arm to a small pouch hanging beside her. She is wearing a beige linen suit and has left her shoes on the floor.

A short man dressed in nurse's whites approaches me, smiling. He takes my paperwork and walks to the table in the center of the room. "Right or left?" he calls back.

"Right seems to work better," I say, following him and taking the chair on the left that looks out the window. Through the blinds, two rows of saplings line the parking lot, their branches still bare of leaves. It's been a cold winter, and a long one.

He brings over the blood pressure gauge, pushes up the sleeve of my shirt, and wraps the length of the pressure cuff around my upper arm. By now I feel compelled to pay close attention to this blood-giving process. He pumps the squeeze bulb a few times, watching the dial. I've always found that tightening feeling reassuring, a secure grasp. Then he lets the air escape, unrolls the cuff, and takes it away.

When he comes back to my side, he is unwrapping the cord from around an empty bag. He hooks up the bag to the chair, lays out strips of tape along the edge of the chair's arm, cleans the crook of my arm with a large swab coated with disinfectant. It's all very orderly, there is no hint that anything could go wrong, that people die slowly from infected blood, that people die quickly from loss of blood. The disinfectant is cool on my skin. I can't help but think of Anna in the hospital, her unconscious body straining to survive, her face with Rachel's features. I rest my head on the back of the chair and take a deep breath.

"Nervous?" my nurse asks. I shake my head. He smiles. "Squeeze," he says, handing me a cylinder of rolled-up paper towels secured by a couple of rubber bands. As I squeeze and let go and squeeze again, he taps the vein on my forearm encouragingly. "Great. Keep it up." I turn my head to follow his movements, watch him pull the wrapping off my needle, the apparently simple process of assembly. I don't mind the needle, its length or thickness. I almost look forward to it. Needle pricks have never fallen into the category of pain for me, like menstrual cramps and migraine headaches. What do I know about pain? I stop squeezing the roll.

The nurse, his needle poised at an angle above my arm, glances up at me. "You don't have to look."

My heart is beating hard. "I want to look," I tell him. He nods and pierces my skin. I scarcely feel it. I watch the sharp point sink in, finding the vein. Holding the needle still, he gently places a square gauze pad over the puncture site and attaches the first six inches of cord to my arm with the strips of tape. By now my arm seems barely connected to the rest of me. The plastic cord fills with my red blood, which looks as if it stops there, astonished by the light.

Rachel stopped painting after her sister died. Her brushes dried out, abandoned next to her tubes of paint. On the easel, she left the canvas she had been working on unfinished. She never went into her studio anymore. On her better days, when she wasn't pinned down by the weight of her sorrow, I tried to coax her into mixing some colors or taking out her charcoals just to find out what might happen. Usually she didn't even bother to answer me. Well into October, she decided she wanted to throw out her old paintings; she said they had never been any good. She took down the six on the wall of her living room, yanking out the nails they had hung by with the claw of a hammer, throwing everything—paintings, nails, hammer—carelessly into one of the corners with the other canvases stacked there. In the end, she only got as far as offering the paintings to me. I could take as many as I wanted. I was mortified enough by her indifference to her own gift that I refused them.

I think now that she always believed—she would say trusted—that she would find a way to return somehow, circle back and approach her painting from another direction. Late in the long fall she did begin to paint again, but this time without a canvas. Instead she painted what was already in the rooms, leaving the white, empty walls unfilled. In her living room she painted the towering bookcase, including the spines of the books wedged on its shelves, and it became a bright mosaic of greens and blues that reminded me of the ocean from beneath the water. She wound leafy vines up the legs of the stools in the kitchen, and on the seats painted a tangled jungle of perpetually blooming flowers. She covered the butcher block table with muted colors, adding streaks and sprinkles of paint, creating a star-filled sky, its comets falling to a pink horizon. Rachel painted her desk, the couch by the window, the bean bag chairs on the porch. When she ran out of furniture, she painted her quilt—hands, feet, breasts, faces with long, unbound hair—and some of her clothes: jackets, scarves. I bought her curtains so she could paint them too. She painted jars and bowls and canisters of tea and flour. She painted anything she could lay her hands on that had some use, some meaning in the everyday world. For weeks her apartment was awash in oil paint and turpentine fumes. The same music thundered over and over from the living room speakers. Rachel painted in furious concentration, accompanied solely by Brahms's German Requiem, which I had given her the week after Anna died.

At first I sat in the room with her, watching her paint. I liked the way her forehead furrowed, how perfectly still she could hold herself, how decisively she mixed colors and brushed them onto the surface in front of her. I saw again how beautiful she was. Eventually she would become aware of me, glance over, and blush a deep red. Or I would approach and touch her lightly, kiss the back of her neck, raising goosebumps. At times she admitted she liked knowing I was there, close by. At other times she told me I was too much of a distraction.

"Would you mind staying in the other room for a while?" she asked the third or fourth time she felt me observing her. It was a chilly, foggy morning; what was left of the brilliant red leaves on the oak outside her window looked dull, rust-colored.

"I could leave if you want me to," I offered.

"No, I don't." She looked at me closely. "What's the matter?"

"Nothing." But something was. I started reading in the next room, waiting for her to finish. I was glad for her burst of creative energy, but at the same time she was ruining expensive pieces of furniture and good clothes. I was scared by her obsessive need to paint over everything in her possession.

I blame myself not so much for sleeping with my new friend in the principal's office but for not anticipating the depth of Rachel's rage when I told her. It only happened once; we didn't start our rather clandestine affair until Rachel moved away. I just didn't expect Rachel to mind so much.

I often wonder: If I had loved Rachel more, would I have known how to stay with her? Or did my failure of imagination limit how well I could love? I still think of writing to Rachel; I want her to know I am sorry. Maybe she would write me back.

After my revelation and the bitter argument that followed, Rachel refused to speak to me. A few weeks later I ran into a friend of hers who told me that Rachel had moved back to Ithaca to be near her family. She wanted to be with people who had also known and loved Anna, who knew what Rachel meant when she said she missed her sister.

I feel cold. The air conditioning is always on too high here, probably to help keep the blood fresh. Or perhaps a person's body temperature lowers as she loses blood. I look at the needle in my arm, the cord sluicing my blood from my body. I hold the roll tightly; I can see the cord below the tape jerk with each pump of my heart. Even when I stop squeezing, it twitches rhythmically, steadily, reliably, proof of the internal motion of my body despite my outward stillness. I can feel the heat of my blood too, as it lies sheathed in plastic taped against my forearm. I knew that blood turns from blue to red on contact with oxygen; somehow I imagined it would cool down once it left the body. I watch the warm red cord pulsing, disappearing over the edge of the chair.

Sex Less

TERRY WOLVERTON

Your herbalist swears it's *Qi* deficiency.

Your best friend accuses you of going back to men.

Your therapist tells you you're acting out, rebelling against mom.

Your gynecologist insists you're depressed.

Your lover's convinced that it's all her fault.

Everyone has an opinion, so eager to give you advice, though you never asked for it. Each is sure she can solve your problem, even if you don't think you have one.

They don't get it.

But why should they? Here, in the closing moments of the twentieth century—after five thousand years of patriarchal rule, five thousand years of being owned and sold and traded and bred like cattle, five thousand years of being defined as wanton and evil or as sexless, devoid of desire—women have stolen back sexuality. It's happened in your very lifetime: from the Pill to the Sexual Revolution, from vibrators to sex clubs, from *Our Bodies, Our Selves* to *on our backs*, women have spent the last thirty years reclaiming lust as a birthright. How could any sane lesbian renounce it?

You say: you're tired. You've done more than your share of sucking and fucking, moaning and throbbing, creaming and cumming for one lifetime. Now you're content to think of it as something that you used to do, like drugs or the Hustle. Now it seems more like your favorite Motown song from the sixties after it's been played to death on the Classic Soul Oldies station: it no longer makes you wanna dance.

You're strangely not upset about this. It's everyone else who's upset.

Your best friend asks, "Is it Angela? Maybe you and Angela should go to couples counseling."

Your gynecologist says, "Ten years is a long time to be with the same woman. Maybe you need to be non-monogamous for a while."

Your herbalist brews you a potion so strong that, once you drink it, you smell it in your sweat for days.

Your therapist suggests you up your appointments to three times a week.

Their efforts bemuse you. Nobody ever tried to intervene during those years you brought home from the bar a different woman each week. No one even blinked when you had three lovers at the same time and cried on the phone every day at work. None of them seemed concerned about too much sex.

And yet, when you think back on those years of chemistry and cruising, all that groping and straining and saliva, you can't help wondering—what was the point? Night after night of dissolving into neural explosion—does that constitute a life? Now it seems the body was not home but a mask, and you long to step out from behind it.

Angela is beside herself. She cannot see that this has nothing to do with your love for her, nothing to do with wanting anyone else. Her dark eyes follow you, ponds swollen with spring rain. She questions you whenever you return home: did you meet someone? Fear changes the shape of her beautiful mouth.

You wish you could explain it, to her, to the worried others, even to yourself. You search for words that would form themselves into the precise shape of your history, a bulk and density that pulls like gravity at your flesh, but the flesh is mute as lead, and the words fall to the ground in heaps, unformed, unheard.

She cannot, as you can, imagine a love relieved of the weight of lovemaking, a love as light and full as breath. You trace the curve of her hipbone and know that she will leave. You already miss the smell of her hair.

Your therapist recommends that you lie on the couch, abandon the upright safety of the chair; she wants you to go back, to walk again the long road of bodies that has led you to this spot. It embarrasses you to remove your shoes, you who've gone topless at the public beach, nude at music festivals, who have rarely overlooked an opportunity for sex in a bar restroom or a parked car on a busy street. Your stockinged feet feel naked here in the small air conditioned room.

Oblivious to chronology, you begin with a story from about ten years ago, just before you met Angela. You were at a party given by someone who worked with you at the sound studio. The party was full of musicians and engineers and hangers-on, not so different from being at work. When the blonde with one walled eye walked in she noticed you immediately. You recognized her; you'd been with her before, uncountable years earlier. You hadn't liked her, you remembered, not before and not then, her personality as sharp and pointy as her face. Still, before the party was over, you'd had sex with her in the shower of the California bungalow's sole bathroom.

Your therapist asks, inevitably, "And how did you feel after you were with her?"

You are bored by the story, not just this chapter but the whole saga. You seem to yourself a cartoon figure, a female Bullwinkle with a permanent hard-on that you followed like a compass arrow. You remember more of the faces than you would have predicted, more of the names. You can recall certain details, the black tile that lined the shower, the blonde's scream of laughter as it shrilled in your ear, but you can't seem to recall the sensations that coursed through your body, lighting up neurons like a pinball machine, the explosions and whistles.

"Maybe we're all programmed to endure only so many orgasms," you suggest, "and I've used up my quota." It's as if you're recounting a story that was told to you, nothing you ever witnessed, your voice low and uninflected. Your eyes study a crack in the ceiling, try to follow it to its source.

Your best friend invites you to dinner, lures you with her offer to make spaghetti with clam sauce, her grandmother's recipe. Her girlfriend's away on business, Angela has been working late for the past month. "Just the two of us," your best friend urges.

You arrive with a bottle of wine, expecting to see the dining room table set for two. Instead, places have been laid on the coffee table, in front of the big screen TV. "I've got a surprise for you," your friend announces before disappearing back to the kitchen.

As the spaghetti steams on a plate before you, the tender clams redolent of cream and garlic, the wine pale in a thin-stemmed glass, your best friend pops a black cassette into the VCR. An image rises before you, a naked brunette climbs atop a naked redhead, pink flesh dragging across pink flesh, the focus is soft, the lighting is dim, and close-ups of breasts and stomachs and thighs and buttocks threaten to come rolling out of the screen into the living room.

"What is this?" you ask your friend. The soundtrack gasps and moans like a tired accordion. The brunette is plunging her fist into the redhead's vagina, inserting her arm past the wrist, her elbow pumping.

It's pornography," she tells you. She explains that she and her girlfriend often watch it to "put themselves in the mood."

"It's gonna make me spit up my dinner," you warn. Glumly, she turns, clicks the remote, and the images collapse into blessed darkness.

"This is serious," she suddenly explodes. "It's not like you're eighty years old. You're way too young to lose your sex drive."

Apparently your gynecologist agrees, because she calls you at home. This strikes you as odd, but then she says, "I've been thinking a lot about this thing you've got going on with your libido. I want you to come into my office for a consultation."

You try to protest until, misunderstanding your reluctance, she proclaims, "I won't even charge you for an office visit. I've run across some information I think you'll find interesting."

You show up the next Tuesday morning, an 8 A.M. appointment since you still hope to be on time for work. Your gynecologist greets you in her office, not an examination room, and pulls out a file folder marked "Testosterone."

Inside are photocopies of half a dozen articles, their type gray and fuzzy, regarding the use of this hormone to stimulate the libido of menopausal and post-menopausal women. You notice the articles all seem to be from popular women's magazines, not scientific journals. They are full of glowing testimonials from women who found that "sex is better than ever" and "now I want it almost every day" since the treatment.

You've been seeing your gynecologist for years. You originally chose her specifically because she is a lesbian. She has told you that she jettisoned her long-term relationship once the sex waned. She's now involved with a woman twenty-three years her junior.

You stare at your gynecologist across the desk. "Testosterone?" you ask. The bile in your tone wipes the self-congratulatory grin from her face.

Does it seem to you that everyone's gone crazy?

You're trying to explain this to your herbalist, when she takes your hand in her moist palms. She moves her chair closer, stares deep into your eyes.

"What my guides are telling me," she begins in the disembodied voice which means she's going metaphysical on you, "is that this whole situation with your sexuality represents a creative block that you're wrestling with."

You hate it when she brings her "guides" into it. She's a terrific herbalist; she's gotten rid of your PMS and your hay fever, and moved you through a couple of bouts of flu, but you'd just as soon stay on the physical plane, in the realm of the observable.

You never meant to work on this with her. It just came up one day during an examination; she was studying your tongue, its color, shape, and coat, when she asked, "What's your level of sexual activity these days?" So you told her.

Now you're sorry. You've been privy to the havoc of her own romantic life, and are certain she's not the one you would turn to for this sort of advice.

"For years you've been facilitating the music of others," she intones as if dictating the words being channeled through her. "Now it's time for your to allow your own music to spill forth."

"You need to learn to trust yourself, your creativity." Her eyes flutter behind her thick glasses. Your herbalist is a frustrated painter, too busy always, she insists, to do what she swears she longs to do. If her "guides" are speaking, you believe, then this must be a message for her.

It is only Angela you can't dismiss. One night you arrive home and she's dressed in red bustier and garter belt, long black stockings.

She's taken extra care with her make-up, piled her dark hair on top of her head. Her breasts threaten to spill from their padded cups; a saxophone throbs from the stereo speakers.

She looks so like a little girl in borrowed clothes, imitating something she saw in her mother's movie star magazines that you want to laugh. But you know this effort is all for you and instead you begin to cry.

At first she's confused at the sight of your tears; she straddles your lap, attempts to cajole you. You remember how your body once opened to hers. You tell yourself to reach for her. You've slept with many women in your life without feeling it, what could it hurt? But you know that Angela will not be fooled by a cheap show of technique; Angela will search your eyes and find you missing. And besides, you just can't make your body lie anymore.

You cry harder, watch the realization spread across her face that she's once more failed to win you. Her eyes narrow, the jaw hardens, her humiliation masked with fury. Her high heels click out of the room, recede down the hall. You hear water running in the bathroom, the sound of clothes slammed back into drawers. The saxophone evaporates into air.

Your mother once told you that she never had sex again after she turned forty.

"Didn't you miss it?" you'd asked at the time. You were twenty-seven at the time and the revelation shocked you. You thought sex was like vitamins, a daily dose essential to your health.

"I was relieved," she confided. "I never liked it all that much. I think your father found . . . other ways to get it. He needed it more. I just told him not to tell me, and it was fine." There is not a shade of regret in her voice.

You wondered then if it wasn't a matter of generation, your mom born in a time when women weren't expected to like it, when the predominant values were duty and sacrifice, not gratification and individual fulfillment. Then, you strutted your era's freedoms like a badge of superiority.

Your mother is now almost seventy. Your dad has been dead for twelve years. You stare into her still-blue eyes and find serenity. She has her garden, her book group; your brother has given her grandchildren. Her life is full; she is content. There is no chance of finding porn tapes on her coffee table, testosterone prescriptions in her medicine cabinet.

Another friend calls you; she's been celibate for six months. She groans into the phone receiver, complains that she's "horny." Your try to imagine your mother horny; it's impossible.

You wonder if it isn't something to do with lesbians, with definition. If a woman is queer because she has sex with her own gender, then pride and propaganda require she have sex as often as possible, an affirmation of identity. Maybe that's what you've been doing all those years. And without sex, who do you become?

Maybe that's what riles your best friend, what worries your gynecologist. They see you as a defector, not holding up your end of the queer covenant.

Any of them might be right: therapist, herbalist, gynecologist, friend. Perhaps you should be as distressed as they, scrambling to shore up your sexual identity. You wonder whether this change is permanent, if, like your mother, you should take up gardening. Odd, that even this prospect doesn't frighten you.

Stretched out in the bath, you stare at your naked body, the skin surprisingly unmarked from its years on the battle lines. You examine the parts—breasts and pubis and thighs—once the sites of desire, but now they seem without landmark, the old maps obsolete.

Beyond the door, Angela moves about the house, making her preparations for sleep. Rejection rings in her every step; you hear bitterness in the way she pulls back the sheet. You'd like to call to her, tell her how much you cherish her laughter, and the way she cries at movies and during sappy commercials, the heat of her skin in sleep, but she won't hear you now.

Submersed in the steaming water, you cup your small breast. Your nipple does not harden, nerves do not ignite. You feel only a vague comfort, like an arm wrapped around you in sleep. You sigh, settle back against porcelain, steeped in the relief of feeling nothing.

Breasts

ELISE D'HAENE

Lynette and Athena are comparing their breasts. They are supposed to be helping to pack boxes in my apartment. I'm moving into C.J's house this weekend. Lynette and Athena are both a size D cup—double D. Lynette is a 36DD and Athena is a 34DD. They are commiserating about lower back pain, shoulder stress, bra shopping woes, and the veritable wasteland of push-up, strapless bras for the D-cup woman. I am a B-cup, although during the bloatation phase of my cycle, a C cup will do in a pinch.

Lynette and Athena have a lot in common: Both are small-framed women. Both have tiny waists. Both have strong muscled legs (developed, I imagine, through the Sisyphean efforts of lugging around their breasts). Each is a double Scorpio, and each define themselves as bisexual, though presently they are both engaged to men.

I am sweating, not because Lynette and Athena have their blouses open and they are palming their breasts, displaying them to each other like prize-winning loaves of bread. I am sweating because I am doing all the work. No one has asked to see my two dinner rolls.

I'm standing on a stepladder, grasping armloads of books off the top shelf, and noisily depositing them to the floor. Lynette and Athena are sitting on a pile of boxes that need to be assembled, leaning against the couch that needs to be wrapped in plastic covering. Perched atop my ladder, I look down and think of ski slopes.

Breasts have been on my mind a lot lately. Everywhere I go I see, smell, imagine, and dream of them. It began with my friend Pauline. She's thirty-three years old. One week she told me she felt a lump. The next week, it had been biopsied. Four days later, the results. Then surgery, seven lymph glands removed. Sixteen weeks of chemotherapy and radiation. Total hair loss. Skin became the color of light ash. Lips chapped. Eyes dulled. Six months later, her arm is still numb, her breast, sore to the touch. Her hair grew back, bristly and coarse, and she burned her impressive collection of vintage men's hats because they became a reminder of hiding her bald head.

We spin around her question over and over, will it come back? The scar disgusts her. Sometimes I wish I could hold her breasts, trace a finger, a tongue across her wound and whisper a word that would heal, conjure up a magic of some kind, restoring her breast and her ease, erasing the menace that grips her brow with relentless worry.

"Lynette," I snap, "would you mind wrapping the glasses on the counter with newspaper?" There is silence. Sitting on my floor, in my apartment, amongst my belongings, Lynette and Athena look up at me as if to say, What are you doing here?

I feel I've intruded on sacred ground. As if I have swung down on a rope from the rafters in a church just as the priest transforms the bread into Christ's body.

"The movers are going to be here soon," I continue. "Can we reconvene this breast convention at another time?"

They do up their blouses, shrug their respective shoulders, and start working. I know they think that I'm envious. My glass of milk is half empty. They have gallon-size pitchers of cream. They get cleavage when they breathe. For me to accomplish cleavage, I need the miracle—steel support, wires that pinch and pull, making it difficult for me to breath.

Lynette is dutifully wrapping glasses as Athena inspects the instructions on how to put together the boxes. I'm in between, wiping the shelves down.

"Do you have a lot of feeling in your nipples?" Lynette asks. This irritating question is directed at Athena, I know, because I've had this discussion with Lynette, and part of me thinks she is being passively hostile.

"Oh God!" Athena brays, "I can orgasm with nipple manipulation alone."

I glare down at Lynette, who is beaming. Lynette is also able to accomplish an orgasm in this manner. My nipples are like those wooden knobs on kitchen cupboards; two knobs you can rap and tap and pull and twist and turn. I don't feel a thing. It's genetic, I'm sure, because of the five of my seven sisters I have asked, they too have nipples that are dead as a door nail. I haven't mustered up the courage to ask my mother.

"When I masturbate," Lynette coos, "I always give my nipples that extra tweak to increase the intensity of my orgasm."

"Absolutely!" chimes Athena.

And that's another thing! They have pink nipples. Rosy pink nipples. Rosy pink nipples that conjure up words like blossom, cheerful, blooming, healthy. Mine are brown. Conjuring up words like—brown.

These are petty issues, a voice murmurs deep within my brain. You love these women, the voice implores. Your breasts are perfect because they are yours.

I decide to go into my closet and start sorting clothes.

I wish C.J. were here. At least she has average-sized breasts, like me, just B-cup, no big deal. They're lovely, firm, and perky. Like Athena and Lynette, her nipples are rosy and enthusiastic, and she would be perfectly content to have me suck and pluck them until the cows came home.

C.J. is wild about my brown knobs; she loves to munch and lick and squeeze them. I'm very patient. I often wait to see if all of a sudden some kind of sensation will erupt. When she's grazing on my breasts, and her hair is blocking my view, it's anybody's guess as to what she is doing.

"Honey," I'll say curiously, "are you sucking my nipple?"

"Uh, huh," she groans dreamily.

"Which one?" I ask. My preference is to watch. That turns me on. When I'm on top, I love to dip my breasts into her mouth, then into her cunt, rubbing my hard brown doorknobs against her swollen clit. When I see my breasts give so much pleasure, a lusty power ripples down my spine.

I dump my bra drawer on the closet floor. I have at least fifteen usable ones, yet I only regularly wear two of them, and my black sports bra. I have six white bras, five black, two flesh-toned, one dusty peach, and one bright screaming fuchsia. The last was bought during a phase when I felt I needed to be trashier, to explore my inner slut. I bought a matching pair of underwear too. It was a pseudo–g-string panty that rode up my ass, pinched and pulled at my pubic hairs, and left me with a rash. I was allergic to the crotch lining. After that, I only bought 100 percent white cotton briefs. I know for a fact that Lynette and Athena have all those girlie get-ups, complete with lace and leather and those thingamajigs that hook hose to panty. I've seen their underwear drawers firsthand. They know something I don't, and neither one of them is coughing up her secrets.

I sit among my bras and pick through those I never wear. There's no use keeping them. I slip my hand under my sweatshirt, then under my sports bra, and hold my left tit, squeezing the mass gently, as if to hold hands with an old friend.

I'm trying to make peace with them, stop the relentless scrutiny that has infected my thinking over the years. As a teenager, I would stand in front of a mirror, naked. I would hoist them up, using my hands as a crane, and smush them together and stare. Though average in size, my breasts are droopy, hanging down mid-torso. It's a result, I imagine, of years of weight fluctuation. C.J. says it's just where they happen to fall.

Your breasts are perfect because they are yours.

What C.J. doesn't know is that while we make love, I surreptitiously give her a breast exam. I can't seem to shake this anxiety. My hands, my tongue, my lips, become frantic instruments, tools for detection. I've read the research. We're at that age. We're not child-bearing. I scrutinize our bodies. Are we pear-shaped, too? I can hardly hug her without my hands wandering up for a swift exam.

Pauline asks, over and over, will it come back? All I can do is circle her question and get dizzy. All I can do is circle C.J.'s nipple with my tongue, circle my own breasts with a calculating finger, press down until it hurts. Looking. Furiously searching for something I don't want to find.

And then this phone call from my mother last week about Katie O'Brien. We were best friends in high school but lost touch. I was in love with Katie back then, but I didn't know what to call it. I just knew I wanted to eat her up like a bowl of sugary Cheerios.

Katie has multiple sclerosis. As this newsy tidbit came hurling through the phone line, a part of me began sinking. My mother's words: "Well, it turns out it was caused by silicone breast implants . . . they disintegrated," my breath jammed in my throat. "They've removed them, but all her breast tissue was absorbed, so everything had to be taken out."

As my mother spoke, I fell into a memory, pushing her voice away like an offensive intruder. Katie and I are in her father's speedboat out on Lake Michigan. It's August, a still and sweltering summer day. Both of us have one leg hanging over the boat dangling in the cool water. We're way out, no other boats around.

Katie takes her bikini top off. We're frying our skin, slathering on layers of baby oil. She squeezes more oil into her hand and rubs it all over her gleaming breasts. "Brad thinks my tits are too small," she says. "What do you think?"

I take off my blue sunglasses, turn toward her and stare. I'm embarrassed, flushed red, but it isn't noticeable because I'm totally sunburned. I want to touch them. I want to rest my hot face against her. I barely whisper, "They're beautiful."

A slow smile unfolds across her lips. She runs her finger in the slick oil, around her nipple drawing little circles. "I think so too," she says.

That night, Katie touched my breasts. We were high and drowsy lying in soft sand, the ground was cool and she was spraying Off! all over our clothes because of mosquitoes. After she sprayed herself, she pointed the can at me but the aerosol stopped working and a thick stream hit my T-shirt in the front. Before I knew what was happening, she was unbuttoning her top. Underneath she was wearing a man's undershirt and no bra. "Take off your shirt," she said. I was practically passing out from the bug spray fumes, but I said, "No, no, I'm okay." She insisted, so I took it off. She grabbed my shirt, hooted, and threw it into the lake, but then, wouldn't give me hers to put on.

"Wow," she said.

"Wow, what?" I said. My face was heating up as her eyes scanned my breasts.

"You've got great ones." My body temperature jumped, and I started sweating. Then she touched my nipple through my bra, and it sprouted, swelled up under her index finger like a fast-rising nub of bread dough. She slid her body on top of mine and my lips opened and she pressed her nipple between them and my legs shook. When she finally peeled off her T-shirt, her breasts tasted like beer and mosquito spray. I was wet and wanting and it felt like a part of myself, dormant since birth, popped out like toast. That was the only time we ever touched like that.

When Lynette comes into the closet, I have my bras wrapped around my neck like scarves. I have both hands under my sweatshirt, as if holding two orphaned babies. Katie can no longer walk and Pauline has started collecting sleeping pills—just in case.

Lynette links her arm underneath mine as Athena comes up behind. She swings one leg then the other over us, and sits down at my other side. The three of us crammed into my shoebox of a closet.

I've started crying. I'm still holding my breasts; they swell with each aching breath. Athena pulls me toward her, guiding my head onto her chest. I press my face deep into her bosom; my sorrow like a prayer pounding at the wailing wall, and I imagine curling my palm into the hollow space left over Katie's heart.

Finally C.J. arrives with the truck and two male movers. All is packed. These guys are paying a lot of attention to Lynette and Athena, bowing to their every wish. I want them to hurry. All I can think about is being in my new home with C.J. and we're in bed, and I push her down, glide on top of her, slide my tongue across her nipples and pray.

Memory Like Ash Borne on Air

ROBIN PODOLSKY

As soon as she arrived at the meeting, Joan was cornered by Tom, a tall stringy man whose drooping mustache did nothing for his already long face. As though in answer to a question she had asked, he told her, "Kenneth's just about the same. I talked to him this afternoon and he said that he'd still love to see people."

Joan forced herself to stare directly into his eyes. Focusing on her tiny reflection, wavering in dark brown irises, she said, "He's still in the hospital? How long has it been?"

"Three weeks, honey." Tom's smile tightened. "I think that the more company he gets, the more energy he'll have to feel better, don't you?"

Joan's inner ear set up a tingle. She felt as though, having locked herself into an empty house, she heard footsteps on the floor. Through closed teeth, she said, "Of course. At least I'd like to call him."

Tom drew from his breast pocket a handful of yellow paper squares, each with Kenneth's name on them, the name of the hospital and its address and the phone number for Kenneth's room. He gave one to Joan and watched while she tucked it into her wallet.

"Let's go sit down, shall we? It's twenty-eight after." They walked toward concentric circles of metal folding chairs surrounding a long table. Crowning the table was a yellow cardboard sign that read: Alanon Spoken Here. Most of the chairs were already claimed with rings of keys, a territorial marking recognized in 12-Step programs throughout the country.

. . .

At the door to her mother's apartment, Joan's shoulders began gnashing their muscles in time to her pulse. Alone in the thinly carpeted hallway, she tensed her nostrils against its anonymous, frightening odors. She listened as her mother undid the door-chain and locks.

At her mother's inevitable, "Hello sweetheart," Joan's shoulders turned to granite. As always, she wondered if she imagined the throb of reproach in those words.

. . .

One of Joan's newfound Alanon friends, Jerry, began to lead the Serenity Prayer that opened the meeting; "God, grant me the serenity to accept the things I cannot change . . ." The group's regulars liked to tease Joan and Jerry by calling them The Twins. They had the same carefully layered blond hair and pampered skin and they wore the same crisp shirts, cotton pullovers, and sweater vests. Both of them spoke, as Tom said, like newscasters.

Joan never wore dark clothing. She favored spring tones named for living things like salmon, coral, and mint. In 1978, she had begun to style her hair in imitation of Dorothy Hamill. Ten years later, at the age of thirty-seven, she had not much changed her cut. Joan adapted to fashion's broadest contours, she went along with shoulder pads, waists, and epaulets as they turned up and went away, but she was never the first or last to sport a trend.

. . .

"So, what do you want to eat?"

At her mother's question Joan's stomach swelled and hardened. She didn't know whether she most hated the kitchen or the living room of her mother's apartment.

The entire place smelled of chicken fat, talcum powder, and sweat. Her mother never opened the windows or the old-fashioned paper shades. When she was little, Joan had loved to play with the shades, pulling the string up and down and wearing the loop like an oversized ring. Her mother had lived in that apartment for forty-five years.

Joan decided that she hated the kitchen most. The pits built into the linoleum floor had widened to gashes and pocks, packed with grease and dust. Everything cooked in that room yielded to digestion with spiteful reluctance, sitting in her stomach for hours and coating her tongue. The living room, a cavern of shadows and mahogany, could provide a numbing comfort when it did not provoke her imagination.

"Whatever you're cooking. I'm not really hungry yet, though."

They sat in the living room, on opposite ends of the plush quilted couch that had faded to dusty pink. It had been deep burgundy when Joan was a little girl; a soft, richly odorous cave to hide in, covered up with pillows.

"So. You're feeling all right?" Joan aimed an invisible snarl at her mother's question and the smile that came with it. The smile insisted that any answer she might give be a placating lie.

"Sure, Mom, I'm fine." She felt the familiar pressure on her neck and shoulders snuggle in like a spoiled cat. "How are you?"

"How am I?" Joan set her teeth at the sigh whistling behind the words. A needle lanced her jaw. "I'm fine, honey. Are you eating? You're thin. All the time working, no boyfriend, you're going to make yourself sick."

• • •

Without telling anyone, Joan had begun to see a therapist. For over two months, she had been seized by a brute need to wash her hands, with a mechanical, painful thoroughness, four or five times a day. More if she read a newspaper, shook the hand of another person or—to Vivien's bewildered and aggrieved pain—if she made love.

Somehow Sharon, the therapist, had gotten her started on her mother. Joan wasn't surprised. Sharon was her first paid counselor, but she had heard that therapists always got around to your mother.

Joan was relieved to say aloud, with Sharon's help, that she had never heard her mother utter a single word that did not hold a well of bottomless disappointment. That breakthrough did not stop her from taking her mother's disgust with life as a judgment against herself, but it did increase her self-contempt for doing so.

• • •

Sitting with a straight back at her mother's formica kitchen table, doggedly chewing on the wet, gray leg of a boiled chicken while her mother talked about a neighbor's surgery, Joan held her fork high. She was afraid that the back of her little finger would touch some of the juice on her plate and she would have to get up and wash.

Shame at her body's weakness to her mind's assaults returned Joan to her own apartment, two nights earlier, cornered by Vivien's rage. Vivien had shrieked at her while Joan said nothing. She was sick, right then, of Vivien's presence and the obscure, terrifying void of her needs. She really expected to vomit on her lover's shoes.

"Take some more." Joan's mother dropped an extra spoonful of canned vegetables onto her plate.

Now, after two days, the absence of Vivien, the fear of losing her for good, held Joan stiff with pain.

• • •

Joan had never told Sharon about the numbers that were inked into her mother's arm. If anyone had asked why—but few people in her life had any idea about her mother's past—Joan would have said that the subject had never come up.

• • •

Bill, who was leading the Alanon meeting, started to speak. Not everybody liked to be around Bill. He was tall and angular, but not handsome in the way that big-boned men are expected to be. His eyes stuck out. He dragged his frame around as though it were a burden, covering it with polyester uniform-like things of dark brown and sky blue and bumping it into furniture. Bill spoke artlessly and in long bursts, blurting intimate revelations and familiar Alanon slogans with equal gravity, segueing between subjects without pause. For a few people, he was egoless inspiration incarnate, a kind of holy fool. He got on Joan's nerves.

One night, Joan had come to the meeting early. Her mother had kept her longer than usual. It was too late to drive all the way home and change her clothes or even to stop for coffee.

No one was in the room when she got there except for Bill, who was arranging literature on the table. Joan told him hello and found a chair in the back circle, next to the wall.

Bill was trying to pile too many pamphlets into stacks that constantly collapsed and had to be grouped again. Without stopping his work, he called out, "Do you want to talk? You look like you have something going on."

Her temples beginning to flutter with an incipient headache, Joan muttered, "I just got back from seeing my mother." She had no energy to continue.

"What?" Bill yelled over his shoulder.

"I. Just. Got. Back. Fromseeingmymother."

Bill strode to her side, knocking several chairs out of place. He sat down and stared so intensely that Joan was nudged out of apathy to the edge of fear. Bill didn't move or speak. To kill the silence, Joan began to tell him about the evening with her mother, about trying to talk to her mother about Vivien, about no longer being sure what the truth of her relationship with Vivien really was. When the secretary called the meeting to order, twenty minutes later, Joan was still talking.

• • •

As her mother spoke, Joan dropped her head and closed her eyes, visualizing her desk at work. She was employed as an office manager by a mail order company that sold men's hairpieces. At the end of every day, Joan knew that adequate supplies of every grade of paper, of manila, mailing, and billing envelopes; of pencils, pens, outliners, and markers were on hand and stored in their correct place. Every shade, consistency, and style of frontpiece and toupee was in stock and all orders had been filled on the day of their arrival. Joan's desk had locking drawers, into which went her rose-colored ceramic mug, pen and pencil set, and desk clock, along with her ledgers, before she went home.

Keeping her breath even, she saw herself locking up her possessions, heard the clean, soft click of the drawer shutting tight, as her mother said, "If I was young again, like you, with your looks, that blond hair, hair like that, it would have saved your Aunt Hava's life, you don't know how fortunate you are with that hair and such pretty hazel eyes, that at least you got from me. Work. Never any men. For all I suffered, at least I had your father with me for a long time."

"Not this tonight," Joan told herself. "Not again." She made herself say, "You know Vivien, Mom."

"Sure, your best friend. Another old maid, like you. Forgive me, my unkind mouth, she's a good person. I'm glad you have a friend like that. So, how is she?"

"She's fine, Mom. She sends her love."

"Tell her hello for me. So you don't go out with nobody at all, not one young fella?"

"Mom, I've told you. All about me and Vivien."

The lines around her mother's mouth deepened and her cheeks trembled. "A friend," she said. "A friend is nice, but at your age to live alone and not even a boyfriend. Before I die, I wish I could see you have with a man what I had with your father."

Joan felt tears assemble behind her eyes. "The one beautiful thing in my life," she thought, all memories of the argument with Vivien obliterated, "the one thing special. And I told her all about it, I tried to share. It's not my fault we're not close, she's the one who won't look at anything.

"We hear only what we're ready to hear," Sharon always told her. Her Alanon friends said the same thing. Joan felt her cheeks sting and itch. A tear dropped off her chin.

"Oh, sweetheart, I know," her mother said. "You miss your father, don't you? So do I. Every day, I miss him."

Joan was dazed. It took her a moment to place her mother's remark next to the one that had preceded it. She sighed and began to wonder. Did she miss him, her ghost father? So pale, as if the confinement in Auschwitz had bleached even the potential for color right out of him. Rice paper skin and chalk dust hair that, according to her mother's recollections, had once gleamed russet.

Joan remembered her father as a stillness. She knew that they had spoken during her childhood, but, of the conversations themselves, she had no memory. She remembered his hushed jailhouse monotone. Joan had wondered how the men at the print shop, a haven for Workman's Circle socialists and holocaust refugees where her father had worked since the war's end, had ever heard him over the clamoring machines.

. . .

Joan first saw Vivien maneuvering a leaking paper plate at a lesbian singles potluck. In the only act of gallantry she could remember having performed, she came to the rescue with a straw plateholder. They found seats and she asked what Vivien did. She had to keep this composed woman, who had the kindest smile she had ever seen, talking to her. She wanted to watch that wide supple mouth produce strings of quiet sound forever.

With her clear skin, sloe eyes, and inky hair, Vivien was pretty, but not intimidatingly so. She was sensible and she liked to do things that Joan understood. They went to more potlucks and to volleyball games. They went to first-run movies and to a Chris Williamson concert. They went shopping for barbecues and coffee makers. Within a month, they had decided not to date anyone but each other.

• • •

Bill, as leader, was kicking off the meeting with his version of the Alanon story; of how his attraction to drunks and drug addicts had made his life miserable until he had found the program. Joan let her eye wander to the door, checking out the latecomers as they either tiptoed to their chairs in horror of creating a disturbance or strode boldly to the front, noisily acquiring attention.

When Emma walked in, Joan abruptly snapped her gaze back to Bill and held it there. She had rearranged her meeting schedule to avoid Emma. She no longer liked to remember that Emma had started her with Alanon in the first place. That had happened six months ago, when Emma was still the closest thing to a best friend that Joan had.

• • •

It was heaven for Joan when she and Vivien watched TV in bed and talked about their day. Joan loved knowing that Fernando, who scored higher on reading tests than the rest of Vivien's fifth graders, was the one whose ears stuck out, and that Nancy, who never talked without being asked, wrote poems. She loved to make Vivien laugh at the news that Janine, the receptionist at Joan's office, had two guys calling her at work again. She had always dreamed of evenings like those that she and Vivien shared during their first year—placid, secure stretches of undemanding companionship.

• • •

Although shorter than Joan, Emma was larger by half and, contrary to all that Joan knew to be fashion wisdom, wore strong bright colors, swirled and spiked into brazen prints. An unrestrained cloud of light brown curls wreathed her face.

They had met at an open-house brunch hosted by a lesbian and gay synagogue. Joan had gone to the function with Vivien, because Vivien wanted to learn more about her lover's culture. That visit to the temple had been Joan's first and last.

Emma, who had helped to organize the event, spotted Joan and Vivien, standing near the refreshment table by themselves, aiming nervous smiles like rotating beacons around the room. She introduced herself, found out what they did, and spent the next two hours answering their questions about her job as a social worker for an underfunded county agency, her prolonged sojourn through graduate school at night, the difficulty of finding dates in a community of couples, and the life stories of her two most troubled clients. One of those tales, that of a horrific procession through divorce to depression, unemployment, and homelessness was enough to make Joan feel, for a moment, that she was glad to be in her own shoes. By the end of the afternoon, phone numbers had been exchanged.

• • •

Joan hardly heard the Twelve Traditions of Alanon as they were read aloud. The sight of Emma had somehow moved her to worry about Kenneth, one of her first Alanon buddies. She wondered if he was reading Alanon literature in his hospital bed.

It was odd, when she considered it, that in a few months of meetings, she had become friendly with so many men. Men had always been a separate breed. Like all natural forces, they could be dangerous or benign, but never comprehensible or comprehending. But a certain group of the gay men she met in Alanon were different. They made sense to her.

They shared her preference for subtle colors, easy listening music, and deliberate behavior. Like the women she knew, they had endless appetites for the details of personal life and, like most Alanon people, they accepted the confidences she offered without pushing for more. And—unlike women—they did not, with their presence in her life, deepen the streak of worry down Vivien's forehead that divided the finely arched brows.

Joan's one and only attempt to become friends with a lesbian Alanon, a shy, wanly pretty blond who was new to Los Angeles, had marched them right up to a fight. Vivien had demanded to know why Joan would not consider either giving up her own apartment or inviting Vivien to share it. Joan could give no clear answer, but swore that her commitment to the relationship was rock solid. She was astonished and hurt at Vivien's fear that she might have sex with someone else.

"What do you have against this woman?" she asked, adding, "You never get jealous of Emma."

"Oh well," Vivien said, "Emma isn't the kind of person you get jealous of."

Joan knew that Vivien meant Emma couldn't be a sexual threat, because she was fat. She also knew that Emma, whose Fat Dykes group conducted workshops on the health hazards of weight-loss dieting, would have been incensed.

Joan changed the subject, guiltily and resentfully aware that Emma expected her to stick up for fat dykes. She promised herself to make coffee dates only with Alanon men and to see the women only at parties that she and Vivien could attend together.

. . .

Joan loved her apartment. It was made of wide, white rooms, brightened with French doors that opened onto a patio with southern exposure. The doors were open all day when the weather was warm, and until she went to bed, the slim blinds stayed up. Joan had furnished the room with blond wood, upholstered in shades of tangerine, orange, and rose. She had bought the prints that hung on her walls at an art supply store and chosen them to match her bedspread and couch.

"What else is new? You make it through another day, you thank God you're still alive."

What was her mother talking about? Joan had completely lost track.

Her mother was smiling the smile that Joan hated, which, guiltily, she thought of as "the Jewish smile." Sad, knowing, infuriatingly patient. Joan waited for the words that captioned the smile, fingernails scoring her palm. Finally, her mother brought them out. "What can you do?"

. . .

After that first, unbelievable, precious year, Joan became irritated and mystified by Vivien's increasing questions about her childhood, her internal life, and whatever ambitions she may have hidden. "We're lovers," Vivien would say. "I want to know more about you than I do. You always act like you're still on a date with me."

"What's wrong with that? Why can't we just be happy?"

"You never talk to me about anything important. You tell me about things at the office and stuff in the papers, but you never talk to me about how you feel."

Joan began to wonder if Vivien had really decided how she felt about her, if there was still some test of character she had not passed. "Don't you want to know more about *me*?" Vivien would ask.

And, eagerly, Joan would say, "Sure," and wait for Vivien to tell her something. She liked hearing stories about Vivien's childhood, growing up with six brothers and sisters in one of East L.A.'s oldest families, one of the first to claim the name Chicano as something prideful. Joan liked to imagine the child Vivien spending every summer in Sonora with her grandparents or watching her father being honored for his work with the American G.I. Forum. It all sounded so blessedly ordinary.

As a desperate teenager, stalking the secret to popularity, Joan had read that people will enjoy talking with you if you get them to talk about themselves. She became a master interviewer. Joan could suck on Vivien's stories like hard candy, making one last for an entire evening.

. . .

Emma's mother, Ruth, had named her for an anarchist. Ruth was a professor of sociology at UCLA. She was also a lesbian and one of Emma's best friends. On National Coming Out Day, they hosted a Mother/Daughter Debut.

To Joan, Emma and Ruth acted more like sisters than any mother/daughter pair she had ever known. They talked on the phone every day, analyzing every wrinkle of their lives and personalities and those of their friends. They argued passionately about convoluted issues that Joan never understood, and they were always next to each other, snuggling in a way that, Joan thought, came close to being incestuous.

The Debut was held at Ruth's house, a California stucco classic, full of alcoves and arched ceilings. Ruth had loaded it with pottery from Peru, rugs from India, and framed posters, including one of a flower, captioned, "War Is Not Healthy for Children and Other Living Things," that Joan remembered from her high school days.

Joan had no way of knowing how much Ruth's house resembled those of all her friends who had been Communists in the early fifties but had managed to escape the witch hunts and achieve tenure. To Joan, Ruth's house was a triumph of originality, a captivating and aggravating reproach to her own carefully assembled rooms.

Joan had come to the Debut by herself. She and Vivien had argued that morning over Joan's suppression of a multiple orgasm the night before. Forty-five minutes after her arrival, Joan left the party after carefully hugging Emma goodbye. Her breath stopped for a full second when Ruth swept her into a surprise hug of her own and said, "You have to make Emma bring you back. Or just come over."

Ruth's grin took a decade off her face. Her soft fuzzy skin had fallen into a veil of lines, but hung on a dramatic frame of forehead, cheekbones, and chin. Joan's clenched abdominals fluttered.

Ruth ruffled Emma's hair. "We can talk about her," she added. Emma matched her mother's grin, and a tremor of annoyance and desire tweaked Joan in the crotch. Panicked, she said that of course she'd love to come back, while her throat swelled and she felt around her pockets for her keys.

• • •

Tom was telling the group about his decision to try, one more time, to make it work with his lover of five years who had, once again, joined Alcoholics Anonymous. His dogged loyalty exasperated Joan. Watching Tom, she felt the weight of her wallet with the square of yellow paper inside it. Joan decided that she would call Kenneth at the hospital in the morning. But why was he suddenly so much sicker? He had been fine the last time she'd seen him. It felt as though that wasn't so long ago.

She and Kenneth had last met for lunch sometime after tax day, toward the end of April. It was now mid-June. Before that lunch date they had seen each other or talked on the phone every few days.

She had known for two and a half weeks that Kenneth was in the hospital. Tom had told her at a party. She hadn't been sure of what to do about it. Some people like to be left alone when they're sick. And Tom had said that it was nothing to worry about.

• • •

"How can you say, 'I love you,' when I make you sick," Vivien sobbed, her voice climbing to a shriek. That shriek knocked Joan torpid with despair. Vivien loosened her grip on self-control now and then, but not ungracefully. Usually, anger made her small voice grow more precise than ever, as she extruded syllables through adamantine lips. Joan reflected that, if she could push someone like Vivien into screaming hysteria, her chances of making anyone happy were slim.

"Look at you, you're so cold," Vivien wailed. And Joan was cold. She was chilled to the bone. Cradled in the apathy of frozen death, she watched Vivien tug her clothes on and leave. It was two o'clock in the morning. Characteristically considerate of the neighbors, Vivien did not slam the door.

Joan wanted to stay frozen. But, as soon as Vivien was gone, she felt the grating shock of an inexorable thaw. Trying to wrench her memory away from the argument, she found herself recalling it with a vivid urgency that had eluded her while the actual calamity happened.

The night had been so perfect before it fell apart. They made love so good. Joan screamed into her lover's cunt, while Vivien's tongue scoured hers.

They came together. Joan's teeth rattled and her hands and feet buzzed with rushing blood. For a heartbeat, she was drained and peaceful, safely pinioned under Vivien's passive weight, gulping rich waves of vaginal mist with every breath.

And then she was wriggling out from under Vivien, making tracks to the bathroom. Joan flushed the toilet, so Vivien would think she had gone. How could she blame her for washing her hands after that? But Vivien heard Joan brushing her teeth.

• • •

Why did Vivien have to take it personally? This was about Joan, not her lover or anybody else, Sharon always said. Joan had repeated Sharon's pronouncement to Vivien. Therapy was her high card, her proof of being willing to change. After she started therapy, they had been happier for a while.

Therapy reminded her that Vivien's passionate side had come as a surprise. No surprise was entirely pleasant to Joan. She realized further that she subscribed to a nasty stereotype; she had thought that all Catholic women were sexually repressed.

"Have you ever heard of reaction formation?" Sharon smiled at her. Joan hadn't.

"But I thought all Jews read Freud."

It took Joan a little while to get the joke. When people she met at work asked what her background was, she told them she was born in southern California.

. . .

Emma was always trying to get Joan to be more Jewish. She invited her to the frequent dinners she cooked for her friends on the Sabbath, which she called Shabat. For Hanukkah, she gave Joan a copy of *Nice Jewish Girls*, an anthology of writing by Jewish women. Joan gave Emma a matched set of potpourri, hand lotion, and perfumed soap from Crabtree and Evelyn.

. . .

After she washed her mother's dishes, Joan kissed her goodnight and made an escape. She promised more than once, as she always did, that she would come back at the same time on the following week.

Her answering machine held two messages. One from a newcomer in Alanon who suspected that her lover was out drinking. The other from Vivien. "I miss you. I'm sorry I ran out like that. I'm getting scared about us, honey. Call me tomorrow, okay?" And, resentfully, after a pause, "I love you."

Joan stroked the phone, rocking a little. Vivien would already be asleep. One more night to sleep alone, trying to know how to make everything all right. She could call Vivien before they both went to work. And go to a meeting the next night.

. . .

On the day that Ruth spoiled everything, Joan had dropped by her house and begun the visit by saying almost nothing. Soon after showing up, she told Ruth that she had been to see her mother and then fell into a miserable silence. After a while, Ruth asked, "What did your mother do during the war?"

Joan knew that Ruth didn't mean Vietnam. For several nights afterward, she would drag herself from sleep, trying to discern what she had done to make Ruth wonder. Ruth knew that Joan's mother lived in a neighborhood that Jews had settled after the Second World War. She knew that Joan's mother didn't get out much. That was all. Joan would insist to herself a thousand times that she hadn't told Ruth anything else.

When they first met, Ruth had asked why Joan's mother hadn't come to the Debut. Joan told how stubbornly her mother ignored her attempts to come out. Ruth had commiserated with a story about her own parents, who had taken the news of her sexual emergence at forty with cosmopolitan aplomb. They had invited Ruth and her lover to a party and then tried to fix Ruth up with another guest, a male writer and Bohemian legend whose entire output documented his voracious and, to Ruth's mind, narcissistic heterosexuality.

When Ruth asked about her mother and the war, Joan became an animal, listening in the dark. She heard the processes of her own body; the rush of air through the bones of her face, the inhuman click of her tongue behind her teeth, her heart's thick echo.

And then the cool outrageous softness of Ruth's neck embraced her forehead, and Joan was held and rocked. "It's all right, baby. Nothing terrible's going to happen, I promise. It's going to be okay."

Joan funneled all of her will into her eyes, trying to draw back tears. Ruth didn't let go, and they sat that way for a long time, Ruth murmuring and Joan willing her body rock hard.

"I have to leave," she said, when Ruth released her. She walked out without saying anything else. Joan never saw Ruth without Emma after that, and they never talked about that day again.

• • •

Joan was seven years old. She was on the playground, raising her hands to strike a tetherball that appeared to float high above her head, when it crashed between her wrists, effacing sight and sound in a wall of pain.

The wall splintered to a babble of voices, the metallic taste of blood and the shock of wet towels on her nose. "Better take her to the nurse," she heard. And then, as she was led away, "If that was me, I'd be crying my eyes out." And a third voice: "She's too weird to cry."

Joan sat in silence as Mrs. Moore, the nurse, swabbed her face clean. She winced at the bite of Mercurochrome, but made no sound. She watched goose bumps grow on her bare arms. Mrs. Moore had taken her dress to soak, and Joan shivered in her thin slip, the metal chair cold against her thighs.

"Everything's going to be fine, honey," said Mrs. Moore. Joan could think of no response. Her pain had begun to ebb. Over Joan's head, Mrs. Moore met the eyes of Mrs. Reed, who worked in the Principal's office. With more exasperation than admiration, Mrs. Moore said, "Any other child would be screaming bloody murder."

Mrs. Reed studied Joan with suspicion. She told her, "Don't worry, sweetie. We called your mommy and she's coming right down. It'll take her a little while on the bus, but she'll be here before you know it."

Joan's eyes filled. Her lower lip, already puffy and cut, swelled painfully. She looked desperately from one grown woman to the other.

Relieved and gratified, Mrs. Moore regarded Joan, for the first time, with real affection. She said, "You wanted your mommy, didn't you, honey?"

"No!" Joan's emphatic squawk bounced against the nurse's honeyed croon. "No!" she shrilled again.

Mrs. Moore and Mrs. Reed arched eyebrows at each other. They left Joan alone to wait. Dry-eyed again, she waited for a long time.

Without warning, she was covered by blackness and sound. The noise, a bottomless wail, rolled over her in waves. The blackness scratched at her skin. Then she was thrust backward, her shoulders gripped in her mother's strong, gnarled hands.

In a silent fury of mortification, Joan stared into her mother's face. The mouth was drawn downward, like the "tragedy" mask over the school auditorium stage. Joan's saliva shone on the black ribbed sweater that her mother had knitted for herself at home.

Moaning intermittently, her mother led Joan down the hall. Children stared from open classrooms at the crying woman in black, whose skirt hung to her calves. They pointed at Joan, whose fingers hung passively from her mother's grip. Joan looked at no one.

• • •

Ruth must have told Emma. In her good-natured, obdurate fashion, her friend began urging Joan to join a support group for children of Holocaust survivors. Joan hated the phrase. She found it pretentious and overwrought. As she was beginning to find Emma.

One day, for no reason that Joan could fathom, Emma asked her, "Have you told Vivien about your mother yet?"

The question turned Joan coldly furious. "Of course not. What for?"

"Don't you think she'd want to know? That's a very significant thing about you. And she's going to find out anyway. You know they talk on the phone now, whenever Vivien's there and your mother calls. And Vivien's working on getting invited over. How do you think she's going to feel when she finds out you haven't told her all this time?"

A seed of apprehension had, irrevocably, burst. Joan wanted to slap Emma for it. "I'll tell her when I'm ready," she said, as flatly as she could. "Let's talk about something else."

After that, Joan began to consider her friendship with Emma, like her relationship with Vivien, to be a matter for, alternately, resignation and worry. And, gallingly, for the few spare scraps of happiness she enjoyed.

• • •

At the previous meeting a week earlier, a woman named Beth had told the group that she had gone to visit Kenneth. She said that he'd been glad to see her and wanted company. Joan had resolved to drop by. Remembering that decision, she felt her neck grow cold, as though someone angry and larger than herself stood just behind her sight.

• • •

When she gave up on the children of survivors idea, Emma suggested Alanon. "It's a support group for people who work harder at pleasing others than at pleasing themselves," she said.

"Just because I'm polite," Joan thought. She didn't believe Emma's story anyway. She had heard that Alanon was a haven for eccentrics and losers. She decided that, by suggesting such a thing, Emma was telling Joan what she really thought of her. And that Emma had gotten sick of hearing Joan talk about her problems with Vivien and wanted to share the load. The fact that Emma herself had three years on the Alanon program was no refutation of her suspicions. She assumed Emma had joined Alanon to meet women.

When she first spoke up at a meeting, Joan had been unnerved to find herself in a circle of undivided attention. When she began with the traditional, "My name is Joan," and twenty people had fielded a hearty, "Hi, Joan," right back at her, Joan was stunned into silence. Nobody stepped in to take her turn. Finally, she began to speak.

"Things have been really bad with me and my lover lately," she heard herself say to a roomful of strangers. "I don't understand it, because we really love each other and I don't see why we're not getting along." She stopped, terrified. She was certain that she had betrayed Vivien and jinxed their love, that her words had brought some dormant horror into solid being. She was astonished to see that the circle was composed of distinct faces, half of whom were nodding at her words, comprehension and concern in their eyes.

Part of Joan had been convinced that Emma would dump her as soon as she made enough Alanon friends to have a social life outside of herself and Vivien. When that didn't happen, Joan allotted herself little tastes of hope. She had a lover and a best friend. She had joined a crowd that did things on weekends. Maybe everything would work out.

• • •

Joan dreamed that Emma stood naked by her bed. Emma's breasts swung easily as she rocked on columnar legs, legs like trees. Her vulva peeped like an anemone from a smoky mass of hair. Joan was naked too. The bed was in her living room, which had grown to twice its size. The patio was a wide terrace, a cliff, and below, lit by moonlight, was a plain that met the horizon. Far away, Joan could see a ziggurat, a pyramid of several levels with steps cut into it, and people climbing those steps toward a bonfire burning at the top. Joan turned to Emma and reached for her, sucking a bulbous nipple and touching the pink vulva, making them swell.

Everything changed. They were no longer in a wide hall, open to the night sky. They were locked into a tiny room with wooden walls. Joan was not surprised to hear the thump of boots on stairs and pounding at the door.

She looked at Emma, now crouched in a corner. Emma, who had aged into a flabby crone, her brown hair limp and laced with gray, her fine round cheeks fallen and trembling, watched the door with vacant-eyed passivity. Joan knew that she had to wake up before she saw the faces of those who were breaking in, but she couldn't move or make a sound. Finally, she achieved a tremble down the length of her rigid body and forced a moan past her throat. She woke to the image of a boot splintering wood.

The next time that Emma called to ask Joan to lunch, Joan said that she was sick. When Emma called again, Joan said that she had something else to do. She and Emma still said hello when they had to face each other at meetings, but they never made plans to socialize anymore. And Joan could no longer touch anyone without washing her hands.

. . .

Bill had opened up the meeting for discussion. The woman sitting next to Emma began to speak. Unwilling to look in her direction, Joan watched Jerry, her Twin. His face was red, as though he'd been sunburned. As it had been the week before.

Joan found herself staring at Jerry's neck. Under his buttoned collar, it was swollen. But the rest of him had become quite slim. Joan began to feel her heartbeat. Her thumbnail dug a channel into her forefinger's padded tip.

Tom was speaking again. Joan brought her attention to his words and heard, "So then he tried to get me to say I'd quit smoking. I told him, 'What's it going to do, kill me?' "

The eruption of laughter that followed mangled Joan's weary nerves. She had a headache. What was so funny?

Joan looked at Tom and her heart bounced hard against her ribs. Suddenly, she was engulfed by emotional clutter—anger, dread, and a strangling nausea that smelled of her mother's kitchen. Tom wasn't Jewish. What was he smiling like that for?

Joan looked at Jerry, at his hollow reddened cheeks. He was smiling too, and nodding. With that same insufferable patience. When had his blue eyes grown so dark with pain? Joan looked around the circle at Darryl and Bill, Arturo and James—did Darryl always have that spot on his forehead? All nodding and smiling. All cheekbones and bright, haunted eyes. The air grew thick with the smell of grease.

. . .

She had last met Kenneth for lunch at a West Hollywood outdoor cafe. They sat under a canvas umbrella, eating broiled chicken with something that called itself salsa and tasted like tomato aspic. He talked about Garth. She talked about Vivien.

Interrupting Joan's musings about unconditional love, Kenneth's beeper went off. Joan expected him to get up and find a phone, but he pulled an enamel box from his pocket and swallowed some pills. Kenneth said nothing about the medicine. Joan continued to talk about Vivien. Before they got up from the table, Joan said, "Well, no matter what happens, we'll both get through it. We'll find the right people for us. Maybe when we're fifty."

Kenneth smiled. Sadly, patiently, into the face of something dreadful. Joan dropped her eyes. When she raised them to Kenneth's thin, ruddy features, her shoulders pulled toward each other. She had become silently enraged.

. . .

She had not seen Kenneth since that afternoon. Now, he was in the hospital. Three weeks. And she hadn't called.

Joan's stomach spasmed hard. The room slid suddenly before her eyes. She was afraid that if she opened her mouth, she would vomit, but her lips had to open, because she couldn't breathe.

Gripping the sides of her chair, Joan began to rock stiffly forward and back, bending more and more sharply at the waist. Swaying forward and back, gasping for air, Joan looked hopelessly upward, aiming her face toward a sky she could not see and, in a voice that she had never known was hers, began to wail.

Learning the Hula

ALICE BLOCH

I couldn't stop looking at the photograph. Women in two lines, arms akimbo, fists digging into their hips, waiting to begin the dance. Garlands of green ferns and deep red leaves twining around the head, neck, wrists, ankles. Long dark hair flowing over the shoulders. An amulet at the throat. The eyes alive with intelligence and concentration; the set of the chin fierce with purpose. A strong stance.

I couldn't stop staring. I studied the photograph until I could feel the dance the women were about to perform. I saw them step off the page and into my living room, two lines of barefooted dancers swaying and bending and reaching, moving with the perfect sensuous power of women who know their own bodies.

I had begun dressing in flowing garments that felt good on the skin. I was letting my hair grow, enjoying its light touch on my neck. My feminist friends disapproved. I tried to explain to them what I was just beginning to understand: that my femininity was the source of my power, rather than its antithesis. I needed to become more like my mother and less like my father. His kind of power had gone cold in me, couldn't give what I needed anymore. I wanted to retrieve what the women had. I wanted to find in myself the power of my emotions and my body.

I stared at the photograph, and I knew these women would lead me back to my mother, back to her mother.

Grandma was the hula queen of my childhood. She was the one who sang and swayed. The one of flesh. The one with springy hair, with moist brown skin that smelled of creams and lotions. The one with large soft breasts and strong, broad hands and feet. The one who dug in the garden and knelt in the soil. The one who sang of waterfalls and rainbows and trees rustling in the wind, of orchids and plumeria, gardenia and maile. The one who loved the warm sun and the tall grass. The one who ran into the receding tidal wave to steal some of the shells exposed on the wet sand.

Crooning *hapa haole* songs from the radio, Grandma held me to her bosom and danced around the front porch. She knew nothing of hula beyond what she had learned from the Arthur Godfrey show, yet she was my first source of hula knowledge. She had never visited Hawai'i, had probably never even met a Hawaiian person, yet she came to represent Hawai'i for me.

Now she is shocked by my interest in hula. "A vulgar dance," she says. "Why would you want to write about such an unworthy subject?"

Grandma, what happened to your sea-green chiffon nightgown with the tiny pink rose between the breasts? What happened to your tropical nature, your warm, lusty, irrepressible spontaneity? What has Hadassah done to you?

Kathy and I met on the rabbi's couch. We were learning to chant from the Torah. The rabbi assigned us different parts of the same portion, to be read at the same Shabbat service. We became study buddies, practicing our chants together.

Our meetings were awkward and constrained. We hardly knew what to say to each other, so we didn't say much; we practiced chanting. Kathy brought her *tikkun*, the reference book that helps Jews prepare to read publicly from the Torah. The *tikkun* contains all the Torah portions of the yearly cycle, arranged in two columns on the page. One column shows the portion in the flame-shaped letters of the Torah scroll; the other, in normal book type, with marks to indicate the melody of the chant.

We sat leaning together over Kathy's *tikkun*, our heads and hands almost touching, practicing our chants, covering one or the other column as we became more proficient.

Kathy was then working for her father, excavating a strawberry field that was being turned into a business park. It was sad, unsatisfying work. She brought me a box of sweet red strawberries, the last that would ever grow in that field. She was courting me, and I didn't know how to respond.

On the appointed Shabbat, we approached the *bimah* together and chanted our portion. Kathy was the first reader. Her voice was thin but true; she read flawlessly. By this time I knew her part as well as my own, so I chanted silently with her.

Then it was my turn. The *gabbai*, the person whose job it is to correct any error made by the Torah reader, gave me the silver *yad*, and I used it to find the beginning of my part. My hands were trembling. My whole body was trembling. I was seized with awe, the awe of standing in a holy place, touching a holy scroll, searching for the holy word I needed, preparing to chant in public with my own female voice. No woman in my family had ever performed this act. I was the first. I was about to perform a holy, forbidden act.

I took a deep breath and sent it to my shaking hands, to my quivering throat. I opened my mouth and chanted.

In the traditional way of Jewish learning, there is no such thing as silent reading. One (and the "one" here is a boy) learns the Torah by learning to chant each verse; the words and melodies are united; the portion is chanted and discussed; the entire Torah comes to live in the student's body.

No prayer is completely silent, either. The Talmud says you should pray loudly enough to hear your voice with your ears, not just inside your head. Hearing the words in your own voice makes them real to you, makes you responsible for them, makes them part of your body. In the traditional way, Jews are taught to move the body while praying, to stand and sway and bow while saying the prayers aloud. Anyone who has attended a service in an Orthodox *shul* knows what a riot of sensory impressions this method creates, as each person sways and prays in a separate rhythm.

Beth Chayim Chadashim, the gay and lesbian synagogue where Kathy and I learned to chant Torah, is not an Orthodox *shul*. The majority of its members, like most Jews today, know little Hebrew. Congregants with Torah-reading skills are greatly valued and are expected to read publicly at least a few times a year.

Kathy is a quiet, shy woman who suffers terribly from stage fright. Nonetheless, she made herself brave enough to chant publicly on a number of occasions. I am not so shy, but the awe that shook my body when I first faced the Torah scroll to chant from it has never left me. Every experience of reading from the Torah has been highly charged with emotion.

For three years in a row I was one of the Torah readers for Rosh Hashana. The portion for that holy day tells a crucial story: the *akedah* (binding), in which Abraham nearly sacrifices his son Isaac.

The part I chanted is the most traumatic part of the story. Abraham and Isaac are hiking up the mountain to the place of sacrifice. Isaac says (and the chant here has a tentative, questioning lilt), "*Avi*? My father?" In a steady, calm cadence, Abraham replies, "*Hineni, b'ni.* Here I am, my son."

When someone says *hineni* in the Torah, a very serious conversation is beginning. When God calls, Abraham says, "*Hineni.*" So Abraham responds to his child, whom he is about to kill, in the same way he responds to God: "Here I am."

Isaac now asks where the animal for sacrifice is. Abraham says that God will provide an animal; the melody here is nervous and evasive, climbing all the way up and down the scale to look for a way out. Then Abraham and Isaac reach the place, and Abraham builds an altar. He ties Isaac to the altar, takes up his knife, and raises it to slaughter his child.

This is where my part of the reading ended. With Abraham's knife still raised, I had to step away from the scroll and hear someone recite the *bracha* that thanks God for giving us the Torah of truth and planting the life of the universe inside us. Then the next reader came to Isaac's rescue.

Every year I practiced chanting this tale of horror, using the complex, brooding melodies that are reserved for the High Holy Days. Every year I was afraid I would crack while chanting the *akedah* in front of the largest congregation of the year. I was afraid I would crumple into sobbing, or my voice would retreat to a tiny place inside me, or I would freeze and forget everything. And then every year I chanted in the clearest, deepest, surest voice I have ever had. The power of the text entered and strengthened me.

Because my lungs and voice and eyes and hands have held its words and sent them out to the congregation in melody, the *akedah* lives in my body. When I see those words in a Hebrew Bible, I hear them being chanted in my own voice. The chant resounds in my head, in my mouth, in my trunk and arms and hands.

The *akedah* is my portion. It haunts me. It has its own special place in my broken chest.

Before we'd gone to Hawai'i together, before Kathy had ever been there at all, friends sent a postcard showing the Napali coast. Kathy would stop before that picture on the refrigerator and do the stereotyped *haole* version of the hula: arms waving to one side and then the other side. Her movements became fluid, her hips supple, her joints loose and relaxed. The spirit of hula was already getting to her.

The women who dance for tourists: how does it affect them to be regarded as mindless whores? They seem to know they are doing honorable work, regardless of the attitude of their audience. They don't seem angry, but rather amused and tolerant toward the drunk men with pot bellies who drool over them and despise them.

When Harriet's daughter-in-law Pearl dances in the hotel show, she always wears a missionary dress, high-necked and long-sleeved. The night Kathy and I went to see her dance, a man in the audience called out, "She's wearing too much clothes." He wanted her in a raffia skirt and halter top, like the other dancers he'd seen at other hotels.

Pearl forces the audience to take her dance seriously, to watch her graceful, expressive movements with esthetic rather than prurient interest. I respect this, yet I keep feeling she has given in to the *haole* missionaries' insistence that the body be covered, that the woman be modestly attired and comported. She is assimilated. In some way she is betraying her culture.

But if she weren't assimilated, her dignity would be swallowed whole by the men panting over her, using her and the mai tais to work them up enough to go back to their rooms and screw their wives, pretending their wives were hula girls.

Dishonored. That's the word for it. The hula has been dishonored. Hawaiian culture has been dishonored.

These islands are overrun with honeymoon couples pulled into hula demonstrations, their new spouses urging them into the circle of performance, then videotaping them shaking their hips, plumeria leis dangling from their bright red necks. The videotapes are the evidence: "See, I was so drunk and crazy then, I even did the hula!" And the hula gets no honor, no respect. Hawaiian culture gets no honor.

The hulas of Pele are the most powerful hulas, the ones that leave me gasping for air. Their source is the fire pit, the caldera of the volcano, the home of Pele's lust and jealousy and anger. The other hulas lead only to sighs of pleasure: how pretty, how lovely and graceful. The hulas of Pele are dances of the flame in the loins.

The ascent to the volcano at Kilauea is like the ascent to Jerusalem. You know you are making a journey to a holy place, to the sacred mountain of the origin of the world.

The landscape changes. Along with the ferns and orchids and ginger, now there are *koa* trees and *'ohi'a lehua*, the sacred tree reserved for the pleasure of the goddess and of the scarlet and gold honeycreepers: the *i'iwi, apapane, amakihi, anianiau.* These birds are permitted to flit among the *lehua* blossoms and taste their nectar. We must leave the trees alone. We must not transplant them.

Some cultures transplant well. Italian, Chinese, and Jewish cultures all remain vigorous far from home. They retain their dignity in exile.

A Frenchman once told me that champagne and Roquefort cheese cannot be successfully exported overseas. Other wines, other cheeses, yes. But not champagne and not Roquefort. They lose their savor, their proper texture, their essence.

Hawaiian culture is like that. Hawai'i absorbs other cultures well, is kind to them, adopts their best qualities. But Hawaiian culture does not transplant well. To appreciate it, you have to be in Hawai'i. You have to feel the tender breeze on your skin and smell the red soil after a rain. You have to hear the music and see the hula in its proper place. In Hawai'i it's all of a piece, all precious; elsewhere, it becomes silly and trivial.

The cassette tapes of Hawaiian music don't sound the same on the mainland. I try to listen to the music in my office. I can't. Is it embarrassment? Is it the knowledge that my co-workers will not respect this music? Or is it something else?

When Kathy and I entered the plane and heard Hawaiian music playing, I felt like crying. I felt as though I'd come home.

The plane hadn't left Los Angeles yet, but it was bound for Hawai'i; in spirit it was already in Hawai'i. We were in Hawai'i, and the music sounded right. If someone had risen from a seat in the plane and begun to dance, it would have felt right. It would have been the hula, the real thing.

Iolani Luahine used to go to the edge of the Halema'uma'u crater at dawn with a bottle of whisky. She drank some and poured some into the crater as an offering to Pele, drank some more and poured some more in.

She danced sometimes in plover position, lying back on the ground with her legs folded under her. She was still dancing as an old woman, beautiful in photographs, only a few months before she died of cancer. She was *kapu hula*: consecrated to the hula. *Kapu*, taboo: separate, holy, special, frightening.

Everybody knows about the hula, but nobody knows about it. Nobody knows what it is. Everyone mentions it, makes fun of it, mimics it, uses it in advertising; but what is it? Even most of those who study and perform it don't seem to know. The few who might know aren't talking much.

It has to do with *mana*, spiritual power. It has to do with storytelling through movement. It has to do with *ka'aina*, the land, each patch of earth slowly rising from the sea to become solid and sacred underfoot. It has to do with a spirituality that is fully sexual, a power that can be graceful and delicate, a grace that involves different parts of the body moving in different ways, in different rhythms, each one true to itself yet all of them performing in harmony.

Writing about hula is beginning to frighten me. Something about the subject touches old, deep emotions. I become shaky, constantly on the verge of tears.

What does the subject have to do with me? I'm not Hawaiian, not a dancer. It's not my people, not my religion, not my culture, not my language.

Part of the fear is that I will lose my hard-won identity. Instead of feeling proud to be Jewish, I will be apologetic for being *haole*, for not being Hawaiian. Sometimes I already feel that way.

I have no business being interested in hula, no business even being in Hawai'i. I am an intruder, an interloper.

How dare I?

How dare I pretend to be something I'm not?

How dare I try to be at home on the earth, in the body, in the sea, under the sky?

How dare I try to be a woman of flesh?

How dare I, a Midwestern Jewish *klutz*, try to be nimble, graceful, enticing?

How dare I be the one to draw my arms around my own body, to hold an invisible lover to my chest, to close my eyes in ecstasy and rotate my hips slowly for the hungry audience?

How dare I be the one to dance from the spirit of the body, from the rhythm of the earth?

When I was three years old, my parents took me to Atlantic City. It was my first trip to the ocean. We had made shorter journeys to water—Lake Pymatuning, Lake Erie, Niagara Falls—but never before had I smelled the salt air and seen the breakers of the Atlantic.

My mother was large with what would soon be my baby brother Eddie, so she mostly sat in a chair while my father and I strolled the boardwalk. During one of those strolls I walked off the end of a pier and into the ocean.

I must have been in the water no more than an instant before Dad jumped in and yanked me to safety. In that instant I looked around as I sank alone, still in a standing position, to the bottom. Below me, half buried in sand, were a greenish Coca-Cola bottle and a brown leather shoe with barnacles growing on it. A few small fishes sniffed at me and swam on. Bubbles floated up from my mouth.

The underwater world was silent, magical, a place of fascination and beauty. I had not yet attempted to draw breath, an effort that would surely have filled me with salt water and terror. When Dad pulled me sputtering to the surface, I felt angry with him for startling me and interrupting my pleasure.

In our hotel room my mother gave me dry clothes and told me how much I had frightened my father. "Good girls don't jump into the sea," she said. I promised never to do such a thing again.

For many years then I was afraid of the water. I didn't learn to swim until I was a teenager.

Recently I dreamed about a mouse in an experiment. The mouse's nervous system was being destroyed from the bottom up and from the outside in, until there was no sensation anywhere but in the head. The body was there but wasn't alive. Only the poor head had any life at all.

Someone once asked me, "When you were a child, did you want to be a girl or a boy?" I don't think I'd ever considered that question in such blunt terms, but I answered without hesitation: "Neither. I wanted to be a brain."

I wanted to be a brain. That's what I was good for. Eddie was prettier. Eddie was better at sports. Eddie got more freedom. I had a brain.

I liked physical activities until either somebody scared me with safety warnings or I found out I wasn't any good. I liked wearing a baseball glove on my hand, softening the glove with linseed oil, smacking my other fist into its warm hollow, admiring its color of a Burnt Sienna crayon, throwing the ball, swinging the bat, trying to catch. I enjoyed practicing in the back yard. I had no sense of failure until I was on a team, playing competitively, and I wasn't any good. Nobody wanted me on the team. On the playground, I was a liability to my friends. I lived in terror that I would miss the ball and let my friends down—and I almost always did.

My vision was no damn good. I must have been born near-sighted, or developed myopia very early, long before my first-grade teacher discovered that I couldn't see the writing on the board. I couldn't see the ball coming at me, and then when I could see it, I was afraid it would break my glasses. I ducked instinctively away from the flying object rather than running to greet it with an open heart and a ready glove.

Meanwhile, I was the smartest kid who had ever attended the school. I think that's the truth. I was the first one they skipped, the first one they sent to the office to help file because the class lessons were boring, the first one they held up as an example of reading skill. In a big-city or suburban school, I wouldn't have been considered so exceptional. But in the small rural school I attended, I was a *wunderkind.*

"She's a brain." That's what they called me. In Cher's town, they called her a tramp and a thief. Me, they called a brain.

There's nothing wrong with *having* a brain, but it's not great to *be* a brain.

I liked the attention, but I didn't like the stigma. And then to be so poor at sports. And to have such poor vision, such thick glasses so early.

It doesn't seem fair. The eyes are a part of the brain, or at least an extension of the brain. If I had to be saddled with a weak, klutzy body, at least I could have had good eyes as an extension of my good brain.

This is why sex has always been so important to me. It's the main way I've been able to feel alive in the body, to get rid of the controlling mind temporarily.

This is why Hawai'i attracts me so strongly, why I long for Hawai'i: it's the place where I feel at home in the body, where the body relaxes and finds pleasure. It's the place where the body is good, where any kind of body is acceptable. It's the place where I can wear shorts in public without feeling that my thighs are flabby, my calves thick.

It's the place where I can be part of nature, a creature of the ocean, swimming in my brightly colored bathing suit among the brightly colored fishes. They aren't afraid of me, and I'm not afraid of them. We're just curious about each other.

Hawai'i is the place of the loosening of the body. But is this the real Hawai'i or the Hawai'i of the mind?

Am I writing about the real hula or about the hula of the mind?

For months I've been trying to contact hula teachers all over southern California. They don't return my phone calls, don't answer my letters. What am I doing wrong? Maybe calling or writing isn't the proper way to approach *a kumu hula*. Maybe I should show up at the door and chant for permission to enter. I don't think I'm brave enough.

In any event, it looks as though I won't be living in Los Angeles much longer. Kathy is sick of this city and wants to leave. I have no objection. We're planning a trip north to decide where to settle. I hope to find a hula teacher after we move.

I've lived in southern California for seventeen years, and I wonder what I'll remember about it, what parts of the landscape, the feel and smell of it, will seem worth recording some day. Very little, I suspect, and that makes me sad and somehow angry, as though the place has been stolen from me by some force other than my own inability or unwillingness to pay attention.

Then of course I might be wrong altogether. Maybe I'll remember a lot. Maybe all kinds of things will stand out as magical, special, worth writing about. Maybe my current feeling of boredom and dissatisfaction masks some deep emotion too threatening to touch yet, just as I once felt there was nothing interesting to write about my eyes, when now I feel that my poor vision is the key to my whole personality.

I'm like Leah, Jacob's unwanted wife, who went down in history as someone with "weak eyes." Period. That's why I'm clumsy and uncoordinated. That's why I daydream, thus why I write. That's why Eddie was the pretty one—because he didn't need glasses—and why I've always felt ugly. That's why I walked off the pier in Atlantic City and was rescued from adventure and excitement. That's why I'm afraid of everything. That's why my sense impressions are sometimes extraordinarily precise, and sometimes lacking altogether, as when I failed to notice that Aunt Rosalind's kitchen floor was torn up and covered with newspaper. That's why I may not remember anything about the look of now, or then again I may remember a great deal, in shocking detail.

I'm worried that the hula writing is too thin, disconnected. That seems odd, to think of the hula as thin. I'm not thin, the hula's not thin. We're fleshy, bosomy, and full-hipped. No bones sticking out, no hard edges.

If I made the hula just one part of the book, I would be less presumptuous. I wouldn't be assuming that I could "become" Hawaiian, or that I could understand Hawaiian culture sufficiently to write a whole book on this subject. I would be appropriately humble, unassuming. No one would ever be angry with me. No one would treat me with distrust. I would be happy and secure again, attached.

I feel like an island, floating away from the shore. Isolated. Once I was connected, but now I'm not. I'm scared everyone will disappear. I'll be all alone and weak and helpless.

The idea of an island is both attractive and frightening. Your world is small. You can walk all the way around it. You can climb to the center where the volcano that created the whole thing still stands, alive or dead or dormant. You can touch it all. Maybe this is why the gods are just like humans except when they go into their spirit state: humans are bigger on an island, more godlike. A visitor from another place is different enough from everyone on the island that she seems bigger than life, more important and exotic and powerful and unpredictable. Pele. The chants call her *ka wahine Pele*, "the woman Pele." If you lived on an island, it might be believable that a person could be a god.

So there you are on your island, surrounded by the familiar. Anything, anyone new is exciting and threatening. But once you were connected, your island was connected. You were connected to your mother, the island was connected to the mainland. Then everything fell apart. You floated away, alone.

Malua'e was a farmer. He raised bananas to offer to the gods and other food for his family. One day his son Ka'ali'i choked while eating one of the bananas reserved for the gods. When Malua'e returned home from planting, there was his son, dead, with a banana still in his mouth.

Malua'e grieved for love of his son, and swore that he would eat no food and would die too. The gods no longer heard him praying and he made no more offerings of food to them. After 40 days the god Kanaloa said, "We were too hasty in punishing this man who grows *'awa* and gathers bananas for us." The god Kane agreed, "Let us heal Malua'e and let him go and get the soul of his son." So the gods revived Malua'e and gave him the *mana* to go fetch his beloved son.

I read this story cursorily, and then the next morning I woke up thinking about it. What a contrast between the Hawaiian patriarch Malua'e and the Hebrew patriarch Abraham. What a wonderful father Malua'e must have been, to have loved his son so much that he would go on strike against the gods to get him back. What confidence he had in his own importance to the gods, and it turned out he was right; they noticed he was withholding his usual prayers and offerings, and they shaped up. Now Abraham had that confidence, too, when the lives of strangers were at stake: witness Sodom and Gomorrah. For the sake of strangers, Abraham stepped forward and challenged God: "Shall not the judge of all the earth deal justly?" But for the sake of his own son? Forget it.

He allowed Ishmael to be exiled without a word of protest. Worse yet, he complied with God's demand to sacrifice Isaac, again without protest. A real internationalist was Abraham. He could speak up on behalf of anyone but his own.

My father was that kind of father. He had plenty of compassion for downtrodden strangers. He pleaded the cause of the unfortunate. But he never defended his own children. Where we were concerned, he was on the side of the authorities. He exacted our obedience. He expected us to obey others in authority, and he had no sympathy with our rebellions. When a fifth-grade teacher told him I argued with her, it never occurred to him to ask whether I had good reason. He came down squarely on her side. "Mrs. Swisher says you sometimes disagree with her in class. Don't do that."

If the gods had taken my life for eating a taboo banana, he would have accepted the verdict. His worry would have been, "Where did I go wrong as a father? Why didn't I succeed in teaching her not to eat bananas?" It is difficult for me even to imagine having grown up with a father whose love didn't depend on good behavior, who would go on strike against the gods to win me back from death.

•

It's decided. Kathy and I are moving to Seattle. Roselle Bailey, the *kumu hula* we met on Kaua'i, has a friend named 'Iwalani who teaches hula in the Seattle area. Now the question is whether 'Iwalani will return my call.

I dreamed we were already living in Seattle, and we went for a drive in the green hills. It was like going up to the volcano: the vegetation became lush, the air misty. Along the roadside were some large, extremely healthy *'ohi'a lehua* trees with enormous feathery red blossoms. What happiness, to find Hawai'i in Washington!

In the hula is a true blend of sexuality and spirituality: a spiritual bodily expression of sexuality, a sexual deep emotional expression of spirituality. No matter how much it is distorted by pandering to tourists or to someone's idea of what tourists want to see, it's still there, hiding underneath, potent and delicate.

In some indirect, obscure way, it leads me back to myself, back to the self I hide, even from myself.

It expresses a power that comes directly from sexual allure. The dancer appeals sexually to the audience, and her power is thereby enhanced, not degraded or diminished.

I've been reading, reading, talking and reading and watching, but some things cannot be learned from books. It is time to learn the hula.

A miracle: 'Iwalani called. She asked the nature of my interest in hula. "I'm a writer," I said. "For two years I've been reading about hula and watching hula performances. Hula is affecting my writing."

She invited me to begin attending her class. "I think you'll find that dancing hula is different from reading about hula," she said in a mischievous voice. What does she have in store for me?

Tourists at a hula show see a woman standing in place, wiggling her hips and gesturing with her hands. They don't see that her entire body is moving. Western culture is so stiff, so hip-locked, that when a dancer moves her hips, all the audience sees moving is the hips.

When I'm practicing hula, I don't think about my hips. I think about my feet and knees. If my knees are bent deeply enough and my feet perform the steps correctly, my hips sway naturally. I don't even notice the swaying unless someone is watching me dance.

Hula is much more difficult, more physically demanding than I'd ever imagined. Every part of the body must be moving independently in exactly the right way at all times. The arms and hands, the head, the torso, the legs and feet; even the eyes must be looking in exactly the right direction. There's a lot to keep in mind, a lot for the body to learn.

I love it. It's good for me. I have no talent for it.

Dancing hula to an ancient chant is like reading Torah in the synagogue. This is the oral tradition, the way the culture was passed down before there was writing and reading. This is the song of the universe, the dance of the universe. This is the sing-song melody of the ancient texts. This is the sound of the texture of the life of our ancestors. "Our" here doesn't mean Jewish or Hawaiian, but belonging to all of us. Belonging to the family of humanity.

I never thought I'd use a phrase like "the family of humanity."

Distinctions and differences have been too important to me. Now I am delving into similarities, into the ways we are all alike.

When I asked Carrell, the other writer in the *halau*, to help me learn a new choreography, she said, "Do you want me to write it down for you?"

"It wouldn't help," I said.

"Let me give you a piece of unsolicited advice," she replied. "Use your strengths. You are a writer. Use your ability with words to help you learn the dance. Don't deny yourself the use of your strengths."

I resisted, but she was right. I watched her and wrote down the steps and the accompanying hand movements, and the next day when I was practicing and couldn't remember the dance, I looked at my notes and was able to figure it out.

I guess it's okay to use my strong side; but I want hula to develop my weak side. The back and neck pains I've been suffering for the past couple of months seem to result from shifting to the left (the feminine side, the side of emotion) instead of relying on the strong right side to do all the work. I have tried to force myself to learn the chants by hearing them before reading them (that is, before approaching them intellectually). I would rather learn the dances by memorizing them in the body. But perhaps I've been too rigid in taking this approach, for the basic method of the class is that of the body; surely it won't impede my growth too much if I take some notes to guide me.

"*Ai ha'a*," calls 'Iwalani. "Dance low to the ground. Bend your knees." My knees say, Oh no you don't! They don't want any part of this hula business. They're busy becoming stiff and old. None of this bending and swiveling for them. They thought I gave it all up when I gave up karate. They thought I'd settle for walks around Green Lake a couple of times a week. And my back thought I would let it become more and more rounded, with my neck sticking out in front, my head poking into the world, testing and inspecting, trying to get a closer view before I let my body move into things. For hula I am learning to keep my head balanced on my body, to go into the world toe first or chest first or pelvis first. When I stand in a balanced position, in what should be a natural position, it feels artificial. It feels as though I'm thrusting my body forward too much, as though I'm leaning my head back, as though my breasts stick out too far. My hips want to arch back, not forward. My knees want to be straight, not bent. My head, above all my head wants to run the show.

'Iwalani helps me position my hands. "Hula position," she says. "Your hands should be at the level of the middle of your boobs." She places my hands where they should be, and I hold them there, stiff and rigid, the wrists and fingers perfectly straight. (Is this a habit I learned from karate? Or is it just that I'm terribly tense, wanting so badly to do it right?) 'Iwalani pulls on my fingers to make them relax into a more graceful posture. Lovely hula hands indeed. Not these stumps of mine. Not these stubby little fingers with the cuticles all chewed up.

The volcano erupts from the belly of the dancer. The caldera is a large circle starting from the dancer's waist and reaching around and forward, the arms forming a circle in front, the fingertips meeting, the palms toward the audience. Pele crunches the ground with a fist on each side pushing down, a strong, angry gesture, while the knees push out in *'uehe*, an astonishing step in which the legs seem to flap open like wings and snap shut again. Sometimes we imitate Pele and she is a woman, sometimes we point up toward her and she is a god.

One of the students asked 'Iwalani a question about the choreography of a recent performance. "I don't know," 'Iwalani said. "I was chanting. I didn't see the dance." Then she asked us why she wouldn't have seen the dance for which she was chanting. I chose the obvious explanation: her position at the back of the stage prevented her from seeing the dancer. But Lena, an experienced dancer and chanter, knew better: 'Iwalani didn't see the choreography because she was concentrating on the rhythm of the dancer's feet, so that her chant and beat would match it perfectly.

Until now I've heard and read accounts only from the point of view of the dancer: the dancer is connected to the chant as if by a thread that causes her to move; the chanter beats the *ipu*, and the dancer's body reacts as if automatically. Here is the flip side: the chanter isn't really in charge. It's a collaboration, like chamber music. The dancer senses the beat and responds to it, and the chanter focuses on the dancer's feet and beats to match their rhythm.

The simple *kaholo,* the basic stereotypic hula motion, looks as though it would be boring to do, but it isn't, at least not to this beginner. It's a deeply satisfying movement that pulls the whole body into alignment and creates its own swaying state of grace. It's a more active movement than it appears, curving but not excessively soft, gentle but strong in the posture, close to the ground but moving, moving, coiling and uncoiling in a lovely serpentine motion that just plain feels good to the body.

The *kaholo* increases communication with the audience. When we do this step, we move back and forth across the performing area, in front of the audience, and thus they can all see and we can make eye contact with all of them. The effect is similar to that of a teacher who moves around in front of the class; more students are "touched" by the roaming teacher than by the teacher who stands behind a podium.

The hand gestures that often accompany the *kaholo* also foster communication: gestures of unfolding or of presenting forward. *Here, this is for you. This dance is for your pleasure.*

"Focus your eyes, Alice," says 'Iwalani. "You are moving correctly, but you're not focusing. When you don't focus, you are pretending it's not you doing the dance. It is you. You're dancing. Focus."

It takes a long time to find the right teacher. Sometimes it takes one's whole life.

And here I'd thought I was just doing research.

Kathy and I hiked a couple of miles from the end of the road, over the 1990 lava flow, to the place where fresh red lava was pouring out into the ocean. The *pahoehoe* lava under our feet was shiny blue-black, opalescent on top, with an iron-red underlayer. In some small fissures there were glassy golden strands known as "Pele's hair"; in others, gemlike chunks of translucent rock with a blue-gray cast: "Pele's tears."

The rivers of lava, hardened where they cooled, formed graceful, swirling shapes, each one ending in a rounded knob (*ihu,* or "nose" in Hawaiian). We walked crosswise over them, past the rubble of a visitor's center, to where the rock became warm. Small fountains of steam escaped from cracks in the ground. When I put my hand down into those cracks, I could feel the heat of the molten center, the red core.

I wanted to remove my shoes and dance *Kua loloa*, an ancient hula portraying Pele, in a jealous rage, destroying Hi'iaka's beloved *'ohi'a lehua* forest with a huge, destructive eruption of lava.

Ihu e ihu la, hulihia la i kai
Ihu e ihu la, hulihia i uka
The nose of lava flows to the ocean for comfort;
The nose of lava turns back toward the mountain.

The lava rolls over the landscape, devouring it. The torn-up branches are gray from the heat of the goddess. The Woman heaps fragments of rock in a smoky jumble.

Ua wawahi'a, ua na ha'aha'a
Ua helelei, helelei, helelei
All is crumbled, smashed, shattered,
Leveled into dust.

There were too many people around. I didn't dare to dance. Instead, I formed the hand gestures as I hiked: fists pushing down slowly from the armpits to the hips, the hands then opening to cross in front and spread to the sides. In these gestures I imitated the goddess strewing lava over the land. In these gestures I became Pele.

At the edge of the island, the black rock opens in a great gash. Red liquid pours into the sea, where it explodes into tiny fragments of black sand. The black finger of rock probing the sea grows larger; the red lava pushes forward from it. Thus the land grows, in convulsive gushes of red.

In Auntie Nona Beamer's version of the Pele legend, Pele's uncle Lono taught her to make fire. Armed with this secret knowledge, and carrying her baby sister Hi'iaka in her bosom, Pele went out in search of a home. The sea goddess was jealous and traveled about, quenching Pele's fire on each island until Pele arrived at the one place where water couldn't reach: the caldera of Halema'uma'u on the Big Island of Hawai'i. In the fire pit Pele found a congenial home for her fiery nature.

So Pele, the goddess of the volcano, did not create the volcano. She took possession of the volcano. She assumed control over a force of nature that already existed. She had to search for the right place to exert her power, the place where she could become a goddess.

She consorted with humans, so her body form must have been human-sized. Pele the goddess is simply a woman with special authority and special powers. Her *mana*, her spiritual power, is exceptional, but her body is a normal female body. Therefore, each of us has the body of a goddess; can we also attain the power of a goddess? How large a spirit can we aspire to?

If the body is the vehicle of spirit—not just its container—if the spirit of the body is *the* spirit, then our bodies give us the means to that power.

In a traditional *halau hula*, students are taken to the beach to begin learning to chant and dance. They rise early and walk down to the ocean, where they practice swaying with the motion of the water. They kneel on the beach and chant into the waves.

If you use your deepest, most powerful voice, the outgoing waves carry your spirit all the way across the ocean, to all the other islands and to all the continents of the world. If you chant from your very center, your voice merges with the voice of the sea. Your voice changes the world. Your voice changes you.

When you fill your chest with air and chant in a good strong voice, the shark flips his tail in rhythm. The surface of the water undulates. The palm and pandanus trees wave their branches in the breeze. The long-haired seaweeds flow through the graceful curve of hip and waist. The dancer weaves a perfect dance through the waves of sound.

When you chant, the gods hear you. The world hears you. Nature hears you.

When you beat the *ipu* and chant, you follow the rhythm of nature and you change the rhythm of nature. The dancer moves to the rhythm you create, and you watch the dancer's feet and make your rhythm match her dance.

When you use your voice as it was meant to be used, you create harmony. You are whole. You are at one.

Poker Face

ROBIN STROBER

I don't have a girlfriend because my hair is falling out. My hair is falling out because I don't have a girlfriend. Chicken-egg. Egg-chicken. Bok. Bokbokbok Bok.

I've attributed *the thinning* to smog, caffeine, hair dye, fluorescent lighting, anxiety, not enough sex, and way too many Snak-Wells cookies. I've tried endless combinations of elixirs, potions, and powerful salves to stave off this ebbing tide, but nothing seems to work.

I'm at Anna's house. She's a wigmaker. Joe and Twig Eddie are on their way over to pick me up and take me to Las Vegas. We do this once a year, go to Vegas. We are Wayniacs and Liberace-lovers of the first order. We are also low on cash.

Anna makes expensive lace-front wigs for film and TV stars, and not all the wigs are worn on the set, if you catch my drift. I've got the 411 on their hirsute histrionics, but Anna's sworn me to secrecy. When inquiring minds want to know, she lets me give out initials. Here are a few famous wig wearers: C.L., R.A., P.M., & N.K. Anna says I'm in good company because a very famous runway model, teetering on supermodel status, has one serious female-pattern balding problem and owns ten lace-front wigs made by Anna at a cool $3,000 a pop. The catwalker recently hired a full-time wig handler.

I, however, will not be paying $3,000 for my jet-black bubble bob. The barter system will be employed here. I will trade homemade desserts, movie tickets, and sexual favors.

Well, maybe not sexual favors. Anna broke up with me last year, so I'm not sure where we stand on the sexual favor front, and personally, I think she'd rather have my cherry pie, just like Humbert Humbert did when he saw the sticky sweet Dolores lounging in Charlotte's yard. I must tell Anna to name one of her creations "The Lolita."

I've always maintained that Anna dumped me because of my thinning pate, but she patently denies this. She says, "Bettina, why would I do that when I can outfit you with an exquisite wig that's far, far superior to anyone's real hair?" She did make me a gorgeous wig which I named "The Stanwyck" after B.S. in *Double Indemnity,* but she dumped my follically challenged ass anyway.

Anna is making me a new rug because "The Stanwyck" flew off my head while motoring on the Hollywood Freeway in my Karmann Ghia convertible. It landed on the hood of the car behind me. The guy got my plate number and tried to sue. He said he'd almost had a heart attack when he saw a dark and furry thing flap toward his windshield.

I watch as Anna meticulously weaves in strand after strand of high-quality Peruvian human hair, her hands as steady as a brain surgeon's. It takes weeks to make one wig and the eye strain and boredom are considerable. Anna has taken to wearing jeweler's goggles and listens to books on tape. Last year she learned conversational Portuguese.

"Hurry! They're here," I say, as the high-pitched bleat of Joe's horn fills Anna's incubator-sized workroom. Anna pulls the bandanna from my head. "Whoa! Telly! When did you shave your head?"

"I've been buzzing it for a while now. I didn't want to look like a garmento with a comb-over. I'm not brave enough to walk around without a *schmatte* on, but this feels a lot better than that cotton candy cloud I had before." I tug on a hank of Anna's decidedly non-wig hair, her auburn corkscrews bouncing like little Slinkys.

"Please come with us to Vegas."

"I can't, Bettina. I've got to finish L.T.'s hairpiece and we're not supposed to be spending so much time together. You're supposed to be looking for love."

"In all the wrong places."

Anna lifts the wig from its styrofoam form and slowly, as if bestowing the Miss Universe crown, places it on my head. "Like flies to honey. Don't worry. You'll catch in this one. It's what you wanted. 'The Emma.'"

"Hey, Miss Peel," shouts Twig Eddie from the back seat of his and Joe's Lotus Elan. I am wearing the quintessential Emma outfit—black ribbed T-neck, black vintage ski pants, and black go-go boots. My lips are slathered with Yardley Petals O' Pink Lipfrost. Joe opens the passenger door for me and silently nods his approval.

It feels great to be on the open road, wind in my hair (well, in somebody's hair), flipping off truckers as they shout obscenities at us, twirling the radio dial in search of the perfect easy listening station. We talk about various Vegas ventures: bankrolling a nude in-line skating revue called *Vague-us* or opening a health food cafe called Las Vegans, but we think the joke might be lost on the Mickey Dee crowd.

I met Joe at a cruisy Gambler's Anonymous meeting in West Hollywood. I was looking for Ms. Right and so was he. He was also looking for some serious help. He had just lost $25,000 in a slot machine tournament. Our eyes locked at the coffee urn, me admiring his quixotic good looks, he thinking I bore a striking resemblance to Dorothy Hamill. (An Ice Capades phase. My own hair, thank you very much.) Joe and I became instant friends and before the meeting was adjourned, we were on a plane to Caesar's Palace.

Joe and Twig Eddie have been together for five years. They got married in Vegas on our last trip. I cried when Elvis pronounced them man and machine. (Joe held a minicam to his eye the entire ceremony.) I was so happy for them. But I was sad too. I want to get married in Vegas. I want to register at major department stores and fine specialty shops everywhere. It all seems so hopeless. In my roaring twenties, things were different. I met women. I dated women. I slept with women. There was always an adventure in a Jetta to light out on. But now, at thirty-two, the well seems to have run dry. The women I meet are either cocooned in a couple or are a little bit nutty. But who am I to talk? I sleep with my head wrapped in a mentholated hair regrowth and pore augmentation turban.

Joe always knows how to pace the trip so we reach the bend in the road where the bleached-out Strip hotels rise from the desert floor just as the sun drops behind the hills, leaving the distant city pitched in an eerie pastel light. Joe wants us to think he has an organic sense of timing, like how we slip into town just as the neon clicks on. But I know he consults the Farmer's Almanac.

Twig Eddie asks Joe if we can go to the secondhand shops in search of old showgirl costumes. He shakes his head no. In all of our trips together, we have never seen Vegas by day. Joe won't let us. He says it would jinx the pull. He says we've seen it. It's like L.A., but without all the pretty people. Once, at high noon, I tried to sneak a peek out the hotel drapes, but Joe caught me. He tucked me back into bed and put five crisp $100 bills under my pillow. But that was in the old days, when my stars were better aligned. In those days, we tried to add to our riches. Now, we just try to pay the rent.

"What came first, the neon or the darkness?" asks Twig Eddie, as we pass a busload of Japanese tourists.

"Why neon, of course," answers Joe. "You ask me this every year and every year, Twig, I tell you the same thing. God was in his garage puttering around with some inert gases and glass tubing and he created these wonderful bars of colored light that spelled out words and pulsed pictures. He said, 'By God, this is stark raving beautiful.' But alas, he couldn't see it for the bloody, screaming sunshine. God needed some darkness to admire his creation, so he dreamed up the moon and the stars and a black velvet sky. And since the desert sky is the darkest and most magical of all of God's vistas, he knew this was the place where his neon would really fly. And hence, the birth of Las Vegas."

Twig Eddie got his name while helping his father, an old surfer dude, wax his cherry 1964 Mustang convertible (original owner!). Eddie ran toward the house to answer the phone and walked right into a tree. A branch impaled his left eye and he was rushed to Cedars Sinai. He sat in the emergency room for hours while the doctors tried to figure out how to remove the gnarly bough.

"Call the Mayo Clinic!" his mother cried.

"I need to leave. My wait shift starts in half an hour," Eddie said with a spooky calm. Finally, an Indian doctor with a gentle hand and an even nerve sat Eddie down in an operating theater, and to a packed house, yanked the branch from the socket. Eddie asked if he could keep it, but before the good doctor could answer, his mother grabbed it and snapped it over her knee.

"Luck be a lady tonight . . . ," whistles Joe, as we swoop down on the Krypton Kingdom, gliding through the back streets and alleys in our resolute search for the perfect win. Every year we raise the stakes, blurring the line between self-aggrandizement and self-destruction. We've whittled our ATM cards down to whisper-thin sheets.

We zoom down an alley where boxy condos are linked together like stucco charm bracelets. I see a woman in a window watching a large-screen TV. She is drinking from a 64-ounce liter of diet cola. Joe stops the car. I pull out my binoculars and zero in on her. A plastic nametag hovers above her gummy cleavage. MAGDALENA, Salt Lake City, UT. With one eye trained on some throbbing technicolor tryst, she pulls her damp tips out of a soiled cocktail apron and puts them on an end table. I aim the crosshairs on her long, lustrous locks and ask myself this question. Would I rather live her low-cal life with a wondrous mane of hair or be bald and be me?

I cannot answer this question.

When we get to the room, Twig Eddie inspects the honor bar and Joe lies down and naps. I run a bath, and as it fills, I sit on the edge of the tub and throw playing cards face down on the steamy surface. "Ten of hearts," I say. I turn the card over. It is the ten of hearts. I do this again and again. Each time I am right. I am warming up for tonight. Joe and Twig are counting on me. They need me to make a wrong thing right. The perfect roulette spin. A flawless poker hand. Twenty-one.

"Don't we look like the moddest of squads," says Joe.

"The Avengers," I correct, as we walk down the Strip toward the Dunes Hotel. Joe is wearing a dark, boiled-wool suit. He sports a white shirt, a striped cravat, and Beatle boots. He carries a silver briefcase. Twig Eddie wears all black and an ersatz goatee. I wear a vintage silver Courreges minidress, glittery opaque tights, and white, zip-up-the-back go-go boots. We are headed to see Wayne Newton perform at the Dome of the Sea, a restaurant that is attached to the Dunes. From the outside, the Dome is an exotic-looking structure, a clam-shaped vessel—white and spherical, not unlike a UFO.

We're early for the show so we decide to try our luck in the gaming room. The casino is spread out before us like a bubbling laboratory experiment. The fry cooks and confidence men, the blackjack brides, the dentists and call girls, pickpockets, housewives, loan sharks, all hurrying somewhere. Somewhere to win.

As we walk toward the slot machines, I stop and listen to the sounds. I love the sounds. The gush of metal on metal as slot machines shit quarters. The colors are magical. J'adore the colors. A Royal Flush, red and black fanned out on brilliant green felt; three cherries on the center line; a trio of red, white, and blue sevens; the orgasmic groan of coins being released from the cache, dumped with a spent thud into the copper tray below. I take a shortcut through the endless rows of slots that shine like supernatural gas pumps. I stop at one called *Treasure Island.* It has a bright glow, an aura around it. I sink three quarters in and pull the beckoning handle. Two wooden pirates' chests and a purple mermaid line up. There is a moment's delay while the machine sizes up the situation. Then a rush of coins falls out. I scoop the loot into a plastic bucket. Two-hundred fifty dollars in quarters. I hand the bucket to Joe. "Here's your car payment," I say. "Let's go. Wayne awaits us."

I push on the seashell door handle of the Dome of the Sea.

"Hello, Bettina," says Mario, the wizened maitre d'. "So happy to see you again."

"Charmed, I'm sure," I say, reaching for his white-gloved hand.

"Goldfinger" is playing over the sound system. An ancient bartender stands in front of a gurgling, yet curiously empty fish tank, carefully drying a shot glass. His gold pinky ring clinks against the rim as he holds it up to the light. Mario escorts us to a horseshoe-shaped booth that resembles a teacup or an inverted mushroom. The Dome is nautical and naughty. The room is dark, lit only by candles. A school of slide-projected fish swim round the circular walls in a mad and swirling rush. I feel as if I am sitting on the ocean floor.

An elderly waiter in a cropped black jacket takes our drink order. A sidecar for me, a metropolitan for Joe, and a chocolate milk for Twig Eddie. "Liberace performed here, you know," Twig Eddie says. "He caused quite a sensation in the early seventies coming out on stage wearing red, white, and blue hotpants and knee-high platform boots."

"I think that was at the Hilton, Twig," I say politely. "But Marlene Dietrich performed here in nineteen fifty-three in a men's pinstriped suit. Talk about drag kings. Ooh-la-la."

As we sip our cocktails, we take in the crowd. It's a lively mix of women decked out in poodle perms and sequined sweaters and their tubby hubbies in golf shirts and double-knit pants. But my heart aches for the days, when probably, at this very same table, sat Frank Sinatra, Liberace, a very young Barbra Streisand, and the haughty Prince Romanoff with his wretched little lap dog. The dog apparently ate filet mignon off a gold plate. Liberace cut it up for him into tiny pieces.

I don't tell the boys, but I've had several sex dreams about Wayne so erotic and vivid, I am sure it means (1) I am straight, (2) I am attracted to scary, greaseball entertainers, or (3) I find myself desiring female to male transsexuals.

Although we have seen this show countless times, it always feels like the first. A spotlight shines on a large disco ball and a spaceship floats down from the rafters. Wayne jumps out of it and we three gasp as he strips off his silver spacesuit.

Progressively, through the course of the show, Wayne loosens his bowtie, takes it off, and opens the top three buttons of his shirt, unleashing a clot of gold medallions that rest on his obscenely hairy chest. We exchange knowing glances as he throws his jacket into the wings and turns his back to the audience so we can discover, yet again, that his tuxedo's vest and pants are actually sewn together, a one-piece polyester jumpsuit that zips up the back. We delight in his unnaturally stiff black hair, his gleaming capped teeth, his coal-black, stuffed-animal eyes. We bask in the glow of his fake-and-bake tan and his small, tight paunch. We revel in his high-heeled patent leather ankle boots and how he punches the air with his diamond-ringed fist and shouts, "Jam on it," like some big, bad rap star.

During "MacArthur Park," as Wayne reaches down to the crowd and kisses two elderly women in shimmery stretch pants and midriff tops, I suddenly remember a dream I've been blocking. It is the dead of winter. Wayne lays me down in a Dr. Zhivago snowdrift. "Lara's Theme" is playing. He lifts up my petticoat. I unzip his jumpsuit. . . .

When I snap back to reality, Wayne is on his third encore. The crowd is putty in his hands. I look over and Twig Eddie is cradling Joe in his arms. They are singing along with the swaying crowd. The crowd has come together in a dentured lovefest. Wayne takes a shallow bow and bolts off the stage. The lights go up. People clutch canes and walkers and slowly inch back to the casino.

"We heart you," shouts Twig Eddie, banging on his chest like a crazed marsupial.

"Come on, Bettina. It's almost time," says Joe, picking up the silver suitcase. I wave goodbye to Mario and blow him a kiss.

As we walk through the lobby, we pass a group of pasty-skinned conventioneers. Rick, Nick, Dick, Mick. They are computer programmers with plastered-down hair and drip-dry shirts. Joe stops near them, opens the suitcase, pulls out a small white veil, and pins it to my head.

I circle the tables. My tentacles twitch as I feel out the situation. I become a channel, a vessel for the ebb and flow of chance. I am looking for the sort of Monte Carlo table at which Emma Peel might be found. Gentry in black watch cummerbunds, starlets in tiaras and white fur capelets. But the roulette tables are filled with weary Central Casting types. Men in ten-gallon hats and white-pumped office girls out on stolen sick days.

I begin to chant. "I am a bride. I am a bride. I am a bride." I walk toward the blackjack table, aching to feel twenty-one again. I yearn to see the neat cut, the breezy whir of the shuffled deck, to spew the saucy words, "Hit me," with a pent-up zeal only a virgin could proclaim.

"How about there," says Joe, pointing to a crowded table. Under a cloud of smoke stand two pretty, portly women, possibly a mother-daughter team; a square-jawed guy I recognize from the *International Male* catalogue; a skinhead in an army jacket and white-laced Doc Martens; a uniformed flight attendant with hair enough for three people; and a little man, a midget maybe, with a normal-sized head, puffed-out chest, and a very small body. He is wearing a tuxedo and sits on the lap of another man, his wheelchair cast off to the side, folded up like an origami butterfly.

I settle in next to the two women. They are speaking to each other in Russian; their lilting tones giving the table a much needed air of intrigue.

Twig Eddie and Joe stand behind me.

I am fixating on the little man. He looks like a puppet on a ventriloquist's lap. One skinny leg is haphazardly thrown over the other, his shiny black shoe dangling weightlessly at a contorted angle. He whispers something to his partner, and as his companion leans toward the table to place a bet, the bottom of the little man's shoe becomes visible. The sole is shiny and new, a pristine place which no phlegm, gum, mud, tacks, toilet paper, or dog shit has ever sullied. It occurs to me that these shoes have never touched the ground. They are purely ornamental.

"Okay folks, let's get our feet wet. Place your bets," says the croupier.

The skinhead makes a square bet—four $1 chips at the intersection of four numbers.

The flight attendant, the Russian women, and the male model put their chips down in modest amounts.

I open the suitcase and put ten $100 chips on black number six.

Everyone stops what they are doing.

"You're betting one thousand dollars on a straight," says the stewardess.

"Is there a law against that?" I snap.

"Dollface, it's called the law of averages," says the dealer.

"I'm not average," I retort.

"I can make that kind of money in an hour," says the male model.

I notice he has bet $10.

Passersby with a sixth sense for suicide gather round the table, hoping to watch a bigger loss than their own.

The croupier spins the wheel.

"I am a roulette degenerate," I cry. "Let the chips fall where they may!"

Spectators look away in fear as the wheel takes flight. Twig Eddie and Joe bury their heads in each others clavicles. But I take a different tack. I stare down the little white ball, the pure sphere, the ovarian egg. I dare it to wrong me. The wanton spinning makes me giddy. I see carousels and '45's and spin cycles and race tracks and tide pools and halos. The wheel is a life force and it spins for me. Joe puts his hands around my neck, ready to press the jugular. And then the wheel stops spinning.

"I—am—a—bride," I exclaim.

There was never a question of the outcome. No click of the stick, the fickle spindle brushing back and forth ever so slowly between numbers like Chinese water torture.

"Beginner's luck," says the skinhead.

"It has nothing to do with luck," I say. "Read John Scarne's book on gambling. Pay special attention to the chapter on the concentration system."

"What providence," someone whispers.

"What a great dress," murmurs another. Joe grabs the cash-out slip from the dealer and races with Twig Eddie to the cashier's booth. I walk over to a slot machine, sit down, and reapply my lipstick. The little man whirs by. "Hi," he says, as he pulls up next to me.

"Where's your friend?" I ask.

"He wasn't my friend. He was just some hombre standing around looking bored. I asked him to help me out."

"He didn't mind you sitting on his lap?"

"I'm light. And I don't bite."

"I do. Maybe that's why I can't find anyone to sit on mine."

"Where are those guys you were with?"

"Probably at the used car lot buying a Lamborghini. What's the tux about?" I ask.

"I was best man at a wedding." The little man reaches out to touch the wig. "You've got such bouncin' and behavin' hair," he says.

I sit back, afraid he might accidently pull it off. "Why, thank you kindly," I say in my best southern drawl, tugging at the wig to make sure it's on straight. "You wouldn't mind if I had a little look-see at the bottom of your shoe, darlin'?"

Without hesitation, as if asked this question every day, he puts his foot in my lap. I clutch his ankle and raise the tiny black oxford to my face. The slippery bottom is cool to the touch. I slide it over my eyelids, my neck and mouth, where my lipstick catches and drags a line of pink across his sole.

"What's your name?" I ask.

"Wayne Newton."

"Get out!" I say. "Let me see some form of identification."

He pulls out a Visa card.

"I have got to tell this to Joe and Twig. They just won't believe it. Wayne, are you looking for love?" I ask, as I try to memorize his account number.

He swipes the card out of my hand. "In all the wrong places, Kreskin."

"Well then, why don't you come down the street and have a drink in our room?" I ask.

By the time we meander upstairs it is morning and the boys are sound asleep. The glare from the muted TV gives the room an icy blue glow. "Let's go out on the terrace," I whisper, as we slip behind the drapes.

Joe was right. By day, Vegas is a gnarly city. Flat and colorless, like the hotel rocketed up and then slammed down in some lackluster and alien place. My eyes smart from the glare.

"Bettina, you really do have the most enchanting hair," says Wayne, as he whirls around in circles.

"Hair'em, scare'em," I bellow, as I arch my back over the railing, letting the wig slide slowly off my head, down to the pavement below.

Notes on the Contributors

Nancy Agabian

I started to write "Ghosts and Bags" two years ago when I had to do a reading for *Blood Whispers: LA Writers on AIDs, Vol. 2,* and I wanted to read something in honor of George Stambolian. I struggled really hard to create something the day of the reading and I remember all these false starts with my pencil and large handwriting in my notebook and I cried a lot. I think it is the saddest piece I have ever written. Sadness is okay, but I am a performance artist and part of my love for writing and performing is the opportunity to make people laugh. But I believe this piece is performing one of the most noble duties that art can execute: it is breaking a small pocket of silence in the world.

Pat Alderete

"Victor the Bear" was begun in a Latina writers workshop, in response to an assignment to describe a favorite photograph. Like many of my stories, it has its roots in my life experiences. I am currently working on a collection of short stories that reflect my history as an urban Chicana veterana who was born and raised in East L.A. and came of age during the politically turbulent Movimiento of the 1970s. I am concerned with maintaining the integrity of my characters and with preserving the authenticity of their voices. A dream of mine is to share the gift of writing with teenage barrio girls in East L.A.

Donna Allegra

My poetry, fiction, essay, reviews, and cultural reportage are largely variations on the theme of writing I do in my journal. I've been keeping one since my teens. Fiction has been the song I've been singing most strongly these past few years. The other large part of my life has been spent in the playing fields of dance class: African, jazz, and hip hop. I write a lot about dancers and that locale because my heart lives largely in class. My publications include: *SportsDykes,* edited by Susan Fox Rogers; *Lesbian Erotics,* edited by Karla Jay; *All the Ways Home: Short Stories about Children and the Lesbian and Gay Community,* edited by Andy Rizzo, Jo Schneiderman, Lisa Schweig, Jan Shafer, Judith Stein; *Queer View Mirror,* edited by James C. Johnstone and Karen X. Tulchinsky; *Dyke Life: From Growing Up to Growing Old—A Celebration of the Lesbian Experience,* edited by Karla Jay; *My Lover Is a Woman—Contemporary Lesbian Love Poems,* edited by Lesléa Newman; *Lesbian Short Fiction,* edited by Jinx Beers; *The Wild Good: Lesbian Photographs & Writings on Love,* edited by Beatrix Gates; and *Close Calls: New Lesbian Fiction,* edited by Susan Fox Rogers.

Hannah Bleier

I came back to my apartment at the Simpson Arms after having a colon cleansing and attending my anger management workshop. I turned on the news. The newscaster said Governor Pete Wilson was trying to close L.A. County Medical Center. I turned off the TV, said a few affirmations, and sat down with a soothing cup of tea to pen my daily thoughts. I wrote for a while before becoming sleepy and retiring for the night. The story was there, written in my hand, when I looked at the journal the next morning.

Alice Bloch

"Learning the Hula" is an excerpt from *This Body,* a book I've been working on for nearly ten years. I became fascinated with hula during a fairly typical vacation trip to Hawai'i. As I followed the obsession—seemingly an odd one for a Midwestern Jewish lesbian intellectual—it led me into a wide, deep territory: the intersection of sexuality and spirituality; the sources of personal and communal power, and the forms of its suppression; the nature of bodily experience. Exploring that territory has been difficult, risky, and rewarding work. I am thrilled that the editors of *Hers* have selected this writing for the anthology. My other books are *Lifetime Guarantee* and *The Law of Return* (both published by Alyson). I am a member of the editorial board of *The Lesbian Review of Books.* I feed the birds of Seattle with my partner, Sharon, and make my living as a technical writer.

Mary Bucci Bush

"Love" is a chapter from my novel-in-progress, inspired by my grandmother's experiences on a Mississippi Delta cotton plantation to which Italians were illegally imported at the turn of the century. While life there was "a hell," there were bright spots, including friendly relations between Italians and the blacks who taught them to speak English and work cotton. I wanted to bear witness to the Italian experience and to the love that sometimes bloomed between girls who played and worked together, innocent of the racial biases that would later drive them apart. I am associate professor of English and Creative Writing at California State University at Los Angeles; my short story collection *A Place of Light* was published by Morrow in 1990.

Nona Caspers

Nona Caspers' novel, *The Blessed,* was published in 1991 by Silverleaf Press. Her stories have appeared in *CALYX, Sinister Wisdom, Hurricane Alice, Women on Women 2,* and *Word of Mouth.* She teaches creative writing in San Francisco. "Vegetative States" surfaced after years of school and work fatigue, but was specifically triggered by a phone call from my mother who had spent the day praying the rosary in my Auntie Jenny's hospital room. Jenny now breathes on her own; I have no explanation for anything. I hope that literary bouts of deep fatigue and hopelessness, those little uncomfortable truths among humans, will continue to intensify rather than stigmatize lesbian characters.

Elizabeth Crowell

Elizabeth Crowell has had work published in *Christopher Street* and the *New York Native.* She teaches high school English and serves as faculty advisor to the student gay/straight alliance at a private school in Boston. "Perfectly Good" was inspired by the magic of going to the Boston Symphony, the ritual of the lights flashing and the conductor bowing, and people who don't know each other outside those walls nodding as they take their assigned seats. When parents deny that a child is gay, they too are entertained by a world that is both familiar and strange. The denial becomes a music in which they find comfort, and which their child hears but does not enter. This story is about dancing or standing still to that music.

Martha K. Davis

"Rachel" came into being in part because I wanted to explore grief from the point of view of someone outside it but close by and committed to witnessing it as well as she can, which is necessarily the experience of a reader of fiction. Also, in this time of AIDS and cancer, I needed to address other deaths affecting lesbians and how grief intrudes upon and can often alter our relationships, which I rarely read about. I am a writer of short stories and poems as well as a massage practitioner, a copyeditor, and a career counselor. I have had work published in *StoryQuarterly* and *The Harvard Gay & Lesbian Review.* I am currently working on my first novel.

Elise D'Haene

I really should dedicate this story to two of my closest, dearest friends, Sharon and Wanda. Beautiful women, beautiful breasts. I don't have a breast fetish, but if I happen upon a woman with exquisite cleavage, my eye lingers. It's true, the cleavage seems to almost demand the attention. And why not? If you got 'em, flaunt 'em. I'm terrified of the possibility and reality of breast cancer. I don't examine my own breasts enough. I know I should, but I don't. I still don't have sensation in my nipples, but that's okay, my lover has enough for the both of us. Yippee! My novel, *Licking Our Wounds,* will be published by The Permanent Press in 1997.

Ayofemi Folayan

Ayofemi Folayan is a cultural actorvist and wordsmith. She is also an Artist-in-Residence at the Los Angeles Gay and Lesbian Center, where she teaches creative writing and performance art classes in the Wordplay! program. As a participant in the civil rights movement, Ayofemi was inspired to create *Elmwood,* the novel from which the excerpt is taken, as a living memorial to the courageous souls who suffered humiliation and physical abuse so that they could reclaim their dignity. Her work was previously anthologized in *In A Different Light, Indivisible, Blood Whispers,* and other gay and lesbian works.

Wendi Frisch

"Safe Sex" began as a writing exercise about someone who "stands out in a crowd." As I wrote the piece, the narrator, rather than the woman who stands out in the crowd, emerged as the main character. I was interested to observe how desire continued to assert itself almost in spite of the narrator—much in the same way that a story asserts itself, often in spite of the author. My work has previously appeared in *Indivisible* (Plume Fiction, 1991), *Snakeskin* (Anaconda Press, 1991), and the first volume of *Hers* (Faber and Faber, 1995).

Mary Gaitskill

Mary Gaitskill is the author of *Bad Behavior,* a collection of short stories, and *Two Girls, Fat and Thin,* a novel.

Judy Grahn

Judy Grahn is internationally known as a poet and cultural theorist and is an original founder of lesbian-feminism. Her most recent nonfiction is *Blood, Bread, and Roses: How Menstruation Created the World* (Beacon Press), a new origin story of human culture based in blood. A major collection of her work is due out from Crown Publishing in 1998. Her story "Green Toads of the High Desert" locates two individual and conscious lesbian lovers in the numinous space between "nature's" guidance and the struggle of heterosexual society to "see" us. Judy is expecting to complete a Ph.D. program in Women's Spirituality.

Ellen Krout-Hasegawa

Ellen Krout-Hasegawa attended Occidental College. Her byline has appeared in the *L.A. Times Book Review, Seattle Weekly, Westways, The Lesbian News,* and the *L.A. Weekly,* where she covers books, music, and theater. She is *sansei* with a Japanese-Peruvian mother and German-American father. The genesis for "Noise" was watching a friend's teenage daughter read. Sitting there, she took on an impenetrable quality which fascinated me. Like Rhea, I'm a Nirvana fan. The thought of Kurt Cobain's dying occurred to me as I wrote this story, months before his death.

Ronna Magy

"Family" was inspired by a Mother's Day celebration that occurred ten years after my mother's death. I was nearly fifty. In an extended family such as mine, where each person's story is piled stone upon stone on those of previous generations, how much does the family require us to be "nice," stable, and uncomplaining? How does family accommodate the edges of personality? When does the family stop supporting each member? What is the tolerance for us as writers? As lesbians? I am a Los Angeles–based writer. My fiction stories have appeared in the *Bilingual Review/La Revista Bilingüe* and *Heatwaves.*

Gerry Gomez Pearlberg

"Caravan" is a meditative ode that came into being at the intersection of Passion and Desolation, written while listening to Ella Fitzgerald's eerie, shimmering rendition of Ellington's "Caravan" play over and over and over again. It was as if I were stuck in the song just as I was stuck—quite willingly—in making this story, memory and imagination being caravans lost in the desert at night.

Robin Podolsky

Robin Podolsky is a writer who lives and works in Los Angeles. In 1993 she received an Outstanding Journalism award from the National Lesbian and Gay Journalists Association for her column, "Pollyanna With a Hatchet," which appeared in the *L.A. Weekly.* Her forthcoming book, *Queer Cosmopolis,* will be published by New York University Press. She says, "With the character Joan, I set out to create the anti-Robin, to build an opposite of myself. Of course, I wound up learning all sorts of things about my own psyche and the instability of identity in general."

Robin Strober

My first of many visits to Las Vegas was in 1990, when the town was morphing from raunchy kitsch to homogenous hyper-real. I feel fortunate that I was able to see glimpses of old Vegas (Fremont Street before it became an indoor mall, the bejeweled and twinkly *Stardust* sign pre-Helvetica-zation, the Dome of the Sea restaurant). I witnessed the implosion of the Dunes Hotel and I'll never forget standing in the middle of the closed-off Strip, hugging my friend Stacie, as we watched the infamous structure crumble to the ground. To us, it was the end of an era, to the cheering crowd, it was the start of another. This story is about transition and change. My writing has appeared in *Out!*, *L.A. Weekly*, and the *Baltimore Alternative*.

Carla Tomaso

I'm a writer and teacher living in Pasadena, California. I've written two novels published by Penguin/Plume and a collection of short stories published by Seal Press. I like to write about edgy and taboo subjects because I think we learn more from people who have the courage to make up their own rules. Of course, the real reason is probably because it's safer for me to write about these things than to have to do them myself.

Terry Wolverton

I am by turns amused and made grumpy by the depiction of sex in much of lesbian work—everything is always wet and throbbing, explosive and multiply orgasmic. Sure, sometimes it's like that, but why do we so rarely write about sex that's sad or awkward or infuriating, or about what happens when the impulse disappears? I see "Sex Less" as a kind of anti-propaganda.

About the Editors

Terry Wolverton

Terry Wolverton is the author of *Bailey's Beads*, a novel (Faber and Faber), and *Black Slip*, a collection of poetry (Clothespin Fever Press). She has also edited several successful compilations, including *Blood Whispers: L.A. Writers on AIDS, Volumes 1* and *2* (Silverton Books), and, with Robert Drake, *Indivisible* (Plume Fiction) and the first volumes of *His* and *Hers*. Since 1976 Terry Wolverton has lived in Los Angeles, where she has been active in the feminist, gay and lesbian, and art communities. Since 1988 she has been a writer-in-residence at the Los Angeles Gay and Lesbian Center, where she directs the Perspectives Writing Program. Terry lives with her lover, visual artist Susan Silton.

Robert Drake

Robert Drake is the author of the popular fiction series, *The Man: A Hero for Our Time,* and co-editor of the anthologies *Indivisible, His,* and *Hers.* Since 1984 he has worked as a literary agent, representing among others Robert Rodi and Christian McLaughlin. He is also Books Editor for *The Baltimore Alternative,* a position he has held since 1993. A Quaker, he lives in Philadelphia with his family—a bull terrier named Pudsey Dawson, two cats named (pro)Zac and Brady, and The Most Understanding Man in the World, E. Scott Pretorius, to whom he dedicated his work on the first volume of *His.*

Acknowledgments

The editors would like to thank Valerie Cimino, Mary Bisbee-Beek, and Betsy Uhrig for their belief in these books and their tireless efforts on our behalf. Robert Drake would also like to extend a special nod to Catherine Carter, Liz Wolfson, and Adrian Wood for providing a home away from home (in a literary sense) during the 1996 ABA convention, and for promoting these anthologies so earnestly to booksellers.

We once again extend our deepest thanks to Susan Silton for her stunning cover designs and to Valerie Galloway, whose eye-catching photography establishes the tone of the collection. In addition, Terry Wolverton would like to offer a belated but no less heartfelt acknowledgment to Ana Castanon, whose thought-provoking suggestions led us to the titles of this series.

We are fortunate to have been able to work with the talented writers whose stories are collected within these books. To them, most of all, we offer our gratitude.

All stories are printed by permission of the authors.